The S

Tom Adair

ISBN-13: 978-1469939834
ISBN-10: 1469939835

TO Dwane,
A great guy, Friend, real friends
& teacher. You are a
class act! I hope this
you well. Be fearless!
Tom Adair

Tom Adair

To my loving wife Cindy…
You are the source of my love, my strength,
and my hope.

The Scent of Fear

ACKNOWLEDGMENTS

First and foremost I would like to thank Jennifer Engle. You were a bright light and calm voice during a very dark period and I will forever be grateful to you. To Kathy Flynn for all of your encouragement and advice; thanks for believing in me. Jan LeMay, you are a man of honor even the best of us can aspire to be. Erik Murphy has been my best friend and confidant since I was literally two years old. You have always shown me that imagination has no limits. Bernard Vonfeldt, my kindred spirit, brother, and partner in "crime". Thanks for always being there. Charles S. DeFrance has become one of the best friends a guy could hope to have. I am indebted to my family for supporting my crazy dream. A lot of friends lent their time to read my many drafts or provide helpful advice along the way. They include Silvia Pettem, Joan Dolan, Pat Adair, Sandra Wiese, Dave Maloney, Karen Pearson, Bruce Adams, Rebecca Shaw, Carol Agnew, Clinton McKinzie, Dr. Diane France, Chris Loptien, Lee Horsley, Debbie O'Laughlin, Alan and Linda Sprigg, Lucy Fisher, Cheri Thomas, Shellie Miller, Shannon Norden, Stacy Matte, Stacy Tingle, Grif, John Franks, Steven and Becky Vonfeldt, Ivanie Stene, and Michaela Schanz. Mom and Dad, I wish you could have seen this.

Dick Hopkins Sr., thanks for teaching me so much in so little time. It was an honor knowing you Hoppy.

To the traveling men who showed me the light.

To all of those who still chase monsters. Thank you for standing squarely between us and them.

Finally, to the men and women of the Army, Navy, Air Force, Marines, Coast Guard, and National Guard. Your service makes it possible to live in a country with the freedoms to write this novel and I am eternally grateful for your sacrifice.

Tom Adair

The Scent of Fear

1

Idiot! Contempt seeped through her clenched teeth as Sarah watched the black Mercedes slither back and forth across the snow-packed mountain highway.

The glossy black Mercedes SL550 coup weaved behind a slower-moving Ford pick-up truck, popping his high beams on and off. No doubt this was some rich ski bum from Denver on his way to the ski slopes of Crested Butte, she thought. The old two-tone Ford wasn't budging. Pulling over in this weather would be foolhardy and dangerous. The Mercedes continued pushing and Sarah wondered if the driver was drunk or just stupid. Guardrails were absent along the high mountain highway, so one false move meant a 200-foot death plunge down the mountainside. Traffic was heavy for this late hour; she assumed the cause were several lumbering snowplows ahead, keeping the flow of traffic to a crawl. The mid-October storm had hit much harder than the local weatherman had predicted. Many of the drivers of the cars on U.S. Highway 50 struggled just to maintain traction on the slick, snow-covered road near Monarch Pass, Colorado. The headlights on Sarah's Chevy Silverado allowed for only shallow penetration into the blanket of snow during the murk of the 9:00 PM winter blast.

Her muscles were beginning to ache from holding the wheel during her long drive, but unlike many of the other travelers, her knuckles weren't blanched white; she had considerable experience driving in bad weather on mountain roads; going to her grandfather's cabin, as she was doing now. After three days at a gruesome double homicide scene she was ready for a vacation.

The Mercedes high beams caught her eye again. Prick. Sarah considered flashing her own lights at him but thought better of it. She could hasten a wreck if this guy took his eyes off the road, even for a few seconds. Maybe the Ford would pull off in the parking lot at the summit and let this asshole race ahead on his rendezvous with death.

The Mercedes' driver pulled into the on-coming lane attempting to pass the slower Ford; he pushed down on the gas pedal and his rear tires slid back and forth in a fishtail. It took all his effort to keep control of the Mercedes as he maneuvered back behind the Ford truck. The sleek sedan was built for the speedway, not the ski slopes, and the $100,000 computer and handling software couldn't compensate for the $10 brain behind the wheel.

The driver popped his high-beams in apparent frustration.

The Mercedes tried a second time to pass on the left. This time he accelerated and held his track, advancing on the Ford until he came even with the truck's rear bumper.

The pickup truck slowed. Was he braking? She couldn't see any brake lights, as the Ford barreled into a left-turn curve. The roadway was impossible to discern in the haze of snow and fog. The pickets of snow-covered pine trees provided the only hint where the road's edge was.

Flittering headlights of the on-coming vehicles broke through the snow-laced pines that were blocking the view up the mountain through the curve. Then, a bright set of headlights flooded the windshield just as the Mercedes started into the curve and outside the Ford. The Kenworth T600 tractor trailer was in low gear and moving slow, but the 35,000-pound semi-truck couldn't stop on a dime, even on dry pavement. The trailer began to jackknife and swing into the on-coming lane of traffic after the panicked driver hit the brakes to miss the Mercedes.

Holy crap! Sarah took her foot off the gas and veered to the right, anticipating the crash. The Mercedes wasn't as careful. He pulled hard to the right. His front bumper struck the left rear wheel of the Ford and made what the police call a PIT maneuver: P.I.T: Precision Immobilization Technique, a disabling spin-out maneuver—at least when done by professionals.

It was never intended to be used by brain-dead yuppies in a blizzard at 10,000 feet above sea level.

The Ford started an unrecoverable and wild counter-clockwise spin, and drifted toward the right edge of the road. The Mercedes slammed into the Ford pickup once more, this time hitting him square on the passenger side door. The impact sent the Ford rolling side over side. Sarah caught a flash of color in the headlights.

"Jesus!" she gasped. Someone had just been ejected from the Ford. Sarah had seen plenty of bodies torn apart and scarred from such ejections. Even on a snow-covered road the injuries would be severe. She visualized the broken bones protruding from torn flesh and bright red road rash over all the exposed parts of the body.

The Mercedes stayed on all fours but spun backward, striking a tree on the edge of the roadway about fifty feet behind the Ford. The devastating crash seemed to last for several agonizing minutes.

Sarah snapped back into reality as the massive semi-trailer swung into her lane. She was still veering to the right but there was only so much road on which to maneuver. She cringed and shrieked as the massive trailer swiped the side view mirror of her door and flung it back to the window with a deafening crash. She was lucky that the huge trailer just scraped her door. Thirty feet farther back and she would have been crushed by the massive rig. It took all her skill to bring her big Chevy truck to a stop without becoming part of either wreck.

Coming to a stop after a long skid, her mind was now racing. She prayed the cars behind her would slow in time before striking the massive semi. The trailer blocked her view of the vehicles behind her and she knew that there were injuries up ahead. Without thinking, she grabbed her day pack and a fire extinguisher from the back seat. She always kept a well-stocked first aid kit in her pack and tonight she knew she'd have to use it. As she exited the truck, the bitter wind bit into her exposed skin and ravaged her long Chesnutt hair. She was wearing a long-sleeved flannel shirt while driving, the heater doing its job quite well. Once outside and sprinting toward the wreck, it was too late to turn back for her coat. Lives were at stake and people were surely hurt, maybe even dying.

She came to the Mercedes first. The male driver looked to be in his early 50s, with wavy blond hair draped across the collar of his cashmere sweater. Blood was streaking down his face from a sizeable gash in his forehead. He hadn't been wearing a seatbelt. Dumbass. The air bag had deployed but he must have leaned to his right just before impact, negating the effectiveness of the safety feature. She placed her hand on his shoulder and told him everything would be all right and not to move. She got a gauze pad from her kit and applied pressure to the shallow gaping wound. He was missing a tooth and his pride. His passenger looked worse.

The buxom blonde looked to be on the last leg of a three-day drinking binge. She seemed quite a bit younger than the driver, and smarter, at least she knew to wear her seatbelt. A daughter, she hoped, but doubted. Sarah could tell that, under other circumstances, she was quite pretty. Her hair resembled a bird's nest after a tornado and her makeup was streaked with tears. High-pitched shrieks came between her gasps for air and Sarah figured every dog in the valley must be looking up to the summit by now.

Other drivers began arriving at the chaotic scene and Sarah yelled at one awestruck woman to call 911. She knew that the odds of getting a signal were slim, but it was worth a try. Besides which, people needed tasks in emergencies; gawking was useless. People were gathering around and giving their two cents' worth in triage management. Annoyed, Sarah howled into the storm for a doctor. A man appeared from the crowd and rushed to her side. His silvery hair and composed face reassured her and indicated that he was capable of handling their injuries. She flashed her badge and instructed him to check the couple over while she headed to the Ford.

By the time she made it to the pickup several people had already converged on the wreckage. Some of them must have come from the downhill traffic lane, she thought. The truck was resting upright, awash in a glow of headlights from the downhill facing vehicles. The engine was making a terrible knocking sound as smoke tumbled from under the hood. Pink anti-freeze was running down the road and mixing with the snow. Shattered glass littered the snowy roadway, glistening in the artificial light. Glancing at the cab, she didn't see a driver.

He must have been the one ejected.

To her right, Sarah saw a small crowd gathered. No doubt they found the driver's mangled body. A younger man tried to head her off, sheltering her from the grisly sight, but she thrust her badge in his face and shouldered past him into the small crowd. As she knelt down her mind tried to process what she was seeing. There in the snow lay the naked body of a woman partially covered by a red-colored bed sheet. People in the crowd were mumbling to each other in soft tones. It was clear that the woman was dead. There was blood on her face and a three-inch laceration across her scalp. A woman in the crowd tried to cover her face with the sheet but Sarah stopped her. Something was wrong. She knelt by the woman's lifeless body, careful not to disturb any evidence.

Why was she naked, Sarah asked herself? It took her brain several long seconds to process the information. Then it hit her. The blood was dried! Her wound was not bleeding. Then she saw a reddish brown mark around the woman's neck.

"Ligature," she whispered.

On instinct, a Glock 17 nine millimeter pistol emerged from her waistband as she scanned the faces of the crowd. This wasn't a result of the accident, she thought, this woman has been murdered!

A woman kneeling next to Sarah screamed as the boxy black gun came into view. People scattered like rats in a fire, slipping and sliding as they tried to find shelter behind the vehicles. Sarah trained her gun on the cab of the Ford and advanced one step at a time. There was no cover, no concealment, and she had no body armor to protect her. Adrenaline pulsed through her body and she tried to manage her fear and keep her footing.

Her training kicked in and she started barking commands to the cab. "You in the cab, sheriff's office! Come out and show me your hands," she yelled. There was no reply. Maybe he was dead. Again she shouted her command. "Come out now and show me your hands!" The wind howled in challenge to her. She moved around the front of the vehicle, using the engine block for cover. Thankfully, the truck's windshield was glowing with the headlights from the opposing traffic. This would work to her advantage and make it more difficult for the killer to see her. Peeking around the hood, Sarah kept her eyes on the front sight of the weapon.

Never point the gun in a direction you're not looking, she remembered. Crouching as she approached the door, Sarah thrust the gun through the broken window. The cab was empty. For a split second she sighed in relief. Then it struck her. The dead chick wasn't driving, you fool; he's out here somewhere! She spun back around to the crowd and saw that they were all still cowering behind the scattered vehicles. Scenarios raced through her mind. Has he taken a hostage? There were no screams from the other drivers. She took a deep breath and began scanning the area around the truck, the muzzle of the Glock out in front of her. No clear tracks in the snow, no blood, nothing. Where the hell did he go? She ran to the east side of the roadway and then she saw it: A trail of boot prints traveling downhill to the east. She knew there was an old campground down the hill but it was closed for the season. Prudence told her to wait, to call for back-up, but the thought of letting another criminal slip through her fingers...she just couldn't do it again. Fuck it, she thought, and dashed down the mountain after the killer's tracks. He must have several minutes on her by now. She cursed herself for checking on the Mercedes first.

The dense woods and drifting snow reduced her visibility to a mere thirty yards. She could tell from the gait of his footsteps that he was running at a good pace. She had to catch him. With no way to take a bearing, Sarah rushed down the hill not knowing where she'd end up. Sarah hoped he didn't know, either.

She stopped, straining her ears to detect the sound of footsteps in the crisp snow, or possibly a breaking branch. Maybe she could get a bearing on his position. Not a sound. The dense woods blocked the wind and a forlorn feeling washed over her as she squatted in the calf-deep snow. The cold air was tearing into her aching lungs as she tried to catch her breath. She had tracked wounded animals many times through the woods. Her grandfather had taught her to hunt and track since she was six years old, but there was a big difference between tracking a wounded elk and a human killer. She could see some kind of structure ahead through the heavy white snowfall. She realized that she was coming up on the campground.

That must be the latrine, she thought. Taking a position behind a cluster of short pine trees she stopped again to listen for the suspect but there was nothing; no sound whatsoever.

She reached for her flashlight. It was back at the truck. Damn it, she thought. How could she be so stupid? She was chasing down a murderer in the freezing cold with no backup, no plan, and no gear. At least she had the Glock.

The Scent of Fear

Why did I rush into this? The situation had taken her by surprise, she reasoned, but there was no solace to be found in excuses. She had prepared herself to find an accident victim and instead stumbled across a murder scene. It was a dangerous situation and she knew it, but at this point she couldn't turn back. His tracks were hard to discern through the snowfall. Did they stop at the latrine or go on?

She hesitated for a moment. The smart thing would be to watch the building until help arrived. But she was freezing now and there was no way to tell how long it would take back-up to arrive. She didn't have time to wait. She advanced on the latrine, trying to minimize the sound of her approach. Moving around the left side of the building the trees helped to conceal her movements. Now she could see the suspect trail change direction toward the door of the latrine. She advanced toward it. Each step seemed smaller than the last. Every sound seemed amplified in her mind. Her breathing, her pounding heart, all of it. Her eyes were transfixed on the door latch, looking for any signs of movement. It seemed to take forever but she couldn't risk revealing her position. She took hold of the handle with her left hand. The cold metal bit into her skin as she steadied herself. Her right hand was strangling the Glock.

This was it.

She tightened her grasp on the door handle and took a deep breath, preparing for the unavoidable confrontation. She jerked on the handle and let out a sharp yelp. It was locked!

It was then that she saw the padlock. Idiot! How can a trained investigator miss something so obvious?! She had been so fixated on the latch that she didn't see the padlock inches from it! In another time and place it might have been funny, but not now.

Scanning the ground, she recovered his trail in the fresh snow and dashed along his tracks. She had lost precious minutes in this futile search. Her heart was racing again and it took great self-control to maintain a safe pace. The last thing she wanted was to stumble upon him accidentally. No, she was stalking him, she had to. Her mind changed gears and she calmed herself by taking several deep breaths. She was the hunter, not him. She would be the one to choose their battleground, not him. Like every good hunter she would anticipate his path and get ahead of him.

His tracks headed up the South Arkansas River which flowed into the campground's east side through Camp Site #34. Sarah decided to take the high ground and follow the suspect along a parallel track above. The advantage was obvious: If she controlled the high ground she'd control the battle.

She felt the frigid air invading her lungs and her muscles aching from heat loss. She had to be careful that hypothermia didn't set in. As long as she could feel the pain, it wasn't too late. If hypothermia took hold she'd lose her capacity for good judgment, succumbing to a painless but inevitable death on the mountain. She only hoped someone would find her body in the spring before the bears did.

It was impossible to keep an eye on the faint trail below so she stopped every few moments straining to hear the killer's footsteps. She spotted a dense conifer grove ahead near the edge of the incline which she could use for concealment while she scanned the trail ahead. As she eased up next to the tree she felt an unusual sensation on her left ear. The hairs on her neck stood up and she swatted at the source of the tickle.

"Jesus," she whispered. Looking up, she saw a tuft of Old Man's Beard dangling from the branch above. Letting out a sigh, she recognized *Usnea hirta*. The branches were covered with the hanging lichen which was powdered with snow.

Staring at the beautiful plant, she jerked backward as the breath of a bullet whistled past her face, striking the tree, and showering her face with splinters. The thunderous report of the gun was still echoing through the ravine as she scrambled behind a small group of boulders.

2

"Son of a bitch!" she shouted through clenched teeth.

Crouching as low as she could, Sarah felt a trickle of blood flowing down her face. Without looking, she thrust her Glock over the rocks and fired three quick rounds in the general direction of the report. She wanted him to know she was armed, too.

She fingered the small cut above her right eye as she peeked through a gap in the rocks, looking for her quarry. This bastard was not as stupid as she'd hoped. He had taken the high ground too. The rules had changed. He was armed and aware she was pursuing him.

The odds were not in her favor anymore.

With the murderer out in front, it would be easy to draw her into a killing zone. She had fifteen rounds in her gun, well, twelve, now. The high capacity magazine was capable of holding seventeen rounds but she didn't top it off to help preserve the spring inside. Those two bullets could be the difference between life and death she realized. On top of that her hands and feet were numbing and she was getting further from any meaningful back-up with each labored step. She let out a deep sigh realizing that discretion was the better part of valor. Local deputies could track him down later. He wouldn't make it far in this blizzard she reasoned. Besides, she had his truck and from that, his identity. Unless it was stolen.

Sarah retreated, turning her head every few steps for any hint of the suspect. She couldn't tell if she was shaking from the cold or from her brush with death. She made the slow, agonizing climb back to her truck, refusing to holster her weapon in case she ran across the suspect again. She struggled with each uncoordinated step from the pain and cold. Her jeans were soaking wet and the cut on her head was throbbing. It took her thirty minutes to trek back up the mountain to Highway 50.

As she cleared the trees and came onto the roadway she saw a deputy sheriff was parked by the Ford. The scene was more visible in the wash of his red and blue emergency lights. Yellow crime scene tape had been strewn across the highway and she was sure that traffic was going to be turned around and the pass closed. She could see the suspect's pick-up truck sitting idle, the engine now shut off.

Paramedics had arrived and were giving aid to the asshole that caused the whole mess. She looked for her truck but couldn't see it through the crowd. The thought of someone stealing something out of her unlocked cab crossed her mind but she pushed the image away. Sarah called out to the deputy and in the blink of an eye was looking down the barrel of his Springfield.45 pistol. She had forgotten she was still holding her Glock and dropped it to the road as the deputy began yelling commands. No doubt he had seen the murder victim, too, and was now looking at a gun-toting woman with a blood-soaked face.

I hope to hell he isn't trigger happy, she thought.

The middle-aged doctor emerged from the crowd and called out to the deputy telling him she was a cop. She slowly produced her badge, putting the deputy at ease.

He holstered his weapon, rushed to her side, and began assessing her injuries. The blood flow had stopped. Part of the bullet's copper jacket must have raked her forehead after grazing the tree she thought as she touched the wound she hoped it wouldn't leave a scar. Sarah did her best to describe the killer as the deputy rushed her to his patrol car; thrusting her into the back seat. I must look worse than I feel she thought. As she warmed herself in the back seat of the patrol car she realized the other motorists might think she was under arrest for causing the accident, or worse yet, the murder.

Why didn't he put me in the front seat?

She knew he was just acting on instinct. At the moment, getting warm trumped all else.

Sheriff James "Jimmy" Booth was half cowboy, half lawman. At 6'4 he towered above his officers and commanded their respect. He was a legend in high-country law enforcement. Sarah knew him from a use-of-force investigation in which he single-handedly killed two armed thugs who had barricaded themselves in a secluded gas station after robbing and raping the teenage clerk. He got a bullet in his thigh and piece of tin on his uniform for his efforts. He never asked for either. She stared through the fogged window as his towering wiry frame strolled over to the patrol car. He cracked open the door and peered down on her with deep blue eyes.

"Sounds like you've had quite an excitin' evening, little lady."

"Yes, sir, Sheriff."

"So the suspect is on the loose in this mess, eh? Did you get a shot into him?"

"Truth is, Sheriff, he caught me off guard and got the drop on me. I never got a good shot off." Booth smirked as his eyes looked her up and down.

"Hell; most guys wouldn't have had the balls to run after him in the first place. We're settin' up road blocks on Highway 50 and have a BOLO out for all state troopers. We don't have a description of the driver yet, but we're interviewing folks as we speak."

She was amazed by his calm demeanor, given the circumstances. "This guy's no dummy, Sheriff," Sarah said. "He's armed and he's pretty smart. Please tell your deputies to be extra careful. He's killed one woman and tried to kill me."

"Don't worry about my guys; they're tougher than the back wall of a shooting gallery."

She knew they must be, working for him. Most were local kids who'd grown up in the mountains. Unlike a lot of city officers, these guys never had backup and almost always dealt with armed individuals.

Sitting in the back of the patrol car, Sarah replayed the events over and over in her head. She had never been shot at before, and it shook her. Her fingers trembled as she wrote a witness statement and she wondered if it was the cold or the adrenalin. Sarah had investigated several officer-involved shootings in the past and had witnessed a cornucopia of emotions erupting from each one. She didn't know how she should feel but she was calmer than she had expected. She wondered how she'd feel later once it all sank in. What would her parents think of her close brush with death? Maybe I shouldn't tell them, she thought. Her mother would overreact and might even march into the sheriff's office berating him for not keeping her daughter safe. That just might be worse than getting shot, she realized.

It was late and Sheriff Booth had a deputy bring her some piping hot coffee. The hot cup brought some color back into her fingers. Sarah detailed the actions of the Mercedes' driver, putting the blame for the accident on his shoulders. After all, everyone else was handling the driving conditions. Still, she couldn't help but think that without him, a murder might not have been exposed. Life was funny that way. Sometimes one tragedy has to occur to reveal an even bigger one. She was just thankful that no one else was injured. As she finished the paperwork she couldn't help but wonder about the murder victim. Who was she? Did she know her killer? It was the curse of the criminalist, an unending barrage of questions that were sometimes never resolved.

Her thoughts were interrupted by the young deputy in the front seat. She had felt his eyes lurking on her from the beginning and was a bit uncomfortable with men staring at her. Most of the cops were drawn to her beauty of youth and fascinated by her chosen profession, but few had the courage to talk to her. "Something I can do for you deputy?"

His eyes darted away as a look of embarrassment swept his face.

"So you're like one of the CSIs on TV, huh?" She smiled and withdrew her gaze. "You seem too pretty to be carrying a gun." He bit his lip, realizing how stupid he sounded. His wandering eyes made it clear he was struggling with what to say next. "Hey, is it really like they show it on TV with all those computers and lasers and stuff?"

The corner of her lips curled up as she fought back a smile. If I had a dollar for every time someone asked me that, she thought. The deputy probed further. "So do you think that Casey Anthony killed her daughter?"

This was going to be a very long night, she thought.

The killer was getting angrier with each plodding wet step. His plan had been foolproof, just like all the others, until that son of a bitch tried to pass him. Up until tonight he had been a ghost and the authorities had yet to connect any of his crimes. Now he had been discovered and he cursed himself for not being better prepared. He was in no condition to be running through the darkened woods in this weather.

And who the hell was that guy chasing me? He wondered.

It seemed Murphy's Law had ensured he would have an accident with an off-duty cop or security guard right there. He was hopeful that he'd hit the meddling bastard after opening fire on him by the tree. He had waited a bit farther down the path to see if his pursuer would come along, but he never did. The killer hoped he had struck a fatal blow and the cop would die a slow death in the sub-zero blanket of snow. He never considered going back to check.

His priority now was escape and evasion. First he needed to find shelter. He worked his way over a saddle in the ridge above. Once on the other side he followed it down to another semi-frozen creek. He worked his way along the creek at an ever-slowing pace. Every step seemed less coordinated than the last. He couldn't move fifty yards without slipping and falling to his now bruised knees. He had no idea what direction he was headed. All he knew was that every step took him farther from his pursuers. His mind began to wander with random thoughts, a clear sign of hypothermia. He needed to get warm or he would soon become disorientated and die. Focusing on each footstep, he kept his head down to avoid exposing his face to the blistering cold. Every few minutes though, he couldn't help but look up, hoping to see shelter. His wet clothing was clinging to his body and he realized he didn't have long.

He came to a clearing in the trees and he looked across the creek, noting a faint outline, maybe a cabin, he thought. He hoped it was empty because killing more people tonight would make a messy day worse. If the cops weren't looking for him by now they soon would be. He forced himself to reconnoiter the surroundings despite every fiber of his being screaming at him to get inside and out of the cold.

He scanned the rustic cabin for any signs of life. There was no smoke coming out of the dark stone chimney but it was late and they could have forced heat, he thought. There was a rusty white propane tank on the north side under some pine trees. Their drooping branches almost touched the top of it under the weight of the heavy snow. The windows were covered with thick wooden shutters to keep out the bears and he could see no light emanating from behind their cracked facade. There were no shoeprints or tire tracks in the snow, although the storm may have covered the tracks he thought. Operating under a cocktail of desperation and survivor's instinct, he decided that he would take his chances. He was still armed and he had already killed today so he supposed one or two more wouldn't make a difference. He rapped his numb, bone-white knuckles on the door. Receiving no answer he searched for an inconspicuous point of entry. He found it in a small bathroom window on the back side of the cabin. With any luck the owners would not find his entry until the next year's spring thaw. He found a small gap in the decrepit old shutter that gave him just enough room to slip his fingers behind. With much of the blood gone from his hands it took all his strength to pry the cover off. He looked around for a wedge and found an old piece of rebar near the woodpile that would work. The frozen, rusted metal bit into is skin, letting him know that his hands were still alive. It took all his strength to pry the shutter off and it landed in the deep snow with a dull thud. He knew that sound traveled farther in the cold air, so he wrapped his flannel shirt around the rebar before smashing window glass. Wasting no time, he climbed through the hole to salvation, cutting himself in several places as his beefy hands grasped the wooden sill. He landed in a crumpled heap. It was then that he heard the scuttle of footsteps across the old wooden floor.

The hard plastic seats in the rear of the patrol car smelled of old vomit and bruised her ass but she finished her reports and gave additional briefings to the deputies and highway patrolmen as they mapped out the manhunt for the killer. Her writing was becoming a bit more legible as the blood once again began flowing through her cold fingers.

Deputies were wasting no time setting up roadblocks but with the storm and the scarce resources many of them knew that they couldn't cover all avenues of escape. Some thought they should focus on the major roadways while others thought they should start searching local residences. The officials at the CBI and Colorado State Patrol decided that they would initiate a reverse 911 call to the local residents, warning of the criminal and focus their attention on roadblocks.

She was startled by the rapping of knuckles on the window. Sheriff Booth looked impervious to the freezing wind. His jacket was unzipped and his white Stetson hat somehow stayed perched atop his head.

"Miss, I just talked with the crime lab folks at CBI and it'll take them a little while to get here with the storm. They insisted that we secure the scene but those sons-a-bitches don't realize the mess we're in up here. I just talked to your sheriff and he authorized you to assist us up here in taking some initial photos and preserving any evidence we might have. I hate to ask, considering what you've been through tonight, but I'm plum stretched thin coordinating this manhunt."

Shit, she thought, you called my sheriff? Why not just hit me in the knees with your nightstick? She was supposed to be on vacation and she cringed at the thought of her sheriff hearing of her shootout from Sheriff Booth and not her. She might get time off without pay for that oversight. She cursed herself for not calling her sergeant sooner and figured she'd better help out to appease her boss. What choice did she have, anyway?

"I'm happy to help, Sheriff. What kind of gear do you have available?"

"Deputy Waters." Booth's gaze could have stopped a freight train in its tracks. The young deputy snapped to attention. "Sir?"

"Bobby, this little lady gets whatever she asks for. Treat her like my virgin sister on prom night or I'll have you running a speed trap by the old mine 'til your short hairs turn gray."

"Yes, sir, Sheriff."

Sarah got to work, knowing she had no time to waste. The storm was unrelenting and every minute wasted could mean the difference between saving the evidence and losing it forever.

"Deputy, I need your camera."

"Yes, ma'am, it's here in the trunk."

He fumbled with the keys as he offered her a toothy smile. Opening a small, gray fabric case stained by years of abuse Waters produced an ancient Pentax ME Super 35mm camera with a Metz strobe that was probably older than she was.

"Haven't seen one of these in a while," she commented.

"Ah, no, ma'am,"

She was thankful that her mentor had forced her to learn photography on a manual film camera and not come to rely on a computer chip. The flash batteries were all dead but she replaced

Tom Adair

them with batteries from her hunting light. With a sigh, Sarah noted the expiration on the film was several years out of date. She just hoped the photos would come out. It had been some time since she had used a film camera and even then it was on a clear sunny day, not nighttime during a blizzard. She was longing for her Nikon D200 digital camera as she strained to remember the proper settings for her aperture and shutter speed. She ignored the accident for now and directed her attention to the most perishable evidence . . . the woman's body.

Sarah took dozens of pictures of the body, wounds, and close-ups of her face for identification. Deputy Waters stayed close, scribbling notes on his tiny spiral notepad as she described the conditions she found. Rigor was beginning to set in the joints and neck. Lividity was not yet fixed, indicating that the woman had been dead less than twelve hours. It could have been much longer, however, due to the cold. She was unsure how the cold temperatures would affect these conditions and she regretted not paying more attention to the coroner investigators in her other cases. The victim's nails were long, with a French manicure. The fingernails on her right index and middle finger were broken and she hoped this woman had scratched the killer's eyes out. Her hair was matted and dirty with a strong chemical smell like Chlorine. Maybe the victim had been abducted from a hotel pool or hot tub, she thought.

Kneeling down, Sarah examined her battered mouth. Broken teeth, abrasions on the lips, Sarah couldn't tell if it happened during the accident or during the murder. As Sarah studied the wounds she detected the faint smell of honey and lilac. She wondered if it was a perfume, but her nose soon became acclimated to the smell and the fleeting scent was gone. The ligature mark on her neck was very distinctive; a type of woven or uneven cordage. Could be a thick rope, she thought. Sarah also noticed some red banding, maybe an abrasion of some sort, which followed along the edges of the woman's back. She couldn't get a good photo of the marks without rolling the body over and she didn't dare do that before the CBI investigators and coroner arrived.

She wondered if they ever would arrive after looking up again at the furious storm. As Sarah looked around she couldn't help but notice that several of the drivers had gathered around the crime scene tape and were fixated on the woman's corpse, hoping to catch a glimpse of the body. It was a primal fascination that all humans shared. Several of them were even trying to capture the moment on their cell phone cameras. Thankfully, the falling snow made that all but impossible. Sarah borrowed a new, clean tarp from the volunteer fire truck that had been dispatched to the scene and covered the body to discourage the crowd from staring and to keep snow from accumulating on it. She had done all she could for the woman at this point. It was time to focus her attention on the suspect's pickup truck.

The older Ford had sure seen better days. It's faded, green-and-white two-tone paint hadn't seen wax since the 1980s, she thought, and rust was eating away at the undercarriage. Sarah couldn't get a good photograph of the vehicle identification number, or VIN, so she read it aloud to Deputy Waters as he scribbled on his pad. When she began photographing the license plates she noticed that the screws holding the plate in place were not threaded in all the way. Probably stolen she sighed. Sarah called out to Deputy Waters to run the plates. The dirty interior had the appearance of a bacteria-laden terrarium. A pungent odor hung in the air despite three evergreen air fresheners waging a lost battle from under the rearview mirror. The cab reeked of cigarette smoke and a dozen battered cigarette filters were scattered on the seat and floor from the open ashtray. Worse still, the seats smelled of urine, probably from a dog, she thought. Short white hairs littered the seat fabric. Used Kleenex and moldy snack food completed the dumpster-like ensemble.

Sarah began taking more photos, careful not to move any evidence. With any luck the CBI team would find something useful in this trash heap.

3

Miles Johansson didn't like the snow or cold. A native of the Basking Ridge area in New Jersey, he had hoped that Denver's advertised 300+ days of sunshine would be a welcome retreat from the eastern winters. Much to his father's chagrin, Miles had opted to pursue an education in forensics rather than join the family's successful import/export business along the Jersey docks. He had been born with a silver spoon in his mouth but he wanted something that was his own, not provided by his formidable father. His father had threatened to cut him off from the family fortune but his stubbornness had prevailed and his dad was somewhat impressed by his fortitude. He was a graduate of the University of New Haven forensics program and landed a job as a low-level DNA analyst for the New Jersey State Police; but after several years he began to bore of the tedious case work. Day in and day out the laboratory environment made him feel more like a specimen than an employee. He wanted something more; he wanted to be a "star".

He'd applied for an open position at the Colorado Bureau of Investigation with the hopes that the move out west would allow him to advance his career in a manner reflecting his own self esteem. With the arrogance of an "old money" socialite he felt the people of the West were ignorant and lucky to have his services. The 1984 Dodge CSI van was heavy, which improved its traction but made for a very slow drive through the windswept valley of South Park. Riding shotgun was veteran lab agent, Julie Knowles, who had been assigned to Miles as a kind of mentor while he got acclimated to his new surroundings. As they drove into the mountains Miles couldn't shake the idea that the call out was a waste of time. The idea that a homicide victim was discovered on Monarch Pass, in a blizzard no less, was preposterous. It was just a case of over-reaction to a tragic motor vehicle accident. Cops of small, boring towns looked for crimes where none existed, he told himself." I'm going to be pissed if this is some bullshit car accident," Miles said.

"Booth is a pretty good sheriff. I doubt he'd call us up here if he wasn't sure it was something bad," Julie replied.

"No doubt an observation gleaned from his vast experience with homicides," Miles spat.

He glanced at Julie as if waiting for a reply but none was forthcoming. It was just as well. The biggest crimes these deputies probably investigated was the occasional stolen car or domestic beating, he assured himself.

Arriving on scene Miles noticed how the army of emergency lights and road flares looked to be lashing out at the falling snow. A young deputy waved him over to the side of the road where Miles slid into the ditch. He cursed aloud as the grill struck the snow-covered bank with a deep thud. Deputies rushed over to help while trying to hide their snickers.

"Are you okay, mister?" a young deputy asked.

Miles couldn't hear him through the frost-covered window. He opened the door and brushed off their assistance and demanded to see the person in charge. Sheriff Booth gave them a thorough briefing of the night's events. When Booth came to the part about Sarah processing the scene Miles gave her a dismissive once over.

"Nice job contaminating my crime scene" he griped. Sarah's face crinkled. "You've draped a dirty tarp over the body and trampled God knows how many shoe impressions with your gallivanting." He paused, staring at her. "And now I find you going through the suspect vehicle without any apparent need for a warrant. She stood tall, offering no response. "Well, speak up. Are you deaf or just speechless?" he asked.

"Hello. I'm Sarah Richards with the Arapahoe County Sheriff's Office Crime Lab. I don't believe we've met."

He left her hand hanging in the air, his eyes burned a hole into her head.

"Hi, Sarah, looks like you've had your hands full up here," Julie interrupted. "Thanks a lot for helping us out. I'm sure you'd rather be somewhere else right now."

"Yeah, sure. I'll just leave you to it, then."

"That's probably the best decision you've made all night," Miles said. As she walked away Miles turned to Julie. "That was awful gracious of you considering she's contaminated our crime scene."

"We don't know the whole story yet, Miles. My advice would be to try and get along with the locals. As for Sarah Richards, she may be young but you shouldn't underestimate her. I hear she's good."

Miles brushed away the comment with a wave of his hand and a snort. They had work to do. Back at her truck, Sarah's Nextel phone came to life with the annoying triple beep indicating a two way call was waiting for her. She saw the name "Lopez" on the small LCD screen. Detective Manny Lopez was a cop's cop and handled a lot of the major crimes in Arapahoe County. "Yo, Manny, go ahead," she said.

"Hey, kiddo, how's the vacation coming?"

Something told her he already knew the answer. "Oh, you know. What fun-filled drive in a blizzard wouldn't be complete without a gunfight?"

"Yeah, I heard. You're okay, right, kid?" She heard genuine concern in his voice.

"Yeah, I'm fine. What's up?" she asked as she waited for the proverbial shoe to drop.

"We may have had a young kid killed by a sniper; of sorts"

"A sniper, you mean like a real sniper?" Manny's silence confirmed it was a stupid question.

"You just came back from that shooting reconstruction course, right?"

"Manny, I've just been involved in a shooting. How can I come work one while I'm under administrative leave pending this investigation?"

"Technically, you didn't hit anyone and fired your weapon in self-defense." He paused. "The DA up there has already cleared you for duty."

"What? How is that possible? The scene is still being investigated." She couldn't believe what she was hearing.

"What can I say, kid? Booth made a call"

Checkmate. "All right, Manny, but I'm tired as hell. I need to get a few hours of sleep before I head down."

"No *problemo*. Give me a call when you're on the road again and I'll fill you in."

She didn't even have the mental stamina to answer. She'd been so looking forward to this vacation, but it wasn't meant to be. She returned to the CBI agents to see if there was anything else they needed.

"I think you've done quite enough for one night, Deputy," Miles said.

Julie rolled her eyes at Sarah and gave a short smile "Drive safe going back; its slicker than hell around Fairplay."

"Thanks, Julie, good luck." As an afterthought she turned back to the pair, and said, "I'll have the film processed in our lab and send you the copies."

Julie gave a wave of recognition but Miles never turned around. She walked over to Sheriff Booth, who was standing guard by the open door of his patrol car with his radio mic. "Hi, Sheriff Booth. I need to head back home to work another scene."

"Shit. They give you any time to rest?"

"I do need to get a few hours of sleep. Can you recommend a good hotel?"

"Hold on one second." Booth punched a phone number into his cell. "Liz? Jimmy. I need a room, gratis, for a Miss Sarah Richards tonight. She'll be down in a few minutes," he said, hanging up the phone. "Go on down to the Monarch Inn and they'll fix you up. Have a good breakfast on the county, as well. We're indebted to you for your help tonight." He reached out his bear-like hand, offering her a firm handshake.

"Thank you, Sheriff, but I don't think I helped much."

Booth looked her in the eye "Don't you mind that pussy over there." He said with a nod to Miles. "Son of a bitch is a born complainer, I can tell. Not many people would have run after that scumbag like you did. I'm very impressed. You should be, too." Sarah could see the sincerity in his face. "Now git." Sarah shot Booth a wink before darting through the snow to her truck. On the drive down to the hotel she wondered if her actions that night were commendable or just plain stupid.

The killer thrust his pistol at the steps cutting through the darkness. He let out a deep sigh as he watched the wood rat scurry across the floor and into the shadows.

Shit, he thought, swallowing hard.

He groped the rough wall for a light switch and illuminated the dark interior of the cabin. The thick shutters would block any light from escaping outside. The old cabin was neat but appeared to be something out of an old Western movie. Rustic was a kind description. There was no running water but at least it had electricity. A large cast iron stove sat against the far wall and he thought of firing it up. The room wasn't much warmer than outside but at least he was out of the storm. He found a small cabinet housing a First Aid kit and applied gauze to his bleeding hands.

As much as he wanted to rest he knew that he needed some distance between him and this county. He searched around the outside of the cabin and found an older Jeep CJ5 under a tarp. Thankfully, the owner had left the keys in the ignition and half a tank of gas. The engine groaned with agony but came to life in defiance of Mother Nature. It would be a long drive back to Denver and he couldn't afford any more accidents or roadblocks. As the Jeep engine warmed he took a map book from the back seat and darted back into the cabin. He plopped the *Colorado Gazetteer* on the kitchen table and plotted a route northwest over Cumberland Pass, up to Aspen, and then to Interstate 70. Scrounging through the bare cupboards he managed to locate some honey and crackers. It would have to do. He found a few water bottles in an upper cabinet as well as a six pack of Coors beer. The beer would be a nice reward should he make it through the night. He placed the items in a green duffel bag he found in a closet. After wiping down the areas he touched and cleaning up as much of the blood as he could find he headed out to the Jeep. The killer eased the old four-wheel-drive out of the driveway and guided her up one of many narrow forest roads to come that night.

Sarah reached the hotel and was greeted by a grandmotherly woman named Liz perched behind the counter.

"Oh dear, you must be Sarah. You look dog-tired. Jimmy said you've had one hell of a night." Sarah managed a smile.

"I just want to sleep." Sarah admitted.

"We're going to take real good care of you, don't you worry. I've picked you out our best room and there's no one in the adjoining rooms so you should get plenty of quiet time."

Sarah took the key and headed to her room on the second floor. She followed the outside staircase up to a creaky wooden balcony spanning the length of the building. She walked along the wooden planks dragging her feet through the crunchy snow until she reached her door. With her adrenalin rush over, Sarah was now crashing hard. Once inside the room she dropped her bags and threw herself on the bed. She was sound asleep seconds after her head hit the pillow.

4

After hours behind the wheel the killer was feeling a bit better about his chances of escape. He hadn't seen a soul. The rugged four-wheel-drive Jeep was built for the snow but he still needed to negotiate the icy slopes and rocky roads in near total darkness. He dared not turn on the headlights for fear of giving away his position. His visibility was further hampered by the old, worn wipers struggling to clear the snow from the windshield. Opaque streaks of dirty snow formed on the windshield with each trembling pass. The tiny heater worked overtime to warm his aching body, but the soft top of the Jeep leaked worse than a sieve.

As the sun raised four fingers in the East he pulled into the town of Aspen. It was time to switch vehicles. The decision was based more on comfort and peace of mind than tactics. He parked in one of the public parking lots overlooking City Park. The heavy swarm of tourists would ensure it didn't stick out to the police. Even if they did notice it they would surmise that some young ski bunny was just shacking up with a local celebrity.

Ignoring the risks, he began strolling the sidewalks, looking for a promising victim. It was just after eight in the morning and he found the streets sparse of tourists. He pretended to window shop while scanning his surroundings in the reflection of the windows. After about twenty minutes of searching he found his mark.

The slender blonde in her early 50s had been jabbering away on her cell phone unaware of her surroundings. He followed behind just within ear shot. The tone of her conversation was smug and juvenile and he was sure that she was the type of person used to getting what she'd wanted. Sporting a fur-lined suede coat with spandex ski pants her long legs left nothing to the imagination. Tethered to her wrist, a small brown dog flailed its tiny legs in an effort to keep from being dragged. Its tiny argyle sweater looked ridiculous and was contrasted by spike studded collar that failed to impart any sense of ferocity. The mutt bellowed a chorus of high pitched "yips," and the killer began to wonder which of the two were more annoying.

The Scent of Fear

He followed at a comfortable distance while scanning the streets for potential witnesses. He was beginning to wonder if she planned to walk all the way to the town of Carbondale, until he watched her turn down an alleyway towards a dark-blue BMW sedan while fumbling through a large shoulder bag for her keys.

After one last glance for witnesses he closed the distance.

Sensing his approach the tiny dog jerked towards him, tugging at the leash while barking. The woman glanced casually over her shoulder as if expecting to see an old friend but it was too late. The powerful punch came landed with tremendous brutality. Her body fell limp over the trunk as blood began flowing from her broken nose. Cradling her waist he pulled the keys from her lifeless fingers and opened the trunk. He rolled her listless body onto a bed of new shopping bags and quickly shut the lid. The tiny dog bit into his pant cuff while he glanced around for witnesses. Seeing none he kicked it away. Snatching her cell phone from the pavement he, removed the battery, and tossed it in the closest dumpster. He had to slide the driver's seat all the way back in order to accommodate his six foot two inch frame. As he closed the door and pulled out of the alleyway, the small brown dog looked around helplessly, giving one last defiant bark.

Sarah's body protested as she tried to rise from her slumber. She wished she could have a few more hours but she knew she had to get up. Sarah lumbered into the shower and tried to wash away the sweat staining her body and the doubt staining her soul. Leaning against the cold tile wall she let the hot water cascade down her naked body, hoping to wash away the foreboding sense of vulnerability following her close call with death. A cold shiver emanated from deep within her, daring the hot water to douse it. Was she foolish for chasing after the killer? Was it justice that motivated her, or bravado? A lot of men didn't see her as an equal in law enforcement and it pissed her off. As a woman, some felt she had no place standing on the thin blue line. They thought the world of crime was too dark for a woman to handle. A minority saw her as eye candy rather than a working colleague. Were they right? No one would have blamed her for staying put with the murder victim but her gut chose the chase. Hell, even her parents didn't support her career choice she reminded herself.

The hot water turned cold before providing any answers. Reluctantly, she shut the water off not feeling the rejuvenation she hoped for.

After a quick change of clothes, Sarah hopped down the old wooden stairs to the diner. Sliding into a booth at the back of the room she ordered up a plate of Huevos Rancheros and hot coffee. She tried to look busy by reading the menu and scanning photos on the wall. Sarah always felt uncomfortable eating alone, and couldn't shake the feeling that people were staring at her, feeling sorry for her.

Sipping the top off her second cup of coffee Sarah watched a familiar face come through the diner door. It was Maggie Miller, anchorwoman from the evening news. That didn't take long, Sarah thought. Dressed in a black business suit and leather boots she looked the part of an A-list Hollywood actress. Her athletic body and silky blond hair held the gaze of each man in the room as she leaned against the counter talking to Liz. Seconds later her head swung towards Sarah.

Sarah shoved a piece of gum in her mouth as the newswoman approached her like a runway model.

"Sarah? I'm Maggie Miller from Channel 4" she said. Sarah raised an eyebrow but didn't say a word. "Liz over at the counter said you were involved in that murder scene last night."

Sarah's eyes darted over at Liz and wished she hadn't been so talkative.

"Do you mind if I sit down to talk?" Maggie asked as she took a seat across from Sarah without waiting for an invitation.

"Actually, Miss Miller—"

"Oh, call me Maggie, please."

"Ms. Miller, I was not involved in the scene last night. I came upon the accident and helped direct traffic."

Maggie cocked her head, offering a fake smile.

"Don't be so humble Sarah, my sources already told me everything". Sarah wondered who else she had talked to. "They must have me confused with someone else" Sarah said. Maggie pursed her lips ""It's a great story about women in law enforcement Sarah, think of all the young girls you might inspire" Maggie said. "Sorry, no comment". Sarah knew better than to give any statements during a murder investigation. Those things were way above her pay grade. Looking defeated Maggie slid her card across the table. "Well, think about it alright? If you change your mind I can really put a good spin on this". Maggie said as she slid out of the booth giving a nod to her cameraman. In a flash they were out the door and climbing into their bright blue SUV.

Sarah took the gum from her mouth, put the gum on the card, and folded the two halves together as she waived for the bill.

It took her a couple of hours to finally reach Englewood, south of Denver. The news vans lining the street told her she was getting close abandoned video cameras stood on tripods like scarecrows guarding a field, as reporters gathered in the shadows waiting for some action. Her arrival seemed to qualify as interesting because two cameramen snapped to attention and began filming her arrival.

Standing at the yellow barrier tape an intense-looking young officer held up his hand in the classic "stop" gesture. Giving her a look of extreme annoyance he barked, "You can't come through here lady, you gotta go around the block!"

Obviously, no one thought to give her vehicle description to the officer. She rolled down the window and flashed her badge.

"Arapahoe Sheriff's Crime Lab. I'm here to process the scene."

He eyed the badge with some suspicion. "You're a deputy?"

"No, I'm a civilian."

"I didn't know they gave civilians badges. You got some other form of ID on you?"

Great, she thought, just what I need, some stick-up-his ass cop who wants to prove to me how much authority he has. "No, I don't. Look, Officer—" she looked at his uniform name badge— "Slater, I've been driving all day to get here from vacation. You can either let me in, or I can leave, and you can be the one to explain to Detective Lopez why you turned me away."

The look in her eyes was one of complete indifference. "Just doing my job" he muttered after lifting the tape for her to drive under. Sarah was sure from his tone that the word *bitch* was meant to follow.

She parked behind Manny's green Chevy Impala and walked to the next checkpoint. She didn't bring any gear with her on this first trip in. Unlike the previous officer, this one just took her name for the crime scene log and lifted the tape for her. Detective Lopez was waiting inside the mobile command post vehicle. Akin to an oversized RV the unit was nicknamed the "pope-mobile," because it had been purchased for the papal visit several years earlier. It housed a communications center, conference room, office, and a bathroom, which everyone agreed was the most valuable space on the rig.

Manny was reclined in a folding chair with his feet up on the conference room desk. He held a drooping slice of pepperoni and mushroom pizza in one hand and a can of diet Coke in the other. A phone receiver from the conference table was clamped between his shoulder and cheek. Sarah caught part of a conversation with what she assumed was a reporter outside.

". . . a big black pickup truck? Well, yeah, that would be one of our criminalists . . . She . . . No . . . It's a personal vehicle . . . Well, I can't say how much longer we'll be here . . . No . . . No . . . I can't comment on that . . . We have been waiting on this particular criminalist to assist in the shooting reconstruction . . . Yes . . ." He glanced at Sarah as she took a seat at the table and rolled his eyes. She returned a coy smile. "I know we've had a lot of crime scene people out here working all night . . . No . . . look, not every criminalist can be an expert in every field. Some are experts in shooting scenes, others are experts in blood or fingerprints, or other types of evidence." There was a short pause while Manny adjusted the receiver. "No, I didn't say that we had found fingerprints and bloodstains and you'd better not print that. Yes . . . Detective Lopez. Listen, when I have new information you'll have new information okay?. Thank you." He hung up the phone and let out and audible sigh "Goddamned reporters act as if they sign my paycheck."

"Why do you tell them anything?" Sarah asked.

"Sheriff's orders."

Manny had shed the normal office wear of a suit and tie for tan BDUs, or battlefield dress uniform, pants, and a blue polo shirt emblazoned with a sheriff's badge and his name. Manny was a "lifer," joining the sheriff's office after a six year stint in the U.S. Army. He had never gone to college. He learned how to be a cop on the streets; the only place you could learn. His raven black hair and handlebar moustache framed the chiseled features of a wise and serious face. He was not a man to be messed with as many an unfortunate dirt bag had discovered. His stout size was misleading as he could move with the gracefulness and speed of a puma.

"So have you been up there yet?" Sarah shook her head.

"Wanna grab something to eat before I take you up?"

"I'm good, thanks. How long you been out here?"

"All goddamned night. This one's a real cluster fuck. Mom's been all over the press and the sheriff is expecting some results . . . and soon." Her expressionless face told him to go on. "Anyway, the kid was out tagging last night and it looks like someone shot him from across the river. Might have been a long shot, too; we haven't been able to find any shell casings."

"Did anyone hear the shots or see the shooter?"

"Not a damned soul, just what I told you this morning on the phone. Two bums found the body and reported it."

"Any idea what time it might have happened?" She wrote some notes on her pad.

"Well, the kid's mom dropped him off at about eleven-thirty last night."

"Wait. His mom dropped him off to go tagging?"

"No shit, even bought him the spray paint. Mom thinks it's a great outlet for his creative soul or some shit like that."

"Nice," What a total waste, she thought.

"Ready to go?" Manny asked.

"Ready, Freddie."

He led her up a short trail outlined with evidence flags to keep them from stepping on anything of importance. A familiar face was waiting for her at the end of the line. Andy Vaughn was a veteran criminalist with over twenty-five years' experience. He was an old-school investigator with more common sense than any Ph.D. she'd ever met. Andy looked busy measuring data points on a grid line when Sarah called out to him.

"Hey, there, stranger . . . thought you'd be sitting around a campfire by now."

"Wish I was, but I missed your classy sense of humor."

"Seriously, kid, I heard about last night. You okay?"

29

"Yeah, fine" she said

He eyed her suspiciously but began the briefing without probing further. "Well, the kid was tagging over here. He got about halfway through his moniker—Big D—when he was struck in the back of the head by the bullet."

Sarah studied the wall, seeing the impact site of the bullet. A quarter-sized chunk of cement had been punched from the wall, exposing the matrix of gravel below. Surrounding the hole was a conical pattern of blood spatter and brain matter. Small bits of skull and tissue covered the ground, sprinkled in a darkened pool of blood. It was obvious the boy had died instantly.

Andy traced the movement of the blood on the wall, and thought out loud. "When the bullet struck the victim's head it punched a hole through his skull, but his heart was still beating for a few seconds so the blood was pumped out of the hole under pressure. As the pressure rose the blood arched, and as the pressure fell, so did the blood stream. That's what gives us this arch-like pattern."

Sarah visualized the spurting blood. "Where's the kid now?"

"Hell, paramedics rushed him to Swedish Hospital right after they got here."

"Rushed him to Swedish? They didn't notice the brain matter all over the wall?" She turned to Manny raising her eyebrows.

Manny shrugged. "You know those cheese dicks; no one wants to call a death any more for fear of being sued. Hell, last year they transported a decapitated cyclist to the hospital, remember?."

Turning his attention back to the wall, Andy continued. "I've finished my trajectories on the bloodstains and they all indicate the kid was standing with his head facing the wall. The right hand and forearm, as well as the blue spray-paint can, were up like this" he motioned with his arm "and Mom confirms he's right-handed."

Andy was one of thirty or so board certified bloodstain pattern analysts in the world. He could hold his own on a shooting scene if he had to but he was a realist and recognized that he was not as current on bullet trajectory analysis as he would like to be.

Sarah was still young and inexperienced in shooting reconstruction but she had had recent training and more importantly, Tony Stanford, the lab's senior expert in shooting reconstruction, was out of town at a conference. Sarah stood at the wall examining the bullet impact and surrounding blood until her mental train of thought was interrupted by Manny's sardonic, and much less comedic, timing.

"So what do you think was the last thing passing through his mind?"

Andy and Sarah exchanged looks of disappointment, looking around for a news camera that could end their respective careers.

"I only ask because it sure would be nice to find that bullet. You know, for evidence and such."

"It's on the list, Manny," Andy said. "We've got a couple other things to figure out first."

After a few seconds Manny asked, "So, kid, figured out where the shot came from yet?"

"Shit, Manny, I don't know. Over there somewhere," she said, waving her hand.

"Well, excuse me, I thought you had some kind of Master's degree or something," he snorted.

"It's just a piece of paper, Manny, it didn't come with a freaking crystal ball or anything."

Manny knew it was too soon for her to know the trajectory but he loved getting her riled up. Sarah knew it, too. Despite their differences in age the two had become quick friends when she'd joined the sheriff's office. Manny flicked the back of her head as he passed behind her. Sarah's foot was an inch short of connecting with his shin. Harassing each other had evolved into an Olympic sport.

He walked Sarah back to Andy's Chevy Trailblazer to retrieve his trajectory kit and lasers. Lasers were very difficult to use in daylight but they didn't have a lot of options given the scene conditions. Andy and Sarah could feel the impassionate stare of the news cameras following their every move and each of them prayed they wouldn't trip and fall. Last year, one of the sex crimes detectives had come out of a rape scene carrying a ten-inch flopping dildo and that managed to grace the front cover of the *Denver Post*. The paper saw a record spike in sales as detectives clamored to get every copy they could find. Every day since that poor son of a bitch would find that picture taped to any number of embarrassing locations. His locker desk, the car windshield . . . everywhere. The pornographic Phoenix seemed to rise from the ashes no matter how many times it was destroyed. Neither one of them wanted to be the next sucker in the crosshairs of such a juvenile juggernaut.

As she approached the vehicle she caught site of Lieutenant Bart Manilow, head of the Internal Affairs Division, known better by the innocuous sounding title "Professional Standards Bureau."

"Hey, there, Barry," Manny said, containing his laughter. He used the pejorative every chance he could.

"Give us a minute will you, Detective Lopez?" The official-sounding tone hung in the air. Once Manny was out of earshot, Manilow said, "Ms. Richards, I'm going to need you to come up to our office first thing Monday morning."

"Detective Lopez told me that I had been cleared in the Monarch Pass shooting and kept on active duty."

His eyes narrowed and he brought his head in closer to hers as if about to reveal a secret. He said, just above a whisper, "The DA up there may have cleared you but I have the full authority to investigate any and all violations of professional standards! You'd be on administrative leave right now if it was up to me, but the sheriff thinks you're needed here." He withdrew his head and regained his composure. "Report to my office at oh-eight-hundred hours Monday, Ms. Richards, that's an order."

"Do I need a lawyer?"

"Now, why would you need a lawyer?" His lips parted into a devious smile before turning towards his car.

Shit, she thought. *This is just what I need.*

Manny eyed Manilow like a leper and returned to Sarah's side. "Screw him, Sarah, he has to look into it for liability sakes. He's just trying to get under your skin."

"He's doing a damned good job of it."

"Hell, he's just cranky because he can't be a real cop anymore. You want me to be there with you?"

"No, thanks, Manny. They wouldn't let you be in there anyway."

"Probably not."

Sarah took great pains setting up the trajectory laser. She took meticulous measurements of the impact site but with just the one point of reference she had little to go on. The height of the impact point on the victim's head would be a crucial measurement. It might give her an indication of how close he was to the wall, as well as the bullet's trajectory. She was sure he was standing in an arm's length of the wall, but the direction of the head was going to be important. She gave Manny a defeated look.

"What is it, kid?"

"Well, I've got an idea of the general trajectory but it's just speculation at this point. We need to see the pathway through his head to get a better idea. When is the autopsy scheduled?"

"The pathologist is up skiing this weekend and not answering his pager. The sheriff is trying to get someone to contact him as we speak."

Perfect, she thought. At least someone is enjoying the weekend.

"You said you had a general trajectory. Can you give me a hint where it came from?" he asked with palpable hope in his voice.

"I think it's safe to say it's between here and any one of those houses over there, but I can't testify to it."

"Officer!" Manny turned and yelled. A handsome young officer came up the hillside to the shooting scene. "I need a few of you guys to canvass those houses way over there and see if anyone heard anything last night."

"Yes, sir, right away." The young officer shot off before Manny could give further instructions.

"Young dumb, and full of cum, that one," Manny said to no one in particular.

5

Sarah and Andy spent the better part of an hour documenting and searching the scene. A metal detector would have sped up the search for the bullet if the ground hadn't been littered with metal trash. The pair resorted to scouring the ground on their hands and knees, instead. It was a laborious and time-consuming technique but there was no other way. Sarah winced each time her knees landed on tiny shards of glass and sharp stones as she inched across the dirt.

"Eureka!" Andy exclaimed as he parted the weeds shrouding the lead-and-copper slug.

He snapped a photo of the bullet and marked its location with a small pin flag. He picked it up in his hand and Sarah leaned in for a closer look. The bullet was mangled, but microscopic pieces of bone, tissue, and cement were embedded in the projectile. The torn pieces of the copper jacketing left no doubt about the destructive nature of the event. The base of the bullet was deformed as the bullet struck the wall in a "key-holed," manner, after tumbling through the young boy's head.

Something caught Andy's eye on the base of the bullet. "What do you make of that?" he asked, passing it to Sarah.

She looked at the marking with her magnifier and could see what appeared to be a jagged line. "You got me... I've never seen that kind of marking before."

"I didn't think manufacturer's marked the base of a bullet."

"I don't see why they would," she agreed.

Andy offered a suspicious glance then tucked the fragment away into a coin envelope and secured it with his gear. "Mission accomplished," he said with a sigh of relief.

"Do you think we need to keep searching?" Sarah asked, unsure of the answer.

"Well, the evidence seems to suggest a single shot was fired. However, some defense attorney could argue that the bullet impact site on the wall was from a shot that missed and that the head shot was from a second round. Come to think of it, the sheriff will ask the same thing," Andy concluded, scratching his

thick brown hair. "Let's finish out the area a few yards in all directions away from the point of impact."
Sarah thought the exercise was futile as it was clear from the bullet fragment that it had struck cement as well as the boy's head, but Andy had the benefit of experience. It took another ninety minutes to finish the search and they had nothing more to show for their efforts. At least they could say that just one bullet was present. Sometimes it was better to spend a few more hours searching for evidence than to have to explain to a jury why you didn't.

The BMW's spacious interior and dark wood trim was luxurious. The plush leather seats formed to his body as if they were custom made for him and him alone. The killer enjoyed the heated seats after the long nights' ride in the old Jeep. The luxury sedan must have cost more than his annual salary and he wondered what her husband's occupation must be.

Taking Highway 82 west from Aspen to Glenwood Springs would put some additional distance between him and his pursuers. Plus, the ski traffic on Interstate 70 would allow him to blend in on his way back to Denver.

His eyes fell upon the mobile phone mounted in the dash as it rang for the third time. The flashing light indicated that messages were waiting. To his amusement, someone had put a label with the phone number onto the dashboard. The killer reasoned that she didn't drive the car very often and needed the label to remind her of the phone number. His curiosity got the best of him and he hit the retrieve button on the keypad. An automated female voice announced there was two new messages and asked for the security code. He entered the last four digits of the phone number from the label. Sure enough the voice began replaying the messages. His reasoning was simple. Anyone needing a label for the phone number would use those same numbers as part of the security code, and he was right. The first message was from her mother calling to see how she was doing. She had a sweet, almost musical voice. The second message was more concerning. A woman with a shrill voice was concerned about being cut off. She must have been the one on the other end of the phone when he abducted the woman in the trunk. Despite his plan he knew he would have to get rid of her sooner than later. It was only a matter of time before she called the local sheriff, he thought. For that matter, someone might find the dog and both reports would raise suspicions. I should have killed that yappy dog, he thought.

As if to punctuate his concern the sound of muffled screams and a pounding fist emanated from the trunk. He was sure the other drivers wouldn't hear her as the cold November air kept their car windows rolled up, but if he needed to stop for some reason things might change. He noticed a snow-covered red Audi on the side of the road, no doubt a casualty of the recent snow storm. The last thing he could afford was another accident. He needed to get rid of this vehicle . . . and the woman in the trunk.

News reached Manny that the neighborhood canvass had been a bust. "Shit, I thought we might turn up something" Manny said.

"I'm not surprised" Andy said. "Most people live in a bubble. They were probably watching American Idol". Sarah smirked.

"So where does this leave us?" she asked.

"Looks like I'm the new mayor of shitsville" Manny said.

"The sheriff is going to blow a gasket"

"At least we found the bullet, right?" Sarah said, trying to reassure him.

"A small consolation for the ass chewing I'm gonna get"

He drove the next sixty miles fantasizing on the ways he could end her life. It was a kind of game he enjoyed, role-playing various scenarios in his mind. It helped to pass the time and keep his boredom at bay.

As he neared the junction with Highway 24 her pounding had become sporadic. Her body was tiring from an emotional drain and her pointless efforts to free herself from the claustrophobic space. God only knows what horrific thoughts occupied her mind as her inevitable death approached. He made the turn onto Highway 24 heading toward Leadville, a historic mining town nestled in the Rocky Mountains at just over 10,000 feet above sea level. Perhaps he could still make some time to fulfill at least part of his desires, he thought. Cresting over Tennessee Pass he began looking for a suitable place to pull off. He would have to work quickly so as not to spend too much time in the frigid cold.

After a mile or so he came to a small road leading off the highway to the right. It led to one of the many summer communities scattered throughout the Rocky Mountains. He examined the road for recent tire tracks. Finding none he proceeded with measured caution. The road cut a path through the neighborhood and he could see a number of small lakes through the dense trees. After ten minutes he found what he was looking for. He parked the car in a small opening with a steep slope leading to the water's edge; the steep pitch of the surrounding terrain told him the pond was deep enough to hide the car.

He opened the door and filled his nose with the fresh scent of pine. He thought he could smell the odor of burning wood but he dismissed the thought as the road didn't have any tracks. He popped the trunk and looked into the woman's wide eyes glaring at him in desperation. Her body trembled as the polar-like winds swept across her. The bruising around her eyes was black and caked with blood. He watched with glee as her eyes dropped to see the knife in his right hand. The drop Tine blade was icy cold as the Damascus steel caressed her neck. Her whimpering was uncontrollable. The killer brought his left index finger to his lips in much the same way a parent shushes a child.

His eyes swept across her shapely figure as he began fantasizing again. His arousal intensified as he imagined her screams and struggles just prior to death.

Janet Easton was born into big money. Until now, a bad day for her was running out of Cristal. She was now in another world, frozen with fear. The last few hours had been a whirlwind of emotion. Her desperate cries for help were answered only by silence and the occasional pothole. She tried to convince herself that all he wanted was ransom money but when he opened the trunk and ran that hideous knife over her skin she knew his true intentions. She wanted so badly to fight but her body was frozen with fear. Janet had to try to talk her way out of this. "I have money, lots of money. I'll . . . I'll give you some of it if you let me go. Please!" The killer brushed the knife against her breast. "No, please don't. I won't say a word to anyone, I swear." Her

Tom Adair

voice trembled and she gasped for air with each convulsion. "Please, let me go. I won't—I won't call the police." The words might as well have been spoken in a foreign language for all the good they did. She looked into his dead eyes and was certain that the fear she now felt would pale in comparison to what lay ahead. Just then the distinct sound of a dog's bark pierced the crisp air, providing her a glimmer of hope. The killer was startled, realizing the implications. A barking dog meant someone was up here with them. He clamped his left hand down over her mouth like a vice. His right hand rotated the blade under her chin drawing a trickle of blood. He strained his ears to locate the dog. It was somewhere off in the distance and didn't seem to be getting closer. It could be a feral dog, he reasoned, but dismissed the thought as wishful thinking. It was time to go. He could not afford to be discovered while indulging in a passing fantasy, especially one involving such a pretentious bitch. A glimmer of hope seemed to fill her eyes just before he drove his fist into her nose. Her body went limp again as a new stream of blood began flowing over her lips.

Time was critical now. He hoisted her limp body from the trunk and placed her in the driver's seat. Leaning over her listless form he accidentally brushed his arm against her silicone breast. It aroused him. His desire to violate her struggled against his need to escape detection. He brushed her long blond hair from her battered face with the care of a loving husband. He allowed himself a brief moment of pleasure as his hand caressed her bosom. As a final act of gratification he cupped his hand over his face and inhaled deeply, trying to capture the scent of her body.

Time to go he thought. He pulled the seatbelt across her body and inserted the buckle. He then turned the ignition and activated the lights. Before putting the car in gear and releasing the brake he cracked the windows about an inch. He watched as it slipped into the black water, the engine pulling it down like an anchor. In a matter of seconds only a stream of bubbles and ripples remained If and when the car was ever found he hoped the death would be treated as a terrible accident.

Once back at the highway the killer flagged a car headed towards Leadville. The middle-aged woman who picked him up would have been more attractive but years of alcoholism had taken its toll. She tried flirting with him, either to get him into bed

38

or steal his money; either way he didn't care. He was just happy to get out of the cold. She dropped him off in town, never knowing the devil rode shotgun.

After finding a phone booth it was a simple enough task to locate the local tow yard for impounded vehicles from the sheriff's office. Like many small communities they had poor security. He lingered about town until dark then headed for the tow yard. Slipping the flimsy lock on the office door was easy and a quick search of the log book revealed the perfect car. A nondescript blue sedan with plenty of gas and current license plates. The plainer it looked the better, he thought. In any case, by the time anyone missed it, he'd be back in Denver.

The hours behind the wheel gave him plenty of time to plan a dumping strategy for the car. He had several such plans already tucked away in his head so that he wouldn't have to come up with a workable one on the fly. It was too dangerous to dump it near his home. He couldn't afford to give the cops any breaks; not now.

The odds were in his favor, though. He was a chess master while the cops were still playing checkers. He reassured himself of his intellectual superiority with a prideful gaze into the rearview mirror. His plan was to involve some local hoodlums in his plans. As he came into Denver on Interstate 70 he turned north away from his home and traveled to Westminster. He drove to a high-crime neighborhood near Federal Boulevard and 72nd Avenue and parked at a low-income apartment complex. The apartments were often featured in the local newspaper whenever there were incidents of domestic violence, shootings, or stabbings. He had scouted the area months before to find this exact spot. The best thing about common criminals was their predictability. Everyone wanted something in life, he reasoned. The criminals wanted an easy opportunity for crime; it's who they are. Likewise, the cops wanted an easy collar. It was the same in nature. The wolf didn't hunt the fittest individuals in the herd. They went for the young and old, the easy prey. By the same token, the fittest criminal would be the toughest catch. Everyone wanted easy. Give the cops an underhanded pitch and they can't help but swing.

If he couldn't hand-deliver the criminals to the cops, he would give them the next best thing: evidence. He stopped at a dumpster and opened a black plastic bag on top. The smells were horrendous. Picking through the contents he found some papers tattooed with phone numbers and names. He slipped them in his pockets for safekeeping. Then he moved silently through the apartment complex until finding his prey.

Hip Hop music blared from one of the ground floor apartments and a few of the partygoers had spilled out to the courtyard. He watched a couple of the rowdy young men strut around like immature turkeys. They were drinking and swearing and dropping their cigarette butts on the ground. Littering pissed him off. They were just the assholes he had been searching for. He waited for them to finish their beers and stumble back into the apartment to replenish their vices. As the door closed behind them he sneaked over and picked up a few of the bottles and cigarette butts and made a hasty retreat to the car. He watched the car from the shadows for several minutes making sure no one was around. He had been careful to park in a darkened corner of the lot away from the old, dim lights that provided a false sense of security. He dropped a few cigarette butts in the ashtray and hid the bottles under the seats. He then sprinkled the interior with the trash he had collected—with any luck the cops would be able to trace either the DNA or fingerprints back to these jerks. A fitting punishment for a litter bug, he thought. Even if they didn't connect the dots the evidence would at least muddy the water.

After popping the trunk he removed the taillight covers and removed both bulbs. With any luck a cop would pull it over for the defective brake lights and catch them red-handed. After wiping down the interior he dangled the keys form the ignition and rolled down the driver's window. As added insurance he left a twenty dollar bill on the dashboard in plain sight. The one thing missing was a bright pink neon sign flashing the words *Please Steal Me*. It was a long walk to the bus stop at U.S. Highway 36 and Sheridan Blvd., but that was the point. Glancing at his watch he noted a few stragglers waiting under a covered bench. He scanned the passengers, looking for any potential threat. The two boys hadn't even started shaving yet. A determined looking Hispanic woman; Janitor he thought. An attractive woman wearing a hairnet and thick soled shoes: waitress. She had a spider web tattoo on part of her neck and he wondered if that helped or hindered her tip jar. He walked up to the lighted route map and planned his connections. The bus was there in less than ten minutes.

Two hours and four stops later the killer arrived home to a mailbox full of junk mail and unpaid bills. He had been gone a lot longer than expected. His elderly neighbor had a habit of stacking his newspapers on the porch, telling him once she didn't want burglars to know he was gone. She was a sweet old woman he thought, misguided, but sweet. The decorum of the house was dated but it was clean and tidy. It was his sanctuary, a place to mend his mind and soul. He did a double take as he caught a glimpse of himself walking past the hallway mirror. His normally clean shaven face was textured with stubble and his collar length black hair was oily and stringy. The rugged look was surprisingly appealing to him.

The killer sunk into an old blue-and-orange padded seat and reminisced about his harrowing adventure. Nothing had gone according to plan but he felt an unusual sense of pride in his ability to adapt to the situation and overcome the obstacles. Preparation, he thought, was the key of success. That and a pinch of luck thrown in for good measure.

He grabbed the remote off the coffee table and activated the stereo. Selecting a pre-programmed set of classical music, he sat back with closed eyes as Beethoven's Moonlight Sonata serenaded him through his Cambridge Sound Works speakers. Reclining back, his mind began to wander through a collage of vivid imagery.

The shooting on Monarch pass, the storm, he was lucky to be alive. The road to Aspen had been difficult. He pictured the drop offs and the stress he felt as the Jeep lingered close to the edge of darkness. Then there was Aspen. The town and its residents were so smug, so entitled, it made him sick. The woman and her rat dog were a perfect fit. Although they were from different species they were cut from the same cloth: bitches. He reminisced about his last moments with her. Her iridescent blue eyes and golden hair was a perfect match for her slim, athletic body. She had been an ideal specimen and he felt deprived for having abandoned her before she could get to know him better. It was her loss, he decided. His hand rubbed the armrest of the chair as he imagined the touch of her supple breast. He brought his hand up to his face in one last effort to reclaim the scent she had imparted on him. As his imagination fueled the evolution of their false romance he began to masturbate. Once finished, he drifted off into a deep, peaceful sleep.

He didn't often dream, but on this night he was haunted by the image of a red-haired lioness stalking him through the woods. He would run and take cover but she was always there, watching him, hunting him. She was relentless and cunning, and then she was gone. He had never felt the fear he experienced in this dream. He could feel his heart rate climb and decided that he liked it. He jolted from his dream at the sound of police sirens racing down the block. Panicked, he rushed to the window and watched with relief as they roared past and slipped out of view. He had only been sleeping an hour.

Then it dawned on him. He hadn't said goodnight to his mother. He was too old to be still living with her but she needed him. They lived on her social security checks and the meager income he came by from contract work. His main job was to keep the house nice and clean for her, and keep her company, of course. He regretted leaving her alone these past few days and he tip-toed down the old, creaky stairs to the basement where she lay.

In the center of the room sat a beautiful mahogany coffin fitted with thick brass hardware. He propped open the half-lid above her head so they could talk about his latest adventures. Unlike his childhood days, his mother now loved him. Surrounding the coffin were arrangements of silk flowers and a colorful funeral wreath. He opened the entire lid and gazed upon her form. She lay in her favorite blue dress, buried in a bed of rock salt. Her neck was adorned by a string of pearls with a matching bracelet on her left wrist. The antique watch on her right wrist had stopped ticking years before. Her hair was stained a light yellow and her blackened skin was spotted with mold, but he just saw the beautiful mother from the past. He was feeling vulnerable from his dream and needed to feel the safety and comfort of her touch.

He placed a thick green wool blanket over her body up to her neckline and the dirty brown teddy bear that kept her company on his frequent trips. The old bear was torn and missing its nose, but beauty was in the eye of the beholder, he thought. He climbed the three short stairs of the pedestal and lay beside her in the coffin. He laid his head upon the bear, nuzzling into her musty hair. Finally safe from the lioness he drifted off into a peaceful sleep.

6

Monday morning came sooner than she had hoped. Sarah sat fidgeting in the waiting area of the internal affairs bureau. The secretary had offered her some coffee but Sarah was too nervous to be loading up on caffeine. It seemed like ten minutes before Lieutenant Manilow finally arrived

"Right back this way, Ms. Richards, this shouldn't take long."

She was led into a drab room for her "interview." The walls were bear with the exception of a clock and a thermostat she was certain held a hidden camera. There was no glass window like the ones seen in television dramas. A single small table was wedged into a corner. The table placement didn't allow for the person being interviewed having a barrier between them and the interrogator, the theory being that the subject would feel more vulnerable to the interrogator. Taking her seat Sarah wished she had taken the coffee, if nothing else, to give her hands something to do besides twiddling.

Manilow plopped a large file folder on the table, and wasted no time in getting started.

"We're investigating your role in a traffic accident and subsequent shooting last Friday night in Chaffee County. The district attorney up there has decided not to pursue criminal charges, apparently following a five-minute investigation, but we have a responsibility to ensure that the members of this department act according to our policies and procedures at all times. I've read your report regarding your traffic accident and subsequent shooting . . . very comprehensive."

"Thank you, sir."

"That was a rhetorical comment, Ms. Richards." There was no admiration in his eyes. "So you get to this 'accident,' find a woman's body that you believe was murdered, and immediately start running down the mountain side looking for her killer?"

"Yes, sir." She wasn't planning on giving him an inch.

"Let's set aside, for a moment, the fact that your initial assessment was correct regarding the woman. Why didn't you secure the scene and call for back-up?"

"Sir, I didn't want the killer to get away."

"But he did get away, didn't he?" He didn't wait for an answer before continuing. "Weren't you concerned that you were leaving a murder victim unattended, opening the door for massive contamination from the people there? Can you even confirm in court that the scene wasn't contaminated by anyone?"

"Sir, that wasn't my primary concern at the time."

"Why not? You're a criminalist, not a cop, right? No . . . instead of doing what you're trained to do you ran off after a murderer, without back-up."

She glanced down to the table unsure of how to answer.

"Let's move on. You tracked this guy down the mountain and into the campground, correct?"

"Yes, sir, his tracks led up to a toilet vault and then moved off to the south beyond the campground."

"Did you make any effort to preserve the tracks in the snow either by photography or casting?"

She cocked her head. His expression was passive as he waited for an answer. "No, sir, I was chasing a murderer, I didn't have any gear with me. Even if I did, I wouldn't stop under those circumstances to snap a few photos"

He made an exaggerated notation on his notepad. "And as you chased him up the ravine you came to a spot where he fired his weapon at you, correct?"

"Yes, sir."

Manilow pulled a topographic map from his notebook and placed it on the table in front of her. "Can you point out that spot to me on this map?"

"Well, sir, it was probably somewhere near here," she stated, pressing her finger to the page.

"That's a pretty big area you're indicating, Ms. Richards. Can you be a bit more specific?"

"No, sir."

"Did you make any effort to mark the area so it could be found later by search teams?"

"Well, I was bleeding there, sir, so they could look for that, I guess," she said with mounting frustration.

He pressed on. "So after getting shot at you fired three shots in the direction you thought the shot came from."

"Was that a question, sir?" What was he getting at?

"It's all here in the report, actually. But what isn't here is where you thought the shot came from. I don't suppose you can pinpoint that position for me, either?"

"No, sir, I can't."

"So you fired three shots blindly in a direction without acquiring a target or knowing what lay beyond."

It was more of an accusation than a question.

As he waited for her to respond his Nextel vibrated on the desk. Annoyed, he looked at the caller ID and excused himself. "Wait here, Ms. Richards, I won't be but a moment." Lt. Manilow seemed to be absent for hours but the clock on the wall indicated only four minutes had passed when the door opened. He took his seat with a belabored plop and let out a dramatic sigh. He stared at her for a few seconds before speaking.

"Have you spoken to Sheriff Booth since the shooting?"

"No, sir."

"You didn't talk to him or anyone in his office?"

"No."

"Do you have some kind of family connection or friendship with him I should know about?"

"No, sir. That night was the first time I met him. What are you getting at?"

He continued, with a defeated expression. "Due to a mechanism which I don't fully understand, this investigation is concluded. Apparently, Sheriff Booth was so taken by your actions that night he felt compelled to call our sheriff and send a faxed letter of commendation for you."

A slight smile began to form on her lips, but she doused it. "So I can go?"

"Ms. Richards, you may have been spared this time but rest assured, any similar behavior in the future would not be good for your career."

She gave him a slight nod. "Thank you for your frankness, sir." She stood and walked to the door.

He opened it in a hollow expression of courtesy.

Manny was waiting for her outside the lab as she bounded down the stairs. "So you still look like you got some ass left."

"Careful Manny, in some circles that might constitute sexual harassment."

"Yeah, right. Aren't you the one that forwarded that email of those naked firemen?"

Sarah laughed and conceded the point.

"So you survived, eh?"

"I guess, but I felt like a criminal. He questioned all my decisions that night. He thinks I should have acted more like a criminalist and less like a cop." Her eyes drifted to the side and Manny could tell she was punishing herself with doubt.

"Hey kid, I want to tell you something and you need to listen to this. No matter what we do in this field there will always be people who say you did it wrong. It is the curse of our profession. Cops attract armchair quarterbacks like flies to shit." He paused, looking for some kind of response but none came. "If you had stayed with the scene and secured evidence then he'd be bitchin' that you let a murderer get away. He'd have questioned your courage and fitness to be the protector of the citizenry or some shit like that." He grabbed her by the shoulders and faced her toward him. "But, hey, it's done. It's over now, okay? You don't have to deal with Barry anymore on this, right?"

His strength of character lifted her spirits a bit. "Yeah, I guess I survived. Oh, but I haven't told you the best part. You'll never believe how it ended."

"Let me guess, Booth called the sheriff and told him he wanted to give you a letter of commendation?"

Her eyes widened. "How did you know that?"

"Hey, who's got your back, kid? I've known Booth for years. We've been hunting a few times together and he was going to put you in for a commendation anyway. I just expedited the process."

"You dickhead," Sarah said, punching him in the arm. "What if Manilow finds out? He's gonna come after both of us!"

"Who's going to tell him? Just you, me, and Booth know about the phone call."

"Yeah, and what if Booth lets it slip out?"

"He's not. Trust me, he has a lower opinion of Barry than we do. They've crossed paths before and as I hear it, Barry was very demanding when asking for copies of your reports from Friday night."

"That's a helluva risk Manny"

"Trust me. Who do you think gave Barry his nickname?"

She smiled and changed the subject as they walked into the lab. "Where are we at with the kid's shooting?"

"I'm glad you asked."

"Why's that?" she asked

"Hey, you're gonna love this. I spoke to the sheriff and told him that this looked like a long-range shot and we didn't have a good fix on the trajectory." He paused for dramatic effect.

"Yeah, so?"

"Well, since you got screwed out of your vacation, and we need some special help on this one, he's agreed to let you take a few days off with pay to head up to the Facility."

"Seriously?" she asked. "But what about Andy? Technically, he's the primary on this case."

"Andy is going to have his hands full with things around here. Believe me, he doesn't have the time to spare."

"And I do? Have you seen my inbox, Manny?"

"I talked to Andy and he's totally on board with you going, plus the sheriff didn't exactly say it was an optional trip."

"So when do I leave?"

"The sooner the better kid."

7

The "Facility," was a nickname given to the Rocky Mountain Forensics Center, a one-of-a-kind specialized school devoted to forensics training and research. Nestled on just over 1500 acres in the Pike National Forest north of Steamboat Springs, Colorado, it was the world's premier forensic training center. The 60-acre campus was comprised of several buildings, most of which were situated around an oval-shaped man-made lake. The lake was fed by the middle fork of the Little Snake River, which ran through the center of the property.

The Facility was privately owned and operated by Dr. Art Von Hollen, and was more efficient and successful than any government run operation. The crippling effects of red tape and bureaucracy were not found here. Students stayed in luxury apartments while attending one- to six-week seminars and instructors were hand-picked from across the globe, each making use of private town homes and cars while teaching.

Art had known Sarah since she was a little girl and promised her grandfather he'd look after her . It was Art who'd gotten Sarah interested in forensics and he mentored her whenever he could. The drive from Denver took almost four hours and Sarah used the time to review the crime scene in anticipation of Art's inevitable questions. She had an open invitation and apartment waiting for her whenever she wanted, a fact that some of her peers and supervisors resented.

Driving through the security gate she pulled into her private garage and dropped her bags at the foot of the stairs. The cobalt blue sky convinced her to leave her truck and walk across campus to Art's office in the administration building overlooking the lake. She entered the plush lobby and took the portico stairs leading to the second floor. The cherry-paneled walls and eight-inch crown molding reminded her of an old mansion. As she entered the outer office she was greeted by the warm smile of Tilly Helton, Art's personal assistant.

"Why, hello there, young lady. Don't you look ravishing."

Tilly was a childhood friend from Art's hometown of Williamsburg, Kentucky, and was his best friend and confidant. She was a true Southern lady with a quick wit and impeccable manners.

"Hi, there, Tilly. You look great"

"Darlin', I'm doing so fine it oughtta be illegal." The Southern drawl hummed across her lips. "You must be looking for Art; he's leading a tour of media folks over by the biological sciences building. He wanted you to head on over and find him. They should be wrapping up pretty soon."

"Thanks, Tilly. I'll see you later?"

"Well, you had better," She said with a wide smile.

Art handled the media like a lion at a three ring circus. It usually took less than ten minutes before he had them eating out of his hand. The successes at the Facility were world renowned and he never missed an opportunity to promote them. Sarah eased her way to the back of the crowd and caught Art's eye. He smiled with a wink and gave her a look of relief. No doubt he had been told about her close call with death a few nights earlier. She followed along as he described the campus buildings with the geniality of a happy tour guide.

After the tour the reporters wandered about taking notes and pictures of the scenery so Art turned his attention to Sarah. "Sarah, I'm so happy you could make it up. Jimmy told me about Friday night. He said the guy was lying in wait for you? I don't have to tell you how upset I'd be if you'd gotten yourself killed up there."

"Thanks, Art. I guess it wasn't the smartest idea to go running off after the guy."

"Well, no, but it was the right thing to do. The killer's just lucky your grandfather isn't around anymore. He'd be up there right now tracking the bastard down."

Sarah recalled the times her grandfather had taught her tracking in the wilderness. He seemed capable of following an animal's tracks over pavement. "I think a big reason I'm still here is because of the lessons he taught me."

"I have no doubt. Listen, something's come up and I was hoping you could do me a favor."

"Sure, Art, name it."

"Can you run Doc over to Steamboat for a doctor's appointment? I was planning to take him but I've got to deal with some administrative issues and you know how he'll get if he has to cancel the appointment."

"Sure. I'd be happy to take him. I'm not sure he likes me, though; it might be a long car ride."

"Don't worry about Doc, he's just old, and stubborn as a mule. Don't give him an inch and he'll respect you all the more."

"No problem. Where can I find him?"

"He's working over on Main Street. I think he's in the bank. We can talk about your case tomorrow, if you don't mind."

"No problem Art. I'll head right over."

Main Street was the name given to the realistic urban training center at the north end of the campus. A stranger walking onto the street would think he was in a small, deserted town. The full-scale city block contained a convenience store, deli, bank, business office, even an ice cream parlor. Each of the businesses was furnished down to bags of potato chips on the store shelves and even personal items from the "employees" working in the stores. There were also several homes situated around a small cul-de-sac at the far end of the street. These buildings allowed instructors to create crime scenes in a realistic setting that Art liked to describe as a "living classroom" environment. The buildings were outfitted with surveillance systems, giving instructors the ability to watch and record the students' progress. Each building was connected to a series of classrooms so instructors could debrief the attendees on the spot in real time. It was a model of efficiency and changed the way in which crime scene investigation was taught around the world.

The sound of her Duramax diesel engine was unmistakable as she pulled the big truck up along the curb outside the bank. A group of students was gathered around a van outside the ice cream shop that looked like it had been blown up with a high explosive. They were busy flagging small bits of the bomb and photographing their positions. One of the students burned her a look as if she'd just compromised the scene but Sarah blew it off. She strode through the bank doors and found Doc on top of an old, creaky wooden ladder, replacing a light fixture above a teller station. She could hear him swearing to himself as he attached the wiring to the fluorescent fixture.

"Hey Doc, how's it going?"

He turned his head and gave her an audible grunt, a pencil clenched in his lips. A small work light hung from the ceiling, illuminating the wrinkled face of a man who had lived a full life. He was wearing a pair of old denim coveralls that were coated with years of dirt and grease. As he turned back to his work Sarah regretted her offer to drive him to his appointment. The truth was Doc intimidated Sarah. It wasn't that he was rude or mean to her, she just couldn't get a read on him. She knew that Art held him in high regard and that was enough, she supposed.

"Art asked me to take you to your doctor's appointment today so just let me know whenever you're ready, okay?"

Doc gave her another grunt. Sarah took a seat at one of the desks in the lobby and waited while he finished his work. The name plate on the desk read Neal Bush and she laughed at the irony. She passed the time looking out the window, watching the students who were now on their hands and knees, searching the street for bomb fragments.

After several minutes, Doc asked, "Hand me one of those bulbs, will you?"

She sprang from her seat, thankful to be of help and breaking the monotony. "What happened here?"

Doc gave her a slight smirk. "Damned instructor thought it would be a good idea to fire a shotgun into the light fixture while the power was on. Damned near started a fire that could have burned the place down."

"Jesus, was anyone hurt?"

"Nope, just his pride, I suspect. Lost a bit of his butt after Art chewed him out, too." He chuckled.Doc climbed down the rickety ladder. "Okay, let's turn on the juice and see if she works." The power kicked on and after a short inspection he was satisfied the work was complete.

As they walked to the truck he opened the bank door for her. He tried to open the truck door but it was locked. Embarrassed, Sarah searched her pocket for the keys.

"Sorry, it's a habit." She clicked her remote entry fob; Doc huffed

"In my day we never had to lock the doors. People had respect for a man's property." He struggled to get into the cab which was a too high for his 5'10" frame.

Sarah selected a classic country station on her satellite radio and headed off campus on her way to Steamboat. She tried to start a conversation as a "Little Jimmy" Dickens ballad serenaded them through her Bose speaker. "Does it bother you that you can't drive anymore?"

Doc shot her a look of amusement. "I never said I couldn't drive . . . just don't like to. There's no courtesy on the roads anymore. Everyone's out for themselves."

She turned her attention to the road for a while, embarrassed by her assumption. Their conversation was strained by Doc giving short answers to her friendly questions. She decided she should just shut up and enjoy the beautiful music and scenery.

"Sarah!" Doc snapped.

"What?" Startled, she wondered if she had been drifting off the road. "The accelerator and brake pedals are progressive in nature . . . they aren't a goddamned on/off switch," he stated.

Sarah realized she'd been tapping the beat of the song with her right foot. "Oh, sorry, Doc." Her smile was met with a short sigh and shake of his head.

Doc was an enigma to her. She knew he'd worked in law enforcement before volunteering for the Army in WWII. Art told her he had been a medic which explained his nickname. He had returned home after the war but she didn't know much more than that. She assumed that Arthur had employed him as a handyman and hunting guide out of a sense of obligation to the old man.

Doc gave her directions to the doctor's office as Sarah came into the city. She took a turn on 8th Street and headed up to Pine Street, where she took a left.

"It's up there on the right. Just pull up to the curb and let me out," he said, pointing a crooked boney finger.

Sarah stopped by the historic brick building that looked to be as old as her gray-haired passenger. The sign on the building read High Plains Veterinary Hospital.

"Here?" she asked in disbelief.

"Yup," he replied dryly, not reacting to her incredulous tone. "Pick me up in a half-hour. Shouldn't take long, it's just a check-up."

So that's it, she thought, the old bugger is senile. Up until now he had seemed quite lucid. This must be why Art asked me to drive she thought. Sarah considered her options and at the risk of sounding rude she decided to intervene. "Doc?"

He turned to look at her with his soft blue eyes.

"This is a hospital for animals, not people."

He stepped back to the open window and leaned his elbows onto the edge. "I'm fully aware of our location, Sarah."

"But, Doc—"

He interrupted her with a wave of his hand. "Look, Sarah, the fact is that I don't like people doctors. You go into the office and all they do is ask questions. 'How're you feeling today, Doc?' 'What seems to be the problem?' 'Where does it hurt?' Vets don't have patients that speak to them so they're better at figuring out what's wrong with you. Plus, it's harder to get through vet school than medical school." He tapped his hand twice on the window ledge as if to say off you go now. "Don't worry, been comin' here for years. Know the doctor well." He started to walk away but turned with a sly grin. "You want me to get you a cookie?" He roared in laughter and disappeared through the front door.

Sarah sat dumbfounded for several seconds before putting the truck in gear and pulling away from the curb. She laughed at her assumptions and couldn't help but think that the enigma just became a bit more entangled.

After a short bout of window-shopping, Sarah returned to pick him up. Doc was standing on the corner waiting for her.

"Sorry, Doc, were you waiting long?"

"Nope, your timing was perfect. I just walked out the door a few moments ago." He seemed to be in a happy mood.

"Everything okay?"

"Yup, fit as a fiddle, as they say."

She had prepared herself for the quiet ride back to the Facility when Doc asked, "So why don't you tell me about your scene the other day?"

Grateful for the conversation she described the condition of the scene where the teenager died when he interrupted her. "No, no, not that one, the murder scene from Friday night on Monarch Pass."

Sarah told him about the accident and her chase. She felt disconnected from the story and she relayed it like a television reporter. The visions were clear in her head but they seemed more like a dream than reality.

"You could have been killed up there. It was the right move to break off the pursuit," he said when she finished.

"Have you ever been in a shootout, Doc?"

"Oh, I hurt someone's feelings one time."

She realized the naivety of her question, given his combat experience.

"You mentioned something about red marks on the victim's body."

It was more of a question than a statement, she thought.

"Yeah, they were about a half-inch wide and looked like a dried ligature mark."

"Where were they, exactly?"

"Um, I saw some running along her back from the shoulder area to the waist but I never got a good look at them."

Doc sat silently for a few moments, gazing out the front of the truck. "Did you notice anything else about the victim's body?"

Sarah thought for a moment before replying. "Well, I thought there was a faint scent of lilacs and honey near her neck. I figured it was maybe her perfume. Also, her hair smelled like chlorine or something. I thought maybe she'd been swimming at a public pool prior to her abduction."

"Maybe," Doc murmured.

It was after dinner by the time Sarah dropped Doc off at his cabin so she decided to head out for a little people watching and a drink. The Lion's Den was the Facility's watering hole, akin to Quantico's Boardroom but with a far more impressive atmosphere. Sarah always felt the Boardroom at the FBI's famed Virginia training academy looked more like a high school cafeteria than the executive decorum implied by its name. By contrast the "den," as it was often called, looked like a sports bar carved into the side of a cliff with rock walls surrounding the bar and table areas. Arcade games, poker and pool tables, and fifty-four-inch LCD televisions dotted the interior. Signed memorabilia from the Colorado sports franchises decorated every free space on the walls.

Sarah picked a chair at the end of the bar next to a framed collection of the first season programs of the Colorado Mammoth lacrosse team. A white lacrosse ball sat in a small protective case autographed by #22, Gary Gait, the famous player from Syracuse University. The location at the bar gave her a good vantage point where she could observe people without being seen. She scanned the room for a friendly face and was happy when an old friend sat down beside her.

"Jenny! What are you doing here?"

Jenny Fletcher was a college roommate who went into patrol instead of the crime lab. She was the first female officer to join the Westminster Police SWAT team in the northern Denver Metro Area. "Oh, I'm taking a refresher course on basic crime scene photography. Hey, did you see that guy at the other end of the bar? He's been staring at you since you sat down."

Sarah rolled her eyes and tried to look over in his direction. He looked away as their eyes crossed paths and tried to appear more interested in his beer. Sarah was surprised to see a man she thought was on the other side of the world.

"Five bucks says you don't have the guts to go talk to him, Sarah."

She shot Jenny a wicked smile. "You're on." Sarah pushed away from the counter and walked the length of the bar, eyes fixed on the rugged, handsome man. She could feel the eyes of a half dozen men glued to her body as she walked. "Is this chair taken?"

The man looked up with a flustered expression. "Ah, no, um, please, sit down."

"I know you, don't I? I've seen your picture in Art's office."

"I'm his nephew, Daniel. Daniel Von Hollen," he said, extending his hand.

She liked the strength in his grip; it was a man's handshake.

"I thought you were in the Army. Last time I asked Art, he said you were in Afghanistan. Are you here for training?"

"Ah, no, ma'am."

"Sarah, please." Daniel shifted in his seat and cleared his throat.

"I'm not in the Army anymore. I got out last month and Uncle Art gave me a job here as a hunting guide, working with Doc."

Sarah caught herself staring at his chiseled features. His muscular frame was toned, but not hulky. The skin on his chin was lighter in color than his cheeks, indicating he had shaved off a beard, and he kept his hair cut short. His deep brown eyes were they type she could get lost in. There was a mystery lurking behind them. He was almost twelve years older but she liked what she saw. This is ridiculous, she thought, you just met this guy. Technically, he wasn't a total stranger, she reasoned. Art had told her a few stories about him over the years and she felt like she kind of knew him.

"I thought Art told me you wouldn't be coming home for another year or so."

His eyes drifted over her shoulder like he was searching for the right words. Did I say something wrong she wondered?

"Well, things kind of changed." He looked up and tried to force a smile "Well...I'm glad" she said, smiling.

Watching him closely Sarah noticed something very interesting. Up close, Daniel had a very strong presence, like he was the only man in the room. But from afar she didn't even notice him. He wasn't loud and boisterous like a lot of the cops in the bar. Sarah wondered if he was just the quiet type.

"You should come out with me and Doc sometime," he suggested.

"I would like that, Daniel." Sarah couldn't hide her attraction to him but hoped it wasn't obvious. She was captivated by their conversation. Then a commotion at the other end of the bar got their attention. A hulk of a man was standing toe-to-toe with Jenny. Sarah sprang from her chair and hurried over to see what was going on.

Mark Blackstone was the SWAT commander for the Boston Police. Technically, his command covered the crime lab as well, and he used his position to attend classes at the coveted facility. Even though Blackstone never worked on crime scenes, he felt attending classes at the posh facility was a privilege he'd earned with his rank. It didn't bother him in the least that his staff didn't get the same opportunity for training. After all, they were just civilians. Blackstone was six beers into his night and Jenny's dismissal of his advances stabbed at his masculinity. When Jenny told him she was SWAT, too, he decided ridicule was better than flirting.

The banter went back and forth like two children until his ego took the last blow. He grabbed her arm just above the elbow. Jenny tried to release his grip but at 6'2," and 225 pounds, he was just too strong.

"What are you, some kind of dyke? You don't know what you're missing," he said with a grotesque snarl.

"I may keep my dick in a drawer, but it's still bigger than yours," Jenny countered.

Sarah was about to say something when Daniel spoke up.

"Sir, let go of her arm. Now, please."

Blackstone turned to face the smaller man. His bloodshot eyes were filled with rage and his muscles were taut. He had the build of a man who lived on steroids. He released his grip from Jenny and decided he'd have a go at this new play toy. "What did you say to me, kid?"

"Looks like you've had a few too many drinks, cowboy. Why don't you go outside and walk it off." Daniel was as calm as if he were talking to a pastor.

Blackstone took a swing but never had the chance to see it connect.

Sarah had never seen anyone move so fast.

Daniel side-stepped the punch and brought his elbow into Blackstone's nose, while grabbing his hand in a classic wrist lock. Blackstone went flipping into the air in a fraction of a second, landing in a crumpled heap.

Sarah heard his wrist snap as Daniel locked up his arm.

Blackstone's nose was streaming blood. Blackstone's friends were stunned by Daniel's speed, and decided they should get while the getting was good. They scooped their friend up off the floor and hurried him out the door.

"Well, that was exciting," Jenny said with a wide smile across her lips.

Daniel could see Sarah's wide eyes and couldn't hide the look of shame on his face. "Ah, I had better go," he said.

Before she could stop him Daniel was out the door, leaving her to wonder about the mysterious man she had just met.

Sarah looked at Jenny, who was still smiling. "What are you smiling at?"

"Do you think he's got a twin brother?"

Sarah dismissed the comment and the two laughed about the night's entertainment over a round of beers.

8

Sarah awoke on her couch with a mild headache from the night of drinking and booming music. She was still dressed, with the exception of one shoe which was lingering by the kitchen. The aroma of coffee filled the air and Sarah realized that Tilly had stopped by before heading to the office. As she rose and stretched her arms she caught a glimpse of the clock on the wall. Shit! She sprang from the couch and cursed. She had less than forty-five minutes to shower and get to the ballistics lab. She grabbed a thermal mug, taking the coffee to go, and arrived at the lab a few minutes before nine. Her hair was tied back in a ponytail and she wore an Arapahoe County sheriff's sweat shirt and jeans. Sarah's natural beauty didn't require makeup.

"Well, good morning Sarah . . . glad to see you could make it," Art said as she burst through the door.

Punctuality was a vice of his and he often lectured late students with a professorial tone while peeking over his wire reading glasses.

"I'm here, I'm here, hold your horses."

He laughed at her pseudo-defiant tone and gave her a hug. "I was wondering if we'd be seeing you this morning."

"What's that supposed to mean?"

"A little birdie told me there was some excitement in the Den last night."

"Yeah, I was going to talk to you about that. Daniel said he wasn't in the Army anymore."

"That's right."

"But I thought you told me that he was going to be serving a few more years in Afghanistan."

His eyes narrowed as a smile emerged on his lips. "It sounds to me like someone is developing an interest in my nephew."

Sarah blushed at the comment. "Ah, noooo . . ." she mumbled, but her eyes told a different story.

Time to change the subject. She knew Art could read her like a book and the last thing she wanted was to discuss her possible feelings about Daniel with him. The truth of the matter was that Sarah had made some bad relationship decisions in the past. Her gut guided her heart. She didn't fall head over heels that often but when she did she fell hard and fast. Art knew it too.

Sitting at an examination table was Walter Haruki, a famed firearms examiner Art had stolen from the FBI crime lab in Quantico, Virginia. He had a reputation for his diligence and attention to details. Walter activated the monitor as he powered on his comparison microscope. The Leica FS4000 scope was coupled with a Nikon digital capture station offering a state-of-the -art platform to examine expended bullets and cartridge cases. "Well, let's take a look at that bullet fragment, shall we?" Art said.

Sarah retrieved a paper evidence envelope from her bag and handed it to Walter. The bullet was wrapped in toilet paper and encased in a plastic 35mm film canister to protect the rifling marks on the bullet jacket. These lands and grooves traversed the length of the barrel, twisting either right or left depending on the make and model of the firearm. Walter mounted the bullet's base to a wax platform that suspended the bullet horizontally under the microscope's powerful optics. He adjusted the magnification and turned the dials to bring the microscopic features into focus. With the click of a button the image was projected onto the eighteen-inch flat screen monitor.

"Uh, Art . . . you may want to take a look at this," Walter said.

Art took a seat next to Walter and studied the monitor. The two looked puzzled as Walter rotated the bullet fragment 360 degrees to see all its surfaces.

"What is it?"

Walter waited a moment before speaking. "Well, there doesn't appear to be any rifling marks on the bullet."

Art and Walter exchanged looks as they considered the implications of this finding.

Sarah broke the silence. "Did we not find the jacket?"

"No . . . the jacket is here. There's just no rifling on it."

"Well, that doesn't make sense. I thought all rifle barrels had lands and grooves," Sarah said.

"Well, most shotguns don't have rifling, and a number of traditional muzzle-loading rifles don't have them, either. Shotguns can fire a one-ounce slug a couple hundred yards but this projectile is no shotgun slug. "I can't imagine why anyone would choose either type of gun to take a shot at a kid at night," Art said.

"I know, I know. It makes no sense. Unless, of course, your shooter was a lot closer than what you originally thought."

Sarah considered the possibility for a moment. "We found no evidence of an expended casing and the ground slopes down to the water and away from the victim's position. So if the shooter were closer the shot should have an upward trajectory, which it didn't," she stated from memory.

"How far was it to the other side of the river?" Art asked.

"Oh, I'd say about a hundred-fifty, two hundred yards."

"I once saw Jim Shockey make a four-hundred-yard shot with his muzzleloader but that was in broad daylight and he had a scope," Walter said.

Sarah had often watched the adventures of the famed hunter Jim Shockey on the Outdoor Channel. He was a legendary hunter who had taken all of the North American big game species with a muzzle-loading rifle, the only hunter to ever do so. Sarah could tell that Art's mind was in overdrive.

"Let's take a look at the sketch and photos you brought. Maybe that will give us a clearer picture of the surroundings."

Sarah brought a color diagram and DVD containing the crime scene images and video taken at the scene. They studied the photographs for several minutes and Art called up some additional aerial photos of the area from the computer network server.

"How is it you have aerial photos of this location on your computer, Art?" Sarah asked.

"We have extensive resources with the assessor's offices throughout the state," he said dryly.

After several minutes of contemplating the images, Art continued with his observations. "Another problem to tackle is the timing of the shooting."

"What do you mean?" Sarah asked.

"Well, look here. The area on the other side of the river between the river bank and houses is pretty barren, except a few scattered bushes and some grass. By the looks of the graffiti the victim was killed a few seconds after he started tagging."

"That was our assumption," Sarah said.

"Well, if he was shot soon after he began painting, then that means that the killer was sitting there waiting for him."

"That sounds pretty unlikely," Walter said.

"I agree," Art said. "You see how this bridge crosses here? Well, that would obstruct his view to the south and he loses sight of the area to the north right here where these trees are."

"So what are you getting at?" Sarah asked, trying to keep up with their thought process.

"Well, the closer you are the more restricted your field of view is. That is to say, the smaller the portion of the wall you can watch. As you back up and get farther away, you can keep an eye on a wider section of the river."

"Yeah, but in either case it would still mean that the killer was waiting for him to show up and we know the victim didn't plan on being there until that night."

The three of them studied the images on the monitor for several minutes until Walter gave them another observation. "I think the guy would have to be lying there in wait. It's almost as if he was—"

"Hunting him," Daniel said from just inside the doorway.

Sarah jumped in her seat, letting out a muffled "Jesus Christ!"

Art had seen Daniel standing behind them in the reflection of the monitor but didn't know how long he had been standing there. He was impressed. It took great stealth to enter a room without being noticed.

"Maybe," Arthur said. "But why would someone choose a shotgun or a muzzle-loading musket?"

"Maybe that's all he had" Sarah offered.

"It would be a near impossible shot from that distance at night with a shotgun or muzzleloader, even with a scope," Daniel said.

Sarah's eyes fixed on Daniel's and a giddy smile came across her face. She was excited to see him again.

"Wait a minute," Walter said. "Let me take some measurements." Walter took the bullet from the stand and grabbed a pair of digital calipers. He first measured the bullet fragment's diameter and then placed it on a small, digital scale. He scanned the books and folders in his office and settled his finger on a spiral-bound book with a government stamp on the cover. He turned the page, dragging his fingers down a columns of numbers. "It's pretty mangled, but from my measurements I would guess that this is a.338 magnum, probably two hundred fifty grains, but don't quote me on that." Placing the bullet back on the wax base of the stand Walter made further observations under the microscope. "I'm not sure why, but my gut is telling me that this might be a Lapua round."

"What makes you say that?" Art asked.

"I'm not sure. I've seen some before and this just looks like it. Give me a minute to think."

"Have you considered the killer was using an ACR?" Daniel asked.

Walter and Art exchanged curious glances, hoping the other had an answer to the question.

Sarah broke the stalemate. "What is an ACR?"

"Oh, I'm sorry. ACR stands for Advanced Combat Rifle. It was the continuation of the Special Purpose Individual Weapon program in the 1970s." Sarah face remained blank. "The ACR program tested the feasibility of replacing the M16A2 infantry rifle. It involved the design of several experimental fléchette rifles with smooth bores. Instead of firing bullets, the rifles fired fléchettes, which were basically tiny darts. The program was abandoned in the 'nineties, but if memory serves, McDonnell Douglas produced a .338 caliber."

"This isn't a dart, Daniel. There is clearly a copper jacket surrounding a lead core. See here . . . " Walter commented as he brought the image back onto the monitor.

"Oh, right you are. That's definitely not a fléchette."

Sarah surmised that Daniel came in the room after they began looking at the crime scene photos.

"I think we're going to have to go to the scene, Sarah," Art offered. "We can only do so much from here."

"Okay, I can give Manny a call and put in the request."

"Don't bother; I'll place a direct call to the sheriff to cut through the red tape. We can leave after lunch. I'd like to see what the area looks like at night."

"All right, sounds good to me." Walter grabbed the bullet off the stand and was about to put it back in the evidence packaging when Sarah stopped him.

"Oh, Walter, I almost forgot to mention it. Andy and I saw what looked like part of an emblem or marking on the base of the bullet."

"The base of the bullet? I've never known a manufacturer to do that." Walter mounted it inverted on the stand so the base came into view. "Oh, look at that . . . jackpot!"

"Do you see it?" Sarah asked.

"No, I mean look at the raised area here in the center. That's what they call a lock base. That confirms it. The bullet is definitely a Lapua .338 Magnum," Walter said.

"What's a lock base?" Art asked.

"It's a proprietary design giving the bullet superior accuracy over very long distances. I would say that if this is the bullet your killer used, then he selected it because he intended to make a very long shot."

"So it could be as far away as the houses across the field?" Art asked.

"Definitely, maybe further. Depends on the scope he used and his skill, of course. Let me check the book here." Walter ran his fingers over the columns of several more pages. "Lapua makes the lock base in a .338 and .308 caliber." Walter clicked a button on his mouse and saved the image on the screen.

"But what about the marking, Walter? Is that consistent with a Lapua bullet?" Sarah asked.

"Um, oh, yeah, now let's see here." Walter adjusted the focus on the lens to bring the area into question. "What, this area here?" he asked.

"Yeah, to me it looks like a jagged line, or a checkmark or something?"

"I'm not sure. It doesn't look like a manufacturer's mark. It's probably not a mark at all, just an artifact from the impact with the wall. Lapua doesn't mark the bases of their bullets as far as I know but I'll check with a buddy to be sure."

Sarah was disappointed. She had hoped the mark would be a significant clue in the investigation. "Sarah, it's almost eleven. Why don't you get your things together and we'll meet in my office in a half hour?"

"Sure, Art, that sounds great. It'll give me a chance to grab a sandwich."

Walter removed the bullet once again and this time put it in the protective packaging. Sarah tucked the evidence into her bag and headed toward the door with Walter. As they approached the doorway Sarah turned back to see Daniel staring at the captured image of the bullet base on the monitor. He was probably intrigued at the mystery of it all, she thought. It was kind of cute. It was her experience that most men were intimidated by her chosen profession but Daniel might be a bit more hardened by his military service. A lot of men these days, even some cops, were more metro-sexual than heterosexual. Forensics was not the most traditional employment choice for women but females were outpacing men, by far, in forensics.

Arthur collected his jacket and headed for the door when Daniel called out to him. "Hey, Uncle Art, can I talk to you for a minute?"

"Why don't you two go on without me. I'll be along in just a few minutes," Arthur stated.

Sarah smiled at Daniel and walked out the door with a half-skip.

Arthur went back to Daniel and could see a concerned look upon his face. "What is it Daniel?"

Daniel looked at the screen for a long second and then back at his uncle. "I need to talk to you about this mark."

9

Most of the highway traffic was made up of truckers and local residents. Coming back on a weekday was much better than the massive traffic jams the highway suffered on the weekends during the ski season. Sarah's Nextel phone beeped that annoying alert tone she had come to loathe. It was Detective Lopez.

"Hey, kid, where you at?"

"I'm just coming up on Floyd Hill just outside Genesee. Should be there in about an hour, I'd guess. Depends on what the traffic is like on C-470."

"Great. I've got to head into a meeting with the brass on this thing and then I'll be out. If you get to the scene before me, just take over. Tony can't get there, but Andy is going out. He may be there already."

"Thank God, I could use the help. Art is behind me somewhere but he might be arriving a bit later. He had some things to get together before he left."

"No sweat, see you when I see you."

Sarah pulled up to the scene and had no trouble getting in this time. Since the scene had been released there was no yellow tape to cross and no guard to pass. She saw Manny's car parked behind it. Across the service road was a black and silver Chevy Camaro SS. The hood was up and Manny was peering over the engine. Sarah could see another man bent over the engine, too. Manny had a knack for striking up conversations with the locals as he worked a scene. If there was information to be had, he would get it. Her heart skipped a beat as the second man stood up at the sound of her approach.

"Daniel? What the heck are you doing here?"

"Oh, I was just showing Detective Lopez my car."

"This is yours?"

"Yeah I picked her up a few years ago and Uncle Art had gotten her in working order when I came out here to work for him."

"It looks pretty sweet," she said.

"Pretty sweet?" Manny interrupted. "This is a '67 big block 502 with dual intakes and Mag wheels," he cooed.

"Careful, Manny, you're already married, remember?" Sarah joked.

"A guy can fantasize, can't he?"

Sarah looked back at Daniel, still confused. "Wait . . . how did you guys beat me down here? I would have seen you guys blow by me in this thing."

"Oh, the car was being worked on at a custom shop in Centennial so it seemed like a good idea to go with Uncle Art. We flew into Centennial airport about an hour ago."

Centennial Airport is the second largest general aviation airport in the United States. The Arapahoe County Sheriff's Office was a few short blocks away, as was the Coroner's Office. The nationally recognized pathologist preferred this proximity, as he did a number of private autopsies from around the country that could be flown in for examination.

"Art has a private plane?"

"Hardly!" Arthur's voice boomed from behind the car as he came into the conversation. "I chartered the flight out of Steamboat. We are driving back to the Facility in this contraption."

Daniel raised his eyebrows and looked at Manny.

"I don't know, Art, it's a pretty nice contraption," Manny said.

"We'll see how well his chick-magnet does during the next blizzard. He should have bought an SUV like I told him."

"You know I'm standing right here," Daniel said.

"A chartered flight, huh, Art? Must be nice to have money." Sarah said with a smile.

"I don't apologize for my success, Sarah. Besides, it pisses the sheriff off that I can fly by private plane and he can't." They shared a laugh.

Andy was already waiting for them when they made it to the river.

"So how did your meeting go?" Sarah asked.

"Typical". "Where we're at and what are you going to do next" Manny said impersonating the Sheriff's voice.

"What are we planning on doing next?" Andy asked.

"My hope is resting on Art at this point."

"How did the bosses react to Art being here?" Sarah asked.

"Art still garners a lot of respect but the bosses want to take the credit for solving this thing. So for the time being, Art's involvement will be 'unofficial.' We are not to give him credit for anything in our reports," Manny said.

"That seems petty," Andy said.

"I agree, but you know how they get about grabbing the headlines. The election is next year and the last thing the sheriff wants is to be upstaged by anyone, even a former employee."

As they approached the murder scene, Sarah recognized a member of the Internal Affairs Division. Lester Davis was a sergeant in the unit and friendlier than his boss, Lt. Manilow.

"What's Lester doing out here?" Sarah asked.

"Barry insisted on it since we have civilians assisting in the investigation," Manny responded, disdainfully.

"I'm a civilian," Sarah said.

"Hey, it's Barry, remember?"

"Do you trust him?"

"Lester? Oh, yeah. He's the only one worth a shit up there. He's not predisposed to think that cops are the bad guys, but remember that he still reports to Barry, so treat him like a mushroom until we have something concrete to go on."

"A mushroom?" Sarah asked.

"Yeah, keep him in the dark and feed him shit." He whispered. "Hey, Lester, sorry you got dragged out on this," Manny said as he greeted the sergeant with a brief handshake.

"I gotta be somewhere during the day. This is a hell of a lot better than my cubicle."

"I hear you."

"Anything I can help with?" Davis asked.

"Nah. This is more of a tour guide sort of thing. Art just wanted to get a feel for the place in living color, so to speak," Manny replied.

"Okay, well, I'll be hanging around. Let me know if I'm in the way or anything."

"Don't worry about it, bud, you're fine."

Art had already passed the group with Andy as they walked up to the wall. The impact site was easy to find. The dried blood surrounding the shattered cement looked almost black against the lighter background. The pooled blood on the ground below was almost gone, having been reclaimed by the earth. Art studied the location of the impact site relative to the victim's partial moniker painted on the wall. He had noticed other graffiti on the wall along the bike path.

"Manny, have you had the gang unit check these other monikers on the wall" Arthur asked.

"Yeah, we checked their photo file and determined that there was no apparent pattern. Some of these are months old and none seem to be repeating. It just seems to be a location of convenience and not territorial to any of the gangs," Manny answered.

Sarah explained to Art what she had seen the night she arrived and where she had located the bullet. Andy pulled out the aerial photos Art had brought and oriented them relative to the horizontal plane of the wall. Art used a dry erase marker to plot the possible trajectories based on the impact angle of the bullet into the wall.

"Manny said you guys think the bullet is a .338 Lapua Magnum?" Andy asked.

"Walter says he's sure. Have you met Walter?" Art asked.

"Everyone knows Walter. He's a legend in the firearms community. Tony's pretty jealous of him for landing a permanent spot at the Facility."

"We're very lucky to have him on board. He's a real asset to the organization."

"Did he have any thoughts on a possible range?" Andy asked.

"No, the deformation of the bullet was not a reliable indicator. Our maximum range could be over a mile but we all thought that the shot was taken from a closer position due to the fact that it was at night and the killer likely didn't have night vision. We should have a better idea tonight when we can estimate the available light at various distances," Art stated, scribbling calculations on the aerial photo. His phone rang. "Hey, did you find something?"

Sarah couldn't hear the other side of the conversation but she could see it had Art's interest.

"Really? I'll send Sarah over to take a look." He hung up the phone and placed it back in his shirt pocket. "Sarah, Daniel's found something that may be of interest over on the golf course.

Do you mind taking a look to see if it's anything we need to follow up on?"

"Daniel? Where is he?" she asked.

"The golf course is about a half mile to the west, southwest. If you start heading in that direction he'll find you."

Sarah had forgotten about Daniel. She figured he had been hanging out by his car. In this neighborhood it might not have been a bad idea. After crossing the river and open field she saw Daniel waiting near the edge of the golf course.

"Hey, there. Art says you found something of interest?" She was trying to be all business.

"Yeah, it's over here by the sand trap."

"What were you doing over here, Daniel?"

"Me? Oh, I was just wandering around. I knew I'd be waiting on Uncle Art for a while."

The two strolled over the dormant yellow grass up a small hill toward the manicured sand trap

"It's right here along the edge."

Sarah crouched down on her heels and examined the area that Daniel had pointed to. There was nothing she could see that was out of the ordinary. There was a wooden coffee stir stick that looked to be months old, a small piece of old paper, and a goose feather. She glanced up at Daniel, who had been watching her intently. She examined the area again for several minutes seeing nothing

"Daniel, I don't see anything here."

"Look right down there in the sand. Right there, just in front of your right hand."

Sarah again looked at the area seeing nothing. "Daniel, I appreciate your desire to help out but we're looking for evidence relating to a shooting. Look, I don't mean to sound condescending, but it's quite normal to find trash in public places and a goose feather on a golf course is about as rare as a chopstick in China."

He looked at her with puppy eyes and she felt embarrassed for talking to him like a new recruit. She reminded herself that he wasn't trained for this and was just trying to help

"No, not the trash, I'm talking about the sand," he said.

"The sand, seriously, what the hell are you talking about?"

Daniel let out a short laugh and crouched down beside her. All of the sudden he sounded a lot more like a professor than a student. "You see this line of demarcation? You see how there is a kind of trench in the sand right here?"

"Yeah, I see it now that you mention it but . . . so what?"

"I think this is caused by a muzzle blast."

"Muzzle blast?" she asked "I don't understand."

"Well, when the bullet passes out of the muzzle it is accompanied by a blast of heat, gasses, and un-burnt gunpowder. I think that blast caused this depression," he stated matter-of-factly.

"No, I know what muzzle blast is, I mean what would make you think this is muzzle blast and not just some depression in the sand?" she asked.

"Well, the orientation of the depression relative to the direction of the victim for one."

Sarah looked up towards the shooting scene. "Daniel, that has to be six, maybe seven hundred yards away."

"I ranged it at eight hundred thirty-six meters actually," he stated, holding up a Swarovski 8x30 rangefinder.

"You just happen to be carrying a thousand dollar rangefinder in your jacket, is that right?"

"Jeez, a thousand bucks? Is that what these things cost? Uncle Art is going to be pretty mad if I lose it."

He was toying with her of course and it annoyed her. "Daniel, we're talking about a night-time shot, remember. I doubt most people could make a head shot at a hundred yards at night."

"Well, somebody shot him didn't they?"

"Yes, but . . ." She could see he was serious about his discovery. "Okay, look. Let's say you're right, and this is a muzzle blast. A court is never going to allow it in. There's no other independent evidence suggesting the shot was taken from here. This could be nothing more than some kind of anomaly."

"I found something else over here on the other side. Come take a look."

She raised her eyebrows and followed him. He pointed toward the yellow grass on the opposite side of the sand trap about ten feet from the depression in the sand.

"You see . . . those tiny orange plastic pieces?"

Sarah couched down for a better look. The three pieces looked like pencil shavings but they were more like fabric than plastic. She gave Daniel a confused look

"Look closely at them," he suggested.

Sarah studied the largest piece of the three. She strained her eyes but all she saw were small longitudinal lines. Then it struck her. "Holy shit! These are rifling marks." She looked up in amazement.

"That's what they looked like to me," Daniel agreed.

She stared at Daniel in disbelief as she radioed for Manny. "Manny, are you there?"

"Yeah, kid, go ahead."

"You're not going to believe this but I think we just found the shooter's nest and some ballistic evidence."

"What kind of evidence?"

She thought for a moment before answering. "This you'll just have to see."

"We'll be right there."

Sarah stared at the evidence in her hand when she realized what a fool she was. "Oh . . . crap!."

"What's wrong?"

"I'm an idiot, that's what's wrong. I picked this up before photographing it in place or measuring its position. Goddamnit. I know better than that."

"It's okay, no big deal, just put it back down."

"I can't put it back down and take a photo!" she cried.

"Why the hell not? That's where you found it," he shot back.

"Look Daniel, there are rules. I can't just put this back there and pretend it hasn't been moved. This is the kind of thing that can devastate a case. It opens a lot of doors for the defense."

He looked at her and shrugged. Obviously, he didn't get it. Well, what's done is done, she thought. She'd just have to write it up in her report and try to give some kind of innocent explanation for her breaking protocol. Something believable like, I was thinking more about the handsome man in front of me than my responsibilities as a criminalist. Yeah, that would sound good, she thought.

Art, Tony, and Manny arrived a few minutes later.

"What did you find?" Art asked.

She handed him the small piece of orange plastic. "Looks like it might have rifling marks on it," she said. "Also, Daniel found a depression in the sand over there that he thinks might be from a muzzle blast," she said with a sullen tone.

"What's with the grumpy tone?" Manny asked. "This could be the thing to break this case wide open, kid."

"I moved the evidence before I photographed it," she confessed, feeling like she had just admitted a crime.

"So put it back," Manny and Art said in unison.

"I can't do that!"

"Why the hell not?" Andy asked.

"Have you all lost your minds?" She couldn't believe what she was hearing. "What about everything you taught us in the classroom, Art?"

"That was the classroom; this is real life. A kid has been murdered. Look, Sarah, I'm not saying you should lie about moving the piece but really, what's the big deal? I mean, sometimes shit happens. You're what, seven hundred yards away from the murder scene?"

"Eight hundred thirty-six meters," Daniel said.

"Really? Anyway, whatever. You saw something eight hundred and thirty meters away and picked it up to see what it was, right?"

"Yeah, but I know better than that," she said.

"This shooting was a couple days ago. We can't say that these pieces didn't move a little between then and now. The important thing is that they are clustered in one location. There is no way for that to occur naturally. If they were moved by wind or foot traffic they would be more dispersed. Furthermore, no one has been out here playing golf so that just leaves the geese." He tried to elicit a laugh from her, but he settled for a smile. "Believe me, this doesn't change a thing."

"I still know better."

"What do I always say to my students, Sarah?"

She could picture him saying it to her a thousand times before as she repeated it. "You can make as many mistakes as you want . . . just don't make the same one twice," she said.

"Exactly. Now, let's take a look at that depression."

Manny felt invigorated by the finding and ignored the back-and-forth argument. A case that had been on life support was now breathing again. With any luck they had found a key piece of evidence that might link the rifle used to commit the crime. "Can Walter do something with the fragments, Art?"

"If anyone can, Walter can. It won't be easy, though."

"You guys have that computer database for bullets, right?"

"Let's take it one step at a time, okay?"

"Sure Art, you're the expert. Anything you can find out would be a big help. Hell, maybe we'll get lucky on this one, huh?"

"Let's hope so."

Andy and Sarah set up a total station to record the location of the ballistic evidence relative to the site where the body was found. Similar to a surveyor's transit the Nikon total station was accurate to within a centimeter even over thousands of yards. They worked for over an hour documenting the scene while Art scoured the ground for other clues.

Daniel kept watch on the group while trying to look disinterested. They were placing the gear back into their vehicles when Daniel finally spoke.

"Who's up for dinner tonight?"

"I've got to get home to the little lady," Manny said.

"I'd love to but I have to get this evidence back to the lab and book it in." Andy said.

" I should be the one to do that. I found it," Sarah offered.

"I can get it. You go. Have a good time. Sarah turned to Art.

"What sounds good to you boys?"

"I'll take a rain check; I have some work to do tonight."

Sarah looked at Daniel and received an encouraging glance.

"Guess that leaves you and me," she said.

"I'm game, if you are. I thought Italian might be nice. I haven't been to Romano's in a long time."

"Sounds good. I just need to go home and change and I'll meet you there."

"Okay, how about an hour? That will give me plenty of time to drop Art off at his place." Arthur maintained his family's home in Centennial and used it when he came to Denver for testimony.

"Great, I'll see you there."

10

Romano's is a local icon in downtown Littleton, Colorado. The family owned restaurant has been a favorite watering hole for the members of the local police and sheriff's departments for over four decades.

Once home, Sarah sprinted through her front door and assessed her clothing options. Laundry day had come and gone and there was little left which remained clean. She opted for a fleece pullover and a pair of denim jeans. Minimal is better, she thought, best not to appear too desperate. Stopping at the hallway mirror she toyed with her hair before putting it in a ponytail. *Slow down!* She told herself.

The night air was crisp and the restaurant was just a few blocks away so she decided to walk. Daniel was waiting for her outside the front door of the restaurant. He opened the door for her like a gentleman. She wasn't one of those pseudo-feminists that were so independent that they couldn't be pampered. She had been taught that a man opening a door for her was a sign of respect and admiration.

"Hey, Sar-bear, I hope you brought your appetite," John, the owner, called from the kitchen as she walked by.

"Been here before?" Daniel asked.

"A few times, yes," Sarah said with a laugh.

They were led to a table against the wall in the old wing of the restaurant. Daniel slid her chair out for her to sit. She could tell that Art must have been making an impression on him. The old wooden chair creaked beneath her small frame as she took her seat across from him. The red-checkered tablecloths were ten years older than she was, but they gave the atmosphere a simple and comfortable feel.

"So . . . what got you into forensics?"

"A friend in college, actually."

"Trying to steal your boyfriend, no doubt."

Sarah eyes drifted down. A minute of silence passed before she spoke. "No, she was raped."

"I'm so sorry, Sarah. I didn't mean to make a joke . . . I . . ."

"I know, don't apologize."

"What happened, if you don't mind me asking?"

Sarah didn't know how to begin the story she had gone over a thousand times before. "It was my fault."

"Your fault?" he asked

Sarah took a deep breath and let it out slowly "I was . . ." Sarah took another long breath as she put her hand to her brow.

"Sarah—"

She cut him off. "I was going to meet a guy," she said, offering a fake smile. "I was late . . . I came back to my dorm room after studying and Annie, my roommate, was sitting on her bed with some guy. We had a signal, you know, when we had boys in the room, but she didn't put it out for me." She paused. "So I walked in there and she's on the bed, she looked out of it . . . . drunk or something. The guy gives me this surprised expression, ya know?" Daniel nodded. "I just felt like I walked in on something so I dropped off my stuff and got out of there."

"It's not your fault. Sarah."

A tear formed in the corner of her eye. "I should have stayed . . ."

"You couldn't have known—"

She cut him off again. "I should have," she said sternly. "My gut knew. My instincts told me something was wrong."

Daniel didn't say a word, but his eyes asked her to continue.

"If I would have talked to her . . . asked her something . . . I would have seen she was in no condition to be with that guy. There were clues, Daniel, and I missed them. I was only thinking of myself. I let her down, and because of that she was drugged and raped . . ." She looked at him, hesitating to speak.

"I'm sure she doesn't blame you, Sarah," he said.

"She killed herself a month later, after she found out she was pregnant."

"Jesus."

Sarah stared at Daniel with defeat in her eyes.

"So that's what drives you to chase murderers through the mountains in a blizzard" It wasn't a question, more of a revelation. He reached across the table and gently squeezed her hand.

The two sat in silence for a minute or so "Look at me" she said with a fake laugh while wiping her eye. "Some great dinner date huh?" Daniel smiled. "I'm not complaining" *Jesus* she thought as she stumbled into his deep brown eyes. Sarah changed the subject.

"So what did you do in the military?"

Daniel shot her an innocent glance over the menu. "Me? Oh, I was a mechanic of sorts. I worked with track vehicles mostly."

"Track vehicles?"

"Yeah, like tanks, earth-movers called Aces, anything with a track." He glanced back down to the menu his eyes darting around the page.

"You weren't a combat soldier, or sniper, or something?"

"Me? Naw that was my dad's career." He paused a few seconds, before continuing. "I'm proud of my service, though. I was good at it and it was a job that needed doing. I just didn't think I was the combat kind of guy." "You could have fooled me with the way you handled that SWAT commander in the Den."

"Oh, that, well, all soldiers go through a bit of self-defense training in boot camp and since I was stationed in Afghanistan, I figured I should keep up on it. You know, just in case."

"You never knew your dad, did you?" Sarah said, making more of a statement than asking a question.

Before he could answer the waitress came up and asked for their order. After the waitress left Sarah apologized.

"All I ever knew of my father were the stories I heard from Uncle Art, Doc, and some of the guys he served with."

"Go on . . . " Sarah encouraged him. "He was a soldier?"

"No . . . he was a warrior," Daniel stated with pride. "He was part of the first Green Beret unit, the 10th SFG, or Special Forces Group. He was fluent in Russian and German and was deployed to Vietnam during the war. I don't know a lot about his operations there but I've heard he was attached to numerous units in counter-insurgency and psychological warfare."

"He died in combat?" she asked in the nicest voice she could muster.

Daniel nodded in silence. "January first, nineteen sixty-eight, during the Tet Offensive. He was at Fire Support Base Burt, also known as the battle of Soui-Cut." Daniel sounded as emotionless as a documentary filmmaker. "It was about four kilometers south of the Cambodian border situated near the river Soui Tanken. Dad had stopped there with his unit to re-supply before making a night excursion into Cambodia to wreak havoc. Of course, the U.S.

military officially didn't go into Cambodia. As it turned out, the re-supply stop probably saved the lives of his teammates. Had they been out walking the bush they would have been overrun by the VC." Daniel paused and took a deep breath. "That night four battalions of North Vietnamese and Viet Cong swarmed the tiny base. The Americans fought all night. From the guys I talked to, the night air exploded from artillery and napalm. Thousands of bullets buzzed through the air like an angry swarm of bees. Dad was last seen firing an M-60 machine gun near the command post trying to protect the company commander." Daniel's eyes trailed off with his voice. "It was a long night but I've been told that Dad saved a lot of men. In the morning his guys took his body and carried on with their mission. Officially, Dad was listed as killed in a training exercise in the south of Vietnam, but I know he was there."

"He sounds like a brave man," Sarah concluded.

"Yes . . . he was."

Just then the waitress returned with the pizza.

"Looks good," Daniel stated.

They ate, and lingered over their empty plates with light conversation until Daniel paid the bill and they walked to the street.

Daniel's Camaro was attracting the attention of dinner guests as they mingled around, waiting for their tables.

"Where did you park, Sarah?"

"Oh, it was such a nice night I decided to walk. I'm just a few blocks away."

"Oh, can I give you a ride home?"

"No, thank you," she said as she started walking down the sidewalk. Daniel stood motionless, staring at her as she walked away. She turned her head turned back " . . . but you can walk me home."

Daniel jogged up to meet her. He listened as Sarah described her childhood adventures while passing various landmarks in the neighborhood. The hobby store in the Woodlawn shopping center; the running track behind Grant Jr. High School; and the games of chase in Sterne Park. Sarah told him of how her grandmother would stand on the balcony over-looking the park and ring the brass bell to signal that dinner was ready. The conversation was light but Sarah had a nagging question from dinner that had yet to be answered to her satisfaction.

"Daniel, how is it that you found that evidence today at the golf course?"

"What do you mean?"

"You show up there and within thirty minutes you find the sniper nest eight hundred meters away?"

"Eight hundred thirty-six . . . never mind."

"I mean, how is that possible?"

"I don't know," he lied. "I guess I was just lucky."

It was a possibility but she wasn't buying it, and her expression conveyed her doubt..

"Okay, the truth is Uncle Art had been looking at aerial photos as we flew in and told me, on a hunch, to go look at some areas over there."

She looked at him, trying to discern the truth.

"Uncle Art just didn't want my name associated with the case since I'm not an expert so I was supposed to keep a low profile. He didn't actually think I would find anything."

It sounded plausible. Art was meticulous in his preparation and she knew he wouldn't sit idle on the plane without doing some work. But there was something about the manner in which he talked about the evidence . . . something that seemed familiar to him, like he had seen it before. She wasn't satisfied with his answer but it would have to do. The walk was over sooner than Daniel had hoped as they reached the edge of her driveway.

"Well, thank you again for dinner," Sarah said.

"It was my pleasure. I don't often get to dine with a lady, just Doc."

"I doubt my mother would agree with your assessment, but thank you anyway."

"You okay walking back alone?"

He smiled at the question. "Yeah, I've been in tougher neighborhoods." There was an awkward pause as Daniel considered kissing her.

"Well, goodnight," she said, making the decision for him and extending her hand.

"Goodnight," he said giving her hand a gentle squeeze. He watched her walk backwards up the driveway smiling before she reached the door and went inside. Daniel was grinning like a schoolboy with his first crush. Some men might have expected more but Daniel was impressed. The last thing he wanted was a one night stand. This could turn into something very special he thought. That is, if he didn't blow it. Hands in his pockets, he strolled into the darkness regretting his lie.

11

Sarah walked through the door amid a whirlwind of emotions. She had wanted to kiss Daniel but her gut stopped her. She wasn't sure he was being truthful with her and that was reason enough to be cautious. The last thing she needed was another failed relationship with a good-looking liar. Still, she couldn't shake the feeling that he was a good man. It was his eyes, deep with emotion, they conveyed both strength and sympathy. She needed more time.

When she dropped her house keys on the kitchen counter, she saw the red light blinking on her phone, indicating she had messages waiting. The first message was spam, but the second was from her mother.

"Hi, darling, we haven't heard from you in a while. Your father and I are a bit concerned. We read in the paper that you were involved in some kind of shooting. Needless to say we were disappointed that you called the paper before you called us."

I called the paper? As if! That's my mother, she thought, more concerned with her feelings than the fact her daughter was nearly killed. She could hear her dad yelling something in the background but couldn't make it out.

"Why don't you come over for dinner tomorrow night, your father really wants to see you. I'll make your favorite."

Sarah chuckled. Her mother hadn't cooked since she was a child. Even then it was simple food. No doubt she was having dinner delivered or catered. Sarah didn't have a favorite dish, meaning her mother was serving one of *her* favorites she assumed Sarah liked, too. Oh, well, she mused, it's the thought that counts.

"Oh, by the way, honey, I took the liberty of hanging a wonderful watercolor by Leonardo Bulé, he's a new up-and-comer who's all the buzz."

Sarah looked into the living room to confront the monstrosity. Sarah's mother hated the rustic interior of her house. It was just the way her grandfather left it. Sarah had grown up in a contemporary home but felt it was cold and without character. Her mother was determined to remake both Sarah and her house in an image more fitting a lady of stature. "I know it's a bit bright, but you could literally design an entire look around it."

Sarah made a mental note to bring the artwork with her to dinner to offload it on her mother.

"Anyway, bring your appetite. Why don't you stop by at seven? Ta-ta," she called, her voice trailing off in crescendo.

Sarah marched into her office with renewed enthusiasm after a refreshing night's sleep. That is, until she looked at her inbox. The small plastic tray was overflowing with laboratory requests. Each one was a story in and of itself. Her sergeant always gave her requests whether she was in the office or on vacation. It didn't matter to him. She powered up her computer and went to find Andy, who turned out to be hovering over a stainless steel examination table in one of the processing rooms.

She found Andy hovering over a pile of evidence in the lab.

"Anything new on the shooting case?" she asked.

"No, nothing yet. Art took those orange fabric pieces back to his lab. I'm hoping we get some answers back today or tomorrow."

"Have you talked to Tony?"

"He's been on a shooting scene since four this morning but he said he wanted to meet before you left today."

"Tony got called out?"

"Yep, he's my backup and since I was tied up on this thing he took his call week a few hours early Sucker!" Andy sang. "I hear that his shooting is a real cluster. I bet he'll be out there all day."

"Well, I'm in no rush. I've got enough work to choke a pig."

"Hey, Sarah, you're famous!" Sarah recognized the voice behind her as Emily Baker, the lab's lead fingerprint analyst.

"Hey, Em. What are you talking about?"

"Oh, I forgot," Andy interrupted. "We made the morning paper."

Emily handed her the cut out photograph. It was taken at the shooting scene as they walked to their vehicles.

"Thank God we didn't trip; it looks like they were locked and loaded."

"Yeah, that would have been classic!" Emily seemed a little too eager for that possibility. "They mention the shooting on Monarch, too. How did they know about that so fast?"

"Oh, I have a pretty good idea," Sarah said, remembering her run-in with Maggie Miller at the motel. She thought it might also be Lt. Manilow getting back at her for skirting his inquisition. "Did they mention the Monarch victim was murdered?"

"No, they just said the driver causing the accident fled the scene and shot at you," Emily said.

Sarah thought of her mother and knew dinner would be served with drama.

The killer awoke early and showered after tidying up his mother's appearance. She had instilled in him an unwavering duty to keep a clean house. His mother would tell them that even though they didn't have money it was no excuse not to be clean. *Elbow grease is free*, she used to say.

He opened the heavy cloth drapes, letting the sunlight shower the interior of the home. Scattered around the rooms were beautiful Parlor maple, African Violet, and Peace Lilly plants. A small, potted moth orchid sat in the center of the old, heavy oak kitchen table. He took delight in wiping the leaves and watering his children. They were perfect to him. They didn't judge him or insult him. They were nothing like his father.

Sitting with a hot cup of coffee he tried in vain to find something interesting in the drab grey morning paper. The stories never seemed to change, he thought, just the characters. Politics, war, crime, they were all symptoms of the same disease; humanity. His favorite section was the comics. As he turned the front page his eyes caught a glimpse of red. He stared at the photo of the attractive female working at some crime scene. There was something familiar about her. He bit his lower lip as he read the reference about the Monarch Pass shooting. He was a woman! She was his lioness. He read every word twice, immersing himself in the story. The paper never mentioned her name but he learned that she worked for the Arapahoe County Sheriff's Office. He chuckled at the sniper's chosen target. How appropriate, he thought, the young punk deserved it. His attention returned to Sarah. He wanted to know more about the woman who chased him. She looked so young. Was it courage or temerity that fueled her spirit? He tore the photograph from the paper, vowing to answer that question.

The Scent of Fear

By 4:00 PM her inbox was back at its fighting weight.

She was gathering her things to leave for the day when Tony came through the door. "Hey, Sarah, glad I caught you. Do you have a minute?"

"Sure, Tony, I was just getting ready to head out but I can stay for a while. Sounds like you had a long day?"

"Oh, just your typical gang-banger party. Three guys exchanging gunfire in the house, and then shooting it out down the block. It was a reconstruction nightmare. I did get a chance to talk with Andy about the shooting scene. I have to say I'm pretty amazed that Art was able to find those fragments on the golf course."

"Oh, Art didn't find them, Daniel did." She regretted saying it the moment it passed her lips.

"Who's Daniel?"

"Just one of Art's employees." She tried to cover remembering that Art wanted to keep Daniel's involvement minimized.

"Well, anyway, I'm just amazed that they could find that location days after the fact. Do you really think that's the shooters position?"

"Geeze, Tony, I have no idea. It seemed plausible at the time but, frankly, I don't have any point of reference to base it on."

"Based on my calculations, I'd say that it's possible if the shooter was using a .338 Lapua magnum, but I just can't figure how he could make the shot at night. Maybe we could go back out there tomorrow to take another look."

"Sure, I wouldn't mind taking another look around myself."

"Cool. I've got to get this stuff booked in. We'll talk more tomorrow, I guess,"

"Great. I'm off to shower and change before dinner with my folks tonight." She said with a detectible trace of gloom.

"That bad huh?"

Sarah thought about that for a few seconds before answering.

"Dinner with my parents…what could go wrong?"

Her black Chevy truck thundered into her parents' driveway at five after seven. Their house was awash in bright, decorative spotlights. A fountain in the center of the circular driveway featured the Greek god Poseidon poised with his trident overhead. The scene could grace the cover of any high-priced home magazine.

Her mother hated guns in the house so she tucked her Glock under the front seat of her truck. Sarah never understood her mother's paranoia regarding guns. She had grown up in a house full of them and Sarah believed it had more to do with the ideology of her social circle than reality. Sarah shut the truck door and walked up the polished cement pathway to the portico. The grand entrance housed two eight-foot-steel doors polished to a mirror-like finish. Each massive door weighed 500 pounds but in spite of their weight, the doors glided with ease thanks to the state-of-the-art hinges. Sarah rang the doorbell and waited awkwardly outside her former home.

Nancy opened the door with a wide smile which deflated as she looked over her daughter's appearance. "Sarah? Look at you. You look like you're on the way to work on the docks," Nancy bemoaned. She noticed the empty holster hanging off Sarah's belt. "For God's sake, Sarah, take that thing off. You know how I feel about guns in the house."

"I left my gun in the truck, Mom," she stated as she removed the holster and dropped it by the door.

Just then the family's Golden Retriever, Gracie Lou, greeted Sarah at the door with a barrage of kisses.

"I was hoping you would have dressed a little nicer for your father."

"What's wrong with what I'm wearing?"

"Jeans and a sweater? Really, Sarah, would it have killed you to wear a dress? No matter, we'll have to go with that. Fix your hair, please, and try not to swear, for god's sake."

Nancy licked her fingers and tried to flatten some wispy hairs but Sarah blocked the hand as if defending a knife attack. "What are you talking about?" Sarah's radar sent an alert to her brain. "Mommmm?! You didn't! Tell me you didn't do what I think you did."

Nancy waved her hand back and forth in front of her face as she dismissed Sarah's comments. Sarah learned as a teenager that her mother heard only what she wanted to, and the hand-waving was a subconscious attempt to erase the words she didn't want to hear.

"Oh, don't be so dramatic Sarah," Nancy said. "I went through a lot of trouble to set this up. Come on, your father is dying to see you." As they walked down the hallway her mother whispered for her to stand up straight. "Sheee's heeere," Nancy sang as she danced into the living room.

Sarah entered the lion's den. Her father was holding a glass of scotch while talking to a young man who looked like he was late for a meeting with the chess club.

"There's my baby girl!" her father proclaimed as he embraced her in a bear hug.

"Hi, Daddy."

"Sarah, this is Jeremy Winters," Nancy offered. "His father is Doctor James Winters, a cardiologist at Sky Ridge Medical Center," she stated as if introducing royalty. "Jeremy's mother Judith is on the governor's beautification council."

"Oh, that's very . . . nice," Sarah said, mentally rolling her eyes.

Jeremy was wearing pressed black slacks with "fresh-off-the-rack" creases, a blue shirt and crème argyle sweater vest with matching socks. The outfit wouldn't be so bad if not for the blue bow tie and polished penny loafers. And her mother was worried about her appearance, she thought.

"It's very nice to meet you Jeremy," Sarah said, admiring his manicured fingernails. He was the picture of metro-sexuality.

"The pleasure is all mine, Ms. Richards," he stated with a slight bow as he raised her hand to his lips. "You're mother has told me a lot about you but I must confess she never mentioned your exquisite beauty."

Sarah felt some vomit rise to her mouth as she withdrew her hand from his clammy grasp. "So Jeremy, what do you do?" Sarah asked discretely wiping her hand on her pant leg.

"I'm a student at the University of Colorado."

"Pre-Med," Nancy interrupted.

"Oh?" Sarah exclaimed. "You must be very smart to get into medical school." She spoke with unfettered praise to make her mother proud.

"Well, I hate to brag, but my MCATs had a combined score of thirty-eight," he stated

Sarah raised her eyebrows and nodded her head, not knowing if that was good or bad. "Ya know, someone told me recently that it's actually harder to get into veterinary school," Sarah said, daring Jeremy to answer. "Let's go into the dining room, shall we?" Nancy said before he could answer.

As they walked to the room, Jeremy moved close to Sarah in an attempt to take her arm but Gracie Lou snuck between them, nearly knocking him over. Good girl, Sarah thought. Jeremy wiped his pants in a futile gesture to remove Gracie's blond hairs.

Jeremy sat across from Sarah while her parents took seats at each end of the sleek, minimalist table. Nancy rang a glass bell and a well-dressed woman in a chef's uniform delivered a fancy-looking spinach salad drizzled with raspberry vinaigrette. The woman was obviously the caterer, but Sarah decided she'd keep her mouth shut.

"Baby doll, I read in the paper that you witnessed a horrible accident on the pass?" her father said.

"Yeah, it was a real cluster fu—" She caught herself as her mother shot her a withering gaze. "It was pretty bad," she recovered.

"I read that one of the occupants was killed," he continued.

Sarah made it a policy never to give out details on an open case, even to family. "A woman was killed after being ejected from one of the vehicles."

"The paper also mentioned that a man shot at an officer and implied it was you. That must be a mistake, right, sweetie?" Sarah could hear the genuine concern in his voice and didn't want to alarm him.

"Of course, Daddy. One of the sheriff's deputies exchanged shots with the suspect while I stayed with the victims, giving aid."

He sat back in his chair with a relieved look on his face. She hated lying to him but she hated seeing him worry.

"Do we have to talk about such things at the dinner table?" Nancy complained.

"Don't worry about me, Mrs. Richards," Jeremy proclaimed.

"I've got a pretty steely fortitude. It's necessary to be a good surgeon," he said, glancing in Sarah's direction.

The Scent of Fear

Sarah was unimpressed. Judging by the look of him a slight breeze might be capable of knocking him over.

They continued with small talk, mostly about Jeremy and his potential as a world-class surgeon and suitor. Sarah wondered how long this torture would continue. There was no way in hell she could imagine herself with a man like Jeremy. Even if he was good looking, which he wasn't, she resented her mother for these lame attempts to pair her up with the progeny of her elite social circle.

"So, Sarah, what do you see yourself doing in ten years?" Jeremy asked.

"We're hoping for a respectable marriage, maybe to a doctor, and some grandkids, perhaps?" Nancy smiled as she planted her suggestion.

Sarah returned the smile while screaming profanities in her mind. "Oh, I don't know Jeremy. I plan on still being a criminalist."

"Oh, Sarah." Nancy waved her hand again. "You can't live your entire life chasing perverts and murderers. It's not good for the soul. Not to mention you could contract some disease from the blood or whatever it is you have to pick up. Honestly, Jeremy, I don't know where she developed this macabre fascination," she said dismissively. "We always encouraged her to be more feminine."

Sarah wasn't sure if her mother ever realized how insulting she could be.

"So do you like your work, Sarah?" Jeremy asked.

"I love it."

"I would think a woman of your . . . beauty, would rather occupy herself with a more traditional occupation," he concluded.

Jesus, she thought. When would she meet a man who valued her for more than her looks? She could feel his beady eyes undressing her as he spoke.

"What do you love about it, if you don't mind me asking?" he continued. His smirk was as prideful as a strutting peacock.

"A lot of things. Using science to protect the innocent, the mystery, shooting guns . . . you know, shit like that." Sarah glanced in her mother's direction.

The caterer brought out a crown rack of lamb. Small vessels of mint jelly, twice baked sweet potatoes, and bundles of asparagus wrapped in bacon completed the presentation.

"The lamb is wonderful, Mrs. Richards," Jeremy said.

Sarah thought it smelled a lot like decomp but she ate it without complaining. As her parents engaged Jeremy in light conversation Sarah noticed him fidgeting and twisting his body. At first it was slight but it became more prominent with each passing minute. The bizarre dance caught her parents' attention as the silverware clanked when his knee struck the underside of the table.

"Is everything all right, dear?" Nancy asked.

"Yep, uh-huh," Jeremy said with a look of growing panic.

His hands darted below the table and Sarah imagined what her parents thought Jeremy might be doing. He looked as if he were about to have a diarrhea attack. Anger was swelling inside him and his face became bright red.

"Can we get you something?" her father asked.

At his wits' end, Jeremy leapt to his feet, and shouted, "You can get that goddamned dog out of here. She won't stop licking my testicles!" He threw his napkin to the table in a hissy fit.

Nancy gasped in embarrassment as Sarah's father put his napkin to his lips to hide his snicker. Glancing at his pants, Sarah saw the wet stain around his groin, not to mention the fact that his legs were covered in blond hair. Jeremy's regal composure was now gone, replaced by a petulant temper tantrum. So much for a steely fortitude, she thought.

Sarah's Nextel phone erupted with the ever familiar alert tone. Seeing Tony's name on the screen Sarah excused herself. Her mother tried to help Jeremy by dabbing his pants with a napkin. Sarah wasn't sure which would be worse . . . having Gracie Lou attacking your crotch, or her mother. "Hey, Tony, what's up?" Sarah asked.

"Hate to bother you during dinner but we've had another sniper shooting. I think I'm going to need your help out here."

Your timing couldn't be better, she thought. "Give me the address and I'll head right over."

Sarah kissed her father on the cheek as her mother took Jeremy to find some seltzer water. Gracie Lou followed Sarah to the door, wagging her tail all the way.

12

The crime scene wasn't hard to find. Sarah spotted the glow of the floodlights and police cars nearly three blocks away. A line of media trucks had already gathered along Santa Fe Boulevard outside the yellow police tape. The wind slapped her face as she got out of her truck, sending shivers through her body. A storm front must be moving in, she thought.

Maggie Miller was there, jockeying for a good position with the police personnel in the background. With some fancy depth-of-field techniques, her cameraman could make her appear much closer to the action. Scattered among the camera crews, local residents hovered for a chance to be on film. No doubt reporters would elicit a meaningless quote to fill the air time and make it appear they were working harder than the cops to solve this crime.

Sarah flipped open her Nextel. "Tony, where you at?"

"Um, I'm on the tracks east of Santa Fe between the light rail elevation ramp and Belleview Avenue. Where are you?"

"I'm out here by all the media trucks. Do you need me to bring you anything?"

"Nope, I think I'm pretty well set for now."

She grabbed some purple Nitrile gloves and her Stinger flashlight, putting them in the cargo pockets on her pants' legs. Sarah ducked between the police cruisers, hoping not to get noticed by the camera crews. She made her way over to a lone deputy standing inside the yellow barrier tape. It was a boring station punctuated by the occasional annoying questions from the media or bystanders.

Unlike the last time, Sarah had no trouble entering the scene. Deputy Carl Mills saw her approaching and lifted the yellow tape.

"Hey, Sarah they got you, too, huh? You should learn to leave your phone turned off."

"I'm glad I got called. It saved me from a horrendous blind date."

Carl offered her a pen to sign in on the log book but Sarah used her own. She'd learned long ago not to use a cop's pen.

With her luck, she'd borrow one used to touch a dead body or worse. The command vehicle was awash in lights. The powerful lights were aimed to showcase the pricy motor home than illuminate the scene around it.

Several commanding officers from both the Arapahoe County Sheriff's Office and the Littleton Police Department were huddled by the door in conference. Sarah knew the media had their powerful microphones trained on the group, trying to glean any information they could from the discussion. She wondered why they never seemed to hold these discussions inside. No doubt the morning paper would have a quote from a "high-ranking source," at the scene that could be attributed to this conversation. The sheriff would then spend countless hours on a witch-hunt trying to figure out who had leaked the information to the media, never realizing it was his own staff.

Sarah made a b-line for Tony's camera flash firing in the distance. She made her way over the light rail tracks and loose rocks of the rail bed to where he was standing. She illuminated her path with her flashlight, careful not to step on any potential evidence. Coming up behind him, Sarah could see the crumpled mass of the victim's body at Tony's feet. As her light fell upon the young man she froze. The victim appeared to be covered in black slime. It was all over the ground too and looked to trail off to the north.

"What the hell is that black stuff, Tony?"

"Believe it or not, the kid was tagging a tanker car loaded with used oil when the bullet struck him in the head. The bullet passed through, penetrating the steel hull, and presto, the oil started spilling out."

The victim was lying flat on his back with his head down slope from the rail bed. Every square inch of his body was covered with the black crude. Sarah was at a loss for how to proceed.

"Where is the train now?" she asked.

"It's about ten miles down the track."

"That's gotta be a lot of spilled oil."

"Yeah. I think it's safe to say that there will be some major ass-ripping over that."

"So . . . what? Was the train stopped here for some reason?"

"Yeah, the conductor stopped while another train down the line somewhere switched tracks. The train cop said they were stopped here for about thirty minutes."

"Train cop? "

"Believe it or not, they're special agents. This guy is with Burlington Northern Santa Fe line and has jurisdiction over thirty-four thousand miles of track."

"How on earth do you know that, Tony?"

"Agent Thomas gave me the spiel when he arrived. He's bringing the train back as we speak."

Sarah wondered how he hoped to get the train back in its original position. She thought briefly of the small orange fibers on the golf course.

"They have to stop the leak first, of course, and the Haz-Mat guys are freaking out that moving the train might cause additional spills," Tony said.

"Well, I guess murder trumps the environment huh? So who found the body?"

"The driver of the light rail train saw the kid and thought he might be a drunk passed out near the tracks."

The light rail system was the state-of-the-art mass transit solution from the Regional Transportation District. . Sarah remembered several cases where people had committed suicide by walking in front of the train. No doubt the drivers were trained to look out for people on the tracks.

"Were there any witnesses who heard the shot?"

"Not sure yet. One of the employees at the gas station across the street heard what she thought was a loud backfire while emptying trash but she didn't see any vehicles. Our only indication is that it came from the west," Tony said, pointing behind him.

"So basically we're looking for a fiber in a carpet factory." She said sarcastically.

"Hey, if this job was easy, everyone could do it."

"Where is Manny?" Sarah asked after looking around.

"He's tied up on a domestic call. Supposed to be out later."

"So who's the detective assigned here?" Sarah asked.

Tony let out a deep sigh. "Vegas."

"Oh, crap."

Sal Vargas, nicknamed Vegas, was a twenty-five-year veteran detective of the sheriff's office and regarded as an expert on doing the least amount possible. Sarah knew him to be an insatiable flirt who loved to skirt the edges of inappropriateness, if not stumble and fall over the edge completely. Suddenly, having dinner with Jeremy didn't seem so bad. Sarah watched as Vargas sauntered over in a cheap looking grey polyester suit and black cowboy boots. His wispy hair, what was left of it, matched his wiry frame.

"What's with the tar baby here?"

Sarah's eyes darted around "Jesus Vegas, the press is right over there"

"Okay, okay, don't get your tampon in a wad. I wasn't planning on giving a statement to the press Richards"

Sarah's jaw dropped as Tony put her hand on her arm.

"Just the same, why don't we try referring to him as 'the victim' before we all get canned," Tony suggested.

"Fine," Vargas said holding up his hands in mock surrender. Sarah tensed as she heard footsteps approaching from behind. The last thing she needed was a lecture on appropriate crime scene behavior from some commanding officer. "Hey, guys, what do ya got for me?" It was Melvin Stokes. He was Sarah's favorite investigator with the Coroner's Office.

"Holy mole," Melvin blurted upon seeing the victim's body.

"I thought we had a drunk that died on the tracks."

"Well, I'd say the dead part's right," Vargas said.

Sarah shot him a look of disdain. It didn't seem to register.

"Is that oil?" Melvin asked.

"Yep," Tony said. "Best we can figure he was standing approximately here when he was shot in the head." Tony motioned to the area near the victim's feet.

"Are you sure it wasn't a suicide?" Melvin asked.

"Well, there's a can of spray paint next to the tracks over there and we didn't find a gun. Plus, the damage to his head is more consistent with a high powered rifle than a handgun."

"It wouldn't be the first time someone came by and took the gun," Melvin said setting his field kit down.

"True, but the location seems unlikely for a suicide by gunshot, and given the fact that it looks like he was tagging, we're assuming this one is related to the murder in Sheridan last week," Tony said.

"Do we have a name?" Melvin asked.

"Try Valdez, I think he's from Alaska," Vargas said chuckling at his own lame joke.

Melvin didn't even look up.

"Nothing yet. It doesn't look like he was carrying a wallet so we're checking the parked vehicles in the area but my guess is he came here on foot." "I suppose we don't have a motive either?"

"Why don't you ask him, Mel?" Vargas joked. "Hey, Slick, who do ya think shot you?'" Vargas snorted.

"Very funny, Vegas."

Melvin leaned over the body and evaluated the grim task before him. Normally, the investigator would examine the victim for signs of trauma or indicators of the time since death. He would check the body's lividity, or settling of the blood, to see if he had been moved. He would insert a liver probe to check temperature. This, however, was no ordinary case. "Jesus, Tony, how am I supposed to conduct an examination on this guy?" he asked.

Melvin focused his light on the victim's open head cavity. He could tell from the crumpled mass of bone that most of the brain missing. The cranial vault was filled with the black ooze and Melvin couldn't even make out the margins of the entrance wound.

"I can't tell where the entrance wound is. The doc is going to have to clean him up first"

Sarah turned to Tony. "What can I do to help out?"

Tony thought for a second, evaluating his mental checklist.

"Head over to the gas station and get the surveillance tapes. It's possible that the killer might have stopped in there at some point and we might have him on camera."

"Okay, anything else?"

With a sheepish grin, he said, "Well, now that you mention it . . . Can you search the dumpsters, too?"

Great, she thought, as she crossed the street. Three years of graduate school and I'm stuck searching through a filthy trash dumpster. She had to cross the road a block to the north so the media wouldn't see and follow her. Aside from all the police lights the gas station was a lone beacon in an otherwise dark neighborhood. The neighborhood was a mix of commercial warehouses punctuated by adult book stores and nude dancing bars. It may not be the armpit of the city but it was a close contender. A lot of dirt bags frequented the local shops but tonight she hoped the bright lights of the police cars would keep them away.

Then she saw the man outside the gas station doors. His grungy clothing and long dirty hair left no doubt he wasn't with the Salvation Army. As she came closer he let out a low cat call.

"My, oh, my! You are much too fine to be walkin' 'round here. You look good enough to slather and bake," he crooned, talking through yellow teeth.

She did her best to walk upright and look him in the eye. Her body language was supposed to convey a sense of self-assuredness but the ugly fact was that some criminals considered that a challenge. She gagged as she brushed past him, and her nose filled with the stench of booze and sweat.

With his right hand he opened the door in a theatrical display of chivalry as his left hand slapped her butt. In one deft move she spun around and caught him off balance, shoving him into a tall pyramid of window washer fluid bottles.

"Bake and slather that, dickhead," she spat.

Sarah remembered her lessons from working crime scenes in the jail. Never show fear. The only thing criminals respected was strength. As she continued through the door it dawned on her how stupid that move was. Had any news cameras caught the act she'd be the one portrayed as the bad guy. She walked up to the counter, looking around for the clerk. Sarah could see herself on an old television screen on the wall behind the counter. A fat, older woman was leaning against the back wall, smoking a cigarette. Her artificial, curly red hair was in sharp contrast to the baby blue eye shadow hovering above her dark, sunken eyes.

"You've got guts sweetie, I'll give you that. That urchin has been parked outside my door for an hour. Maybe now he won't bother the customers for change."

The name tag on her stained uniform read Flo.

"Happy to be of assistance, now I need you to return the favor."

"What do you want?" the old woman croaked.

Sarah produced her badge. "I need to borrow your surveillance tapes for the day."

The older woman just huffed. "You got a warrant?" The cigarette clung to her lipstick-laden lips, just daring the ash to jump off.

"Look, ma'am, we've had a murder across the street and frankly, I was hoping on your cooperation."

"You were, were you?"

"Yes," she answered as the older woman sat emotionless on her stool. "But if you'd prefer, we can shut your business down for eight to ten hours while we get the warrant if that would make you feel better."

The clerk rolled her eyes and lifted her bulk from the chair with considerable effort. "Follow me."

Sarah looked back to the store front as they walked, and saw that the man was now gone. The windows were covered in a hazy film and dozens of dead flies littered the sills. Sarah wondered if the employees had ever even heard of Windex. Flo's cheap sneakers moaned as she crossed the dirty floor to the back office. The room was dark, dank, and smelled of three day old coffee. The old VCR must have had a half inch of dust resting upon it. A small black-and-white television with aluminum foil for antennae bowed the thin wooden shelves under its weight. Sarah noted the time displayed on the VCR clock was eight and a half hours off. She made a notation on her hand so the video tech could adjust his calculation. The tech would be annoyed at dealing with such old technology as it was. In her experience old, overused VHS tapes from stores like this were worthless. She'd be lucky to get a fuzzy picture of the killer, assuming he was even on there in the first place. Sarah jotted down the pertinent information then punched the eject button. Nothing. Using her finger to open the door she peered inside the empty recorder. "Ma'am, where is the tape?"

"What tape?"

"That's what I'm asking . . . where is the surveillance tape?"

"I don't know, it's not my job to keep track of them."

"Don't you load a new tape each night?"

"Honey . . . I haven't touched that thing in years. As long as the little red light is on and I see myself on the TV then I really don't give a damn."

"That little red light is the power indicator, ma'am."

"Whatever, they didn't hire me as an electronics wizard."

No shit, Sarah thought.

Most businesses had made the switch to digital surveillance systems but a few hold outs kept the older technology. Most of those used the same tape day after day until it broke or got stolen, but even a crappy tape was better than no tape at all.

"Well, I sure am glad we didn't wait for a warrant, aren't you?" Sarah said in a sarcastic tone. She gave Flo a look that said thanks for wasting my time bitch.

"I wouldn't want to waste any of the government's time or money." Flo said.

Touché, she thought. Sarah bit her lip before saying something she'd later regret. She walked over to the refrigerator, hoping to find a beverage that wasn't coated in dust. As she peered into the dirty soda cabinet Sarah's phone began to ring. She glanced at her screen and saw Art's name came up on her caller ID.

"What's up Art?"

"Detective Lopez called to give me a heads up. I hear you have another shooting on your hands?"

"Manny called you? We haven't even completed the scene investigation yet," she said.

"I know, I know, I'm not trying to step on your toes, but I took the liberty of pulling up some aerial photos of the scene and found a location you may want to search for ballistic evidence."

"You found a location? Based on what? We don't even have a trajectory yet on the bullet path."

"Daniel noticed a high structure about three blocks to the west. Based on our analysis, it's the highest point in the area that would have a clear view of the shooting scene."

"How is it that Daniel has an opinion? I thought you hired him as a hunting guide, not a shooting reconstructionist."

"You know, Sarah, if I were perceptive I might conclude that someone is in a snooty mood."

Sarah took a breath and calmed herself. She realized she had been taking an accusatory tone with Art that he didn't deserve.

"I'm sorry, Art, I didn't mean to be that way. I'm just frustrated because this gas station clerk didn't load a surveillance tape."

"Let me guess, heavy-set redhead named Flo?"

"I take it you know her, then?"

"Oh, yeah, Flo's been there a long time. A regular fixture, you might say. She's not exactly the brightest bulb in the chandelier, is she?"

"No, not really. So where is this place and why does Daniel think it's the shooter's nest?"

"Let's just call it an educated guess, shall we? You know the old fire fighter training tower?"

Sarah thought long and hard but had never heard of the training tower. She didn't spend much time training with fire fighters and had no reason to visit the training center. "No, can't say I do."

"It's down by the river. It's a plain-Jane cement building about six stories high on your side."

"Okay, so what should I be looking for?"

"You remember those orange-colored fragments from the golf course?"

"Yes, of course, very small flexible fragments like fabric with some rifling marks. Those are going to be hard to find in the dark if we don't have a specific location, though."

"Best we've got, I'm afraid."

"Maybe we should wait until daylight to make a search."

"I'm not telling you how to conduct your investigation, Sarah, but these fragments are tiny and the longer you wait the more likely they'll be dispersed by wind, rain, or something else."

He was right, of course. Trace evidence could be very fragile and many an investigator had altered or destroyed it just by walking about the scene. "Okay, I'm heading that way. Wish me luck."

"I'm confident you won't need it. You were very well trained."

We'll see about that she thought as she hung up the phone.

"Thanks for all your help, Flo," she called out in a sarcastic tone.

Thankfully, the grungy-looking pervert wasn't there waiting for her. She considered going back to her truck to get some evidence packages but truth be told she had no expectation of finding anything. She glanced at the dumpsters, relieved that the disgusting task could be put on hold. She left the lighted safety of the gas station lot and entered the darkened street on her way to the river.

The street was dark and eerie. A few small oases of light came from the occasional security lamp. Tall weeds littered the empty lots and broken glass crunched under her feet. The traffic noise grew fainter with each step she took toward the river and the night's air felt still. The old warehouses were covered in graffiti and most of the windows were broken out behind their security bars. The scenery reminded her of a bad Halloween horror movie. She looked around, half expecting to see a guy in a hockey mask holding a chainsaw.

Sarah wasn't afraid of the dark. She had walked many a late night back to hunting camps with her grandfather. She was walking on autopilot when she detected the faint sound of broken glass being kicked. Her senses came alive, hearing faint footsteps behind her. Was it a deputy? She was walking under one of the few lights and fought every muscle telling her to turn around. The light would just blind her anyway. She waited until reaching the shadows before looking backward. She focused her attention on a small tent of light near the corner of a warehouse when he came across it. Shit. It was the grungy guy from the storefront. Is he following me? Maybe it was just a coincidence. Then she caught a glimpse of movement on the other side of the street. It was another man! He was walking parallel to the grungy guy. This can't be good. There was no way these guys were out for a stroll. She glanced back again and they had cut the distance to her by half.

She reached for her waistband and realized in horror that she had left her gun in the truck. Fuck! How could you be so stupid? She cursed her mother while knowing deep down it was her own fault.

Sarah picked up the pace and began scanning the area for an escape route. She was unfamiliar with the neighborhood. Should she call for help? Maybe these guys were just headed for the river with the other homeless junkies. One way or another she had to know for sure.

She saw her opportunity when she caught sight of an alleyway with lots of pallets and dumpsters littered along its length. They would give her the cover she needed. The entrance was illuminated by a single street light, which presented a problem. She passed the alley and walked a few yards more before angling to the building and backtracking along its edge out of sight from the men down the sidewalk. When she rounded the metal building she broke into a sprint. She was careful of her footing, hoping she didn't stumble and fall. She took cover behind a dumpster that was about halfway down the alley and turned to watch the opening. Even though it was a short run, her chest was pounding from a mixture of adrenalin and fear.

Several excruciating seconds passed. Nothing. Maybe they had veered off. Maybe it was a coincidence after all. She began to convince herself that her paranoia had gotten the better of her when they emerged from the shadows.

Both men were now on her side of the street. They looked around, slowing their pace. It was obvious they were looking for someone, and that someone had to be her. They stopped under a light, looking agitated as they spoke to each other. The grungy man's arms pointed down the street and his partner took off toward the river at a run. The grungy man began a slow, deliberate stalk down the alley.

His pace slowed as he navigated each obstacle. No doubt he didn't want to get knocked on his ass again like in front of the store. Sarah crept backwards, moving only when she saw him looking sideways. She made it most of the way down the alley unnoticed when her heart sank deep within her chest. The alley was a dead end. An imposing chain-link fence blocked her escape. She was trapped.

This is just my luck, she thought. Sarah took cover behind a 55-gallon drum that smelled of old kitchen grease. She tried to slow her breathing. The street light backlit the grungy man as he closed in on her old position. He lunged behind each man-sized obstacle, obviously looking for her. Sarah considered making a run for the fence but she had no way of knowing whether the other man might be waiting close by on the other side.

After thirty tense seconds he reached the dumpster she had been hiding behind and stopped. He looked around but held his position. His stance changed from a crouch to a more upright one and his arms fell to his sides. Slowly, he turned and began walking back toward the street.

She let out a heavy breath as she told herself the worst was over. She imagined the wickedness each man intended for her and she wondered how many unlucky women had been victimized by the pair. The thought of it made her sick. Brushing away the thought, she decided to wait in the alley for fifteen minutes while the thugs got farther away from her. She could then call for help and make her way back to the gas station. Sarah could feel her heart rate begin to slow as fear began to give way to relief. The man had almost reached the entrance to the alley when her Nextel phone erupted.

13

The sound blast amplified off the metal buildings like a thunderclap. She panicked and tore off the battery to silence it.

Looking up, she watched in horror as the grungy man stopped mid-step and turned back toward her. As he started back down the alley she saw the glint of a knife blade in his right hand, and although she couldn't see his face, she imagined the evil grin covering his yellow-stained teeth.

Sarah darted her eyes around for something she could use as a weapon. She had a small pocketknife, but the two-inch blade might as well be a toothpick against the drunken assailant. She used it to cut fingerprint tape and never considered training with it as a weapon. She looked up . . . he was twenty yards away. It was obvious he didn't know her exact position. That was the good news. The bad news was that he knew she was there somewhere. Sooner or later he'd find her. Just then the second man appeared under the street light. Fuck! One was bad enough but fighting two of them would be impossible. He didn't come down the alley, though. She adjusted her gaze to the figure coming toward her. No one would hear her screams, except him. Her options were growing bleaker by the second. She retreated behind another dumpster, and then she saw it.

The handle was sticky from old duct tape, but it was beautiful. Under normal circumstances she would have flinched from the filthy relic but tonight this mop might save her life. Her best strategy would be to get the knife out of his hand. She would have one chance to hit the knife before he took a more defensive position. If she missed she was done for.

As he came closer she lay in wait, trying hard not to give away her position. Her breathing was shallow and painful. Images from her life passed through her mind and she wondered if it were her destiny to die in this godforsaken alley. She promised herself that if she made it through the night that she would carry her gun everywhere she went, even to church.

The man kept his knife hand out in front of him. She grabbed a thumb-sized rock and waited for the right moment.

He was six feet away when he turned, looking at the opposite side of the darkened alley. This was her chance. She tossed the small rock at the dumpster on the other side. It wasn't a hard toss but it had the desired effect. The grungy man spun toward the dumpster and exposed his right side to her. She wasted no time as she swung the mop handle with all her strength. It struck his wrist with a thud and the knife skipped across the ground behind them. His surprised expression was soon replaced by a sneer. "Hey Reggie! Keep a lookout man, we got ourselves a wild one here!" he shouted to his compatriot. He gave a shallow huff, seeing her weapon of choice. "What do you think you're gonna do with that, darlin'?" he asked in a menacing tone.

"Oh, I don't know . . . I thought I might shove it up your ass," she said, trying not to show how terrified she was.

"Gooood, I like kinky girls . . . maybe I'll return the favor," he snarled through his yellow-stained teeth.

In that instant her eyes betrayed her fear, and the rapist saw it.

"You can hit me all you want but it's just gonna make it worse for you. I'm gonna show you a whole new meaning to the word 'pain,' bitch," he said as he crept toward her.

She was frozen with fear. She tried to muster up the courage she had shown on Monarch Pass, but it just wasn't there. It was one thing to chase after a guy with a gun in your hand. You were the hunter. Now she was the prey and she didn't like it one bit.

"I'm gonna enjoy breaking you, little girl. Ol' Reggie ain't gonna have much left to play with I'm afraid." Then he unzipped his pants.

She tensed, expecting him to tackle her. If she was going to act, it had to be now. She'd worry about Reggie later. She swung the mop at his head but he blocked it with his forearm. It was all the opening she needed, though. She planted her left foot and kicked his crotch with all her might. The devastating blow came a second before his right fist came crashing into her jaw. They both collapsed in a heap on the ground, reeling in pain.

"You fucking bitch!" he groaned.

Sarah was dazed by the hit. For a junkie, the guy packed one hell of a punch. He was on top of her in a flash. He grabbed both her hands and pinned them to the dirty asphalt. He plowed his knees into her thighs and forced her legs apart. She could feel the broken glass and trash under her body and tried not to think of the scars they would leave behind. He drew his face near to hers. His oily blonde hair tickled her cheek as his musty breath blanketed her face.

"You're gonna wish you never met me," he rasped.

I'm already there, asshole, she thought. She wondered if he was hopped-up on drugs. She made a feeble attempt to head butt him but she just couldn't get any power behind it. He was just too strong for her. As if to punctuate that thought he slammed his head into hers and sparkles of light danced in her eyes.

Sarah was close to surrender when a blinding light pierced the darkness. The million candlepower spotlight lit the alley brighter than the sun. A short squelch and whoop from the 120 decibel siren told Sarah the cavalry had come.

The grungy man jumped to his feet and stared in disbelief at the blinding light. Sarah heard a familiar voice yell out

"Stop right there, asshole! Move an inch and you're dead!" It was Vargas.

Her assailant turned his head to the fence behind him and took off in a sprint. Sarah heard a gunshot ring out and the distinctive whiz of a bullet as it passed overhead. She tucked her body in and stayed as low as she could. He leapt onto the fence, scaling it with ease. Vargas fired a second shot at the man as he neared the top, but in a blink, he was gone.

Vargas ran up and scooped her into his arms as he knelt by her side. She was trembling and she felt tears welling up in her eyes.

"Sarah! Are you okay?"

"I can't stop trembling."

"It's just the adrenaline. Let's get you to the car and warm you up."

He helped her walk to the sedan where she slumped into the front seat. "David-44," he shouted into his shoulder mic. "I need some units in the alley just east of Wyandot Street. A criminalist has been attacked."

"A-firm, do you need an ambulance?" the dispatcher asked.

"Negative, just send me some cars, code three I've got two suspects at large. Oh, yeah, I almost forgot . . . shots fired."

Sarah could hear the sirens approaching from the murder scene.

"Did you get a good look at the cocksucker?" Vargas asked.

"Um, yeah. He was at the gas station earlier when I went there."

"Good deal. There's a real good chance he'll be on the surveillance tape."

Sarah shook her head as she realized the irony.

Two patrol cars screeched to a halt near the alley entrance and Vargas ran over to give them a description of the two suspects. In a flash, the patrol units sped off shining their spotlights into every shadow.

Vargas came back to the car to check on Sarah. "Don't worry, Sarah, we'll get the sons-a-bitches. We got a K-9 unit on the way; should be here in five."

Sarah couldn't think of anything to say.

"Did they hurt you?" Vargas asked.

"Just my pride," she said, feeling the pain in her back and thighs. "Why didn't you shoot the motherfucker?"

"I left my gun . . . long story."

"Shit, you're lucky I came by when I did. What the hell are you doing out here? You were supposed to be searching the dumpsters."

Under other circumstances the questions would be annoying but tonight they kept her mind off of the attack. "I got a call from Art telling me to check out the fire tower for the shooter's nest. Why were you out here?"

"I stopped by the gas station to see if I could help and Flo told me she saw the guy follow you down the road. I figured I'd better give you a call but you didn't answer your Nextel."

No shit, she thought. "Did you hit him?" she asked, referring to his gunshots.

"I don't think so."

"Vegas, he dropped a knife in the alley up by that blue dumpster. We need to go find it." His eyes were distant and she was sure he didn't hear her.

Vargas stood by the open car window and hollered, "Woo-hooo! Nothing like shooting at dirt bags to get the blood flowing!"

Back to his normal self, she thought.

"I wish I had got my rifle out of the trunk. That son of a bitch would be doing the dancing chicken on the ground over there.

Can't be more than fifty yards to the fence," he said, studying the distance. His caring side had vanished. "Did you see that cocksucker run? He shot outta here like a jackrabbit!"

She couldn't believe it.

He glanced at Sarah and saw the look in her eyes. "What? You look like I just farted in church or something. Oh, you want me to call you a victim advocate?"

She shook her head in disgust. "No."

"Well, what then?"

"Never mind," she said. "Let's go over to the training tower and see if we can't find some evidence of the shooting, shall we?"

"Whoa, wait a minute, girly." She ignored the condescending name. "I don't think you're in any condition to work tonight. Let me call the captain and get someone else out here."

Leaving would be justified but she didn't want to go home. She needed something to get her mind off the attack and working was the best option at the moment. Plus, she didn't want to call someone else out of bed for what she was sure to be a needle-in-a-haystack type search.

"You wouldn't be saying this if I were a male deputy who just got in a fight"

"Yeah, but that's different"

"Why…because I'm a woman?"

Vargas shook his head while letting out a huff. Clearly, he was biting his lip.

"I'm fine. I don't want to go home. If I go home I'm just going to think about it and I don't want to think about it. I need to get my mind off it . . . Okay, Vegas?"

"Okay, okay. But you're not going over there alone. I'm going with you. With any luck I'll get another shot at Br'er Rabbit, eh?" he said playfully elbowing her ribs.

She was not at all amused.

As they were getting ready to leave the alley, a media van pulled up and blocked their way. No doubt they had heard the gunshots and saw the police cars race away from the murder scene. It was a simple task to follow the flashing lights. Maggie Miller leapt out of the blue SUV, microphone in hand. She was dressed in dark business slacks and her employer's trademark yellow windbreaker jacket which was opened to reveal her silk blouse.

Vargas zeroed in on her instantly.

This oughtta be good, Sarah thought as she got out of the car.

Vargas licked his hand and smoothed out his wispy hair as the camera lights came on. He swaggered over to Maggie in his polyester jacket and pants from a decade long past.

"Detective, what happened here? Were those gunshots we heard?" she asked in an agitated voice.

"Calm down now, calm down. I'm Detective Vargas with the Arapahoe County Sheriff's Office Homicide Squad," he said.

Sarah laughed knowing that no such squad existed. He just said it to impress a pretty reporter.

"One of our criminalists was attacked but she's fine."

"Who fired the shots Detective?"

"Please, call me Vegas,".

Maggie smirked as she realized this dope was flirting with her on camera.

"Well, I came to check on my criminalist."—*My* criminalist? Sarah thought—"and I see this guy hanging out by the alley here so I race over and flash my lights. Well, he takes off running but I roll down my window and I can hear my criminalist screaming like a banshee down the alley. So I raced my car into the alley and confronted the second suspect at gunpoint."

"Did he have a weapon?"

"Oh, yeah, he had a knife in his hand." Vargas said, remembered Sarah's comment.

"That must have been terrifying," Maggie said stroking his ego.

"Not at all. I deal with murderers and rapists every day. They don't scare me a bit," he said, sucking in his gut.

"Did he attack you? Is that why you shot at him?"

"No, the son-of . . . the suspect . . . turned and fled the scene toward the fence. That's when I fired."

Maggie gave him a seductive look that said "I'm impressed" and Vargas fell right into her trap. The blood flushed south from his brain to another body part.

"Detective . . . are you saying you shot at him while his back was turned?"

"Fuckin' A."

The Scent of Fear

"Do you think it was wise to shoot your pistol at a man that far away?"

"Well, I didn't have time to get my rifle."

Sarah rolled her eyes as the hole got deeper and deeper. Maggie looked down the alley at the fence. "That looks to be about fifty or sixty yards, Detective."

"Yeah, would have been one helluva shot if I had hit him."

14

Holy shit! Sarah thought she could actually hear the sheriff screaming at his television set across town at that very moment. Just then the police radio came alive and Sarah heard Victor 1 call sign asking for Vargas. It was the sheriff. Vargas is a dead man, she thought. Sarah called out to Vargas and he left Maggie with his trademark cheesy wink. Vargas got in the car and closed the door, knowing that he didn't want the conversation broadcasted. Sarah could hear the sheriff yelling through the closed windows. After a few minutes Vargas opened the door

"Let's go, Sarah," Vargas said as he motioned to the car. He turned to Maggie and yelled out, "I'm sorry but I have to go. We have to continue with our investigation. The public information officer will have a statement for you at the command post shortly. For your safety, we're asking you all to leave the area and go back to the murder scene while we search for the suspects." He closed the door and waited for the van to move out of the way.

"So, are you in deep shit?" Sarah asked.

"Fuck no. I told the old man about the shooting and he said we needed to go find that sniper nest you were blabbing about."

"Seriously?"

Vargas was focused on the media van as it pulled away. "Jesus. Did you see the cans on her?"

"You know that I'm a girl, right?"

"What? You can't tell me you didn't see those. They about knocked me on my ass!"

"You wish. Don't you think she's a bit out of your league?"

"Sure, but a guy can fantasize, can't he?"

"I can't believe I'm talking to you about this. Have you ever heard of sexual harassment?"

"Oh, don't give me that shit. You can't tell me you didn't want to fuck her, too. I mean, even being a girl and all."

Mouth open, Sarah sat dumbfounded. Miraculously, she had all but forgotten her attack fifteen minutes earlier. Vargas drove out of the alley and turned back toward Santa Fe.

"Nice embellishment of the facts back there," Sarah said.

"What do you mean?"

"The screaming, the knife in his hand . . ."

"Oh, that. Look these media types want a good story so I gave it to them. Little white lies, that's all.

"You're not worried that my report is going to say something different?"

"Are you kidding me?" He shot her a disappointed stare.

"Nobody cares about the details. Unless we catch the guys, which I doubt, there won't even be a trial. So don't sweat it."

Amazing. *She* shouldn't sweat it. As if *she* had something to worry about. Sarah decided to get back to business. "So where's this fire tower?"

"We have to cut around Union here and go back around these buildings to the south. Don't worry, I know this area like the back of my hand. I used to take some girlfriends out here in my cruiser."

Sara was sure she was going to be sick before this ride was over. At least airplanes had barf bags she thought.

A few minutes later they pulled into the training centers gravel parking lot. The "training center" was just an old ranch style home that had been remodeled into classrooms.

"Oh, shit, I forgot about the knife in the alley back there," Sarah said.

"No problem, I'll call an officer to go over and get it."

"I should be the one to collect it, don't you think?"

"What difference does it make? We're here, aren't we? I don't feel like making a special trip just for that," he said. He had a point.

A few red lights perched on the stairwell delineated the tower in the night sky. The air was still. The thunderous groan of a locomotive loomed in the distance, signaling the return of the leaking behemoth to the crime scene.

Sarah looked up at the six-story tower with a sense of defeat. Even if someone took a shot from up there the orange pieces could have been carried a block away, if the wind had been blowing. It would take a month to scour this area.

Sarah kept thinking about Art's phone call. It wasn't so unusual that Manny had called Art to get his brain engaged. After all, he was already involved in the investigation, even if from afar. No, what bothered her was his comment about Daniel. Why would Art ask him his opinion about the sniper's position? It didn't make any sense. Maybe Daniel just happened to be there in the lab when the call came in. That didn't make any sense, either, though. Why would he be in the lab at any hour? Maybe he was just hanging out with Art when the call came in and decided to tag along out of curiosity. That must be it, she thought. It still didn't explain why Art would send her out on Daniel's intuition. Vargas interrupted her train of thought.

"Nobody got up that staircase. There's a padlock on the gate"

"What about another way up? Could he have scaled the sides or the cage surrounding the stairwell?"

"I doubt it. He'd want to be able to get out of here in a hurry and scaling that cage with a rifle would be slow going."

"What if he repelled down after the shot?" she asked, playing the devil's advocate.

"How would he get the rope, or whatever, released from up top? No, I don't think he would have repelled, either."

The two meandered around the perimeter of the building, shining their lights in a futile attempt to find some evidence of the shooting. Aside from the tiny orange fragments Sarah wasn't even sure what they were looking for. The lot was huge. Art always said that crime scenes should be measured by the scale of the evidence being searched for. In this case they might as well be searching Mile High Stadium for a piece of confetti.

"Okay, you satisfied Sarah? Can we go?"

"Give it a few more minutes. We're here, so let's make the most of it."

"We ain't gonna find nothin'."

"Well . . . then think of all the overtime you're making," she said, trying to appeal to his pocketbook instead of his dulled sense of duty.

"I'll go check around that old school bus," he said with renewed spirits.

Sarah walked around the structure but found her attention waning as she relived the recent attack in her mind. She could still smell him. His putrid scent pestered her. Am I an idiot for being out here she wondered? She needed to focus on the task at hand. Sarah made a spiral search around the east side of the tower. It was the most probable spot to find the orange fragments but after a half hour of searching she gave up hope.

"Sarah, it's way too dark out here. Why don't we just come back tomorrow and try this again in daylight?

She was beginning to think he was right. "Okay, I guess you're right."

"It just kills you to say that, doesn't it?"

You have no idea, she thought.

As they walked back to the car Sarah couldn't shake the feeling that she had missed something. It was one of the curses of her profession. Every time she left a crime scene she always felt there was something she forgot to do. They were about half way back when it hit her. "Wait. Vegas, you said there was a padlock on the stairwell door?"

"Yeah, a padlock."

"Did you actually go up and examine it?"

"What the hell for? I could see it from fifteen yards away!"

Remember who you're dealing with Sarah, she thought.

"Gimmie a sec. I want to take another look."

"Knock yourself out. I'm waiting in the warm car."

Sarah turned back with a slight spring in her step and a tiny glimmer of hope in her eye. She approached the gated door, looking for anything that might be out of place. The red wire cage surrounded the stairwell and made entry impossible without getting through the gate. The four-inch padlock looked capable of stopping a tank round. Kneeling down, Sarah examined it with her flashlight. It seemed normal until she grabbed it in her hand. The body rotated away from the shackle which had been cut at the base. To the naked eye the lock appeared intact. It might have been several days before the trespass was noticed. She was sure that's what he had intended. By that time no one would have made a connection to the shooting, she thought. Sarah removed the lock and opened the whining door, careful not to damage any fingerprints that might be present on the handle. Vargas must have seen her light going up the stairs because he came running from the car. "Hold up, Sarah! Let me clear the building first!" He began to climb after her, gun in hand.

Each level contained one room measuring twelve feet square. The bare cement rooms were littered with burned furniture and wooden frames used to make doorways. Vargas made it to the top of the stairway where a small ladder led to the roof. Sarah was a few steps behind. He was breathing hard and looked dead tired when Sarah caught up to him.

"It's clear," he said holstering his weapon.

"Don't you want to check the roof?" "Be my guest," he said as he hunched over and put his hands on his knees. Sarah smiled and climbed the short ladder to the roof.

The view was impressive. The Platte River to the west was jet black. She could see the buildings of downtown Denver to the north, and the Tech Center to the east. The crime scene by the train tracks was awash in lights. The train was stopped now and must have been put back in position, she thought.

The rooftop was ringed by a small iron railing. A five foot square sheet of oil-stained cardboard and small bits of trash littered the floor. Considering the padlock, Sarah knew there was a good chance this could be the sniper's nest.

She had a nagging sense that she needed to do something when it hit her . . . she didn't have a camera! Ugh! I'm a total idiot!, she thought. She had left her camera in her truck thinking that it was right across the street if she needed it. Now she was blocks away and she knew Vargas wouldn't leave her alone to go back and get it.

"Hey, Vargas? You don't happen to have a camera with you, do you?"

"Jesus, kid, no camera, no gun. . . no brain? You sure you don't want someone else out here to do this?"

I deserved that, she thought. She was unprepared and there was no good excuse for it. Under normal circumstances she'd just walk out to her truck. She was never this far away from all her gear at most crime scenes. This one, however, was anything but normal. "Do you, or don't you?"

"What's it worth to you?"

"Don't go there, Vegas, not tonight."

"Okay, okay, I've got a point-and-shoot in the trunk. Will that do?"

"It'll have to."

As Vargas climbed back down the stairs she began a careful scan of the rooftop with her flashlight. She remembered what Art had told her when she'd first started this career. Crime scenes are not the dominion of criminals alone. Each scene had a history of activity and the evidence of that activity was mixed among the evidence of the crime. It was the job of the criminalist to determine which items related to the crime and which items were there regardless of the crime. It was one of the more difficult challenges of the job.

Vargas returned in a few minutes with the camera. He was out of breath again. "You better not ask me to get anything else for you down there," he said, lighting a cigarette.

"Hey, do you mind? This is a crime scene," she complained.

"I'm on the stairwell, for god's sake."

"Well, you did sort of save my life tonight so I guess I owe you."

"Now you're talking."

"Jesus, you old hound dog. I meant the cigarette."

"I know, I just like messing with you."

"Those things are going to kill you, ya know."

"Kid, judging from tonight, I'd say you're gonna kill me much sooner."

Sarah grabbed the camera from him and checked the available memory. There were sixteen pictures already on the card but it still had plenty of space on it. "Can I erase these pictures on here?"

The crime lab policies directed all flash cards to be formatted at the beginning of each scene.

"Ah, I'm not sure—"

"Oh, my god!" Sarah exclaimed as she viewed an image of a middle-aged naked woman engaged in a lewd sex act. "Dear God, Vegas, this is a department camera! What if these had been turned in with some crime scene photos?"

"What are you talking about? Gimmie that camera." Vargas took the camera and started flipping through the images. "Oh, yeah . . . her," he said with a devilish tone. "That was a night of red label whiskey and red light debauchery," he stated with pride.

"That's disgusting, even for you."

"Hey I'm a detective . . . not a priest. I don't judge your personal life."

"Yeah, but she's a total hussy!"

"I don't spend time admiring the mantle while I'm stoking the fire," he said, not looking up from the screen. He was still scrolling through images when she snatched it out of his hands.

"Hey, you're not going to erase those are you?"

"No, I wouldn't dream of it, *Detective* Vargas. I thought I'd turn them in with our homicide photos! Yes, I'm erasing them, dumbass."

"Oh, c'mon. Those are classic! Can't you just download them separately at the lab before you turn the others in?"

"*No*! End of discussion."

Vargas conceded defeat. "Oh, well, I guess I can always call her up again."

The mental picture was enough to make her gag. She deleted the images before Vargas could protest further. The compact Nikon Coolpix camera was the on-call detective's camera. It was simple to use . . . even for Vargas. It was fine for photographing people, cars, or small rooms but it wasn't suited for nighttime use outdoors. It was a common problem with all point-and-shoot cameras fitted with so called "peanut," flashes. It just wasn't enough light. She began by photographing the rooftop from all four corners. Then she photographed the trash and debris. Sarah tiptoed across the concrete careful not to damage any evidence. She studied the cardboard sheet, noticing a crease running down the middle and two tennis ball sized indentations on either side. There was something about the indentations that looked familiar but she couldn't quite place it.

Vargas was finishing his second cigarette when he called up,

"How's it going up there? Find anything interesting?"

"Still looking."

"How big is it up there?" he asked sarcastically.

"Overtime . . . remember," she called out.

It must have worked because he lit another cigarette. She was trying to imagine how the shooter would have stood against the railing and searched the metal bars for signs of disturbance. She knelt down and examined the cardboard with her flashlight. Sarah held the light at a low angle so the beam skimmed the surface, highlighting every depression and every pebble lying on it.

She heard Vargas come up the ladder and stand behind her.

"Looks like someone was on their knees," he stated.

She looked back at him over her shoulder. "What do you mean?"

"Those indentations there, they look like they were made by someone on their knees."

He was right, she thought. How could she not see that? She felt stupid missing something so obvious to the mediocre detective. "You wouldn't shoot from a kneeling position, would you?" she asked.

"Not if you want to be accurate. But you're probably going to come to your knees after lying prone," he said, taking a long drag on his cigarette.

Of course! Her head wasn't in the game. Sarah lay down next to the cardboard and held up her arms as if she were holding a rifle. "You could definitely see the victim from here."

"I bet it would have been pretty dark, though, especially against that dark tanker car."

"Maybe he had night vision."

"Maybe," he said, exhaling a blue-colored smoke ring.

Sarah tried to imagine how difficult such a shot would be as she lay on the cold concrete. It was a perfect spot, though. It was high, which allowed the shooter to spot potential witnesses. The commercial nature of the area meant no one would be around to hear the shot. If they did they would think it was a car backfire or some noise coming from a warehouse or the recycling plant. She tried to take a few photographs from the shooters perspective, but they were all too dark. It was a moot exercise anyway unless she found some tiny orange fragments or a cartridge casing if she could be that lucky. Vargas' Nextel blurted. "Hey. Yup, she's right here with me. Oh, I don't think her phone is on. I'll give her mine."

Sarah remembered that she had not thought to reattach her battery. Sarah held the phone with her fingertips. Who knows what vile substances might coat this thing? She thought.

"Sarah, you're on the tower?" It was Art.

"Yeah, and there's some very weak evidence suggesting he was lying prone up here."

"What kind of weak evidence?"

She told him about the cardboard.

"I see. Have you found any of the orange fragments?"

"No, but I'm guessing with the barrel sticking out over the railing they would've been scattered to the wind."

She could hear another voice talking to Art in an excited tone. It sounded a lot like Daniel.

"Sarah, I'm on speaker phone here and Daniel reminded me that a sniper would not place his muzzle out over the railing. Pulling it back over the concrete would help hide the muzzle blast from the road and redirect the sound so that it was more difficult to zero in on. Do you see any dark discoloration on the cardboard or concrete?"

Daniel again? She looked around. "No, nothing."

"Did you look under the cardboard?"

Ugh, nooooo, because I'm a dipshit. Sarah slowly lifted the cardboard and there it was. A darkened area in a cone-like pattern. "Bingo!"

It was gunshot residue expelled from the barrel of the gun as it was fired. There were tiny flakes of gunpowder still embedded on the concrete surface. She was trying to figure out how to collect them when her eye caught the Holy Grail: a single, tiny, orange-colored sliver. Hot damn!

"What's Bingo?" Art asked, waiting for her to elaborate.

"This is the place Art," Sarah reported. "I found gunshot residue from the muzzle blast and a single orange fragment. It must have ricocheted off the railing and come back to rest on the concrete."

"That's great, Sarah. Can you see any powder flakes?"

"Yes. How do you want me to collect them? I don't have any gear up here."

"For now photograph them and cover them with the cardboard, then get with Tony. He'll walk you through the process when you have the materials ready."

"Will do. I gotta go, Art. Busy night."

"Hey, Sarah?" he asked.

"Yeah, Art?"

"Great Job."

"Thanks."

It was an empty expression, she thought. She hadn't done anything. It was Daniel that directed her to the sniper's nest and Art who thought of looking under the cardboard. Hell, even Vargas was more helpful than she was.

15

It was a few minutes after ten o'clock in the evening. The killer sat slumped in his Lay-Z-Boy chair after a dinner of microwave chicken pot pie and a Budweiser, playing solitaire, same as most nights after dinner. The television played in the background; he was usually content channel surfing until something captured his interest. Tonight he was interested in the evening news, hoping to gain a tidbit of information about one of his crimes. He stared at his big toe poking through a hole in his sock while waiting for the trademark jingle from the local news channel.

He grew tired of the phony news anchors with their polished presentation and a spray-on tan in the dead of winter.

The big local story was another sniper shooting. He sat upright in the chair when Maggie Miller graced the screen. She was one of his favorite roving reporters. Her energy and personality were infectious, much like her sexuality. He had once thought of "dating" her. He had even tracked her down to a parking garage one night, but in the end he decided that the world was more interesting with her in it.

The sniper had killed another kid who'd been tagging a train. Miller said the police weren't sure if the two shootings were related but he knew they were. They had to be, he thought. This sniper had panache. Foolish, though. Why risk prison in retaliation for some minor property damage? Vigilantism was a losing game and sooner or later this killer would slip up. Hell, it was a good bet the cops were on to him already. He smiled in self-adulation. He was a professional killer practicing the fine art of murder. He had no question he would one day be immortalized in the history books.

Then on the screen, he saw her. She was in the background but her chestnut hair was unmistakable. Maggie was interviewing her partner. Apparently, she had been attacked again, this time by two thugs, and she'd survived. He was intrigued by her tenacity. He wanted to find out more about her. This might be a woman worth pursuing, but not too soon. He must study her first, learn

Tom Adair

her strengths and weaknesses. This one was not to be taken for granted, he thought.

He watched the rest of the local news with some disappointment. There was no mention of any of his crimes. Hadn't the police found the Jeep in Aspen? Weren't they searching for the owner? He was being upstaged by this sniper fellow, he thought, and found himself toiling in a mild jealousy. After a moment, he dismissed the thoughts and reminded himself that his crimes were committed so well that it would take an army of detectives to scent his trail. In point of fact, his anonymity was the ultimate demonstration of his superiority.

Sarah secured the orange fiber and covered the gunpowder burn before descending the stairs with Vargas. In a few minutes they were back at the murder scene.

Manny was yelling at one of the officers near the tanker car. He shot her a mixed look of concern and anger as she approached. "You okay?"

"Yeah, I'm fine now. No problem."

Manny shook his head and rolled his eyes. "You sure are one hell of a shit magnet Sarah."

"Hey, I don't look for trouble Manny, trouble finds me."

Manny returned his attention to the officer. "I want you up on that tanker with a light, watching him every second!"

"What's going on?" Sarah asked.

"Tony's in the tanker car trying to find the bullet."

"Isn't that dangerous with all the fumes?"

"Yeah, no shit. He's in a level-three biohazard suit but I still don't feel good about it. OSHA would shit a brick if they saw this circus. I've got Deputy Numbnuts up there who's supposed to be keeping an eye on Tony but I keep catching him dickin' around."

"Don't you have com links with him?"

"Yeah, but you know Tony, he's not exactly a Chatty Kathy."

"How is he searching for the bullet?"

"The oil is about two feet deep thanks to the height of the bullet hole, but its slow going. He's feeling around on his hands and knees."

"Why can't he use a metal detector?" Vargas asked.

Sara looked at him, wondering if he was the same guy who had figured out the indentations on the cardboard.

120

"Oh, yeah, I guess the whole tank is one big metal drum."

"Got it!" Tony announced over the radio.

All heads turned to the tanker top, waiting for Tony. The blue-colored hazmat suit was coated in oil and Tony was all too happy to get out of the claustrophobic environment. The decontamination team stripped him to his underwear and hosed him off in a small, rubber kiddy pool. EMT's did one last check before he could dress and make it over to the group.

"What'd ya got, Tony?" Manny asked.

"Not sure yet, I haven't had a chance to clean it off." Tony pulled a fine white cloth from his duty bag and caressed the oil from the bullet. "Looks to be in pretty good shape. No rifling marks," he said "What about the base?" Sarah asked.

Tony adjusted the bullet under the bright spotlights, trying to see through the glare of the oily film. "Let me see here . . . it's pretty deformed, but there might be something. I can't really tell . . . I need to get this under the microscope to be sure." He put the bullet into a protective case and tucked it into his cargo pants.

It was clear that Tony had not been told about her attack, which made working conditions a lot easier. "Hey, Sarah, find anything promising at the gas station?"

If you only knew, she thought. Sarah told him about her findings at the fire tower. "I'll need some help collecting the gunshot residue," she said as they walked toward his car.

"No problem." Tony said. "It's crazy how this Daniel guy is two for two. He should play the lottery."

"I don't know how he does it," she said.

"You mentioned he was in the military. Was he a sniper or something?"

"He said he was a mechanic."

"Must just be lucky, I guess."

"Well, Art vouches for him and that's good enough for me," she said, trying to convince herself

"Any thoughts on the motive?" Tony asked.

"The sniper's motive? I have no idea. It'll be interesting to see if there's any connection between the two victims."

"It's never that easy."

They reached the tower in short order. Vargas was waiting by the stairs with a deputy he had assigned to guard the scene. No doubt Vargas was spinning a tall tale of the evening's adventures fit for the Hollywood screen.

"Exciting night, eh?" Tony asked as he approached the pair.

"So she told you about her attack, huh?" Vargas blurted out.

Sarah slid her hand across her throat, gesturing him to stop. It was too late.

"What attack is that, Sarah?" Tony asked.

"Oh, it was nothing. I'll tell you about it tomorrow."

He stopped in his tracks and gave her a defiant look.

"We've got to get this evidence collected. That is the priority, Tony, so let's get at it."

They climbed the stairs while Vargas kept the deputy company. Truth be told, Sarah didn't think he had it in him for another climb. Tony took a few moments at the top to take it all in. He produced a set of Burris binoculars from his pack and scanned the area around the tanker car, while Sarah set up a tripod to take additional time-exposed photographs.

"Are you going to try to get a trajectory from here?" she asked Tony.

"No point, really. It's impossible to put the train back at the exact spot and since we can't measure the potential error rate it would never see the inside of a courtroom."

"Error rate? I don't get it, Tony. How can we be held to such ridiculous standards in our line of work. Do people really think we work in some controlled laboratory where everything can be measured?"

"Hey, don't shoot the messenger, kid." He knelt down and examined the cardboard sheet.

"Those are the indentations we think are knee marks," she stated, pointing to the small depressions.

"Sure looks like it to me. Good find."

"You can thank Vegas for that."

"It's possible he left some prints or DNA on this. We'll need to check it back at the lab."

It was a long shot but it was a base they had to cover. They lifted the sheet, placing it to the side. Tony switched on his light and examined the cone-shaped muzzle blast. Sarah handed him the small vial containing the orange fragment.

"I see rifling marks but this is a really small piece. I'm not sure Walter will be able to do much with it."

"Even if he can't, it still proves it's the same shooter, right?" Sarah asked.

"It's a working theory. Given the circumstances, though, I'd say we're dealing with the same guy," he agreed.

Sarah knelt down next to the muzzle blast pattern. "So how do you want to collect the gunpowder flakes . . . swabbing?" Sarah asked.

"No, that'll just piss Walter off and I'd like to keep him on my good side," he said.

"What then, a GSR kit?"

"Exactly." Tony pulled out a small plastic case about the size of his thumb and removed the lid. He pressed the tiny pedestal against the muzzle blast so the adhesive coating would pick up the unburned powder flakes. "Soooo . . . Sarah?"

"Yep?" she said, not looking up from her camera.

"What was Vegas talking about down there? Were you attacked by a dog or something?"

"More like two dogs."

He wasn't satisfied. "C'mon, Sarah! You know I'm going to find out sooner or later."

Sarah acquiesced and retold a condensed version of the story. He stared at the Denver city lights while taking it all in.

"Jesus, you are some shit magnet. This isn't your month."

"You can say that again."

"Why didn't you shoot the guy?" he asked.

Sarah rolled her eyes and went back to her photography.

Back at the murder scene, Manny was debriefing Sheriff Brian Westin, who was freaking out. The last thing he needed in an election year was some vigilante killing kids.

Manny's briefing was interrupted every few minutes with orders to perform tasks that had either already been completed, or were on the short list to get done. If there was one constant in the universe it was this: Under-qualified supervisors always developed an insatiable urge to control every aspect of a major investigation. It didn't matter if a detective had hundreds of death investigations under his belt; micro-management was the preferred approach of all the higher-ups. Of course, if mistakes were made and arrests weren't forthcoming, it was the detective's fault. It was one of those "get none of the credit; take all of the blame," kinds of arrangements. Manny was used to playing the game but he still didn't like it.

During his debriefing, Lieutenant Manilow and Sergeant Lester Davis approached the pair, settling in a too close for Manny's taste. "Hey Lester, how's it going?" Manny asked, ignoring Manilow.

Lester raised his head in acknowledgement, but said nothing, not wishing to tick off Manilow.

"Lieutenant Manilow. What can I do for you?" Manny asked, turning his attention to the squatty leader.

"You do for me? Not a thing, Detective. We're here to do our own investigation," Manilow said

"Detective Vargas' shooting?" Manny asked.

"No, no . . . that's been handled already," Sheriff Westin cut in.

Of course it was, Manny thought. He studied Barry's face and saw the look of annoyance and frustration.

"No, we're investigating Criminalist Richards' actions leading to the alleged attack in the alleyway."

"What do you mean, *alleged* attack?" Manny demanded.

"Look, Detective, I know you two are close, maybe too close, but I think you've lost your objectivity here. Ms. Richards should never have been in that situation. In fact, her escapades are placing a great deal of potential liability on the department," Manilow said.

"Potential liability? Is that like getting a little bit pregnant?"

"Look—" Manilow started to say.

"No, you look, Lieutenant, she's been through enough already. She's the victim here, remember? I need her focused on my investigation, not yours."

"Frankly, Detective, you don't get a say in how I conduct the timing of my investigations or on whom."

"No, you're right, Barry, I just figured some sicko going around killing kids would be our priority," he said, making eye contact with Sheriff Westin.

The sheriff stood motionless for a moment, pondering the obvious dilemma. He could either piss off his lieutenant, who worked at his pleasure, over a case where his criminalist was almost raped and killed, or risk hampering a high profile murder investigation that could generate a firestorm of bad press if it ever got out.

Manny knew Sheriff Westin was a master politician, in fact, he was counting on it.

"You know Lieutenant; I think we need to give Ms. Richards some time on this. She's been through two traumatic events recently."

"But, Sheriff—" Manilow started to protest.

"Bart, I've made my decision. Now that's the end of it, understand?"

"Of course, Sheriff, I completely agree with your sentiment."

Manny could tell by his angry stare that Manilow was taking this personally.

"Good to know we're all on the same team here. Our priority is finding the man killing these poor children."

"Continue, Detective," Westin said to Manny.

"Well, as I was saying . . . the victim was shot over there by the train as he was tagging. The kid is a mess. Aside from the massive head trauma, he's covered in oil."

"So is half my county," the sheriff stated rhetorically.

"Best we can figure the shot came from the top of the fire training tower to the west."

"You've already found the sniper's nest?" Manilow interrupted.

"Sarah found it."

"Ms. Richards found the sniper's nest. After being chased down the street and attacked in the alley she miraculously located a sniper's nest in the middle of the night?" Manilow asked in amazement.

"I don't know all the details yet but she got a call from Art Von Hollen, who had been reviewing aerial photographs at my request, and he directed her to the fire tower."

"And how was it that Art was so sure this was the sniper's nest?" Manilow asked.

"Actually, I think it was his nephew, Daniel, who suggested the fire tower."

"Oh, so it's 'Daniel' now. Sounds like you need to get your facts in order, Detective." Manilow turned to walk away but stopped. "Wait a minute—is this the same Daniel that found the sniper's nest in the previous shooting along the river?"

"Yeah. So what?" Manny said.

"Don't you find it odd that the same man was able to locate such a specific scene hundreds of yards from the shooting victim in literally minutes from being told of the location?"

"Not as strange as I find it that you made lieutenant."

"Gentlemen," the sheriff cut in. "We're all on the same side here and I won't get bogged down in these petty rivalries. We have the murder of a young man here. No, make that two young men. Let's try and keep our eye on the ball, shall we?"

Manilow marched to the command post, but not before Lester shot Manny an approving smile.

"I'm going to hold a press conference at oh-nine-hundred hours tomorrow morning and you had better have some answers for me by then," Westin said.

"Well, sir, I'm not sure what we'll be able to tell the press by then." Manny said

"Listen, Detective Lopez, by tomorrow morning the public is going to be scared shitless, and as the protectors of this community we need to assure everyone that the streets are safe, do you get me?" It was more of a command than a question. "I can't afford a DC Sniper-type case, all right?"

"Sheriff, we have no idea who he is or what his real motive is. The fact of the matter is that there will probably be more killings before we catch a break," Lopez confessed.

"Jesus Christ, would you listen to yourself, Manny? Does that sound like the sort of thing that's going to calm the community? I had better not hear that shit tomorrow morning. You know what, on second thought, you just stand there and I'll do the talking. If I need your input I'll ask for it." Westin started to walk away and then turned back. "Oh, and for Pete's sake, wear a nice suit this time, will you?" Westin hustled back to the warm interior of the command post.

"Fuck you very much, Sheriff," Vargas whispered as he came up behind Manny.

"You heard all that, huh?"

"Oh, yeah, got my handy-dandy little super-ear sound amplifier," Vargas said, pointing to the small hearing aid dangling in his ear. The device looked like a Bluetooth but it amplified ambient sounds. "Can you believe that guy?" Vargas asked.

"I can't blame him. He's scared shitless of a rising body count. And since when do you wear a hearing aid?"

"Oh, I don't need a hearing aid, but it sure helps dig up dirt on people who don't think I'm listening."

Manny had heard the rumors for years. Sal Vargas was the J. Edgar Hoover of scandalous information for the local law enforcement community. If there was dirt to be had on you, Vargas had it. Manny always wondered what his own "file," might reveal. He decided it was better to stay on Vargas' good side just to be safe.

"Hey, I got a fresh lead for us," Vargas said

"What kind of lead?"

"An informant called me. He overheard some bartender mention that a customer said he just wanted to kill a kid who had been tagging his building."

Manny perked up at the potential break. "Which bar?"

"Uh . . . Mel's Place."

"Jesus, Vargas. Are you kidding me?"

"Dead serious," he said in an official, yet unconvincing, tone.

"Vegas, we can't afford to screw around here. If the sheriff finds out, and this wasn't a legitimate lead to follow, he'll have both our asses!"

"Well, yours maybe," Vargas said grinning.

"Vegas!"

"All right, all right. I'm on the up and up I remember how much trouble you got into the last time and besides...I said I was sorry."

"I don't know . . ."

"Hey, this could be the break we've been waiting for. But if you'd rather not follow up on such an important lead, I guess the sheriff will understand, right?"

Manny sighed at the thought of returning to the bar that almost got him a demotion. "I can't believe I'm letting you talk me into this."

"It's a good lead, man. Plus, we'll be able to spend hours in there on actual official duty," he said, using air finger quotes.

"This had better not turn out like the last time," Manny warned.

"Hey, man, who's got your back?"

"Not you, that's for sure."

"Nice. You have to admit, though, last time was funnier than hell."

16

Manilow gently grabbed Lester's arm when they reached the front of the command post. "What do you make of this Daniel Van Hollen thing?"

"Well, it's weird, I guess."

"'It's weird, you guess. There is no way in hell that some handyman is going to cherry pick two sniper's nests that fast. No way in hell."

"Who knows . . . maybe the guy is just lucky."

"Lucky?! No one is that goddamned lucky, not twice in a row. We work in Littleton, not Las Vegas, remember?"

"Well, what are you saying, then? You can't think that he's involved in this. I mean, the guy was hundreds of miles away when these shootings happened."

"Was he?" Manilow asked.

Lester had seen this look before. He knew that when Manilow got onto the scent of something he was harder to shake than a bloodhound. "What do you want me to do?" he asked, "Do you still have friends in the military?"

"Yeah, couple of guys, at least."

"Call in some favors and see what we can find out about Mr. Von Hollen and his military record."

"Officially?"

His eyes narrowed as his mind began to churn. "No, let's keep this unofficial, for now."

"Am I intruding?" Sarah asked after finding the two detectives talking.

"Not at all. We were just talking about the case," Vargas answered.

"You two all done, Sarah?" Manny asked.

"Yeah, we got everything documented and collected. The next move is up to Walter," she said. "You guys staying out here much longer?"

"Actually, we're going to a bar," Vargas said.

"No kidding? Oh, after tonight I'd love to get a drink. Do you mind if I go with you?" she asked.

"After all you've been through tonight?" Manny said.

"Actually, I can't explain it but finding all the evidence we did has really put me in a good mood".

Truthfully, she just didn't want to be alone right now.

"We're following up on a lead. It's not like we're going there for fun or anything," Manny said,

"The beer will still taste the same, won't it? Plus you can be my designated driver. That is if you boys don't mind driving me home," she said in a playful voice, knowing that Vargas couldn't resist the implication.

"She's got a point, Manny. I for one would love for you to come along." Not getting a reply he continued. "She's an adult, right, Manny?"

"I'm sure as hell more of an adult than you two," she said.

"It's settled, then," Vargas stated. "My lady, your chariot awaits." He extended his arm as they walked to the car.

Sarah jumped into the back seat and the two detectives stared at each other over the hood of the car.

"This is a really bad idea," Manny said.

"That's why I suggested it, my good man."

The Cooter Shooter was one of the seedier strip clubs along the Santa Fe corridor, not that there was a respectable one. Mel Harris had been the club's owner since it opened in 1971 amid a torrent of community protests. It was home to all the ugly girls who couldn't get hired at the classier strip clubs in Denver.

Sarah did a double take as they pulled into the parking lot but she was damned if she was going to show an ounce of discomfort in front of the two male detectives.

"I guarantee you the beer is good," Vargas said, smiling at her in the rearview mirror.

"Sarah, you don't have to go in there with us. We can call a patrol car to come get you," Manny said, feeling very uncomfortable.

"Don't be silly. Do you think this is the first strip club I've been to?" Sarah hopped out of the sedan walking with bold determination to the bar's entrance.

The neon sign above the door featured a smoking revolver emerging from a pair of burlesque legs.

"You gotta admire her spunk," Vargas said as the two detectives hurried to catch up.

Mel Harris sat smoking a pricy Opus X Double Corona cigar inside the front entrance. Sarah could hear the moans of protest coming from the old wooden stool under his considerable girth. The $40.00 cigar was in sharp contrast to his stained undershirt and wrinkled polyester pants. His wardrobe was accented by a gaudy gold chain necklace hanging from his beefy neck. His wiry, gray chest hair was entangled in the chain like Clematis.

He was a fat version of Vargas, she thought.

His eyes swept her body with indifference as she came through the door. "Auditions are Tuesdays but since you're here, let's have a look at your tits," he stated as Sarah stood before him.

"What did you say?" Sarah asked. He talked like Vargas, too.

"Ah, she's with us, Mel," Vargas said as they came scampering into the dim entry.

"You two again?" He eyed the two suspiciously. "So tell me . . . are you here for business or for pleasure?"

"Business, not pleasure," Manny blurted out before Vargas could answer.

"You sure? 'Cause last time you said that the cops were bashing down my goddamned doors."

"It's not like that Mel, we just need to talk to someone," Vargas said.

"Just talk, eh."

"I swear to you, Mel, we just want to talk to someone and then we'll leave," Vargas said, trying to calm his nerves.

Mel eyed the two detectives through a haze of smoke and decided he didn't have much choice. "Don't go riling up any of my customers, you hear?"

"Got it, buddy, no problem," Vargas said, patting his shoulder.

Buddy? Sarah thought.

The three grabbed a small table in the corner of the dim bar. Every stool at the bar was occupied. Sarah watched as two women paraded between the stage and bar, teasing the men seated below. Four Herculean bouncers stood ready to pounce on any fool dumb enough to jump up on stage. Sarah wasn't sure who was more disgusting, the dancers or the patrons. The dancers were haggard women covered in faded tattoos, dancing with the grace of drunken baboons. The men weren't much better. Most of them appeared to be professional drunks. There was a small group of young men hollering at the edge of the stage that Sarah presumed were from the nearby community college.

"Kind of a compliment ol' Mel gave you about working here, huh, Sarah?" Vargas asked as they settled into their seats.

"Yeah, Vegas, I can't believe I wasted all that time in grad school when I could have been dancing with all these classy ladies," she retorted with a laugh. These were just his type of women, she thought: skanky and desperate.

"Jesus, look at the blonde up there!" Vegas said, waving his arms above his head, trying to keep beat with the retro-rap song.

"I think that's a man," Sarah said.

"We're here on business, remember?" Manny said.

"I know, Jesus, don't be so friggin' stiff. On second thought . . ."

Manny shot him a look that said don't go there.

Their bikini clad waitress came over to the table to take their drink order.

"Sarah, what do you want . . . it's on me," Manny said, trying to salvage some sense of decency.

"Bring me a Coors, baby," Vargas blurted out, not waiting for Sarah.

"Vegas! We're on duty," Manny protested.

"All right, make it a Coors Light," he said continuing in his ridiculous dance.

Normally, Sarah would have been more critical but after tonight she really didn't care. She looked up at the waitress and was struck by the amount of metal dangling off her face. "I'll have a Corona."

"Just gimme a club soda." Manny just knew he'd be the designated driver.

"Seriously, Manny, what do you think of that blonde?" Vargas prodded, not caring that Sarah was there.

"I think I'd rather jack off with a handful of razor blades," he said.

"You're no fun tonight, man," Vargas said.

"Who's your contact here?" Manny asked, trying to get back to business.

"Some bartender broad named Starlight."

"Starlight? That's her name?" Sarah asked.

"Apparently . . . I'm going to go try and find her at the bar."

"Ya think, Sherlock?"

Vargas sprang from his chair and danced his way over to the bar, sporting his beer and the classic white man's overbite.

"So you two have been in here before, huh?" Sarah asked Manny through the blaring music.

"Once," he said, not making eye contact.

"It sounds like it was quite the evening. Want to tell me about it?"

"No, not really."

"Okay, I'll just ask Vargas when he gets back."

"Okay, all right already."

His eyes darted around the room before whispering.

"It was a couple years ago. Vegas tells me that he's got a hot lead at this bar on a sex assault case we were working. So we get in the car and come over here and I don't think anything of it because our victim was a stripper. So I come to find out that it was all a ruse. Vargas was bringing me here for my fifteenth wedding anniversary and he had paid a stripper to, well, give me a lap dance."

"Seriously? What did you do?"

"Well, it took me off guard, of course. I mean, I come into this joint and start to interview this chick and she starts talking dirty and acting really inappropriate."

"What do you mean, inappropriate?"

"You know, she's touching my leg and oh, I forgot to mention, she's topless and wearing this pair of red crotchless panties."

"No shit?" Sarah asked, laughing harder now.

"It's not funny!" Manny protested. He felt like he was confessing to his daughter.

"Okay, I'm sorry, go on."

"So she starts getting all touchy-feely and starts grinding on my lap."

"That's hysterical, Manny."

"Oh, yeah, it was hysterical right up to the point the FBI busts through the friggin' door."

"The FBI?"

"Apparently, they'd been staking the place out with hidden surveillance cameras, trying to bust a human smuggling suspect they thought was scouting girls in the joint. One of the agents recognized us and thought the operation would get blown if we stayed in much longer so they decided to bust the place with us inside."

"You're shitting me? And it's all on camera?"

"Yep, I think I have all the copies accounted for but I have a feeling Vegas still has one."

Sarah couldn't contain her laughter. "How come I've never heard this from anyone before?"

"Because I've worked my ass off keeping it quiet. Only Vargas, the sheriff, and the field agents knew about me and my involvement."

"I'll bet that cost a few favors to keep quiet."

"You have no idea."

She glanced over at the bar and saw Vargas talking to a young woman with long, blue-green hair and black nail polish.

"Do you think he can get her to talk to him?" she asked, nodding toward the bar.

"Who, Vargas? He's the Pied Piper of crazy bitches. Believe me, that guy could sell her a bag of leaves in the fall," he stated.

"I just don't get it, Manny, the guy is repulsive."

"I know, but skanks respond to him. It's like he knows he'll never get with a pretty girl and he's just accepted his lot in life. Like a third-string quarterback or something. He'll take whatever playing time he can get, even if it's on the practice field."

"That's pathetic."

Once at the bar, Vargas ditched the Coors Light for a double shot of bourbon.

"What else do you want, *cop*?" the bartender said adding the emphasis.

"Are you the one they call Starlight?"

"Yeah, that's me," she said even more annoyed.

He was fascinated by her Goth look. The tattoos, black fingernails, even the dark eye shadow had an erotic effect on him.

"I like your jewelry," he said, stroking the dozens of thin bracelets on her wrist. "So how did you get that name?"

"You know, like the children's rhyme?"

"Oh, yeah, I wish I may, I wish I might, have the wish I wish tonight!" he said in a pseudo-sexy growl.

Her eyebrows rose a bit. "No guy's ever known the meaning of my name before. But look, my boss told me I can't say nothing to you cops without a warrant," she said with the hint of a smile.

Like a lion sensing the kill, Vargas prodded further. "Well, we wouldn't want you to get in trouble with your boss, now would we? How about you just whisper it in my ear and pretend you're telling me about your heavenly body."

The comment would elicit a stream of vomit from a decent woman, but Manny's prediction was right. Within minutes she was smitten with him. "My shift ends in five minutes. Maybe you'd like to talk about it somewhere quieter."

Sarah could see the two laughing and touching from her seat and thought she might be witnessing the eighth wonder of the world in action. He was old enough to be her father but she didn't seem to care. So much for Darwin's Survival of the Fittest model, she thought.

Vargas came bouncing back to them plopping his keys on the table.

"So did you get any good information from her?" Manny asked.

"Oh, yeah, real good information," he said in the same annoying growl.

"About the case?" Manny asked.

"Oh, that, not sure yet. To be honest it doesn't sound like our guy. Some old fart bitchin' about a warehouse up in Arvada. I'll know more by morning."

"Jesus, I knew it!" Manny threw up his hands

"Take my car. I'll have her drive me home. All the way home, if you know what I mean," he said, poking Manny in the ribs.

"Yeah, Vargas, we get it. Isn't she a bit young for you?" Sarah asked.

"Hellllo? What's your point?" he asked, blowing Starlight a kiss from the table. "Tonight, I'm going to show her how to do an Australian kiss."

"You mean a French kiss, don't you?" Sarah corrected him.

"Well, it's like that, but down under!"

Sarah nearly gagged.

As Vargas danced back to the bar, Manny and Sarah made a hasty retreat to the car. Sarah caught Manny looking up at the ceiling several times and thought he must be worried about hidden cameras "Man, am I glad to be out of there," he said.

"Ditto. You want to go somewhere without naked ladies and finish that beer?" she asked.

"To be honest, I just want to go home and take a shower. I've got this press conference in the morning and I'm sure it'll be a joke. Anyway, after tonight I'd think you were dying to get home."

"You'd think so, wouldn't you? I don't know, I guess I just didn't want to go home to an empty house."

"You want me to drop you off at your Mom's?"

"God no!" She could envision her mother allowing Jeremy to stay the night while she pampered him after his traumatic ordeal. "Just drive me back to the scene and I'll get my truck."

17

The 9:00 AM press conference came much too early for Detective Lopez. The sheriff met with him at eight to get an update. "You're not giving me much to go on, Detective. You had better generate some leads on this thing if you want to continue as lead detective," Westin said.

He was getting under Manny's skin. He had convinced the sheriff to withhold information about the Lapua magnum and orange fragments so the killer would not try to dispose of the evidence. Most criminals had the media and complacent department heads to thank for reminding them which evidence they needed to destroy.

No less than ten cameras lined the media room's back wall. All the major networks were there, including a national correspondent from FOX television. Local reporters described the victims as innocent boys being hunted by a madman. The headline for the *Denver Post* read: TERROR STALKS THE CITY, and citizens were devouring the hype with their morning coffee.

The glaring camera lights and flash bursts made it difficult to see people in the crowded room, which was a blessing of sorts. Manny spotted Sal Vargas, wearing the same rumpled clothes from the previous night. He sauntered down the aisle, nestling up to Manny's side. Moments later, the sheriff strolled out in regal poise, creating a thunderous roar of questions from the media. Sheriff Westin motioned for silence as he began to address the anxious crowd.

"Ladies and gentlemen, evil has trespassed among us. Through a senseless and tragic series of events our community has lost two of our beloved sons. Andrew Ramirez was sixteen years old. He loved going to school and taking care of his grandmother . . ."

As the briefing continued Manny wondered if there'd be any mention of the criminal history of assault, carrying a concealed weapon, and burglary that already graced the teenager's rap sheet.

"Hey," Vargas whispered.

"Shhh."

"Hey," he repeated his voice a bit louder.

"Shut up, Vegas. Stop screwing around while the sheriff is talking," Manny whispered tersely.

"You want to hear about my date last night?"

"No!"

"You sure?" Manny was sure he would regret asking.

"Fine, how'd your date go?" he asked.

"Smell for yourself," Vargas said holding his fingers up to Manny's face. Manny swatted away the hand.

"Goddamnit, Vargas," Manny whispered loud enough to alert the undersheriff's attention, standing foursquare behind the sheriff.

They both looked away as the under-sheriff gave them a look that could have stopped a grizzly in its tracks.

Vargas continued with his unsolicited debriefing.

"This chick was wicked, man. She sleeps in a frickin' coffin-shaped bed!"

"Shhh!"

"So, she tells me she's got to freshen up and goes into the head and I hear the biggest fart I've heard since last year's Christmas party, remember?" Manny's wide eyes pleaded with him to stop. "It sounded like a damned elephant or something. So I just figure she's getting warmed up, right?" Manny didn't say a word. "Anyway, we start getting down to business and the Goth freak has a visitor at home."

Manny raised an eyebrow.

"You know . . . she's on the rag!"

Good, serves you right. Manny glanced at the under-sheriff and seeing he was looking elsewhere he chanced a question. "So what the hell did you do?"

"Oh, so you were listening. Well, I'm thinking what a minx. She knew she was sporting a mouse and just wanted to test my resolve. Well, I don't back down from a fight, you know me." He paused waiting for a response. None was forthcoming. "So I grabbed the string in my teeth and pulled the little bastard out, kicking and screaming."

Manny's tongue curled as he winced. Composing himself, he tried steering the covert discussion back on track. "What about the suspect? Did you find out anything?"

"Oh, him, I almost forgot. Nope."

Manny needed more. "Well?"

"Turns out it was a neighborhood punk. Since our vics don't live in Arvada I crossed this guy off the list. Plus, from Starlight's description, this guy is way too old and fat to be the sniper."

The under-sheriff stared at them again and Manny tried to look interested in the press conference.

"Detective Lopez?" Sheriff Westin's lips pressed firm against the microphone.

Manny almost forgot where he was when he glanced over to the podium. "Yes, sir?"

"Can you answer Miss Carter's question?" He was annoyed.

Shit. Manny recovered quickly. "My apologies, Ms. Carter, I was conferring with my partner on this case. Could you repeat the question, please?"

"Can you tell us if the shooting in Sheridan is related to the murder last night?"

"We haven't ruled that in or out. Right now we are analyzing evidence from both scenes to see if we can link them together," he stated in the most official tone he could muster.

"What kind of evidence have you recovered?" she asked.

"We have no comment on that at this time."

"C'mon, Detective, you must have ballistic evidence right?" she persisted.

"As I said, we have no comment."

Another reporter chimed in. "Detective, are you aware that the FBI can search for fired bullets through a computerized database?"

Really? Thank God you showed up today or I'd be totally lost on how to do my job! "Yes, I am aware of that."

"Have the bullets from the two scenes been compared yet?" another reporter asked.

"That is being done as we speak," the sheriff answered.

Great, let's confirm what evidence we do have, Manny thought. "Detective, assuming that these two crimes are related, what can the public do to protect themselves?" another reporter asked.

"We are pulling out all the stops," the sheriff answered. "I have stepped up patrols in the area and we're checking the registered sex offenders in the neighborhood."

What? A sex offender . . . is he serious? Does the sheriff know something I don't?

Even Vargas was stumped by that one. "I have an alibi for last night," he whispered, giving Manny a nudge with his elbow.

"Detective, two young boys have been murdered. What would you say to the parents of other children out there listening?" the reporter asked.

Searching for the perfect answer, Manny opted for the truth. "Well, if the two killings are related, I'd say the killer is targeting kids engaged in spray painting. So I guess I'd tell them to make sure their kids don't go out tagging."

The sheriff's eyes popped out of their sockets. "I think what Detective Lopez meant to say was that parents should hold their children close until we catch this killer."

The press wasn't biting.

"Detective? Are you suggesting that these boys are somehow to blame for their own murders?" an angry reporter spat.

Before Manny could answer the sheriff stopped the press conference. "Ladies and gentlemen, I want to thank you for coming today, but I'm afraid we are late for a very important meeting on this investigation. We'll have another briefing tomorrow at the same time."

As the detectives descended the stairs, a middle-aged woman confronted Lopez. It was just what the television cameras had been waiting for.

"How dare you blame my boy for this? He is the victim, not a suspect!"

Manny knew better than to get into a yelling match with the victim's mother in front of the media so he just kept walking.

"That's right! Walk away . . . *A tí no te importa mi hijo. Lo único que te importa es protegerte tu culo. Eres un racista!*"

Manny lost his composure. "*Estás bromeando? Señora, se dió cuenta que soy mejicano.*"

"*Tú no eres mejicano. Eres un maldito policía.*"

Vargas grabbed his arm to hustle him out of the room before Manny said something he couldn't take back. Once they were in the car, Manny couldn't hold it in any longer.

"God! Do you believe that woman? Calling me a racist?!"

"She's emotional, man—losing your kid can do that."

"Yeah, she lost her kid because she let him grow up to be a dipshit and then drove him out to vandalize other people's property. Maybe if she played games with him or made him do his damned homework he'd still be alive."

Vargas let him vent.

"You know, its parents like that that keeps us in business. These kids grow up thinking they can do anything they want to anyone. They take, and steal, and rape, and kill; whatever they want they think they deserve. Don't get an education, don't get a job, just take from those that do and make your own rules! She's raised him to believe that the world owes him something instead of teaching him to earn his way."

"Yep," Vargas agreed.

"Argh! I just can't stand people like that!" he stated with finality.

Neither detective knew what to say anymore. The rant released a building frustration in both of them.

After a brief moment Vargas broke the silence. "She was kind of hot, though, don't you think?"

It was just what Manny needed to hear to lighten his spirits.

"God, Vargas, you are one sorry son of a bitch."

"I meant when she was yelling and stuff. Angry women just get my juices flowing."

Amy Summers was a woman on the road to recovery. Determined to shed the unwanted pounds gained during her pregnancy, she woke early every morning to go jogging. Her ex-husband's infidelity had been a huge blow to her self-confidence and after eight long months she wanted to look good, even if she wasn't dating. Living with her mother didn't help, either.

She slid on her skin-tight body suit and running jacket after checking on her newborn Emma. While most joggers ran to the beat of their iPods, Amy preferred the sounds of nature. Her favorite path was a seldom-used stretch of an urban greenbelt along the South Platte River. She loved to hear the song birds and see the occasional deer or fox along the trail. Coyotes were becoming a big urban problem but her dog Mandy would protect her. The five-year-old Belgian Malinois had been a constant companion for Amy during her turmoil. Like the old cliché, Mandy was her best friend.

The path had a remote and mystic feel when the fog drifted in as it did this morning. The river bank was choked with willows, reeds, and small trees that conspired to form an impenetrable overgrowth. To Amy it was the closest thing to the real outdoors in the city.

As she rounded a bend she noticed a man walking along the edge of the path in the grass to her left. Head down, he was dressed in a pair of jeans with work boots and a heavy wool coat. He sported a dull green backpack shouldered over both arms. He looked homeless. She moved to her right to give the man a wide berth but he stepped out onto the trail at the last moment and knelt down. Amy quickly wound the leash around her arm to restrict Mandy's reach.

Most people were intimidated by the look of her breed but this man didn't show an ounce of fear. Mandy began barking but Amy jerked the collar on instinct. "No! Mandy, be nice."

"Oh, she's all right. I used to have one of these beauties but she passed away about a month ago. Her name was Koko."

Amy felt sorry for the man. He seemed to be in his early 40s and his friendly demeanor suggested a calm and loving soul. Why couldn't all men be this nice? she asked herself

"You have a lovely dog. She looks to be about sixty pounds or so."

"I guess so," "How old is she?" he asked as he played with her snout and rubbed her head.

"She's five, how old was Koko if you don't mind me asking?"

"Almost fifteen!"

"Wow, that's pretty old. I hope Mandy makes it that far."

"I doubt it." His face didn't show the slightest hint of humor.

His left hand clamped down over Mandy's muzzle as his right hand drew a concealed knife from his boot. He plunged the four-inch stainless-steel drop point blade into Mandy's neck, severing her arteries and spurting blood all over his jeans, boots, and the pathway. Mandy's whimper was barely audible over the horrified gasp of her owner.

"What are you doing?!" Amy screeched.

The Scent of Fear

She tried to run but the dead weight of the dog cinched the leash coiled around her arm. Amy flinched as the man leapt to his feet and punched her face. The devastating blow knocked out two teeth as it clubbed her face. She hit the ground with a dull thud losing consciousness.

He sliced the black nylon leash with his knife and dragged Amy's limp body into the heavy brush and out of sight from any would-be joggers. The bare branches and cactus tore into her lower legs as he hauled her to a small, grassy patch. He returned to the path and dragged the dog's lifeless body by the leash dumping the blood-soaked canine alongside her owner. Amy stirred, and he kicked her in the head.

As the two bodies lay placid in the tall grass, the killer returned to the path to cover his tracks. He gathered some water from the river, using a coffee can he had planted on an earlier trip, and poured it over the blood on the groomed dirt path. He ground the diluted blood into the dirt with his boot. Once dried, the blood would be indistinguishable from the surrounding soil. He melted back into the brush after scanning the path for witnesses.

The rape would last thirty agonizing minutes. He started by slicing off her skin-tight running suit, exposing her ghostly white skin. Her warm, soft skin was a comfort from the cold morning air as he smothered her body with his. She was almost picture perfect, he thought.

Warm blood from Mandy's body seeped onto Amy's leg as the killer removed his belt. It was a dated-looking macramé weave from the early 1970s. Handmade by his mother, it was the preferred disciplinary tool of his abusive father. He could recall it being whipped against his bottom or wrapped around his neck with regularity.

The belt tore into her neck as he violated her womanhood with the Buck knife. Her body thrashed as she struggled against the wicked assailant. Freeing one arm, she lashed out at his face but she had a limited range of motion. Her screams were muffled by the constricting belt, not that anyone was around to hear her. Images of her daughter, Mandy, and the future she would never realize raced through her mind. It was a desperate and painful thing to know you were about to die. She could feel the energy being sapped from her muscles and prayed for the relief of death to halt the unbearable pain.

Then it was over.

With her heart now stopped the blood flowed from her wounds by gravity alone. The kill was thrilling but he needed more. He smoothed out her tangled hair and wiped the blood from her mouth. He was far from finished with her. He reached into his coat and pulled out an antique perfume bottle. The sterling silver vessel was decorated with jade inlays and a deer-skin-covered mister. It had been his mother's favorite perfume. The irresistible scent of lilac and honey was from a time gone by. The expensive perfume was meant for special occasions. Like the day he killed his father. He misted her neck and bosoms then did his best to prop open her eyes. He wanted her to see him. The warm blood heightened his arousal as he climbed on top of her. Despite his temptation, he was disciplined enough not to ejaculate until later.

Soon the thrilling sensation was gone and her warmth reclaimed by the cold morning air. He slid off his bloody trousers and pulled a loose-fitting pair of nylon sweat pants and a plastic bottle from his backpack. He poured the clear liquid over her naked body and hair. As a final act he removed Mandy's collar, and tucked it inside his pocket. He made his way to the path where he stood motionless, looking for witnesses. Seeing no one, he strolled past the drying blood, placed his hands in the warm wool pockets, and whistled through the woods all the way to his car over a mile away. He knew that soon his lioness would come.

18

It was 4:30 when Sarah bolted from the lab and headed for the grocery store for a few last-minute items. Her neighbor Mrs. Langdon was waiting for her as she pulled into her driveway. Marge Langdon was a kind, older widow who kept tabs on everything in the neighborhood. Sarah would sometimes catch her using binoculars to spy on the neighbors or kids in the park. She was nosy but Sarah got along with her quite well.

"Hi, Sarah, I saw your mother this morning," Marge said.

"Did you? She said she might be stopping by."

"She took out a big painting." Marge's tone was almost accusatory.

"It's hers. She was just letting me try it out in the living room for a few days." No need to fuel the gossip fire, she thought. "How are you doing, Mrs. Langdon?"

"Oh, you know since Martin died I do get lonely sometimes and my back hurts now and again."

Sarah knew it was an exaggeration. That woman had friends over all the time and she'd even seen a few men come around now and again. "Well, we should have breakfast sometime," Sarah offered.

"That would be lovely, dear. How about tomorrow morning?"

That was quick. Mrs. Langdon was intrigued by the darker side of Sarah's job and was always trying to get her to talk about recent crimes she'd read about in the papers. "Well, I'm having some girlfriends over tonight and I may not be up all that early tomorrow. But don't worry, we won't be loud."

"I guess I'll take a rain check, then," she said. "Well . . . I'm off to walk Butler," she said, referring to her Bichon Frise. His tiny tuxedo-themed sweater was laughable. Even Butler knew it.

Walking through the front door Sarah was thankful to see the open space on her living room wall. But as she rounded the corner into the dining room she was greeted by a contemporary sculpture of two obsidian stick-figure-like people dancing, at least she hoped they were dancing. Mom strikes again! Her mother detested the western décor of her house but Sarah kept it just as her grandfather left it. As Nickelback's song "Rockstar" coursed through the speakers Sarah got the place ready. Kimberly McFadden was the first to arrive. Kim was a dispatcher with the sheriff's office. They hung around a lot in the dispatcher's lounge after hours when Sarah would come in after a call out. Like Sarah, Kim was attractive and had dated several of the single deputies working in the department.

"Jordan couldn't make it tonight. Some issue with her overbearing boyfriend," Kim stated.

"Thank God I'm single," Sarah exclaimed.

"Amen to that, girl. You know he's been following her around to check up on wherever she goes?"

"Sounds more like a stalker."

"I don't know what she sees in him, he's not at all attractive," Kim said.

Sarah said nothing. Kim's current boyfriend wasn't much better. He was lazy and treated her like property.

Jenny arrived at eight-fifteen. "Howdy, girls, the bartender has arrived!" she proclaimed holding up a bottle of 100 Anos Agave tequila. "Sorry, I'm late, traffic was a bitch."

Westminster was forty-five minutes away with no traffic.

"Don't worry, we were just talking about you behind your back."

"Hey, no fair. You know you're not supposed to gossip without me," she protested.

"Wouldn't think of it," Kim lied.

"Where's Jordan?" Jenny asked.

"Don't ask," Kim said.

"Her boyfriend again? Why doesn't she just dump that loser already?" Jenny wondered aloud.

"We were just wondering the same thing," Sarah said.

"So where's the grub?" Jenny asked, getting down to business. "Are we having some fancy elk dish or something?"

"No, I'm not quite the chef Art is. Tonight the cook has selected Pizza Hut!"

The announcement was met with high-fives". Sarah phoned in the order while Jenny mixed the drinks.

"So how's life at the sheriff's office? I saw Westin on TV again, saying he was going to roust sex offenders to find your sniper," Jenny said.

"I know! It's been the talk of the department. He makes us look like Keystone Kops," Kim said.

"What's the deal with your suspect? Do you have any leads?" Jenny continued.

"Nothing concrete. We have some weird ballistic evidence, but Walter is still working it up," Sarah said.

"What do you mean by weird?" Jenny asked.

"Well, I can't say too much but it looks like the guy made some kind of synthetic jacket or something on the bullet to hide the lands and grooves."

"No shit. You guys get all the cool cases."

"That's not true. Westminster should be called Ripley's."

"We haven't had much of anything lately. It's been pretty boring," she confessed. "The only semi-weird thing is a recovered stolen vehicle I went out on about a week ago."

"What was so weird about that?" Kim asked.

"Well, these idiots steal a car, then park it right in front of their apartment complex."

"I wish they were all that stupid," Sarah said.

"Sounds pretty run-of-the-mill to me," Kim said.

"No, you're right. The weird part was the car was stolen from a police impound lot in Leadville," she said.

"Leadville, why in the hell would you go all the way to Leadville to steal a car?" Sarah asked.

"Who knows? The pricks are denying it, of course, even though we got their fingerprints and cigarettes all over the inside."

"Of course, the old Mystery Man defense . . . *he* must have stolen it, right?"

"Right. Say, speaking of mystery men . . . whatever happened to that stud in the Cave?"

"Daniel?" Sarah asked.

"So it's Daniel, now. Did you sleep with him?" Jenny prodded.

"NO! Jesus, Jenny I'm not a slut."

"Bet you wanted to though huh?"

Sarah gave her a sarcastic smile.

"Wait a minute. Who is this Daniel?" Kim asked.

"He's Art's nephew or something, total dreamboat. He was undressing our little Sarah at the bar with his eyes," Jenny taunted.

"No, he wasn't! He's just a guy I met. He's nice, that's all."

"Nice? He's *nice*?! My God, she's in love!" Kim screeched.

"Am not!" Sarah said in her best imitation of a six year old.

"Are too!" they joined in chorus.

"Have you talked to him since then?" Jenny asked.

"Actually . . . we had dinner the other night," Sarah said, blushing.

"Was diner followed by breakfast?" Kim asked with a coy tilt of her head.

"Stop it, you guys," Sarah said. "It's a bit complicated. He seems great and his manners are top notch but I don't think he's being honest with me about his past," she confided.

"Oh, you're such a Nancy Drew, Sarah!" Kim chided. "Every guy has skeletons in his past he wants to bury. Old girlfriends, one night skanks, fights he's lost, whatever."

"I don't think this guy has lost many fights," Jenny said.

"Oh, yeah, why don't you tell Kim about your boyfriend?" Sarah said, trying to change the subject.

Jenny adjusted her position in the comfortable chair, removing her FNP-45 pistol and placing it on the end table.

"This is getting good. Tell me everything!" Kim said.

"Nothing to tell really. Some east coast SWAT dick tried to get fresh with me and he paid the price," Jenny related.

"Oh, you're so tough! Wasn't it Daniel that broke his wrist?" Sarah reminded her.

"Moot point. I was just toying with the guy. Another few seconds and I'd have drop-kicked his ass off the planet," Jenny said.

Even though she was joking both Kim and Sarah believed she was capable of doing it.

His curiosity got the better of him after standing motionless in the trees for almost thirty minutes and the killer moved closer to the patio doors in the hope of hearing their conversation. A light snow had begun to fall and it was chilling him to the bone. With slow, careful turns, he unscrewed her patio light and he disappeared in the darkness. Unless or until they turned off the interior lights, he thought. The girls were quite pretty and he fantasized about each of them as he stood on the wooden, snow-covered deck. He wondered if he could subdue all three but decided it was unlikely.

The one with the handgun looked tough and he was sure she was a cop. She had that edgy look. Most women wouldn't choose a.45 caliber pistol unless they knew they could handle it. It complemented her masculine body language and turned him on. She would put up a good fight, he decided. Briefly, he wondered if she was a lesbian. The thought was enough to suppress the fantasy he had been developing and he returned his attention to the others.

He knew the mysterious, red-haired beauty from Monarch Pass could handle herself. She was a hunter, he thought, a worthy adversary. She was the reason he had come tonight. He wanted to study her, to understand her. She was the first woman, besides his mother, who wasn't intimidated by him. He glanced around the room at the taxidermy and animal hides and realized she had taken a life before, just as he had. She has had blood on her hands. She could pose a very real threat but he was sure he could handle her.

But the other redhead, the sweet one, she didn't look threatening at all. She looked . . . innocent. He studied the way she tossed her hair when she laughed, her mannerisms, her eyes. It was her. She was the one. His thoughts grew wicked as he adjusted his surging manhood. Like a wolf, he had subconsciously selected the weakest member of the herd. It was an instinct that all killers shared; man and beast alike.

He knew they were armed and one was prepared to shoot at him for sure, but he couldn't help but wonder if he could get closer.

Sarah and the girls never saw his beady eyes through the window as he reached down and inserted his knife between the panes.

19

The old and tarnished brass latch gave a half inch before the lock engaged. Damn it! Should have known a cop would keep her windows locked. He longed for the victims too lazy or naïve to take such a simple precaution against an intruder. He moved farther away from the French-style patio doors by creeping below the side window. Once in the corner of the elevated deck, he reached up and unscrewed the second patio light. The warm, glass bulb eased the chill in his fingers as he twisted it. Peering through a pane of glass, he spied a coffee pot and double sinks. Must be the kitchen, he thought. Sometimes people left kitchen windows unlocked to air out the room and he again tried to pry up the window. Damn it! He was more determined than ever to get into the house.

Just then Sarah bounced to her feet and headed to the kitchen. He stood frozen.

"Hey, guys, how about some dessert?" Sarah asked as she rose from her seat on the floor.

"Now?" Jenny asked. "This is a good part."

"I can see the TV from the kitchen," she said.

"Hey, Sarah, doesn't this actor, the hitchhiker, look a lot like Daniel?" Jenny yelled.

"Yeah, sort of," Sarah said.

Who is Daniel?
Sarah had fond memories of her childhood in this very kitchen. She peered out the window and caught a hint of falling snow through the glare of the kitchen lights. She flicked the patio light switch. Nothing. Great, Sarah thought. One more thing I need to put on the To Do list.

He was inches from her now. A woman who had stalked him, shot at him, was now separated by a thin sheet of glass. The proximity was maddening to him. He could see every freckle, every turn of her long, beautiful hair. His arousal heightened his bravado as he made no effort to hide his face.

The Scent of Fear

Staring out the window, Sarah felt uneasy. The hairs on her neck stood up as she felt the eerie sensation of eyes upon her. The snow falling outside reminded her of the night on Monarch Pass. She thought of that poor woman's killer and wondered if he would ever be caught.

Sarah imagined the chase from the killer's perspective. The last thing he'd expected was an armed "victim," she thought. Most criminals dreamed of an unarmed society so they could safely ply their wicked trade. Sarah marveled at how criminals talked tough until they were staring down the barrel of a gun. She wondered if he ever made it out of the storm. Hopefully, he'd died in the valley and some turkey hunter would discover his rotting corpse in the spring. No, he seemed too resilient to die. It didn't matter anyway, she thought. He was a thousand miles away by now.

He jerked his head jerked back from the glass as a light came on. Sarah caught the movement, or so she thought, and looked across the yard as Marge Langdon came out on her deck with her black cat, Spooky. Sarah had always loved that name and thought it appropriate for that particular feline. Bad luck seemed to follow that cat everywhere.

The killer saw Marge, too. He didn't panic or run the way some voyeurs might. Almost by instinct he gave her a friendly wave and put his finger over his mouth. Always snooping, Marge had caught a glimpse of the person standing on Sarah's deck and watched him as he looked through the glass at Sarah. Had she seen him unscrewing the lights she might have realized he was a threat.

Kids, she thought. Always playing pranks on each other. She returned the friendly wave, seeing that Sarah still had a house full of friends.

Sarah waved back, unaware of the danger inches from her.

"Sarah!" came the cry from the family room. "You're missing the best part!"

"He's got that big Indian by the balls in the bathroom!" Jenny cried.

"Okay, hold on a sec!" Sarah yelled as she rushed back into the living room.

His heart was pounding with excitement now. What a fucking rush! With the old woman watching, he snuck back around the corner of the house and out of her view. If he waited any longer the old hag would become suspicious and call Sarah. The killer used the well-manicured bushes to conceal his escape. Stopping in the driveway he jotted down the girls' license plates before making a fast-paced getaway.

20

The sun was setting when Daniel entered Art's office. "Hey, Tilly, you coming out with us tonight?"

"At my age? Heavens, no, but you boys have fun, whatever it is you're doing."

Daniel found Art behind his desk reading a book with a tattered and worn leather binding. "Whatcha reading there, Unc?"

Art glanced up from behind his reading glasses. "Beck's *Elements of Medical Jurisprudence.*"

"Looks old," Daniel said.

"Eighteen thirty-six. Almost two centuries ago. Just researching a case."

"Wouldn't something more . . . modern be better?"

"Murder is an ancient crime, my boy. Sometimes we have to look back if we are to move forward." Art stood up from his desk and walked over to look Daniel in the eye. "Tonight, however, you will be the teacher and I'll be the student."

The stables were still and quiet. The horses and pack mules were kept for the hunting guides but the truth was Art had a soft spot for the beautiful animals and would have kept them regardless. Art's horse was named Wicoha Waste, the Lakota words for miracle. Art had acquired him and four others from a Mustang rescue center in Nevada.

The operation was in reality a sham designed to capitalize on federal and private funding sources. It was an abomination and thirty-two horses were found in a malnourished and impoverished state. Sixteen were found dead in the pastures outside the corals. Three of the horses Art rescued died within a week but his miracle horse survived.

Daniel's horse Revelation, named after the biblical reference in the Book of Revelation 19:11, was an anomaly of nature. An albino Mustang as wild as a tornado. The trainers Art had hired to rehabilitate him were unable to break his spirit and two had broken ribs to prove it; until Daniel came along, the white steed had been impossible to approach. Daniel was the one man able to ride him. From the moment they met the two were like old friends. Daniel always said that they sensed each other's pain. His majestic white coat reminded him of the Masonic apron and the purity it symbolized. Similarities between its biblical namesake and Daniel's choice of pistols were not lost on Art either.

Darkness was falling as the two men saddled the horses. The antique western saddles were decorated by a master leather smith time had forgotten. After opening the old, wooden corral Art followed Daniel up an old game trail to the hills above the Facility. Daniel had been making preparations for this night for several days and was happy to be of some help to his uncle's investigation. It gave him a sense of purpose again. Much like Sarah did, he thought. As Revelation moved through the Aspen grove his acute senses detected the presence of others. Daniel sensed it, too. No one is supposed to be up here after dark, he thought. He held up his arm with a closed fist, indicating for Art to stop.

Art looked around, unable to detect any possible danger. Silently, he moved his horse alongside Daniel. "What is it?"

"Don't know. Heard some voices, I thought. Could be poachers."

Art's eyes narrowed as he gave Daniel a look of disdain.

Both men sat silent, trying to discern the faintest sound.

All Art heard was his pounding heart.

For Daniel it was a matter of training. He could discern two voices, one was a woman.

Art now heard it, too, and wondered how Daniel could hear the voices over the repetitive thuds of horse hoofs.

Daniel tapped his Sig Sauer 1911 Target Nitron pistol as he motioned for Art to follow.

The two dismounted and crept through the trees toward the mystery voices. Entering a small clearing in the trees, Daniel could see two forms entangled on the ground. His powerful Surefire tactical light illuminated the pair as a bare-chested woman screamed out in surprise. The buxom blonde looked no older than twenty-one and Art recognized the older married man as a criminalist from the Miami-Dade police department.

"If you two don't want to get thrown out of here you'd better hightail it back to your rooms . . . alone!" Art barked. The two gathered their clothes like kids grabbing candy at a parade. "And

Charlie . . . don't ever let me catch you cheating on your wife again," he said in a serious parental tone.

The two lovebirds bolted down the trail.

"Pretty exciting, huh?" Daniel asked, holstering his pistol

"Exciting is not the word I would have chosen. I can't abide a man who so easily discards his vows," Art said.

"Must happen a lot up here," Daniel said, stating the obvious.

"More than I would like to know, I'm sure. Seems that some men can't resist the siren's call when they're away from home."

"I saw this with a few guys I served with. Maybe you don't know the whole story. His wife might be a bitch; maybe she won't touch him with a ten foot pole."

"You really think that matters? If the marriage is bad you get a divorce, or separate, I don't care, but do something. A man who breaks his vows is forever a slave to temptation."

"I guess so." After a few minutes of quiet Daniel asked a question. "Do you still miss her?" Daniel was referring to Art's wife. She had been killed by a drunk driver years before. Art never fully recovered from the loss of his high school sweetheart.

"Every day," Art confessed.

"Yeah . . . me, too." Daniel agreed, remembering his favorite aunt who always found time to send him letters and care packages when he was overseas.

The two rode in silence until reaching the rocky outcrop Daniel had selected for his experiment. They dismounted their horses and tied them to a small fir tree. As the horses snorted Daniel retrieved a rifle from the old leather scabbard hanging from his saddle. Art gazed upon its sleek lines with wonderment. The Barrett 98Bravo was a prime example of American craftsmanship and ingenuity. Chambered in .338 Lapua Magnum it was a formidable rifle in the hands of an expert. Daniel lay out his canvas bedroll as a shooting mat and pulled down the bipod legs. Art stood in silence as Daniel checked the rifle and scope and adjusted the butt plate to his body.

"That's one helluva rifle," Art said.

"Oh, yeah, me and Maggie here are going steady," he said.

"You named your gun Maggie?" Art asked.

Daniel considered explaining it for a brief moment but decided not to "It's a long story, Uncle Art."

He pulled three rifle cartridges from a small pouch on his belt and laid them side by side on his shooting blanket.

"What are we shooting tonight?" Art asked.

"Two hundred and -fifty grain FMJs with a lock base design just like the killer used," Daniel said, holding up one of the shiny brass cartridges. "I'm not replicating the coating he used; I just wanted to show you the shots are possible."

"That's fine."

Daniel handed Art a pair of night vision goggles, or NVGs, with a 9-power telescopic attachment. He placed another attachment over the rifle scope.

"What's that?" Art asked, trying to adjust the goggles.

"It's a magnification device. U.S. military issue only, very restricted. It gives me night vision out to two kilometers," Daniel said dryly.

"And just how did we come by this?"

"According to Army records the damned thing went missing in the Tora Bora Mountains of Afghanistan. Along with those goggles you're wearing," he said, offering his uncle a sly grin.

"You don't say?" Art asked, raising an eyebrow.

"Damnedest thing."

"So how far away is the target?" Art asked.

"Tar*gets*, actually. The one on the left is eight hundred thirty-six meters, the same distance in the first shooting. The target on the right is about seven hundred sixty-five meters, which is software's guesstimate of range based on the aerial photos of the second shooting at the train."

Art peered through the green-colored fog of the glasses, trying to see the targets Daniel described.

"And . . . where are the targets?"

Daniel glanced up to see Art looking too far to the north. It was common for new recruits to get disoriented when first using the NVGs.

"Uncle Art?" he asked as Art looked down at him. "That way." He motioned with his hand. "The targets are coated with a special IR paper that lets me see my hits in the dark. There's about a two-inch border around the edges that should glow milky white in your goggles."

Art scanned the darkness, adjusting his eyes "Oh, there they are, I see them now," he said.

"I'm gonna shoot the one on the lef'
"That looks pretty far away. I can '
"Reach up with your right han'
above your nose with small, scallor
"Yes, I have it."
"Turn the knob clockwise while looking ⸜
"Oh, my. Yes, that helps a lot."
"The target got bigger?"
"Yes, quite a bit."
"Okay, just stay focused on it. If you move your head you might have a hard time finding it again. If that happens just back off on the magnification and try again."
"Got it," Art acknowledged.
"You want to practice first?" Art asked.
"Nope," Daniel said.
"You're gonna shoot cold bore?" Art asked with a hint of skepticism.
"Yep."
"Suit yourself."
Daniel's training taught him to control his breathing. There was a natural "wobble," of the scope that many shooters noticed. Good shooters knew to accept the wobble and time their shots to hit as they wanted them to. His index finger graced the trigger as he began to pull back.
"Care to make this interesting?" Art asked, knowing he was interrupting Daniel's concentration.
"I don't like to gamble," Daniel answered as the words were drowned out by the report of the heavy rifle.
The ingenious muzzle break reduced the recoil of the rifle so much that Daniel felt as if he were plinking a .22. Art watched the target as a white dot erupted near the center a second later.
" . . . and neither should you," Daniel said, looking up and smiling at his uncle.
"I'll be damned," Art said. Daniel repeated the feat on the second target.
"Boy, I sure would like to get some of that paper for some experiments."
"Good luck with that."
"Hard to find?"

n't tell me you found that in the mountains of
istan too."

Something like that," Daniel said, laughing.

"So, just how many guys in the world can do that, Daniel?"

"Not sure, really. Probably quite a few in our military, not as many in others." Seeing Art's dismayed look Daniel continued. "It's not like we have a Facebook page or anything. A lot of guys are under the radar. Hell, a number of civilians could make that shot with ease."

"What about the night vision?"

"Well, it's nice. He wouldn't have to use it, though. Both victims were partially lit by street lights and the moon. A guy with a good, low-light scope could make the shot."

"So we have zilch, is that it?"

"Not exactly. You're forgetting about the mark."

"Ah yes . . . your mysterious symbol. How can you be sure that's what it is? Walter thinks it's just an artifact from the impact."

"I've seen it once before. Granted, it was a number of years ago, I was bleeding and running from armed insurgents . . . but my gut says it is." Daniel confessed with sincerity.

"Well, until we have more to go on it's just a theory."

"One scary fucking theory for sure," Daniel reminded him.

21

The girls woke late, their heads aching from the alcohol. Jenny was the first one up and started a fresh pot of cinnamon-hazelnut-flavored coffee. Sarah and Kim soon awoke to the aromatic sweetness from their spots on the living room furniture. The three gathered around the old wooden dining room table and gazed upon the snow-covered park. The morning sun had not yet risen but the faint light was accentuated by the white powder.

"That sure was a lot of fun," Jenny said as she poured a round.

"Yeah, we need to do that more often," Kim said.

"I agree, but maybe a little easier on the tequila next time," Sarah said. "Some of us have to go to work this morning."

"Sucks to be in the lab, I guess," Jenny prodded.

"You guys want some breakfast?" Sarah asked.

"What would that be? A bowl of Cheerios and some cold toast?" Kim asked.

"Hey, that was a long time ago," Sarah explained.

"It was two weeks ago," Kim said.

"Whatever, I'm just saying if you want something, feel free to find it, make it, cook it, whatever."

"Thanks, I think we'll take our chances at home," Jenny said.

The three finished their coffee and Sarah walked them out to their cars. As she watched them drive away Marge came out of her house

"Good morning Sarah!" Marge called out.

"Hi, Marge, I hope we weren't too loud last night," Sarah said.

"Oh, no dear, I slept like a log. You girls get enough sleep?"

"Yeah, I'm the only one who has to go to work this morning," Sarah said.

"Well, I'll let you get to it, then." Walking back to her house Marge turned back to Sarah and called out, "Oh, Sarah?"

"Yes?"

"I hope that young man didn't give you too big a scare last night."

Sarah looked perplexed. "What man?"

"Your friend . . . the one who was trying to scare you through the kitchen window?"

"Marge, we didn't have any men over last night," Sarah said.

"Well, he was standing on your deck plain as day."

Suddenly they both realized the gravity of the revelation.

"Where exactly did you see him?" Sarah asked.

"He was standing outside your window, looking at you. He waved at me . . . and you did, too!"

"It's all right, Marge, just tell me, what was he doing?"

"Let's see . . . he was looking at you through the window, and then I came out, and then he went around to the front. Oh, dear, I thought he was playing a game."

"It's okay, Marge. I'll check it out."

"Oh, dear, I'm so sorry. I should have called you, or the police."

"No problem, Marge. It must have been Kim's boyfriend checking up on her,"

Sarah knew Marge liked to over-dramatize things for attention and figured there must be a reasonable explanation. She walked up onto her deck and saw the boot impressions. He had stood right next to the windows. She could envision the man peering into the kitchen and then she remembered how uneasy she felt while making snacks. Shit, she thought. That's when I waved to Marge. Who the hell was it? Kim's boyfriend, or some Peeping Tom that spied us from the park. Nothing appeared damaged and Sarah walked back to the front of the house. As she grabbed the storm door handle her eyes caught a glimpse of something. Wedged between the door and step was a small white envelope. The name Sarah was scratched in blue ink on the front. Looks like a child's writing, she thought. She opened the envelope and pulled out a small note. As she did small green fuzz dropped from the note gliding to the snow below. She reached down and picked it up. Her hands began to tremble as she stared at the tuft of Old Man's Beard. Her face became serious as she unfolded the note. Her right hand came up quickly to cover her mouth as she read the words

Sorry, I missed you on Monarch.

Sarah's eyes darted around, half expecting to see the killer standing nearby. Get a hold of yourself, she thought. She ran inside the house and grabbed her Glock and cell phone. After checking her weapon she hit Manny on the two-way radio.

"Manny!" she called. It took a few agonizing seconds for him to answer.

"Morning Sarah, you're up early, aren't you? I was thinking—"

"Manny," she cut him off. "I need you over at my place now. Something has happened," she said. The thing about Nextel's is that you never know who is able to hear you on the other side.

"What is it, kid? Is everything okay?"

"No, it's not okay . . . not by a long shot. Just hurry," she said. The fear in her voice was almost palpable.

"I'm on my way," he said as he made for the door.

Sarah sat huddled on the floor in the corner of the room. Normally, she had a very strong exterior but this was her home! The son of a bitch knew where she lived! Thank God she wasn't alone last night. Having the girls over probably scared him off and kept him from trying to come in. Fear gripped her soul as she sat shivering on the floor reading the note over and over again. Then it struck her . . . fingerprints. Damn it! How could I be so stupid?

Manny arrived twenty minutes later and found Sarah on the floor still holding her gun. "Jesus, kid! What the hell is it?"

Sarah pointed a shaky finger at the note on the floor.

His eyes widened as he read the short message. "Jesus! He was here?"

"Last night," Sarah said in a low voice.

"Did he get in? Are you okay?"

"He just stood outside the window looking in. I never even knew he was here. My neighbor saw him late last night."

"Can she give a description?" he asked, hopefully.

"I doubt it."

Wasting no time Manny picked up his portable radio and called dispatch for back-up.

Manilow was irritable and tired when Sergeant Davis knocked on his door.

"Hey, boss," he said.

Manilow waved for him to enter and sit without saying a word. Lester dropped into the uncomfortable seat that had occupied the office longer that Manilow had.

"What did you find out, Sergeant?" Manilow asked in a huff.

Good morning to you, too, Lester thought. "Some interesting stuff, actually. I checked with a buddy I have in the army and he did some looking into this Daniel Von Hollen character. First, he was discharged a few months back."

"Really?" Manilow now looked interested. "Dishonorably discharged?"

"No, but it wasn't honorable, either. Technically, it's called OTH, meaning 'other than honorable.'"

"What the hell does that mean?"

"My buddy tells me that it's used for soldiers who depart from the conduct expected in the military. He thinks Daniel was some kind of screw up or embarrassment to the army and they told him to take a hike."

"What was his assignment?"

"He was a mechanic. Fixed track vehicles like tanks and Bradley fighting vehicles, even earth movers."

"So how does a mechanic know so much about long-range shooting? Were you able to get a report or transcript regarding his discharge?"

"No, and that's where it takes a weird turn. While my buddy is conducting his search he gets a call from a base colonel wanting to know just what the hell he was doing. When the colonel found out he was doing me a favor he shut the whole thing down."

"Did he say why?"

"No, but he sounded pretty scared. The last thing he said to me was to leave this whole thing alone."

"Leave it alone? Now that's got my interest. Why would a colonel shut down routine questions about some mechanic that's been discharged?"

"It doesn't make sense," Davis agreed.

"Maybe they have their own investigation and don't want us getting in the way?"

"Something else," Davis continued. "I checked his financials which was no easy task. He has a couple of credit cards he uses but they get billed to the Facility so it's hard to figure what is personal and what is work-related."

"Isn't that illegal? Mixing business and personal finances?"

"Since they're a private organization Art can pay for whatever he wants to, I suppose. I have no idea how much cash he has access to because I didn't want to send up a flare to the staff at the Facility."

"So what did you find out?" Manilow asked.

"Ah, in going over his most recent statement I saw that he paid for a dinner at Romano's down on Windermere Street."

"I know where Romano's is . . . get on with it," Manilow said, becoming impatient.

"Yes, sir. I talked to the wait staff and showed them a picture. They remember seeing Daniel Von Hollen and Sarah Richards in there together. The records indicate it was the night they were at the crime scene."

"Is that a fact?" Manilow said, rubbing his chin.

"Yeah, and get this. The waitress said they were real smitten with each other, touching hands and stuff. Apparently, they looked pretty into each other."

"Is that all?"

"No. The busboy saw the two leave, I guess he knows Ms. Richards as a regular customer and has a crush on her. He saw them walking hand-in-hand toward her house. Then this same busboy sees Daniel return to his vehicle a little over two hours later."

"He remembered the guy?"

"Actually, he remembered Van Hollen's Camaro, which is pretty distinctive. I saw it out at the crime scene and you couldn't miss it."

"Interesting," Manilow said as he stood up and began pacing across the office. "So we have an army mechanic who knows way too much about shooting scenes. He's discharged from the army under less than favorable conditions and when we try to check him out, the door is slammed in our face. He has access to unlimited funds, and he's sexually involved with one of our criminalists on the very same shooting scenes. Does that about sum it up?"

"Why do you say they are sexually active?"

Manilow shot Davis a disapproving glare. "Well, what in the hell do you think they were doing for two hours? Playing Chutes and Ladders?"

"Do you think he's involved in the shootings?"

"Yes, I do."

"And you think Richards is, too?" Davis asked.

"One way or another. Sarah Richards is a young, naive feminist who likes to go off half-cocked. I swear, I miss the days when the women just answered the phones around here," he confessed.

Lester Davis offered no response to such a ludicrous statement. Manilow sat back down at his desk. Davis could see the wheels turning in Manilow's head.

"You know what, Sergeant? I think it's about time we had you go up and take a closer look at this Daniel Von Hollen character," Manilow said, picking up the phone.

22

Sarah's house looked like a three-ring circus to the neighbors. Three police cruisers sat on the street with flashing lights as the patrol deputies canvassed the neighborhood. Neighbors on their morning walks stood and wondered what had happened. Perhaps someone was murdered or a child molester was on the loose? Of course the deputies lied and said they were just investigating a suspicious person seen in the neighborhood.

Sarah's mind was filled with "what if" scenarios. What if she had been alone? What if he had tried to force entry? What if he came back? It was a confusing potpourri of fear and despair. Why . . . no, *how* did he find out who I was . . . where I lived? A victim advocate for the department came by to try to ease her mind. The problem was she didn't want to be a victim. Victim is a past-tense term, she thought. It denotes a person who has been harmed by another, either physically or financially. I'm not a victim yet, and I don't plan to be, she thought, trying to build her resolve.

"How ya doin', kid?" Manny asked

"I'm fine," she lied.

"Sure you are. I got a call from the sheriff and he said he's posting a patrol car here twenty-four/seven for the next few weeks. Even when you're not here."

"Great, that's just what I need. I'm sure the neighbors will be thrilled."

"Who cares? This guy is a killer and he's stalking you."

"My question is why?"

"Might have something to do with you shooting at him."

"He shot at me first."

"I'm on your side here, Sarah," Manny said, holding up his hands.

"I'll bet the patrol guys will just love me for this."

"Are you kidding? Have you looked in a mirror? I'm guessing the wait list for this assignment is gonna be two pages long."

Sarah shot him a disbelieving look. Manny always made her feel better. He was like that older brother that was always there to watch your back. Her eyes drifted out the window when she saw the Colorado Bureau of Investigations crime scene truck arrive.

"What the hell are they doing here?"

"You didn't think our guys were going to process this scene, did you?"

"I was hoping," she said with a smile.

Her mood grew dimmer as she watched Miles Johansson exit the vehicle with his clipboard. He strode to the front door with the regality and posture of royalty, his CBI emblazoned windbreaker announcing to everyone who he was. Sarah noticed with some humor how he slipped and almost fell on the slick snow because of his polished dress shoes. "Not that dick again," Sarah lamented.

"You two know each other?"

"You could say that."

Manny could tell from her tone that the relationship was not friendly.

"Well, if it isn't Ms. Richards," Miles announced in a condescending tone. "It's nice to see you again so soon."

"Is it?"

Miles offered a fake smile before looking around. "So I understand we have a Peeping Tom you need help with?" Miles snorted.

"He's no Peeping Tom. It's the same killer from the Monarch Pass murder," Manny offered.

"That hasn't been determined yet. Not until we find fingerprints or something linking that killer here. This could be a practical joke or something," Miles offered.

"A practical joke? You can't be serious?"

"Maybe someone you work with wanted to get a rise out of you. Frankly, I don't see why this killer would supposedly come here and just stare at you through the windows. It's much more likely someone was looking for a cheap laugh and now doesn't want to 'fess up with all the hoopla," he said.

"It's not too fucking funny if you ask me," she said.

"Nonetheless," he said as he began walking along the deck. Manny took her by the arm and gently squeezed. "Calm down. He was right, of course. Making a scene would just make things worse." To Miles, he said, "These are the suspect boot prints along the wall. We've stayed away from them."

"There seems to be two sets here," Miles said.

"The smaller ones are mine."

Miles shot Sarah a disapproving look. "Seems you haven't learned anything since we last met."

"We think he loosened the light bulbs." Manny said, pointing.

"Why do you say that?" Miles asked.

"Normally, they come on when you flip the switch" Sarah said. *Dumbass.*

"Could be that the bulbs are burned out. I doubt we'd get anything off those even if he did touch them. The killer probably wore gloves last night, considering the cold weather," Miles countered.

"You want to check them anyway?" Manny suggested.

Miles shrugged his shoulders. "What about the note?" he asked.

"It's inside on the kitchen table," Manny said.

Miles donned a pair of purple Nitrile gloves and examined it with a magnification loupe. "And how many people have touched this?"

"Just Detective Lopez and myself," Sarah said.

Miles didn't even look up from the note but Sarah could tell what he was thinking. Trade places with me, asshole, and we'll see how you do, she thought.

"Uh-huh," he said.

"What? Did you find something?" Manny asked, looking over Johansson's shoulder.

"This looks like a child's writing," Miles said.

Sarah and Manny exchanged looks.

"Well, are there any kids in the neighborhood?" Miles asked.

"You still think this is a prank? You think a kid knew I was on Monarch Pass with this prick? You think a kid on the block knew about the tuft of Old Man's Beard I was holding when he almost killed me?" Sarah asked, her voice becoming louder with each question.

"I don't know, Ms. Richards . . . whom have you told?" he responded.

Okay . . . That's it! *Game on, motherfucker*, Sarah thought.

Manny grabbed her arm and led her outside before she said something they'd both regret. "Okay, kiddo, just calm down and let me deal with this dipshit okay?"

"Can you believe that prick? Do I have to connect every fucking dot for him?"

"Just let me handle it, I won't let him off the hook here, all right?"

Sarah leaned against the wall gazing out onto to the park, trying to control her emotions. She was damned if she'd let anyone see her cry.

Miles began photographing the scene with Detective Lopez in tow. "Sure are a lot of dead animal parts in here."

"What's your point?" Manny asked.

"Just an observation. Seems Ms. Richards likes to shoot her gun off nearly as much as her mouth."

"Three things. First of all, this was her grandfather's house. Second, hunting is a scientifically valid management technique." He paused.

"And the third?" Miles asked.

"You're a dick," Manny said.

Miles didn't have any words ready for a comeback and kept shooting pictures as if nothing happened. He made his way out to the porch after he put the envelope and note into a plastic evidence bag. Miles examined the snow impressions with disdain. He disliked footwear evidence and wondered why anyone even collected them nowadays. Placing a small "L" shaped scale, or ruler, on the snow next to one impression he took a photograph from above.

"Don't you want to put that camera on a tripod?" Manny asked.

"No, I don't, Detective."

"Well, shouldn't that scale be down lower in the snow?" Manny asked, remembering something Sarah had showed him once.

Annoyed, Miles stopped what he was doing and looked up.

"Detective, I have a Master's degree in forensics from one of the finest universities in the country and I've been trained by some of the best experts in the world. Where exactly did you get your degree from?" he asked.

"Well, nowhere, I—"

"Then why don't you leave the forensics to the experts, all right?"

Manny bit his tongue.

Setting the camera down, Miles took out a bag of premixed dental stone from his crime scene kit. The gallon-sized Zip-Lock bag held two pounds of dental stone which was the amount typically used to cast a single shoe impression. He then went into the house and filled up a plastic cup with twelve ounces of water. Miles nearly slipped on the ice as he walked back onto the deck, almost spilling his cup.

"Don't you need to put that water in the snow to cool it off?" Manny asked, knowing it would annoy the petulant crime scene investigator.

Miles shot him a withering stare. "It'll be fine."

It was clear that he didn't mix the contents well enough as large blobs of the mixture plopped out into the fragile snow impression. If Miles had seen the blobs he didn't say anything.

Sarah had stormed out to the sidewalk by the deputy's car, hoping the distance from Miles and cold air would settle her down and cool her temper. It was working, too, until Sal Vargas showed up.

"Jeez, Sarah, I can't leave you alone for a second, can I?"

"Nice try, Vegas, but you can't stand guard inside the house."

"Shucks, and I thought this might be my way in," he joked.

She was warming to his demeanor, sort of. He wasn't all that bad, she thought. Pathetic, but not a bad guy. She was filling him in on the details when a familiar car drove toward the house. The deputy had lifted the yellow crime scene tape high in the air so the driver could pull up to the driveway. The silver BMW M-class sedan cost more than her college tuition but her mother worked hard for it. Plus it was great for impressing her wealthy clients. Her mother tiptoed through the snow, wearing her skin-tight workout suit and bright white tennis shoes.

"Mother! What are you doing here?" Sarah asked, surprised.

"Jesus! That's your mother?"

Sarah elbowed him in the ribs. "Don't even think about it, Vegas," she snarled.

"I should be asking why you can't call your mother when a Peeping Tom is looking in your bedroom windows! I have to hear about it from Mrs. Langdon?" she snapped.

"She called you?"

"Of course she did. She's always looking out for you when I'm not here."

Sarah filed that useful tidbit away.

"Why, hello there, are you one of Sarah's work friends?" Nancy said.

Sarah's eyes widened as one of her worst nightmares was about to come true.

Vargas' mind was busy undressing her when he realized the question was for him. "Uh, yeah. We work together, Mrs. Richards. I'm Detective Vargas. I'm the one who saved your daughter's life the other night."

Shit, Sarah thought.

"Saved your life? What on earth is he talking about?"

"It's nothing, Mother. Right, Vegas?"

"Um, right. You can't possibly be her mother. You 're much too young and pretty."

Too pretty? What the hell is that supposed to mean? Sarah thought.

"Oh, my, aren't you…something. Now run along so Sarah and I can talk," she said, waving her hand dismissively.

Finally, her rudeness pays off, Sarah thought.

"Well . . . I'll be right over there if you need me," Vargas said, sucking in his gut before walking away with his tail between his legs.

"Sarah, dear, what happened?"

"It was nothing, Mom. Marge saw some guy looking in the windows last night."

"Did he try to get in?" Nancy asked.

"It doesn't look like it. Jenny and Kim were over watching movies. It might have been Kim's boyfriend just checking up on her."

"Is Jenny that lesbian from Thornton?" her mother asked innocently.

"No! She's not a lesbian, and she's from Westminster, not Thornton."

"Oh, all those cities are the same up there."

The Scent of Fear

"Look, Mom, I appreciate you stopping by, I really do, but I'm fine. I'm sure it's a prank," she said, trying to ease her fears.

"Prank or not I've already called the handyman. I'm having one of those security systems put in this afternoon."

"A security system? Mom you don't need to do that, really," Sarah said, grateful of her generosity, though.

"Nonsense, what if he had gotten in?"

"Then either me or Jenny would have shot him dead."

"Oh, Sarah, really. This is something for the police to handle. This system calls them automatically. I got the very best," she said proudly.

"Mom, in case you've forgotten, I work for the police."

"Well, maybe I shouldn't have wasted my money on my daughter's safety after all? I mean, if I'm not appreciated . . ." Nancy said, laying the guilt on thick. "God forbid you let your mother help protect you."

Sarah was sure the crocodile tears were mere seconds away. "I'm sorry, Mom; you're right, of course. I'm fortunate to have such a caring mother," she said, giving her a hug. Nancy's expression changed in an instant.

"Thank you dear, I'm only doing what a mother has to do to protect her baby."

"And I promise . . . if he comes back I'll call the police before I shoot him."

"Sarah, why don't you come stay with your father and me for a few days?"

I think I'd rather take my chances with the killer. "Thanks, Mom, but I won't be scared out of my own house."

"Oh, you're as stubborn as your grandfather."

Thanks, Mother, I'll take that as a compliment. "I'll be fine. The sheriff is posting a guard outside the house and by the end of the day I'll have that great security system you bought."

Nancy's cell phone rang. "Yes? Oh, Claude, dear, did you get my message about . . . Yes? You have it? You are an absolute angel. Oh, I'll come right over and get it. Don't let Harriet Reid lay her bony fingers on it." Nancy hung up the phone and almost turned to leave before remembering where she was. "Sarah dear..." "Gotta run?" Sarah asked.

Tom Adair

"I hate to go but the gallery has an exquisite piece by Charles Magdon that I simply must have."

"Sounds like an emergency."

"I've got to get over there before another designer gets their grubby hands on it."

"No problem, Mom, I'm fine here."

"Great, I'll call you later so we can set up another dinner at our place."

"Can't wait. Bye, Mom."

"Ta-ta, dear."

And with that her mother hopped in her sedan and sped down the roadway, driving straight through the yellow crime scene tape.

23

The doors to the Department of Motor Vehicles Bureau opened right at 8:00 AM.

The government office's drab surroundings reminded the killer of his junior high school cafeteria. The dank air reminded everyone just how decrepit the old building had become. Laughter and hope were scarce commodities dampened by their straight-laced boss, Stanley Phipps.

The killer was sure that he'd have made a great factory manager in the old Soviet Union. Stanley was under a lot of pressure to bring costs down while increasing productivity. He was a bottom-line kind of guy, which suited the killer just fine. He'd approached Stanley a year before, posing as a retired computer programmer looking to volunteer some time and serve his community. Stanley was in a pickle trying to update his computer database to a new records management system. The work entailed tedious data transfers, a kind of copy and paste exercise, that few of his employees relished and his overtime budget couldn't accommodate.

The killer's impromptu offer was a dream come true for Stanley. Once a week he spent a few hours in his bare cubicle, entering data. His involvement was kept off the books and hidden from Stanley's boss's downtown. The killer knew his way around the software and designed a simple program to transfer the data with a few key strokes, which allowed him the time to pursue his true objective.

Looking around to be sure no one was watching, he minimized his screen and pulled up the main database. He punched in the license plate of the BMW he'd dumped in the mountain pond. The record appeared on the screen in seconds, complete with the woman's photo and home address. Her face was quite pretty, reminding him of the regret he felt over their unfinished date that night. He looked around one last time before punching the delete button. That was that he thought; another record gone forever. If the police ever did find the BMW, it would complicate the identity process. They'd spend months trying to recover the record, assuming it got misplaced in the data transfer process.

"Good morning, John," a voice sang over his cubicle wall.

He used the name John Rogers around the office.

Molly Rupp was what government unions referred to as a "lifer." Content with her menial job she would come in day after day with no hope of advancement until the day she retired . . . or was forced to. The DMV was her life. She was perky, likeable, but much too friendly. She was always probing for personal stories; it was a full time job to keep her queries at bay. He had hoped that her curiosity would have dwindled by now but she was nosy to a fault. That, and he was sure she was flirting with him. Even if he could have a "normal" relationship, it would never happen with a woman like her.

Her bright, primary-colored dresses and costume jewelry were in sharp contrast to the drab office surroundings, but not her gaudy makeup. Molly had long, artificial nails which she decorated each week with a different theme. This week's theme was Thanksgiving: turkeys, pilgrims, and Indians.

"I brought in Krispy Kream glazed and chocolate doughnuts."

"Ah, okay . . . thanks, Molly. Maybe I'll get one later," he said, while trying to look busy.

"Oh, do you want me to get you one? I'd be happy to."

It was an annoying cadence that reminded him of a mother talking to a young child. "No, thanks. I'm not sure which I'd like. Maybe when I take a break," he said, not looking up from his screen.

His fingers danced across the keyboard for several more seconds while she relayed the weekly minutia of her life. To any other person it would be obvious that he was ignoring her but she droned on for several more minutes before running off to answer her phone. Thank God, he thought.

He pulled the folded paper out from his pants pocket and entered the first license plate into the database. The computer drive hummed for several seconds until the record came up on the screen. Ewe, the dyke, he thought, as Jenny's picture popped up on the computer screen. "Jenny Fletcher," he whispered. He punched in the next license plate number. There she was. He entertained deviant thoughts as Kim's photo and driver's license record came up on the screen. Most people hid their driver's license photo but she had nothing to be ashamed of. Her eyes welcomed his perverted stare, he thought, as he imagined their first date.

"I went ahead and brought you one of each!" Molly said as she entered his cubicle unannounced.

His surprise was evident.

"Who is she?" Molly asked.

"Ah, just a corrupted file. A few always get dumped in the transfer and I have to go back in and re-enter data by hand."

"Oh, I hear you! I'm entering stuff all day. My fingers are always sore. You know what really helps me?" He didn't answer "I like to wind down with a nice glass of Chardonnay at the end of a long shift," she said, fishing for any interest. He raised his eyebrows in acknowledgment but kept his eyes on the screen. "Would you like to join me sometime?" she asked, sounding desperate now. Her first move was as clumsy as a drunken chimpanzee sliding into home base.

"Me? Oh, thanks, but no thanks. I don't drink." She offered her best puppy dog eyes. "I take care of my elderly mother and have to go right home after work," he said, not knowing why he was making excuses.

"Oh, isn't that sweet. Well, maybe some other time."

"Um, sure . . . maybe." He couldn't believe he'd left the door open.

"Okay, well, I'd better get some work done myself," she said as she turned to walk away.

Looking back to the screen, the killer once again gazed into her eyes. Kimberly McFadden, he hummed. I've always loved the name Kimberly. The killer jotted down her address and vehicle information. He inserted a tiny thumb drive into the USB port on the computer and saved a copy of her image file. It would make a nice addition to his scrapbook. He would add more from their date afterwards.

Sarah was on the verge of being late for work when she grabbed another slice of bread and jogged to the door. She gave a brief wave to the deputy stationed outside her home and wondered how long the sheriff would keep them there. Twenty-five minutes later she entered the high-fenced parking lot and found her assigned parking space outside the crime lab garage. She caught her sergeant's disappointed stare when she came through the door five minutes late. Sergeant Leonard Marshall had been put in charge of the lab because he'd burned every other bridge in the department. He was by all accounts intellectually challenged and his favorite pastime was making the criminalists' lives miserable.

Sarah snapped a casual salute as she hurried to her cubicle.

"You're late, Richards," Marshall said, peering over the cubicle wall. "Don't think that because of your situation you can just stroll in here any time of the day. Like it or not, we have work to do."

Sarah was too tired to be sarcastic. "Sorry, Sarge, won't happen again."

There was nothing new on her case. Detectives had been searching in vain for a useful lead, but had come up empty. The killer was a ghost. Sarah's parents had dealt her another blow this morning, adding more stress to her life: Instead of spending Thanksgiving together as a family, they were headed to Hawaii. Alone. On Thanksgiving. The one family holiday she looked forward to and they were going on vacation.

"Hey, kiddo . . . Wow, you look like shit,"

"Nice to see you, too, Manny."

"Just wanted to drop by to see how you're doing, but I guess I don't have to ask."

"No, I'm fine, really."

"Now why don't I believe that?" he asked.

Sarah let out a big sigh. "It's my mother again. They're flying off to Hawaii for a vacation . . . on Thanksgiving, no less."

"They ditched you on Thanksgiving? Man, that's cold."

Sarah put her hand to her forehead and stared at the computer screen.

"Well, that settles it, then," Manny said.

"What?"

"You're joining our family for Thanksgiving."

"Listen . . . that's really nice and all, but I don't want to be some lonely pathetic loser mooching a free meal."

"Shit, you just described half the family."

A faint smile curled her lips. "Well, shit . . . in that case . . ."

The Scent of Fear

It was a bold move, but the killer cased Kimberly's neighborhood, hoping to see her again and study her routine. It was just the neighborhood he had expected. The neat and clean yards anchored older homes from two generations past. The daylight surveillance was risky but less suspicious than at night. He'd used this same tactic to study Amy Summers' place several weeks earlier. People were creatures of habit with predictable routines. He had been watching Kim for days. Mostly he watched her in the dispatch windows at night as she walked the floor. He listened to his police scanner and it didn't take long to determine which voice was hers.

He'd spent hours listening to her sweet voice on the radio and imagined her talking directly to him. Then one night her voice was gone. Then another. He thought he had plotted her days off but this was an unexplained break in the chatter. Could she be sick, did she quit, or was she just on vacation? He walked along her sidewalk, hoping to see some evidence of her whereabouts. No stack of newspapers or solicitors' coupons graced her porch. The mailbox was empty, too. Her yard was basic: A few evergreen bushes and a small stand of aspen trees were its only occupants. A few well-placed flower beds would do wonders for the place, he thought. A tire swing arched from a fifty-foot elm in the neighbor's yard and a small girl giggled as she spun. Parents must be close by, he thought.

There was no Beware Dog sign on the wooden picket fence and no alarm placard in the yard. Kimberly, you're making this too easy, he thought. He peeked through the garage window and saw only emptiness. He decided a look through the front window was warranted. The big bay window allowed him to see a great deal of the main floor. A drooping *Spathiphyllum*, or peace lily, indicated it hadn't been watered for several days. "Can I help you with something?"

It was the next door neighbor. No doubt the bored housewife had spotted him snooping around and summoned the courage to approach. Options raced through his head but he played it cool.

"Oh, thank you. Maybe you can help me," he said in a friendly tone. "Is this Kimberly McFadden's house?"

"Are you a friend of Kim's?" the woman asked.

He thought it comical that, while trying to be coy, the woman just confirmed it was Kim's house. *If I were a friend wouldn't I already know it was?* "Actually, I'm an old friend of the family. I'm just in town for the day and thought I'd surprise her."

The woman's uneasiness gave way to a helpful neighborly demeanor. "Well, isn't that nice of you. Ya know, you missed her by a couple of days. I think her dad rented a cabin in the mountains for the whole week. It's a new Thanksgiving tradition," she said.

"Oh, that's too bad. I'm sorry I missed her. I'll try her on her cell and see her next time I'm in town."

Normally, a criminal might be worried about being spotted but he knew that the woman wouldn't remember him. He was blessed with an average face that few could describe with any meaningful detail. His car was three blocks away, but he relished the warm November day. By the time he reached his car the killer had formulated his next move.

24

Sarah pulled into Manny's modest Centennial neighborhood right at 2:00 PM. His extended family had turned the quiet street into a parking lot and Sarah had to park a block away. Even from that distance Sarah could hear the festive Ranchera music hanging in the air. She could almost envision the partygoers dancing in traditional clothing from the State of Jalisco where Manny's family originated.

Manny's spirited niece, Anita, answered the door and took Sarah's coat. The air was thick with a heavenly aroma. Sarah found Manny's wife, Marielos, laboring over an outdoor oven on a beautiful rosette tile floor.

"Marielos? Happy Thanksgiving," Sarah said as they hugged.

"*Bienvenidos a nuestra casa.* Welcome to our home," Marielos said.

"Thank you so much for inviting me."

"Sarah, you look absolutely stunning. I have many a nephew who would pursue you to the ends of the Earth."

"Well, just remind them that I'm armed," she said, laughing.

"Come, come, Manny is in the yard, showing off his new toy."

"Do you need any help in here?"

"Not to worry, I have everything under control. Not as many people showed up as expected. Go . . . go enjoy yourself."

Sarah gazed in wonderment at the thirty-odd guests drinking beer and singing in the back yard. So this is a small family gathering? Manny was standing by the addition to the garage.

"*Hola,* Sarah, come check out my *nueva moto,*" An olive-drab Harley Davidson motorcycle with black leather saddle bags was balanced on a chrome kickstand.

"Cool. It looks like an older-style bike. Is it new?"

"Yep. Oh-eight model. They call it a Softail Cross Bones. This was one of the last in the country. I had to get it delivered from a dealer in Oklahoma City."

The polished chrome pipes accented the black metal frame nicely. The custom seat embroidery and wheels rounded out the unique look of the bike.

"This thing has an air cooled 1500cc twin cam engine," he said as he started it up for the twentieth time. His neighbors must have thought it was a biker rally. "I even added a GPS."

"I'd like to see you work it while you're cruising down the highway at seventy miles per hour!"

"You wanna take a ride?" Manny offered.

"Maybe later, for now I'd settle for a beer."

"*Una cervesa, para senorita, por favor!*" he yelled into the air.

Two young men sprinted for the cooler in an apparent attempt to impress their stunning visitor. The older one returned with a Negro Modelo, nearly stumbling over a lawn torch. He puffed out his chest as he handed her the bottle.

Thanksgiving had always been a special time for Sarah. Her grandfather spun fanciful stories of the frontier and man's shared journey of discovery. He had always insisted on her dressing up for holidays and she honored that memory. Sarah wasn't comfortable in fancy dresses so she opted for a pair of slim-fitting boot-cut tan slacks and embroidered white and brown western style shirt. A pair of custom Ghost Rider boots gave her outfit an added dose of flair. Made in Denver the expensive boots were a birthday present from her mother. Her long, chestnut-colored hair and slim figure captured the attention of every man at the party. Young, single men were drawn to her deep and hypnotic hazel eyes. She would never have want of an empty glass or plate at this party.

Sarah engaged several family members in light conversation but soon lost track of everyone's names. It was kind of pathetic that a criminal investigator could have such a poor memory. She reminded herself that she was bad with names, not case details.

"Can I have everyone's attention?" Manny said as he tapped a knife on the side of his Corona bottle. As the conversation settled he stood high on the bench seat and addressed his family. "I am so happy to see all of you here today. Thanksgiving is a time to reflect on the bounty life provides us and expresses our gratitude to family and friends. To my father, Luis, for teaching me to be a good man, a good husband, and a good friend. Pop,

God broke the mold after you. To my wife, for supporting me and helping me become the best husband and father I can be, and to the rest of you for putting up with me. They say you can't choose your family and that's true. But in the end, family is all you have and I'm very grateful for you all."

Manny's sister Aina hugged him and kissed his cheek. Manny told Sarah once that Aina had practically raised him while her mother worked two jobs. Later in life she claimed that he saved her from a life of drugs introduced to her by a despicable boyfriend.

"That was very nice, Manny." Sarah said, thinking of her own parents taking off on vacation during the holiday.

"It was meant for you, too."

"Me?"

"Like it or not, you're family."

She was touched by the sentiment. The gesture comforted her and erased the loneliness creeping into her heart.

Sarah noticed that several of the young men had made efforts to save a spot for the attractive guest. "Sarah, come join me," Marielos said. Thank God, saved by the bell. "I'm afraid inviting you here was a bit like throwing chum in the water," she said.

Sarah laughed. "I can't say that I'm not flattered by the attention."

"They are good boys, believe me, but none of them are right for you."

"Who is right for me?"

"You need a man who isn't intimidated by your beauty, your drive, or your values," she said, looking up toward the afternoon sky. "A man who treats you like a lady . . . not because of who you are, but because of who he is."

"Sounds a lot like Manny."

"Who, him? Honey, the only things he's good for is changing the channel and drinking beer," she said, laughing.

Sarah knew it was a lie.

The meal was just underway when Manny's Nextel echoed the dreaded alert tone. His body language told her that something bad had happened. He was scribbling on a small notepad when her Nextel went off, too. It was Leonard Marshall.

"Sarah, we've got a report of a dead body down in Littleton by the Platte River. I need you to respond down there and see what we've got."

"All right, is this the same call-out Manny is getting?"

"How did you know that?"

"He's sitting right here."

"I assume so."

"Okay, what do we know so far?"

"I have no idea. Why don't you call dispatch and talk to the deputy on scene?"

Gee . . . I guess I figured you'd do your job and ask a few questions before sending me out on assignment, she thought. Sarah looked over to see Marielos, already making them pork sandwiches to go.

"This totally sucks!" Manny exclaimed as they rushed to her crime scene truck. "I worked all day on that pig."

"Murphy's Law strikes again. Every time you make plans you'll get called out," she observed. "Did you get any information about what we're heading toward?"

"Not much. Apparently, a family was out walking off their turkey dinner when Fido came across a woman's body along the trail."

"Any indication of foul play?"

"I was told the body is pretty bloody but the deputy on scene thinks it's from animals."

"That's more information than I got."

"What did you expect from Marshall?"

They pulled up to the yellow tape blocking the roadway behind the Aspen Grove Shopping Center. A burly deputy with a scornful face was guarding the entrance to the scene. Sarah pulled up as Manny rolled down his window.

"Hey, there, Ed, got us a dead body, huh?" Manny said.

"That's the rumor. I haven't been down there, but it sounds pretty gory."

"Anyone else from investigations show up?" Sarah asked.

"Detective Riley already went down and I heard Andy from the lab was en route."

Oh, I hope Andy wasn't in the middle of dinner, Sarah thought.

"What about the coroner?" Manny asked.

"Hey, that's your job. We haven't called for anyone yet," he said.

"Thanks, the last thing we need is those guys traipsing around before we have our preliminary work done."

"We did let one paramedic in to verify death but that was it," he said.

"All right, make sure we get a report from him," Manny said.

Unlike the previous scenes they had worked there was no media waiting for them. No doubt members of the media were occupied with holiday festivities and not manning the scanner. Manny drove as far down the path as he could before stopping. They were still a hundred yards from the scene though. Sarah grabbed her camera and put on a pair of Hi-Tec hiking boots.

Detective Bret Riley was new to the investigations team. He was still adjusting to the demanding requirements of the job. Most of his career had been spent in Patrol and SWAT. Riley had established a safe walk line with small plastic surveyor flags. The route was supposed to have been checked for evidence but they still kept a close eye out, just in case. The artificial path took them on a parallel course with the jogging path running through the woods. In some areas the path ran adjacent and above the slow-moving river. At other points it was over fifty yards away, separated by a congestion of willows and small trees.

"Nice secluded spot," Riley remarked as the pair arrived. Manny and Bret shook hands as the junior detective relayed his findings to the senior investigator. "The Wilsons over there were walking off their turkey dinner when Zeus got loose and ran into the willows. Apparently, he was on a beeline to the body," he said, pointing to the white Westy Terrier being held by the animal management officer.

"His name is Zeus?" Sarah asked.

"Yeah, he's a little terror, too. Looks like he rolled on the body and in the decomp fluids. I had the officer secure him so you could check him out before releasing him."

"That sounds like fun," Sarah said.

"Did the family touch the body?" Manny asked.

"Nope, they pretty much stayed clear. The father got the closest but he never got past the edge of the small clearing there.

You'll find a pile of his vomit over by that small tree," he said, pointing the way.

Sarah rolled her eyes.

"Any other witnesses?" Manny asked.

"None so far, but the patrol guys have just started the canvass of the trailer park over there," Riley stated.

"I don't suppose we have an ID on the victim?" Manny asked with a glimmer of hope.

"Nothing yet. Obviously, I didn't get near the body until the lab had a chance to look at it. We have a report of a missing woman a few weeks back . . . uh, Amy Summers," he said, flipping through his notebook. "Dispatch is waiting on confirmation she's still missing. Unfortunately, the holiday weekend is making it hard to find folks. There were no cars in the parking lot at the trailhead but she could have parked at the mall," he said.

"Why would she park so far away?" Sarah asked. "The trailhead lot is locked until sunrise so maybe she arrived before then."

While Manny interviewed the family, Sarah returned to her car to get a trace evidence wand. It was a fancy description for your standard sticky lint roller from the local Wal-Mart. The feisty dog was buzzing around the officer like a tether ball in a tornado. His normally clean, white beard and coat were soiled with dark, decomposing fluids. The sixteen-pound dog was stronger than Sarah expected and she needed the officer to hold both his collar and carrot-shaped tail to control him. Sarah knew the likelihood of finding something from the killer was slim. Even if they did find some hair or fiber from the suspect on the dog it would be difficult to connect the evidence to the victim. Some savvy attorney would just argue that the evidence got on the dog at some other time or from some other place. Although ridiculous to Sarah, she knew that some gullible juror would buy into the theory. CYA, she thought.

Manny signaled to Sarah that he was done with the interview.

"Okay officer, I'm done with him. You can give him back to his owners now," Sarah said.

Then they all witnessed something both horrifying and unexpected. Zeus's tiny legs propelled him furiously to the family's young daughter. With an Olympic display of athleticism, the tiny dog leapt into her arms and began kissing her. As his tiny tongue licked her face through the decomp-stained beard, all three investigators gagged at the thought of what fluids were being transferred between them. Sarah almost called out to the girl but the family had already begun walking away. The damage was done, she thought.

"That was the most disturbing thing I've seen in years," Riley confessed.

"How is it possible that she can't smell that?" Sarah asked. "I could smell the stink from six feet away."

"Kids love their dogs, I guess," Manny said. "My dog loves cat shit, eats it like candy. I'd rather have my dog eat nuclear waste, but what can you do?"

"I hope to God she brushes her teeth before bed tonight," Sarah said.

The three sat in silence, detoxifying their brains, when Andy came up behind them.

"Hey, guys, sorry I'm late. What do we have?" Andy couldn't help but notice their disgusted facial expressions. "That bad, huh?"

"You have no idea," Sarah said.

"What's been done?" Andy asked.

"Not much, we just got here."

"Okay, why don't you concentrate on photos and I'll shoot some video. We'll meet up at the body and assess our needs at that point."

"Sounds good to me."

Sarah began taking overall photographs of the scene. She had to be careful not to get other officers in the photos as she moved around. She photographed anything that seemed important. The problem was that this was a popular public use area. Hundreds of people used this path each month, even in the winter. It could prove difficult discerning things like shoe prints left by the killer and those just left by hikers.

Sarah and Andy eventually converged at the entry between the willows leading to the small clearing where the victim lay. She snapped some quick shots of broken twigs at the threshold to hell. Sarah could literally taste the odor of decomp. The dank stench penetrated clothes and skin lasting for hours, even days after showering. "Looks like there's a dog here," Andy observed from a distance.

"Goddamnit," Sarah whispered as she shook her head.

"I just hate to see a dog killed," Andy said.

"Any pet for that matter," Sarah added.

"I don't mind cats so much," Andy noted dryly after brief contemplation.

25

Sarah shook her head at the dark attempt at humor. Sarah studied every twig looking for anything that might yield the killer's identity. The horrific nature of the woman's condition was soon apparent. Amy's once beautiful body was now a macabre heap of unrecognizable humanity. Her contorted limbs and battered privates spoke volumes to an experienced investigator.

"Looks like a rape-homicide," Sarah observed.

"A violent one I'd say, by the look of her va-jay-jay," Andy said.

"Va-jay-jay?"

"Sorry, my wife watches a lot of Oprah. I guess it rubs off."

"Just make sure you don't put that in a report," Sarah joked.

"Duly noted."

The mild afternoon air must have carried the scent of death far away. Several robust flies buzzed around the body. Flies disgusted Sarah; she thought of the last place it had been visiting every time one landed on her skin, hair, or food. She made a mental note to look for maggots or egg masses on the victim. Chances were there wouldn't be any due to the time of year, but she still had to check. Her skin-tight body suit had been sliced open with some kind of knife, she thought. Her hair was tangled and matted with dark coagulated blood that flaked off in the weak breeze. Sarah watched Andy put on two layers of purple Nitrile gloves and decided it was a good idea. A small percentage of latex gloves always failed and Sarah learned it was better to be safe than exposed to an unknown disease.

"Well, based on the way she's dressed, I'd say she was walking or running on the trail," Andy said.

"If that's the case then the killer would have ambushed her."

"Or he could have lured her down here on a ruse of some sort."

The body was free of tattoos, a rare sight with younger women nowadays. Her skin looked like dried jerky sunken and draping over the skeleton below. Her eyes looked like old hardboiled eggs that had dried and withered in a hot sun. Her decomposed facial muscles left her jaw gaping wide open. It was a ghastly expression symbolic of her horrific death.

"Her teeth look like they've been smashed with a rock," Andy said.

"So he's trying to hamper our ability to identify her by dental records. Do you see the rock?" Sarah asked.

"Nope, he probably chucked it in the river. At least that's what I would have done."

"Her fingers look intact, but they're pretty dried out."

"We can plump 'em up. Hopefully, she's been fingerprinted sometime in her life. Look at this ligature mark, Sarah," he said, studying the darkened strip of dried tissue around her neck. "It looks like some kind of woven material, maybe."

"I can't make it out very well, but it looks like there may be more than one cord. See how there's a gap here between these two indentations?"

"Yeah, I see it," Andy said.

"What would that be?" Sarah asked.

"I don't know. Maybe he had a long piece of cord that was double or triple wrapped," he said.

Sarah studied the ligature with a sense of déjà vu. She slowly leaned over the victim's head and took a deep breath. It was a rookie mistake. Her nose was filled with the stench of death and she gagged.

"What are you doing?"

It took Sarah a few seconds to compose herself. It was a sensation similar to having water going down her airway, she thought. "I think I've seen this kind of ligature before."

"Really, where?"

"The victim on Monarch Pass," she said with an air of trepidation.

"Seriously?" Andy said.

"Well, I guess I can't be sure due to the decomposition but it at least reminds me of it. That's why I was trying to smell the body for chlorine," she said.

"I guess that plan backfired," Andy said, laughing.

"Fuck you, okay?"

Andy kept laughing as he began examining the face again.

"Looks like there may be some bruising from a punch or something. I can't tell with all the damage." He continued his examination, covering every inch of her body while Sarah snapped several close-up photographs.

As the two continued their investigation, Sarah caught a glimpse of people coming through the willows. It was Miles Johansson from CBI, along with another technician she'd never met.

"Andy, did you call CBI?" Sarah asked.

"No. Whoa, guys, this is a crime scene," Andy said, holding up his hands as the pair walked toward them.

"It's our crime scene now," Miles declared.

"What the hell are you talking about, Miles?"

"Why don't you go ask your detective," Miles suggested.

"Sarah, can you go find out what the hell is going on here?" Andy asked.

Miles began unpacking his gear to get started.

Sarah dashed off until she reached the established walk line. In minutes, she'd found Manny talking loudly into his cell phone with a finger in one ear.

"Sir, I don't understand. Yes, sir, I hear you on that, but this is our scene. We don't have any identity on the victim. We've been here two hours. Yes, sir. Yes, sir, but again we haven't established that yet."

Sarah thought he looked worried.

He saw Sarah out of the corner of his eye and motioned for her to come over. "Sir, hold on a sec. Sarah does the victim have vaginal trauma?"

"Yes, looks pretty severe, too."

"What about her mouth?"

"Looks like it was bashed in with a rock."

"Is there a ligature on her neck?"

"Yes."

"Yes, sir, it appears all three of those indicators are present. Yes, sir, I understand," Manny said as he hung up the phone.

"What's going on?"

"CBI is taking over the investigation," he said with a deep sigh.

"On whose authority? They have no jurisdiction to just come in and take over."

"The sheriff requested that they take it over."

"What the fuck? Did we do something wrong?" she asked.

"No, this is politics, kid, plain and simple. Apparently, there have been a series of murders that have taken place all over the state. All of the victims display the same type of trauma. They think they have a serial killer. The governor has created a special task force to investigate the murders and CBI is taking the lead on all field operations."

"How long have these murders been happening?"

"Over the past six months, it seems."

"Why haven't we heard anything about this?"

"He said the connection between the murders was just made in the past few days."

"How on earth did they find out about this scene? Good news travels fast I guess."

"C'mon, we need to go talk to Andy and the CBI folks," Manny said, walking off toward the scene. Manny motioned to Andy when they came into the clearing. "Andy, come on over here a moment."

Miles sauntered over as well.

"Per the sheriff, we are relinquishing control of the scene to CBI," Manny said.

"What? This is bullshit. Are you telling me that after all the work we've done we're just giving up?" Andy asked, looking at Miles.

"Listen, Andy, this wasn't my idea," Miles said. "Tell you what. You and your partner can help us out by working the perimeter."

The perimeter? What a total prick, Manny thought. "We'll help in any way we can," he said.

Miles didn't bother hiding his smug smile as he walked back to the body.

"Look, before you say anything, Andy, let me explain something: The sheriff made his decision. There's nothing to be gained by trading jabs with these guys okay?" Manny said.

"I know, Manny, but the whole thing just pisses me off."

"Look at it this way: You just got out of a lot of work."

"*This* is my work. This is why we're here, Manny. I want what's best for the victim and this ain't it."

"Hey, it is what it is. At least by working the perimeter you two can keep an eye on them." Manny touched Sarah's shoulder as he walked back to his vehicle.

"Well, I guess we'd better debrief them on what we've found," she said to Andy.

Andy looked her in the eye. "Fuck 'em. They can read it in our report." After a deep sigh Andy calmed himself and determined their next course of action. "I'll head back to the parking lot to have a look around. Maybe she dropped something between here and there that might give us an idea of where this thing started."

"All right, what do you want me to do?"

"Take a walk around the edges of the bushes and trail and see if you can find tracks or something he may have dropped. Maybe he came and left by another trail."

"Got it," Sarah said as she took on her new assignment with enthusiasm.

She began at the trail in front of the opening to the willows. There were a number of overlapping shoe impressions but none of them were very detailed. None except those of the paramedic and the first deputy on scene. The Vibram soles were in sharp contrast to the others. As Sarah made her way around the back of the willows she was struck by the beauty of the freezing river. Sporadic breaks in the ice revealed pockets of slow-running water. In other areas the thin ice was more of a window than a barrier to the air above. While a band of snow existed along the banks, the rest of the area was devoid of snow pack. Sarah noticed that the ground beneath her was firm but not frozen. Earlier in the day she was sure that it would have been much muddier.

Then she saw them: A set of shoe prints along the willows within sight of the victim. These footprints looked different because they were obviously made when the ground was muddy. There was still no obvious tread detail but the edges of the tracks were sharp and distinct.

Sarah got down on her knees to take a better look. The tracks were from a single individual coming from the south. The victim had come from the north, they presumed. She was amazed at how fresh the tracks looked even without any detail. Then she remembered something Art had told her months ago about observing the suspect's walking path. These tracks came to the relative position of the victim then went back south again. She could see a point where it appeared the person had stood stationary, facing the victim. The right and left prints were aligned side by side. Sarah looked through the willows from that spot to see if the victim was visible. Jackpot. Sarah could see the victim lying a mere fifteen yards away! Sarah snapped a photo to document the find. Maybe this wasn't a waste of time after all, she hoped.

Miles and his assistant didn't seem to notice Sarah until her flash went off. "Have you found something back there?" Miles called out.

"Yeah, I found some shoe impressions that may be important," she called back.

"Hold on a sec, let me take a look at them," he called back. As he made his way over to her she figured he'd take the credit for the find with his superiors.

"Where are these prints?" he said, out of breath.

"Right here," she said, pointing. "They come in from the south to this point and then stand facing the victim's position, then head back to the south again."

He stared at her in disbelief for several seconds before taking her down a notch. "Are you shittin' me? I came all the way over here for this? Richards, these prints don't go anywhere near the victim," he snapped.

She was taken aback by his blunt dismissal. "I know, but they come in and stop here facing the victim. You can see her right through there. Why would someone walk to this specific point, turn to face the victim, then go back the way they came?" she asked.

"First of all, you can barely see the victim at all. Second, this guy wasn't facing the victim, he was facing the willow. Did it occur to you that this is just some guy coming down the trail and taking a piss?" he asked in bewilderment.

Sarah hadn't considered that. Her excitement was crushed. But it still didn't make sense. Why here? If the guy was taking a piss he could have done it anywhere. Why walk to this point then turn back and leave the way he came?

"I still think we should cast them. It seems like too much of a coincidence," she said.

Miles dropped to a knee to inspect the impressions. "You want to cast this shit?" he sneered. "These things are so old there's not even any detail left in the tread. Just what do you think the examiner is going to compare this to?"

"I just thought the edges looked fresh," she said, trying to justify her reasoning.

"The edges . . . the edges? You think we're going to compare edges?" he asked, almost laughing. "I see now why your sheriff called us in."

It was a low blow, she thought.

"You want to cast this crap, be my guest, but don't waste my time with any more of your discoveries. I've got serious work to do and I can't be wasting time holding your frickin' hand," he said as he walked away.

Sarah stood silent with her tracks. A sea of anger and embarrassment boiled within her. He seemed to enjoy belittling her. Miles could be right, she thought. Maybe the guy was just taking a piss. But it just didn't feel right. If she made a cast of the impressions and they turned out to be nothing she'd be the joke of the week. Screw it, she decided. If I'm a joke, I'm a joke. At least no one can say I didn't try. She made her way back to her crime scene vehicle and grabbed her casting kit. She picked out the two best impressions and poured in her casting material. She checked her watch and calculated it would take an hour before the cast was dry enough to lift. She decided to use her time to update Andy.

"Hey Andy, where you at?" she called into her Nextel.

"Over in the mall parking lot by the William Sonoma store."

Oh, I love that store, she thought. "Need any help?"

"You're done already? Yeah, come on over."

They spent the next hour walking the empty lot, looking for something of value. Like most parking lots, it was littered with cigarette butts and assorted trash. She relayed her story of the footwear but he didn't seem interested. Maybe he thinks I'm out of my mind, too.

Sarah made it back to the scene just as night began to fall. Manny was standing by the opening to the willows.

"Where's the CBI guys?" she asked.

"Hell, they're gone."

"Gone? They're done already?"

"Yep, took some photos and talked a lot. Once the coroner got here they scooped her up and away they went," he said, pointing off to the road.

"Wow, that seems kind of fast, don't you think?"

"You could say that. But hey, they're the experts, right?"

"I guess."

She pried the cast from the cold ground and carried it back to her truck. After dropping Manny at home she made her way back across town to the crime lab. She was exhausted. She had missed a great meal, been taken off a case, and then belittled by another criminalist like she was a ten year old. As she downloaded her photographs from the crime scene Sarah couldn't help but think that this Thanksgiving day had been the worst ever.

26

It was ten to eight when Sarah sprang out of bed to the high-pitched screech from her new home security system. Holy shit! She thought. She snatched her Glock 9mm pistol from the nightstand. Her cell phone was nowhere to be seen; at least the alarm company had been alerted, she thought.

Sarah pushed forward to the bedroom door with the sleek black pistol leading the way. Taking the corner wide she tried to catch a lucky glimpse of the intruder. The blaring alarm echoed loudly down the narrow hallway. Was the killer back?

Unlike the alleyway, she was armed now and didn't plan on being a victim again. There was a fire in her eye as she moved forward. Cold air struck her pale skin as an eruption of goosebumps warned her that the front door was still open. She could hear a faint tapping sound under the wailing alarm. This was it, she thought as she neared the living room. He has to be either there or in the kitchen. Once she broke cover from the hallway she would be totally exposed. Summing up all her courage she decided it was now or never. In a flash she was around the corner. In a chorus of alarms, the two women screamed in unison.

"MOTHER!" Sarah yelled.

Nancy Richards was punching the security keypad. She grabbed her chest in surprise at Sarah's shout. "My code doesn't work!"

Sarah switched the gun to her left hand and punched the proper code into the system. An eerie silence followed.

"Good heavens, Sarah you nearly gave me a heart attack," Nancy complained.

"*I* gave *you* a heart attack? What are you doing here? I thought you were in Hawaii."

"Oh, we were but we flew back late last night."

Sarah decided it didn't matter. Passing her mother she slammed the front door shut. "What code were you trying to enter?"

"My code, of course. I had the young man program it in when the system was installed," she said "I'll tell you this for sure, I didn't spend all that money for a faulty system. I'm going to call that manager right now and give him a piece of my mind. He'll be over here in fifteen minutes to fix the problem if he wants to keep his job."

"Mother, I set the alarm code myself once it was installed."

"You changed the code? Why would you do that?"

"Geeze, Mom, I don't know, I guess I figured it would be better to have a code I'm familiar with."

"Can you change it back?"

Sarah couldn't believe what she was hearing but decided it was easier to learn a new code than it was to continue arguing with her. After all she had bought Sarah the system. "Sure."

Just then her cell phone rang. It was the security representative from the alarm company.

"No, no, I'm fine. My mother came in to surprise me and didn't know the code," she said.

"I knew the code, dear," Nancy whispered at her.

"Okay . . . No, it's all right. You don't need to call the police. Thank you, sir," she said, hanging up the phone. Sarah wondered why the deputy outside hadn't come in. She plopped onto the soft leather couch and forced a smile. "So, Mother . . . to what do I owe this surprise?"

"Oh, I brought you a new furniture catalog. I thought we could look for a new kitchen table together," she said.

Sarah was in no mood to argue, at least not yet. "Do you want some coffee, Mom?"

"Yes dear, that sounds lovely."

Sarah caught her mom staring at the pistol lying on the table. "Problem, Mother?"

"Can you please put that thing away somewhere before one of us gets shot?" Nancy had always suffered a type of hoplophobia, which was odd given her proximity to guns growing up. Sarah had even seen photos of her shooting skeet as a young girl.

"Mother, it can't hurt you just sitting there."

Nancy retrieved a white handkerchief from her monstrous handbag and laid it over the gun as if it were a dog turd. "I don't know why you need that thing anymore now that you have the alarm."

"It's not like the TV commercials, Mom. In my business we have a saying: 'When seconds count, the police are only minutes away.' The bad guys don't always run away just because the alarm goes off."

"I just don't want you to get hurt, dear."

"I won't, Mother; I'm very careful." The coffee-maker chimed and Sarah rose to get them each a cup.

Nancy took her cup and searched for a coaster on the table.

"You don't have a saucer, dear?"

"Just use a magazine, Mother."

Nancy looked across the room and cringed. "Dear heavens, Sarah, what is that monstrosity on the wall?" she asked, pointing a boney finger at a large metal bear trap hanging next to the mantle.

Sarah was amused. "Oh, I found it in Grandpa's stuff in the attic . . . cool huh?"

Nancy offered a fake smile as she opened her catalog.

"All right, now what do you think about this one?" she asked.

"Oh, that's nice. It'll look great in your place."

"Sarah, I'm doing this for you."

"And just what's wrong with my table?"

"Oh, please, it's older than me. The wood is so weathered and worn it looks like it belongs in a barn."

"Grandpa made that table, remember?"

"All things eventually change, my dear. I just want to fix your place up and make it more 'hip,' as you kids like to say."

"Mother, seriously, why are you here?"

"Oh, all right." She waved her hand in front of her face. "If you must know, I felt bad about leaving you alone on Thanksgiving."

"You did?"

"Well, of course, dear."

"I appreciate that, Mother. I . . . I don't know what to say."

"You don't need to say anything. I'm the one who left in such a hurry. I'm sorry, dear. I should have been here for you," Nancy admitted.

It was a rare moment between mother and daughter.

"Then why did you go in the first place?" Sarah asked.

Nancy looked ashamed. "To be honest, I've been so busy lately I forgot about the holiday. I'd already paid for the tickets and hotel when you reminded me it was Thanksgiving," she confessed. Sarah smirked as she recognized the simple mistake. She knew first-hand what it was like to lose track of time when work had you swamped. Her mother was human, after all.

"Thanks, Mom," Sarah said, laying her hand on Nancy's.

"So did you have a nice time at your friend's house?"

"It was interesting," she admitted after some consideration, not wanting to worry her mother with the details, something criminalists often did.

"You don't want to look at tables do you?" Nancy asked.

"How about if we just talk a bit and catch up?" Sarah suggested, not sure what they would talk about, though.

"I know, let's go clothes shopping! There are a ton of sales today; its Black Friday, remember?" Nancy exclaimed.

"Oh, thanks, Mom but I don't really need any clothes."

"Oh, dear, but you do . . . you really do," Nancy said. "C'mon, it'll be fun."

It was a rare moment for Sarah. Her mother actually wanted to spend quality time with her. It was an opportunity Sarah decided she couldn't pass up. "All right, why not? Give me a minute to shower and get dressed,"

Tilly Helton came in early to the office, hoping to catch up on some paperwork. The school was closed, and she didn't have to be there, but she relished the peace and quiet. She started a fire in the stone fireplace which filled the room with a romantic ambience. She was none too surprised to see Art already sitting at his desk. As she entered the room she heard a melodic classical song piping softly from his stereo.

"Good morning, stranger. What time did you roll in this morning?" she asked.

"You assume that I left last night," he said smiling. "I've been here about two hours," He confessed.

"Mozart?" she asked, nodding toward the stereo.

"Mozart? No. That piece is entitled 'Finlandia,' by Jean Sibelius. So Tilly, are you enjoying your week off?" Art asked sarastically. "You know me. I don't know what to do with my time off," she said.

"You and me both," he said.

"Can I help you with anything?"

"No, I'm just putting together some fact sheets for this task force meeting on Monday."

"Oh, those killings sound just terrible. He's a dirty son of a bitch that's for sure and for certain. I'll be at my desk if you need anything." Art nodded without looking up.

The two worked in peace and quiet for about an hour when Tilly's phone rang. "Hello? Well, . . . yes, he's right here, hold please," she said. Tilly punched the intercom button.

"Art . . . the governor's office is on line one," she said.

"All right, thank you Tilly," he said, pressing the lighted key on his phone base. "This is Dr. Von Hollen. Yes, Governor, what can I do for you? Ah-huh . . . Well, I can't say I'm surprised. No, It had to happen sooner or later. Where did you say the body was found? I see. Sir, I need to ask you a favor. I want to add someone to the task force. Yes, sir . . . but this one might cause a little friction with others in the group. Yes, sir, I do think it's imperative to the investigation. Yes, sir, I'm aware of that but I'm afraid I must insist. Thank you, sir; I knew I could count on your support. What's that? Yes, I did hear that Dr. Huxley and his assistant are joining the group. I'll make them very comfortable here. No, sir, that won't be a problem. The meeting is scheduled for Monday at oh nine hundred. I'll keep you posted."

Art held the phone for several seconds before hanging up. Any number of his colleagues around the world would have cautioned him against making such a decision. In his gut, though, he knew it right.

It was nine o'clock in the morning but Dr. Jeremiah Sheppard thought it felt more like six. Normally, he would have put off the autopsy until Monday due to the holiday weekend but the governor had made a personal phone call to his residence late last night. He couldn't possibly refuse the request. The office had been buzzing after investigators from several agencies descended on the least-appealing medical office in the county. Even the sheriff was present. Everyone was interested in the autopsy, except the victim, he thought. He would often tell his students that on the bright side, his patients had no co-pay. Sheppard placed the investigators and higher-ups in a large conference room with a fifty-two-inch flat-screen TV on one wall. He punched some keys on a control pad in the middle of the table and brought up an image of the autopsy suite.

"Ladies and gentlemen, you'll be able to watch the autopsy from the comfort of the conference room. Please help yourself to coffee or a Danish," he said, pointing toward the small kitchenette. "If you would like to switch camera views push this button here. The microphones will be hot during the procedure so you can just ask me questions like I'm right here in the room All right?"

They had all heard it before. Miles Johansson and CBI Agent Jacob Tyler were the only ones allowed in the autopsy room besides the pathology assistants. Agent Tyler was the go-to investigator in the agency and inherited most of the major cases.

As Sheppard changed into his surgical scrubs, he wondered about the woman on his table. She was someone's daughter, after all. On a day when she should have been out perusing all the hyped-up holiday sales she was instead the victim of a horrendous crime. At least, that's what they told him. Technically, a death could be classified as a homicide, suicide, accident, natural, or undetermined. Judging by the information he'd received Dr. Sheppard doubted very much if it was natural. The final decision was his to make.

Miles Johansson, Agent Tyler, and his assistant, Jennifer, were waiting by the body as he came through the door. The room was awash in the morning sunlight. He had pressured the county commissioners to add a number of skylights to the autopsy suite. Nothing beat natural light for his examinations. It didn't hurt for photography either. Even with the skylights the room was still frigid. Miles snapped photos of the body bag and evidence seal as Sheppard read the serial number into his tape recorder. His assistant, Jennifer, carefully removed the body bag, leaving the victim and her tattered body intact on the table. Miles was photographing every step of the procedure. Agent Tyler stood several feet back. Many an investigator had made the mistake of crowding out the doctor as they studied the body. It was a mistake few made twice in Sheppard's office. The autopsy began as it always did; the external examination. "Looks like she has a circumferential ligature covering her neck," Sheppard said, bending over the marks, illuminating them with his powerful examination light. "It is a woven fabric of some type. I want to say that I've seen it before but I just can't put my finger on it. Are you going to cast it?" he asked Miles.

"I think photographs will suffice," Miles retorted.

"You can cast that impression, Doctor?" Agent Tyler broke in.

"Yes, of course."

Agent Tyler gave the younger criminalist a withering look. No doubt Miles had told him it wasn't possible. Jennifer mixed up a batch of Mikrosil casting paste and spread it over the neck like cake frosting.

"She has petechia in both eyes," Sheppard noted.

"I'm sorry, Doctor . . . what was that again?" The unidentified voice came from the microphone piping in from the conference room.

"Petechia are small, pinpoint hemorrhages in the eyes that support a finding of strangulation," he noted dryly. "Her dentition is severely damaged due to blunt force trauma," he continued.

"We never recovered a weapon," Agent Tyler said, anticipating his next question.

"We'll take X-Rays. Do we have any idea who she is?" Sheppard asked.

"One local missing woman matches her description. Agents are following up on it as we speak. Her car was found in the mall parking lot too"

"Don't forget about the dog," Miles added.

"Right, the dog matches, too, but there was no collar," Agent Tyler confirmed.

"Did you scan the body for a microchip?" Sheppard asked. The CBI investigators exchanged worried looks as each realized that that simple task had yet to be done. Miles had released the dog to a local vet for disposal. He would call them after the autopsy to check for the microchip.

"There are no visible tattoos and the fingers are desiccated. Jennifer, will you remove the thumbs and index fingers for re-hydration?"

"Yes, Doctor, I'll take care of it right after autopsy."

"Looks like massive, sharp-force vaginal trauma," he noted.

"Can you tell if it's perimortem or postmortem?" Miles asked.

"Definitely perimortem," he answered, looking at the hemorrhaging in the tissue. "Jennifer, let's make sure we get a sample of the pubis for the anthropologist. With any luck, we'll get a description of the weapon used in the rape."

27

Sarah's hope of bonding with her mother while shopping was not to be. Nancy was bonding with expensive jackets while treating the sale's staff like hired help. Sarah's Nextel rang. The caller ID told her it was Art. "Hey, Art, how are you? Did you have a nice Thanksgiving?"

"Nicer than yours, I'm told."

"Yeah . . . You heard about that?"

"It's the reason I'm calling, actually."

"Really?" She thought the comment was strange. "You know CBI took over the case per the sheriff so you should probably ask them if you have questions," she said, not wanting to waste his time.

"Yes, I'm aware of that. Listen, Sarah . . . we think the man who murdered the woman you found yesterday is the same one you chased on Monarch pass."

"We?" she asked, puzzled.

"The governor has commissioned a multi-agency task force to catch him. The whole operation is being run out of the Facility."

"Okay. What does that have to do with me?"

"We're having our first meeting Monday and I'd like you to be there."

"Why me?"

"I think you'll be valuable to the group."

"I don't know, Art. I mean, I'm flattered and all but I'm not sure I'm experienced enough to make a difference. Plus, there's no way in hell the sheriff is going to let me go. I'm on call through next Tuesday."

"It's already approved," Art assured her

"Mind if I ask how you managed that one?"

"It wasn't me. I don't think Sheriff Westin could muster enough courage to say no to the governor."

"Jesus, you had the governor call him?"

"Not at all; I just suggested that I would."

"What about my on-call? I can't stick someone with that."

"Good news: Andy volunteered to cover you from now through the end of your schedule. He mentioned something about having you cover a weekend for him in January."

"Really? Well, I guess I can do that. When should I come up?"

"I thought you might want to come up to the Facility today and stay for a few days."

"Today?"

"Doc and Daniel are hunting Magdalene Gulch for elk and I figured you could tag along for the weekend."

"Seriously? That's one of your sanctuary spots!"

"I know, but the herd is getting too big up there and we need to manage their numbers or we'll lose a lot of calves to starvation this winter."

"I don't know what to say, Art." The thought of getting a hunting trip, not to mention one in Magdalene Gulch, was very tempting. She hadn't forgotten the last vacation this job had screwed up, not to mention Thanksgiving dinner.

"Say yes then."

"Okay, yes. Hell yes, I'll come. I'm out with my mom right now so I'll hit the road after lunch. Should be up there by six or so, I'd think."

"Great. We'll have your room stocked and ready for you".

Sarah stood speechless for several minutes as she contemplated the implications of this new assignment. A governor's task force? It sounded important although she had no idea how common they were. Some politicians loved creating committees and task forces for everything from homicide investigations to recycling programs. She wondered who else had been asked to join.

Nancy was scrutinizing a fur jacket when Sarah interrupted her. "Mom, I hate to do this but I need to get on the road."

"What is it, dear? You're not having a good time?"

"No, it's not that. I just got a call from Art and I have to head up there for work stuff." Sarah decided it was better not to go into any more detail than that.

"Well, all right, but you haven't bought a single outfit."

"Next time, Mother, I promise." She gave her mom a kiss on the cheek and raced for the exit.

Once back at her house she packed a full suitcase, not knowing what kind of weather she might run into. Then there was her hunting gear. Sarah punched the combination into the digital pad of her Redhead gun safe and opened the heavy metal door. The fabric-lined shelves housed an array of handguns, rifles, and shotguns; most of which had been passed on to her from her grandfather. She selected a heavy Winchester 1917 rifle which had been updated in the '50s with a "sporterized," wooden hunting stock. The 30-06 rifle was plain and simple, but it shot true. The metal bluing had been rubbed off the muzzle area and the old leather military sling was silky soft from years of use. The deep-colored Walnut stock was nicked and scraped but was more beautiful to her than any new rifle.

She never noticed the man sitting at the picnic table across the lake. If she had, the gentle nature in which he fed bread crumbs to the geese wouldn't have aroused any suspicion. Not unless she noticed the few times he lifted the compact binoculars to his eyes. The park was deserted and the spot offered him a good view of her home while maintaining a safe distance. The last thing he needed was to be spotted by another neighbor. He watched as she loaded her car for an apparent trip. He took special notice of the rifle case. Now where are you off to? He often liked dropping by to check in on his girls as he made his daily errands. His volunteer work at the DMV allowed him to select women based not only on their looks but also by their geography. It made his work more . . . efficient. He watched the red-haired beauty climb into the big black truck and speed away.

Soon, he thought.

Traffic was heavy on the Interstate as hordes of Denverites scampered to the ski resorts for the extended Thanksgiving weekend. Once past the town of Silverton, however, she made up lost time. The weather turned gloomy as she drove farther north. The low cloud ceiling let loose a frozen drizzle of sleet that would soon give way to snow once night fell. To most people this kind of weather was depressing, but Sarah knew it would make the hunting trip outstanding. It was about six PM when she turned down the gated drive to the Facility. The parking lots looked strange without any cars. Sarah drove straight to her reserved condo and put away most of her bags. A note from Tilly on rustic-colored stationary asked her to call Art at his residence when she got in.

"Hey, Art, I'm here," Sarah said, not trying to hide her excitement.

"Have you had a chance to settle in?"

"I dropped off my bags, but I figured I'd be heading out early in the morning so I haven't really unpacked anything."

"Tomorrow morning? I figured you'd be heading out tonight."

"Tonight? Oh, I'd love to but I haven't been up there in a while. I'm sure I'd get lost. Plus, I have no idea where Doc and Daniel are."

"As luck would have it, they're standing right here waiting for you."

"They are? I thought they went up days ago."

"They did, but they came back for some supplies and now they're ready to guide you up to camp if you're game."

"Yeah, I'm game. Just let me grab my stuff and I'll come right over."

"See you then," he said hanging up the phone.

"What are you going to tell her?" Art asked Doc.

"The truth."

"The whole truth?" he asked, raising his eyebrows.

"Just enough to scare her into the right perspective, I guess," he said, spitting his chewing tobacco into a spittoon.

"What about you?" Art asked, looking at Daniel.

"What about me?"

"Exactly. Are you going to tell her the truth, too?"

"I haven't decided yet. I think it's too soon."

"Look, Daniel, you're family so I love you no matter what. But Sarah is like family, too. So if you think the two of you are going to get serious you need to tell her everything, understand?"

"I understand."

"In the meantime, I'm counting on you to keep her safe."

"I will."

"I'm deadly serious about this, Daniel."

"So am I,"

Daniel's eyes told Art that he would sooner die than let anything happen to Sarah. It gave him instant comfort and he pitied the killer if he ever happened to cross paths with Daniel.

28

Sarah arrived at Art's cabin twenty minutes later and entered the foyer without knocking. Art had insisted she treat the home like it was her own. A massive bull moose Sarah nicknamed Rudy stared at her from the wall as she entered. She was serenaded by sweet smells wafting from the kitchen and could hear the familiar sound of classical cello on his stereo.

"Hey, guys, sorry I got here so late," Sarah said as she entered the living room.

The three men were lounging in leather furniture around a roaring fire. The massive stone hearth had an opening large enough to drive a Mini Cooper through and reminded her of the old Hansel and Gretel fairy tale.

"No worries. Doc here can find that camp in the middle of a blizzard," Art said as he gave her a big hug.

Doc rose and gave her a smile but didn't offer his hand or say hello as he walked toward the door. Daniel extended his hand and gave her a very warm greeting but both could tell it was awkward. Sarah had thought of him often since their dinner date but still had some reservations. She hoped a little time together on this trip would reveal more about him. He could just be shy, or as Kim had observed, had some skeletons he didn't feel comfortable talking about.

"What do you say we get this rodeo going?" Daniel suggested, still holding Sarah's hand.

"Sounds good to me."

He must have realized he had been holding her hand too long because he quickly released his grip. "We've got all the gear down at the stables. Camp is already set up so all we have to do is eat and sleep. "But you'll have your own tent, of course, you don't have to sleep with us."

"No? Well, I'm sure I've slept with worse," she said with a gaping smile as she walked past him. What are you doing? she asked herself. Thirty seconds and you're already flirting? *Slow down!*

They took an older white Ford Bronco down from the house. The well-cared-for vehicle looked like it had just rolled off the showroom floor. As Doc drove down the steep dirt road, Sarah couldn't help but make a joke.

"At this speed I kind of feel like OJ Simpson fleeing a murder scene."

Doc gave her a penetrating stare in the rear view mirror. "You think he did it?"

"Of course," she said.

His grunt suggested she had just passed some test. Doc seemed distant, like something was nagging at him. It wasn't like they had a close relationship or anything, she hardly knew him. He'd been much friendlier on her earlier visit, though.

The Bronco pulled up behind the old wooden barn and Daniel got out, guiding Doc in backing up to the stable.

"Make sure I can see you in the mirrors," he snorted.

"Okay, Doc . . . just back up 'til it sounds expensive," Daniel called out.

Doc shook his head in dismay as he backed to within a foot of the barn wall. He put the Ford in park and Daniel came up to help Sarah with her gear.

"I'll get this," Daniel said, grabbing her pack. "Go and meet your horse," he said.

Doc waited a few minutes before asking, "How will she know which one is hers?"

"Oh, shit," Daniel said, realizing how dangerous Revelation was to strangers.

Daniel took off in a sprint to the stable with Doc following as best he could. What they saw upon reaching the stable defied belief. Sarah stood next to the white stallion wrapping her arms around his neck as the horse bobbed its head.

"He's beautiful. Is this one mine?" she asked, almost giggling.

"Looks that way, don't it?" Doc whispered to Daniel.

Daniel was speechless. Until this night Daniel was the only man Revelation had responded to.

"Actually, I have you set up on that horse over there," he said, pointing to an old paint. "Her name is Bailey."

"Oh, well, your loss, my friend," she said, patting Revelation's mane as she walked out of the stall.

As Doc came around the stall with his horse, Sarah couldn't help but notice the dead deer draped in front of the saddle.

"Looks like you two got started without me," she said.

"What her? She's tomorrow night's dinner, that's all," Doc said.

The three hunters mounted up and began the slow trek up the hills under the gibbous moon. The forest was quiet and still. It took an hour to reach their camp which was marked by an old cowboy boot and spool of barbed wire nailed to a tree. It had been a quiet ride but Sarah relished the silence of the woods.

"Here we are," Daniel said as he dismounted his horse.

Doc rode over to a meat pole where he dumped the limp deer to the ground. Sitting in an open meadow were three white canvas-wall tents. Daniel helped Sarah down and then began lighting the cylinder stoves in each tent.

"What can I do?" she asked.

"How about getting a fire started in the pit over there?"

She loved building fires and made her way over. The fire pit was not the normal metal fire ring one might find in a campground. The rocks were arranged in a "keyhole," pattern which was ideal for cooking. As the fire burned in the circular area, coals could be moved to the rectangular end for cooking. It was a traditional cowboy set-up, she thought. A spit and tripod sat over the cooking end and Sarah thought about the pulled pork dinner she had missed at Manny's.

Doc made quick work of skinning the deer and by the time he made it back to the others the camp was roaring back to life. Sarah's gear was placed in a comfortable 10'x12' tent while Doc and Daniel shared a slightly bigger one adjacent to hers. The cook tent was 14'x16' which held a dinner table, camp kitchen, and supplies. The three tents were arranged in a triangle creating a kind of courtyard between them. "So what's for dinner?" Sarah asked.

"We're having elk loins in a molasses glaze with garlic mashed potatoes and a fresh Caesar salad."

"You two really rough it up here, don't you?" she joked.

"Nothing in the rules says you can't have a nice meal in camp. Frankly, I never did take to beans and hotdogs," Doc said. "Now the kid here . . . he'll eat the ass end out of a dead rhino if need be."

"I'd prefer elk and potatoes any day," Daniel said, brushing off the comment.

After dinner the three sat around the fire engaged in simple but nice conversation. The roaring fire was their one ally against the approaching storm front.

Sarah asked a lot of questions about the terrain and Doc was happy to impart his knowledge of the ranch. But there was something about his demeanor which told her he was still uneasy.

Doc pulled out a hefty cigar and chewed on the end, never lighting it. "So I understand this son of a bitch paid you a visit the other night."

The question took her by surprise. "That's right, he came to my house."

"Left you a note, too, I hear," he said, spitting into the fire.

"Yeah, he did."

"What did it say?" The flickering flames cast an eerie light on the old man's wrinkled face.

"'Sorry I missed you on Monarch.'"

"Was that it?"

Sarah got the distinct feeling he already knew the answers to these questions. "No. There was a tuft of old man's beard in the envelope, too."

"What do you think that was all about?" Doc asked innocently.

"I was holding a tuft of it when he shot at me that night on the pass." The images and sounds of that night began rushing through her mind.

"And he hasn't been back since?" he asked, raising his head now to meet her gaze.

"No."

"You sure?"

"What is this about, Doc? You're starting to freak me out."

"You should be freaked out. He's hunting you."

"What?"

"He's hunting you," he said with finality, staring her dead in the eye.

Sarah didn't know where this conversation was going. "Why do you say that?"

"Doc," Daniel said. "Why don't you tell her?"

"Tell me what?"

With a deep sigh, Doc continued. "I've seen this kind of guy before. A long time ago."

Sarah realized in an instant that the uneasiness he displayed earlier was trepidation for the story he was about to tell.

"You used to be a cop?" she asked, already knowing the answer.

"Of sorts, more like you but we didn't have fancy titles." Doc shifted his seat and stared into the flames as he relived the evil tale he was unable to vanquish from his memory. "It was the summer of forty-seven. I was an old soldier in a young man's body and like a lot of guys back from the war I went into law enforcement. Seemed like the right fit, ya know?" Sarah nodded. "Anyway, I was pretty green when it came to investigations. In the war, if you saw a bad guy you just shot the mangy dog. Weren't nothing real complex about it. Back in the states, we had rules and such we had to follow. Mostly it wasn't a real problem—the criminals back then were not the same as they are today. Back then they expected a beating. Just the way it was, I guess. Weren't no Miranda back then," he said. "Everything changed that summer." His eyes took on a distant stare and Sarah could see his pain even through the roaring flames.

"What changed, Doc?" she asked.

"The face of evil," he said. "That was the year I met Dorothy Dickenson."

"And Dorothy was evil?" Sarah asked, confused.

"What? No, no, I'm getting ahead of myself. It was June twenty-sixth in the town of Leadville. Well, the outskirts, actually. Old man Taggert came riding into town like he was on fire. He was sweating and he had blood on his hands. He face was white as a ghost. 'Bout took the office door off the hinges when he barged in yelling that he found his daughter dead inside the stable. Lizzy Mae," he said as a tear welled in his eye. "She was just fifteen when she was murdered. Old man Taggart had been herding cattle for three days with his boys about ten miles to the west. Wasn't nothing in those days to leave the young ones behind to look after the place. When he came back though he found a sight I wouldn't wish on any father."

Sarah saw Daniel's cool composure as he gazed into the fire. "What did he find?"

"Me and Jed, another deputy, headed out to Taggert's ranch and found her in the stable just like the father said. I never saw anything like it. Not even in the war." His eyes were distant and cold. "Lizzy Mae had been raped, real bad. 'Foreign object insertion,' I believe you call it these days. An old billhook, nasty sickle-shaped tool," he said, making the shape with his fingers. "It was covered in blood. She was naked, dressed in tack, and suspended from the rafters in the barn."

"Tack? You mean horse tack?" Sarah asked.

"Yep, the bridal, snaffle bit, even a saddle. Son of a bitch made the bridal from barbed wire. She had welts all over her backside from the crop," he said, shaking his head. "Looked to us like he had her tied up for at least a day while he violated her. Found evidence of several cooked meals in the kitchen where he took his breaks."

"Jesus," Sarah said.

"That ain't the half of it," he said.

Doc seemed reluctant to go on until Daniel spoke up. "Go on, Doc, tell her the rest."

"We never could figure out how long she'd suffered, but in the end he field dressed her. Did it while she was still alive, according to Doc Winters."

"My god, gutted her alive? What kind of man would do such a thing?" Sarah asked.

"A monster," Daniel answered.

"A monster . . . right," Doc repeated gazing far off into the flames of the fire.

"The tack was hers; belonged to her horse, Mischief. I don't know about nowadays but back then there wasn't nothin' coming between a girl and her horse. It was almost a love affair, but not in a sexual way, mind you. It was a bond as strong as a mother has with her daughter. Now I don't know if he killed the horse first or last but based on where the body lay I'd say he did it in front of her so she could watch."

Sarah had never heard such a horrible story and tried imagining what it must have been like to watch her best friend killed right in front of her. Sarah knew that evil existed in the world but most murders were the result of drunken arguments or petty jealousy. The motives and intentions were seldom complex.

It was a disturbing tale of murder and suffering but Sarah failed to see what Doc was getting at.

"That's a horrible story, Doc, but what does that have to do with the Monarch Pass killer?"

"Sarah, I'm just getting started here," he said. He couldn't seem to get the words out of his mouth. He hadn't told the whole story in years and it was becoming much harder with each passing word. "You need to tell her, Doc," Daniel said.

"What? Was there something else?" Sarah asked

"Yes . . . there was."

"What?"

"Her hair smelled like bleach."

29

Sarah was dumbfounded by the revelation.

"I hadn't thought of it in years but when I saw those pictures of the woman on the pass I knew I'd seen it before."

"Seen what?" Sarah asked.

"Those red marks on her body. That line that looked like rubbed skin or how a ligature might look on other parts of the body."

"Are you saying it was bleach?"

"Yes, ma'am," he said, staring up at the moon. "I am."

"How does it work?" she asked.

"Just like it does on living tissue. You know, like when a kid accidentally drinks bleach and it burns their esophagus?"

"Yeah, I've read about that but never actually seen it."

"Well, you have now," Doc said, reminding her of the woman on the pass.

"So you saw the same type of red marks on your victim, Lizzy Mae?"

Doc sat motionless, staring into the flames of the fire. He turned to their picketed horses as Revelation let out a neigh. Even the horse could sense the foreboding story to come.

"Vic-*tims*," he said. "There were at least four of them before we caught the son of a bitch."

"You caught the guy? Who was he?" she asked, engrossed in the story.

"His name was Roger Everett, but I don't know who he really was."

"You mean he was using a false identity?" she asked.

Doc looked up surprised at the comment. "No, that was his given name all right, but I didn't recognize his nature as having anything in common with the humanity I knew of," he said sounding philosophical.

"He's a cancer," Daniel offered, stoking the burning embers once more.

"Yeah, I guess so. Since then I've seen that cancer growing in our society. Debasement, narcissism, and an abandonment of the golden rule infecting souls and spreading like crabgrass throughout our culture. Criminals mock our laws and show utter contempt toward a society that indulges their true nature." He stoked the fire. "In my day, people treated one another with respect. You didn't lock your door. You never feared a neighbor might steal your livelihood because people had respect for one another and more importantly, for themselves. Today, most of us don't even know who their neighbors are, as people. Parents didn't used to excuse and defend their children's bad deeds. Somewhere along the line the seeds of cultural destruction got sown and continue to grow out of control."

Pretty deep, Doc, Sarah thought, but didn't dare say. Sarah could see the pain seeping from the old man's soul. He didn't understand the world around him and yearned for a day long gone that might never return. "How did you catch him?"

"Who, Everett? Oh, he was a ranch hand in the next county over. For a while we had no idea who it was. Lizzy Mae was missing one of her socks. It was Canary yellow with embroidered flowers and fringe. Her mother had made them by hand as a Christmas gift and they were quite distinctive. We always figured he wiped his hands with it or kept it as a souvenir. Then the second girl, Joann Coberly, was killed about a month later. She was a sweet young girl with a sterling reputation around town. I remember she used to skip down the sidewalks with tight little pigtails in her hair. Blue ribbon . . . that's what I remember most. She always wore blue ribbons in her hair. She always had a smile and nice word for a stranger. Needless to say the community was fit to be tied after her murder. The locals formed a lynch mob but we managed to quell the emotion before some innocent person got strung up from a cottonwood."

"She was killed the same way as the other girl?" Sarah asked.

"Worse." His gaze sent a chill through Sarah's body. "He took a lot longer that time; much more brutal. Her folks were gone on a roundup and left her older brother in charge. Of course everyone in town was on edge about Lizzy Mae but the sixteen-year-old brother didn't know the details. It wasn't something parents talked about with their kids. He decided to go to the lake with friends asking an elderly neighbor to check in on Joann from time to time. He never did forgive himself for that decision. He hung himself about three weeks later."

"What made it worse?" Sarah asked, trying to imagine a scene worse than the one she'd already heard of.

"Oh, it doesn't matter, Sarah," he said, not wanting to go into the details. "What matters is how I acted during the thing."

"What do you mean?"

"We started looking for similarities between the two girls. Back then people's lives were much simpler so it didn't take long to notice the connection. At each crime scene there were new bales of Timothy hay stacked in the hay shed."

"What's Timothy hay?" Sarah asked.

"It's just a higher grade of hay grown for horses. You can feed it to cattle but most people don't because it costs a lot more. So we tracked down the shipments to a rancher in the next county and started poking around. At first, we thought he might just be a witness, you know? Help us with the time line. But as we started talking to the old man he said he had taken on a new ranch hand in the spring that was causing him consternation."

"What did he do?" Sarah asked, hanging on his every word.

"Apparently, he had quite the temper. The rancher would find him beating the animals for no reason at all. Everett was some kind of dandy, too."

"A what?" Daniel asked.

"My god, don't they teach English in schools anymore?" Doc exclaimed.

Daniel smiled at him and looked down at the fire, stirring the embers.

"You know, a dandy. What do you call them now? Metrosexuals or some such. Everett was obsessed with his appearance. The rancher says he'd change his shirt if it got the tiniest spot on it."

"That must have been pretty often working on a ranch," Sarah observed.

"You ain't kidding. The rancher said he might change his shirt eight-ten times a day. The rancher's wife also told us that she had caught him staring at her often and it made her feel very uncomfortable."

"She's lucky to be alive," Sarah said.

"Well, that place was his bread and butter. He wasn't about to do anything to get tossed out on his butt, although I'm sure he thought about it. She was in her forties and looked to be in her sixties after a hard ranching life. I guess she was just too old for his taste," he said, spitting another wad of tobacco juice into the flickering flames. "Well, we didn't have anything concrete to go on so we started watching him. We searched his room for the sock, but didn't find it. The rancher told us where his deliveries would be going and we checked out the ones with young girls in the home. It didn't take long.

"There was a poor family down the valley toward Twin Lakes. They didn't have much, just a shanty of a shack to live in. But they had a plow horse and a fourteen-year-old daughter, Emma. Everett owed the man some money from gambling and said he'd pay in feed. The daughter was a real wild rube. Crazy as a coyote under the full moon, that one. She didn't come into town much and most folks just ignored her when she did.

"We were about a ridge over to the west, watching him with our pocket scopes—you call them monoculars," he said, looking at Daniel. "We had to keep a fair piece away from him so he couldn't see us.

"At first we thought everything would be fine because the girl ran off to the river while Everett was pulling up to deliver the hay. He must have been watching her, though. Hell, he may have even fixated on her in town, for all we know. Anyway, mom and dad were busy in carnal discussions, as it were, which is probably why the young girl ran to the river. We always suspected the father took turns with her, too, but could never prove it. Well, old Everett must have heard their raucous tryst because he hung out by the window for a few minutes then headed off in a trot toward the river with a lariat in hand." Doc threw out his tobacco and pulled out a small flask, offering it first to Daniel.

"It took us a few minutes to get down there, even on horseback. God, it felt like an eternity. I couldn't get the images of the other two girls out of my head." Sarah could hear his voice tremble. "We got there just short of too late. Apparently, she had gone down to the river for a swim. She was naked as a jay-bird. She had piled her clothes under a big ol' cottonwood that shaded the whole river from the hot summer sun. Everett tried convincing her of his intentions through charm and when that didn't work he roped her like a calf. When we rode up he had that rope tight around her neck and was slapping her hard with his open hand."

"My god, what did you do?" Sarah asked.

"I froze . . . that's what I did." He was ashamed. "I raised my Winchester rifle and leveled the bead on his head as I called out his name. 'Roger Everett! Stop right there and let her go.' That 45-60 bullet would have put a hole in him the size of a melon. He dropped the rope and took off at a run through the trees. I followed him with my rifle for a good hundred yards but I couldn't pull the trigger. God as my witness, I just couldn't do it. Jed had gotten off his horse and was tending to the girl. I guess he thought I would take the shot, too," he said, looking confused.

"Hey, Doc, I'm sure that was really hard on you, but you saved the girl. That's gotta count for a hell of a lot," Sarah said, trying to console him.

"No . . . I killed her." Doc saw the horrified look enveloping Sarah. "I may not have pulled the trigger but I killed her just the same. You see . . . he got away. Then later, he came back to finish what he'd started. Even more brutal. Emma put up a good fight and she paid a heavy price for it. We found her three days later hanging from that same cottonwood. He killed another girl in the valley before we finally trapped him in an abandoned cabin up in California Gulch. I should have burned the place down with him in it but the sheriff wanted a trial."

"I've never heard that story before," Sarah admitted.

"I'm not surprised. The whole thing was covered up and the trial was a joke. Turns out Everett was the nephew by marriage to a former Denver mayor. He wasn't in office anymore but still had a reputation to protect, and he had money. The mining barons and politicians paid off the rancher and intimidated the rest. The local press followed suit and said the police were incompetent and trying to frame an innocent man. We thought for sure the bastard was going to get off. You should have seen him in court. Fancy suit and a clean-shaven face to show off his smug smile. Makes me sick just to think about it."

"So he got off?" Sarah asked.

"In a manner of speaking. We found him hanging in his cell the day before closing arguments with Lizzy Mae's missing yellow sock draped over his genitals. I guess the pressure got to be too much for him or something," he said, pondering the old mystery.

"How on earth did he get that sock in his jail cell?" she asked.

"We always figured his lawyer brought it to him or one of the family members paying the bills."

"He doesn't sound like the type of guy who would hang himself just as the trial was winding down. Especially if he was getting a rigged trial in his favor," Sarah said.

"I think you're missing the point, Sarah," Daniel said from his quiet post at the outside of the fire light.

"Which is?" she said.

"Everett was a killing machine, plain and simple. His empty soul could never be filled, no matter how many women he slaughtered."

"The only way to stop a man like that is with a gun," Doc said. He leaned forward as if to make a point to the young criminalist. "If I had just shot him that day on the river those two girls would still be alive today. God knows how many more girls would have met the same fate had he been set free."

Sarah knew there was a greater point she was missing. "Doc, all that aside, what are you getting at?"

Doc glanced at Daniel and took deep breath. "I see the same traits in your killer," he said. "Frankly, I'm afraid for you. He's stalking you, hunting you. Knowing that, you need to be very aware of your surroundings. He won't go away until you're dead," he said as she gazed into the fire. "When he finally does show himself you need to put him down. You cannot hesitate. You cannot reason with him or ask for his surrender"

Sarah didn't know what to say.

"Do you understand?" Doc asked, staring her straight in the eye.

It was more than a question, she thought. He was asking for a commitment, a promise. She wasn't sure she could keep such a promise.

"We're just trying to keep you safe, Sarah," Daniel said.

Sarah looked at them, nodding in agreement. Several minutes of silence followed until Doc finally spoke up.

"Well, I think I should hit the rack. I'm not as young as I used to be," Doc's bones creaked as he rose and hobbled into the trees to relieve himself before bed.

30

Daniel moved around the fire pit and sat close to Sarah.

"That was quite a story."

"It's not easy for him to talk about his past. I think he carries a lot of pain inside. He doesn't even tell me that much and we're close. His past is comprised of secrets stacked upon secrets," Daniel said.

The irony didn't escape her. Sarah stared up at the constellations, pondering Doc's story.

"What are you thinking about?" Daniel asked.

"I'm just wondering if I would have taken that shot. The one by the river."

"Well, you shot at him before, didn't you?" Daniel asked, speaking of the events on Monarch Pass.

"I guess so," Daniel was overwhelmed by her beauty in the soft firelight. He loved how the small freckles dotted her face and her curly hair graced her slender shoulders, cascading toward her supple breasts. Her smile was so inviting and he longed to kiss her lips. The firelight cast a romantic glow that even Sarah was aware of. Just then a shooting star streaked across the night's sky.

"Look . . . a shooting star!" Sarah said.

"You know legend says if you wish upon a shooting star the wish will come true." Daniel said. He was pleased to see her smile as she closed her eyes while squeezing his hand.

"Do you know much about the stars?" Sarah asked.

"Yeah, a bit."

"What's that one up there?"

"That's Andromeda."

"Sounds Greek."

"That's right. Andromeda was the daughter of Cassiopeia, who claimed to the gods that her daughter was more beautiful than Nereid's, Poseidon's daughter. Angered by the claim, Poseidon flooded the lands and sent a sea monster to kill Andromeda, whose parents offered her up for sacrifice to appease the gods."

"So this beautiful young woman gets sacrificed by her parents to a monster, eh? Sounds familiar."

"What do you mean?" he asked, chuckling.

"Never mind. So what happened to Andromeda?"

"Oh, well, a hero named Perseus, the mortal son of Zeus, happened upon Andromeda chained to a rock by the ocean and killed the sea monster."

"Saved by her knight in shining armor?"

"Something like that," he said, smiling at her.

Sarah wondered if she would ever meet such a man. She hoped she was sitting with him now.

Daniel reached over and grabbed her hand. "C'mon, I want to show you something." They walked over to the camp table and Daniel pulled out a spotting scope and mounted it to a small tripod. The 20x60 Swarovski scope was aimed at the partial moon. He adjusted the focus. "Take a look."

Sarah was dazzled by the lunar surface. "That is amazing."

"Yeah, you see an awful lot more detail away from the city lights. You see that lone crater above that larger area above those three bigger craters?"

"Yeah, I see it."

"That's called Mare Crisium."

"Pretty knowledgeable for a mechanic."

If the comment bothered him he didn't show it. "Sometimes when I was out alone I'd stare up at the moon and fixate on that crater. It reminded me of home and no matter how far away I was I didn't feel alone anymore."

He's a softie, she thought.

"Now look to the edge of the horizon."

"Okay."

"Look just into the darkness."

"Oh, cool, the craters look like halos," she said.

"Yeah, as the moon orbits the earth and the edge is plunged into darkness there is a brief moment when the sunlight only hits the upper part of the craters, giving them a halo appearance."

"We use the same technique when photographing shoe and tire impressions. It's called oblique lighting."

"You see, we both learned something tonight," he said.

A light snow began falling.

"I just love it up here, don't you?" he asked.

"It is peaceful."

"It's not just that. When I'm here I feel like I'm safe from the world. Like nothing bad can ever happen."

"You're so lucky to live here full time."

"Tell me about it. I don't know what I would have done if it wasn't for Uncle Art."

"So why did you leave the Army, Daniel?" The question had been biting at her for weeks and she figured asking him now was as good a time as any.

It took him by surprise. He knew that the issue would come up sooner or later but he had hoped it would be later. "It was just time for me to move on."

"No, you don't get off that easy. What does it was 'just time to move on' mean?"

He sighed and paused, knowing she wouldn't let the issue drop. "It means that war ain't pretty. Even on base we got shelled every day or two. There were snipers, IED bombs, and friends who came back from patrols with missing limbs . . . if they came back at all. I guess I just got burned out," he confessed. It wasn't a total lie, he told himself.

31

Reggie Winters was angry at the world. The school counselor called him as an under-achiever but the truth was that he was just lazy. His role models were thugs pretending to be musicians who glamorized the gangster life of doing drugs, objectifying women, and displaying a general disrespect for everyone. Instead of acknowledging his own failures in life he blamed others, convincing himself that society owed him. It was the type of mindset that most criminals used to justify their crimes.

He was perpetually unemployed. It was easier living off government checks. If he needed a score, Reggie and his friends would mug a woman in some parking lot or beat up a homeless man for his daily take. The sniper killings had presented him with a rare opportunity to settle an old score. A rival tagger had been covering his monikers around town and won the brief lust of a girl they were both competing for. It was the ultimate form of disrespect and required the ultimate response.

To his way of thinking, his rival's actions were a direct challenge to his manhood. The only way to respond was with decisive violence. It seemed so simple to him. The previous night he'd painted his Dope moniker in chartreuse green letters on a wall commonly visited by his rival, Spider. Then he spent all day bragging on the street about the bold move and Spider's timidity to respond. It was like putting cheese on the mousetrap.

Now he waited. The thought occurred to him, hiding behind a dumpster, that by tagging the wall he had exposed himself to the real killer. The brief exposure was well worth the risk if all went according to plan. The one wild card factor would be if Spider came alone or in a group.

He was beginning to wonder if his rival would ever show as he watched the moon arch past its apex. Reggie was missing a small party that presented the possibility of hooking up with some junior high school girls that were too young and naïve to resist his charm. It was just after one AM when he saw the dark figure approaching. He recognized the distinctive gait as that of his prey.

The dark form was carrying something in his right hand that Reggie hoped was a can of spray paint. Spider was known to carry a knife, but no one had ever seen him with a gun; it was a fatal move he'd soon regret.

As the figure loomed closer Reggie pulled his Kel-Tec P32 pistol and readied himself. He had never shot anyone before but he'd done it plenty of times on his Xbox. How hard can it be?

Reggie let him get about halfway through the ugly glyph before making his move. He could have shot him in the back but he wanted Spider to know who had won the rivalry once and for all.

"Yo, Bug! It's time for your extermination!"

The voice startled Spider and he spun around. To his horror he saw the flash of the muzzle a split second after recognizing the face of his nemesis. The 88-grain .32 caliber bullet spat from the barrel. Reggie kept firing one after another at the scum who had caused him so much consternation.

He fired without aiming, holding the gun sideways like the real gangstas on television. It sure looked cool but the orientation was very inaccurate, especially in the hands of a moron. The first two bullets struck Spider in the right arm and shoulder. The third and fourth missed him completely, striking the wall behind. Reggie saw the brick dust popping behind his foe and adjusted his aim. Reggie was still closing the distance. The fifth bullet found its mark, passing between Spider's ribs, through his left lung, and penetrating the pericardium of Spider's heart before coming to rest. Death wasn't instantaneous, but the Reaper had been paged. Spider collapsed to the sidewalk, dropping his can of spray paint with a sharp clank. He moaned while writhing on the ground.

Reggie put the small gun to Spider's head for the final *coup de grâce*. Click . . . "Shit!" he screeched. Reggie jerked the trigger three more times before seeing that a spent cartridge was lodged in the action—the malfunction was known as a "stove pipe." Panicked, he yanked back on the slide twice to clear the obstruction, freeing the bent casing to fall to the ground and sending a live round following close behind.

A stream of frothy blood began erupting from his nose and mouth as Spider pleaded for his life. Reggie lowered the muzzle one last time and pressed it hard against the dying man's forehead. With a simple pull of the trigger, he sent the weapon's final round through the frontal lobe of his brain.

The rivalry was over.

Reggie stared into Spider's eyes as Spider's life-force fled with his last gargled breath. Even after Spider's cold heart stopped beating, his body twitched from muscle spasm. Once the reality of the moment set in, Reggie ran from the scene like the coward he was.

32

Sarah awoke to find a foot of snow against the canvas walls. Unlike many of the lightweight tents sold at yuppie camping stores, her canvas wall tent was very well insulated and got warmer with deep snow against the walls.

Doc was already up, warming a coffee pot on the kitchen stove and making hoe cakes to compliment the elk breakfast burritos he'd brought.

"Morning, Doc, how'd you sleep?" Sarah asked.

"At my age, I'm more concerned with getting up than with sleeping," he joked.

"Is Daniel up?"

"I'm not sure he ever came to bed. Sometimes when he's got something on his mind he doesn't sleep. His tracks head out of camp, so I'm guessing he's checking on the horses or doing some quick scouting. Grab a chair, I'll pour you a cup," he said, pulling the stainless steel pot from the hot stovetop. "I'm sorry if I was a bit out of line with you last night."

"It's fine, really. I've seen this guy's handiwork and I know what I need to do if he comes after me."

"*When* he comes after you."

"Morning, sunshine. You ready to head out?" Daniel sang as he walked past the tent flap.

"Here, take a few burritos and some hoe cakes," Doc said, gathering them up in a cloth napkin. "You're not coming with us?" she asked.

"Naw, let's see if the kid here can find 'em on his own," Doc joked.

"It shouldn't be that hard to track them with a foot of snow on the ground, Doc," he said.

"Well, get going . . . early bird gets the worm, you know."

"Do I need some snow shoes?" Sarah asked as the two walked out of the tent.

"Nope, we're going by horseback, then we'll dismount and make our way on foot. I've checked out some areas already and the walking should be pretty easy."

The Scent of Fear

As Sarah reached her horse, Daniel caught her arm. "I thought you might like riding Revelation."

"Great!"

They spent the next few hours riding and sharing stories. Mostly they talked about her. She shared gory details of her job and stories from the office as Daniel listened while forging a trail through the snow.

Truth be told, he'd listen to her read from a phone book. Sarah looked elegant on the white mustang, her pale skin pure like the snow, her beautiful chestnut hair peeking out of a knit cap. It was like something out of a fairy tale, he thought.

Sarah felt something special, too. Like a lot of people in her profession, Sarah put up a protective barrier with most of the people she met. But with Daniel something was different. He had a natural, disarming nature that Sarah responded to.

Daniel kept the horses moving in a line just inside the Aspen trees along the edge of a snow-covered meadow. They noted fresh gnaw marks in the delicate tree bark, proving the elk had been in the area. Daniel stopped his horse and Sarah pulled Revelation up alongside so the riders were abreast.

"There," he whispered, pointing to the trees on the other side of the meadow.

Sarah lifted her binoculars and spied-out the area. "I see them."

"Let's move in from the south," Daniel said, making a hand gesture.

The two dismounted and made a slow trek to flank their prey's position. They made it to some downed logs that provided good concealment and offered a steady platform to shoot from. Then they waited. As the sun warmed the valley the elk made their way along the edge of the field feeding on the buried grasses below the snowfall.

"Anytime you're ready," Daniel told her.

She selected a nice-sized cow and laid the old Winchester rifle across a log. She was lying flat on the ground and Daniel couldn't help notice her sexy form. Daniel put his own binoculars up and tried concentrating on the elk.

"Which one are you aiming for?" he asked.

Tom Adair

"You see that group of five on the right? Last one in line."

"They're moving away from you right now. Might not be the best shot to take," he said, ranging the shot at 234 meters.

"For you, maybe," she said, feeling very confident. Her finger eased the trigger backward until the separation of the sear sent the firing pin plunging into the primer. The 150-grain bullet rocketed on an arched trajectory from the old, worn barrel, striking the cow in the back of the head between the ears. Sarah watched the mighty animal fold in her scope.

"Holy shit!" Daniel muttered. "Did you mean to do that?"

"Hey, I'm not just another pretty face, you know."

Truer words have never been spoken, he thought.

The herd scattered to the north as the report echoed through the trees.

"Not bad for a ninety-one-year-old rifle, huh?"

"In my experience it ain't the gun . . . it's the shooter."

After an hour of field dressing, they continued in their pursuit of the herd. Tracking the stampeding elk was like following a marching band through the snow. They came upon the herd two ridges over from where they started.

"This looks like a good spot," Daniel said.

"Here? Don't you want to get a bit closer?"

"Yeah, I thought we'd hike down this game trail and use the trees and slope to our advantage," he said, pulling his rifle from the leather scabbard.

"How far away is the herd?"

Placing his laser range finder over his eye, he said, "Looks to be about seven hundred-fifteen meters to the small group near the center."

"Hey, I have an idea. Wanna make this interesting?"

"What do you mean . . . a wager?"

"Yeah."

"For what?"

"I'll bet you that you can't make the shot from here," Sarah said, throwing down the challenge.

Daniel studied the herd below. "What are we betting on?"

"Let's see . . . if you win you get to take me out for a nice dinner with some dancing."

"Boy . . . that sounds fair. What if I miss?"

"Then I get to ask you anything."

230

"And I have to answer?"

"Of course you do, silly."

"Sounds like a win-win for me." Daniel again looked at the elk below, considering the shot. "All right, you've got a deal."

Daniel unsheathed his Barrett 98Bravo and laid it out on extended bipod legs, taking a prone position in the snow. After getting comfortable, he flipped open the plastic scope cover and adjusted the high-priced optics. With his breathing controlled, he began timing the shot. His finger was just pulling the trigger back when Sarah interrupted his train of thought.

"So have you ever been married?" she asked, hoping it would spoil his concentration.

"No."

"Do you have any children?"

"You realize I haven't lost the bet yet, right?" he asked, looking up and smiling at her.

"Oh, right, you need to concentrate . . . sorry," she said, smiling back.

I better not miss this shot, he thought.

Jason had been Kimberley's on-again off-again boyfriend for the past two years. It was a volatile relationship at best. He disliked her shift rotations in the dispatch center and often pressured her to take a day job somewhere. He had his own apartment but he often crashed at Kim's meager house for days on end. Most of Kim's friends considered him a lying moocher. Kim had caught him in bed with one of his co-workers almost a year ago but took him back on a provisional basis. Since that time he just got better at hiding his promiscuity. He never helped around the house or offered to pay her bills. Kim's neighbors grew to hate Jason but never confronted the perky dispatcher who was always baking for them.

On this mild Sunday afternoon, he decided to use her driveway to change his oil. His 1965 Chevrolet El Camino had numerous patches of Bondo which had never been painted. The one thing of value on the wreck was the new Konig wheels he'd paid for with her credit card. Drinking Kim's last beer, he jacked up the front end to gain access to the oil pan below. The vehicle frame rested precariously on a battered and unstable 3.5 ton floor jack. Jason never used stabilizer jacks, thinking they were unnecessary. He flattened himself on an old wooden mechanic's creeper and slid under the heap while rap music blared from his boom box. The rusty undercarriage was coated with a heavy layer of grime and dirt. The dangling exhaust pipe was a reminder to get more bailing wire.

Even the killer could tell Jason was an asshole. He had become an unwelcome obstacle to the killer's plans. He'd watched Kim for several weeks and found the boyfriend's unannounced visits troubling. Jason would cause problems if he showed up at an inopportune time. He looked around the area for witnesses, grateful that the deep bass thumps masked his approach. The horrid music—a lurid and unoriginal rant of debauchery that just happened to rhyme—violated the otherwise peaceful neighborhood. That alone was justification for his death in the killer's mind.

He approached from the vehicle's rear, hugging a fence along the side of the driveway. He saw Jason's feet tapping to the vulgar sounds as he rounded the hood. This punk made it all too easy, he thought. Jason never saw the killer twist the jack handle but he sure felt the full weight of the car as it came crashing down on him. Were it not for the elevated creeper he might have survived. His chest was compressed to one tenth its normal capacity as the air was pushed from his lungs. Even if he could have screamed no one would have heard him over the boom box.

The killer was two blocks away, whistling a show tune from the play *Girl Crazy* when an elderly woman walking her dog stopped him.

"Oh, my, isn't that a lovely tune? I know that I've heard it before somewhere. What's it called?"

"It's Gershwin's 'Bidin' my time,'" the killer answered as he continued around the corner to his car.

33

It was dinner time at the Manilow residence when Lester called in his report.

"L.T., I think we may have something here," he said.

"Hold on a second," Manilow said as he excused himself from the dinner table. "You didn't phone in yesterday," he complained.

"I know, my battery died in the cold and I didn't want to leave my position to go back to my room," he said.

"Cut to the chase, Sergeant."

"I have two very interesting things to report. First, Sarah Richards went out hunting with Daniel Von Hollen and they stayed in the same camp for two nights with some old guy."

"Did they sleep in the same tent?"

"Not that I could tell, but they were very touchy-feely. Saturday morning I heard a rifle shot in the distance and seeing that the horses were gone I started to tail them from the next ridge over. It wasn't easy catching up to them with all this snow on the ground."

"I thought you were an ex-Marine."

Veteran Marine, asshole. "Yes, sir, I did catch up to them. This guy Daniel made an amazing shot on an elk."

There was a pause while Lester let Manilow absorb the information.

"That's it? He made an amazing shot?"

"Sir, let me explain. He made a head shot on a moving elk from six- maybe seven-hundred yards away. Put the bullet right in the back of the head."

"Is that so?" the wheels were now turning.

"Yes, sir, never seen anything like it. Now a trained Marine sniper could make that shot but a mechanic? I don't see how that's possible."

"Interesting. Are you still watching them?" "Yes sir, I'm going to stay on him. Maybe we'll get lucky."

"All right, but be careful. This guy is a killer," he said, already convinced of Daniel's guilt.

"Wilco, sir."

"How's that?"

Lester rolled his eyes. "I will."

It was 6:32 PM Sunday evening when the Gulfstream G150 touched down on the concrete runway at Hayden Airport west of Steamboat Springs. Fields of snow stretched as far as the eye could see as the jet-lagged passengers peered out foggy windows from their soft leather seats. The flight was smooth with almost no turbulence. Dr. Reginald James Huxley and his assistant Jared exited the plane feeling a bit like royalty. They had never been treated to such luxuries. Dr. Huxley was the director of forensic studies at the University of Connecticut at New Haven. Although a native of England he had been in the United States following his retirement from the Metropolitan Police a decade earlier. England was still his home though.

With Jared in tow, Dr. Huxley descended the air stairs with the grace of a prince. He walked with a long, black cane, not because he needed it, but because it added to his image. Jared followed him across the tarmac to the light-blue-colored terminal while tugging at the heavy suitcases with the tenacity of a sled dog. A young male intern stood inside the warm terminal building with a small cardboard sign bearing the good doctor's name. It was totally unnecessary but Art knew Dr. Huxley would relish the status it conveyed.

"Well, there, lad, I suppose you're to be our driver?" Dr. Huxley waxed in a heavy Welsh accent.

"Yes, sir, Dr. Huxley."

"Would you be so kind to help my assistant Jared there with the baggage?" he asked.

"Right away, sir, I mean, Dr. Huxley."

The young intern scurried over to help the burdened man, who in return dropped all the bags on the terminal floor catching up with his ungrateful mentor. The pompous pair waited impatiently as the young man struggled with the baggage into the parking lot. Stopping at a black SUV, the intern popped the cargo door and began lifting the heavy bags without so much as a finger of help from his guests. Once inside the comfortable Suburban,

Dr. Huxley lit an old pipe. Being English he had a fascination with the fictional character Sherlock Holmes and felt the pipe made him look sagacious.

Dr. Huxley had visited the Facility only once before. He had assumed upon its opening that a coveted teaching position would have been offered to him. When one never came, he developed a loathing for its founder and took great pride minimizing Von Hollen's accomplishments. He was convinced that Art was jealous of his status and didn't want to be upstaged in his own kingdom. The lie made the truth a more palatable pill to swallow.

"So what am I supposed to call you, lad?" he asked.

"Oh, I'm sorry, my name is Ed. Ed Stevens."

"Ed" he repeated. "How drab." He gazed out the windows at the deserted city streets.

Ed was too star-struck to notice the insult.

"What do you call this little village then?"

"Oh, this is Steamboat Springs. It's a super nice place with friendly locals and great activities."

"Quite. How fitting Art's Facility is settled among the Boer of this land."

Ed didn't know what he was referring to, trying instead to find the right moment to ask for an autograph. The uneventful ride ended outside the apartment Art had assigned the pair.

"Well, here we are," Ed announced.

Dr. Huxley gazed up at the tasteful, yet dorm-like dwelling, and began to protest. "Here? No, my good man, there must be some mistake."

"Ah, let me see," Ed said, fishing a piece of paper from his pocket. "Yes, this is the place we have assigned to you."

"Well, this simply will not do. Get me Dr. Von Hollen on the phone," he demanded.

Art was in a meeting with Tilly when the call came through. "It's okay, Ed, put him on. Dr. Huxley? I trust you had a pleasant flight. How can I help you?"

"I think there has been some mistake with regards to our accommodations."

"How's that, Reginald?" he said with a trace of annoyance.

"Well, it simply won't do, Art. First of all, a scientist of my status should be afforded one of the townhomes, and second, I cannot be expected to share a room with my intern. It's beneath a man of my stature."

"Well, the townhomes are reserved for instructors, you know that. I can get you another apartment, if that would suffice?"

"No, I don't believe it will. I was called in here to assist you with these killings on the recommendation of your attorney general, no less. I'm sure that he would expect me to be treated with some common courtesy, don't you?"

"Reginald, let me put you on hold while I check our availability list . . . hold on one sec," Art said, punching the hold button.

"Now we're getting somewhere," Huxley snorted to Jared.

Tilly rolled her eyes at the thought of the pompous prick making demands of them. "I guess the leer jet and shuttle service weren't enough," she said.

"I should have just hung up on him but in the spirit of cooperation, not to mention the promise I made the governor, let's try to accommodate him. What do we have available?" Art asked.

Tilly punched the keyboard and studied the colorful Excel table. She was a master organizer who kept the whole place running smoothly. Art couldn't help but notice the sly grin creeping across her lips.

"What is it?"

"Why don't we put him in Dr. Ingraham's town home?"

"Kind of a poke in the eye, isn't it?" Art asked.

"On the contrary, I think he would appreciate the connection to his forefathers," Tilly said with delight.

"God must really like me," he said, bringing the pompous Brit back on the line. "I have good news, Dr. Huxley. We have found a town home that is available for your stay. Unfortunately, it's just the one so I'm afraid your intern will have to settle for the apartment. I'm sorry we can't accommodate you both into the townhomes."

"That's quite all right. Jared will be fine here."

"May I speak to Ed, please?"

Huxley passed the cell phone with a gloating stare. After getting instructions, Ed drove the scientist to his new domicile on the edge of the complex.

"I'll bring your car over in a few minutes, Doctor, and leave the keys in the ignition."

"That will do nicely Ed," he stated with a thud.

A framed American flag bearing the original 13 stars of the colonies greeted him as he entered the foyer. Dr. Ingraham was a renowned geneticist who traced his family tree back to the Jamestown colony. A proud member of the Sons of the American Revolution, his townhome was awash in patriotic art, history books, and symbols of the American defeat of the British Empire. Dr. Huxley noted with amusement the colorful surroundings. *Touché*, Art . . . *touché*.

Daniel dropped Sarah off at her town home late Sunday evening after returning from camp. He opened her door, grabbed her small bag, and carried it to the front porch.

"Daniel, I had such a great time this weekend. Thank you so much for everything,"

"It was my pleasure. Doc's dropping the meat off at the restaurant and I suspect Art will have them do something special with it."

"Maybe you'd care to join me tomorrow night for dinner," she said with a smile.

"Uh, I don't know . . . let me check my schedule."

"Screw you," she said, punching his arm.

"Okay, Okay, I'm just kidding. I'd love to."

Sarah was dancing inside. "Great!" she said.

It was an awkward moment standing in the doorway, but Sarah was prepared to spend all night saying goodbye if need be.

Daniel wasn't sure what to do. He so wanted to kiss her but his conscious told him no. They hadn't even talked about dating, and his last relationship ended badly. He decided he'd try a hug. "Well, I guess this is goodnight," he said as he performed the most awkward hug of his life. He smiled at her and began to turn away.

Sarah grabbed his arm. She closed her eyes and leaned in to kiss him. At first the kiss was awkward but then all of the passion that had been bottled up inside was released. Holding her tight, he held her head in his hand while the two continued to kiss. "I think you should come inside," Sarah said.

She caught the hesitation in his eyes. "What?" she asked.

"I...I don't know"

"I do" she said lying to herself.

Daniel put his hands gently on her shoulders and pushed her back to arm's length. "Listen Sarah, I really like you". He sounded like a dipshit. "But I'm not sure you want to put all your eggs in my basket right now"

Sarah couldn't believe what she was hearing. She thought she had read all the signals. "I thought there was something between us" she confessed. "There is, there is...I just need some time to figure some things out"

"Fuck, you're married aren't you?"

"No! It's nothing like that."

"Then what?"

"I just want to go slow. I don't want to fuck this up".

It sounded good but Sarah didn't want to hear it. She put her hand to her head and pushed her hair back. "Fine".

"Look, don't be mad".

"I'm not mad, just confused"

Me too he thought.

"Look, let's not spoil an otherwise great day" she said. The disappointment was thick in her voice. As pretentious as it sounded, Sarah had never been rejected before. Sure, she had fallen for some real losers but she was the one to finally break it off.

"I swear, it's not you Sarah. I just have some things to work through first". Sarah smiled and hugged him as if to say it was alright. She had to admire his self control. After a final peck on the cheek he turned down the walkway. Watching him leave Sarah couldn't help but wonder. *What the hell are you hiding?*

34

John Simmons had worked sixteen uneventful years at the small tooling shop. The days were filled with grease, grime, and sweat, and the same monotonous work day after day. "CSI" was his favorite television show. At first he thought the crumpled mass next to the building might be a drunken bum. Then he saw the blood. He had never seen a real dead body before and he was transfixed for several seconds. He nudged the body with his foot. There was no response.

"Goddamn!" He felt the urge to study the scene for clues but his conscience got the better of him and he dialed 911.

Kim had fifteen minutes left in her double shift when the panicked call came in.

"Police? Yeah, I came to work and there's a real dead body here."

"Okay, sir, can I get your name, please?"

"Ah, it's John . . . John Simmons."

"You said there is a dead body. Are you sure that the person is dead?"

"Yeah, I know for sure. I shook him and he's dead, all right."

"Okay, Mr. Simmons, where are you calling from?"

"Uh, I'm at the Tyler Tooling Shop over here on old Hampden Road and Federal."

"All right, I have deputies on the way to you, sir. Just hold on. Now, do you know this person?"

"No, he looks like some kid. There's a can of spray paint here and a bunch of shell casings."

Kim recognized the significance of the call and had another dispatcher call Captain Karl Evans. "Okay, sir. I need you to stay on the line but don't touch anything at the scene, all right?"

"Yeah, I watch CSI all the time; I know what I'm doing."

If I had a dollar for every time I heard that one, Kim thought.

Sergeant Leonard Marshall was on his way to the office when his Nextel went off. Captain Evans' number appeared on the caller ID.

"Yes, sir, what can I do for you?"

"It looks like we've had another sniper shooting on the west side. I've sent detectives out but we'll need some lab techs, too," he said.

"I'll get right on it, sir."

He rang Sarah. No reply. He sent an alert tone. Still no reply. Then he remembered she was up at the Facility and cursed under his breath. He resented having to adjust his schedule for the task force assignment. Sarah was way too green to be selected for such an assignment. He had little confidence in her abilities and couldn't understand why anyone else would. He assumed it was because of her looks and figured Art was banging her. Why else would he help her career?

The patrol deputies had done a good job of securing the scene and witness by the time Detective Bret Riley showed up. It was his first assignment as the primary detective on a homicide scene and he was a bit nervous. He decided he should compensate by acting in control. By tomorrow the case would get passed off to Lopez, but since he was the on-call detective he was in charge for now.

Andy showed up a few minutes later.

"I'll bet you wish you hadn't covered Sarah's on call now, aren't you?"

"Naw, she's doing me a favor by covering me later in the year."

"So what do we have?" Andy asked.

"Looks like another sniper killing," Riley said as they walked over to the body.

Right away Andy was troubled by what he saw. "Hmmmm."

"What?" Riley asked.

"Take a look. These shell casings are for a pistol, indicating a close-range killing. The sniper takes long-range rifle shots."

"Maybe he's just changing his M.O."

Andy studied the body and wall above. The victim did appear to be spray painting a spider or something on the wall above. But what struck him most was the inaccuracy of the shots. "Look at these wounds, Riley. He's got two in the arm, one in the head, and one in the chest. The head shot looks to be the last one fired."

"Why do you say that?"

"Look at all the soot and unburned gunpowder around the margins of the wound. This was a contact or close-contact gunshot wound. Plus, look at the blood pooling . . . it all emanates here on the ground from the head wound. Then there are at least two impacts on the wall above," he said, pointing to the small divots in the brick.

"Couldn't those just have passed through the victim?"

"Maybe, too soon to tell, but I doubt it, based on the damage." Andy bent down and looked at one of the shell casings: .32 caliber. "This makes no sense at all," Andy said.

"What doesn't?"

"The killer used .32 caliber rounds? None of this looks like the sniper killer to me."

"Well, like I said, maybe he changed his M.O."

While the two investigators were talking, Evans arrived on scene and plowed through the yellow crime scene tape. "Goddamnit. The press is gonna have a field day and scare the public into a frenzy," he lamented. "What do we know?"

"Not much, sir. Looks like the kid here got shot several times at close range while tagging on the wall there," Riley said, pointing to the four-legged spider.

"So the bastard is back," he said.

"Captain, it may not be the same guy," Andy said.

"What do you mean?"

"Sir, consider what we know. The victim has been shot multiple times with a small caliber weapon at close range. Also, it looks like the shooter missed at least twice," Andy said.

"It could also be that the killer is changing his M.O. to mask his involvement sir," Riley offered, trying to appear open-minded.

"What do you mean?" he asked the younger detective.

"Well, think about it. What better way to throw us off the trail? The evidence is a hundred-eighty degrees from what we have come to expect. It's made to look like some incompetent petty criminal with piss poor aim killed this kid," Riley stated.

"Yes. I like the way you think, Riley. That makes a lot of sense," he said.

"Sir, most criminals aren't that sophisticated," Andy said.

The captain cut him off. "Vaughn, you're just a civilian. Your job is to collect the evidence that the detective tells you to."

That was it then. Andy knew that any further debate was pointless. All he could do was document his findings and hope that cooler heads prevailed.

"You're doing a great job, Riley; keep it up," Evans said, praising his young detective with a pat on the shoulder.

"Sir, I could use some help out here doing a canvass," Riley said.

"Go ahead, whatever you need."

The morning had already gotten off to a bad start for Leonard Marshall and he was in a crankier mood than usual. His phone buzzed and he snatched the receiver from its base. "Sergeant Marshall," he snapped.

"Sir, this is Donna in dispatch. We need s criminalist to respond to Kim McFadden's home for a dead body call."

"Kim's house? Is she all right?"

"Yes, sir, she just went home and found her boyfriend dead in the driveway. It looks like a car fell on him while he was working on it."

"Oh, God, that's terrible." He had supervised Kim several years ago when he'd been in charge of dispatch. He always liked her work ethic and thought she was a good employee. He'd also had fantasies about being her lover. While much older that the younger dispatcher, Marshall believed his position of authority was all the aphrodisiac a woman needed. "I'll send someone right over."

He spent the next several minutes calling his criminalists. One by one each of them had some excuse. Two were in court, one was home sick, another was in training and Andy was in the field. Then there was the matter of Sarah Richards. He cursed her name again. Everyone was tied up except him. The sergeant weighed his options and decided he would respond to the scene himself. I have more experience in law enforcement than most of my staff, he thought. Anyway, it's just an accident. He grabbed one of the spare lab cameras and hurried to the scene.

Kim was sitting in her living room, talking with a victim advocate when Marshall arrived. Her eyes were filled with tears, causing her mascara to run. She looked tired.

"Kimberley, I am so sorry for your loss," Marshall said as he tried to hug her.

She leaned in with her shoulders so he couldn't cop a feel. He had always been an ass of a boss and was an insatiable flirt. "Thanks for coming out, Sergeant. Who's here from the lab?"

"I'm going to be handling this one."

"You?"

"Of course, the department takes this seriously and I'm here to make sure things get done right."

Kim was too upset to care. Anyway, how bad could he screw up an accident scene?

Marshall left her with the volunteer and walked out to the driveway.

"Hey, Sarge, surprised to see a supervisor out here," a young deputy said.

"Well, someone has to work the scene."

"*You're* working the scene?"

Marshall ignored the comment. He snapped a few shots, showing the victim's position and the dilapidated jack. "Nice rims."

"They're probably worth more than the car. Not sure why he bothered fixing this piece of shit," the young deputy said, trying to make small talk.

"It may be ugly now but the El Camino is a helluva ride," Marshall stated. "Have the neighbors said anything?"

"Mostly that this guy was an asshole. He blasted his radio day and night and was generally a jerk."

"Did you turn off the radio?" Marshall asked, concerned about contamination of the scene.

"No, sir, the power button is on but it looks like the batteries died."

"How late was the radio playing?"

"Ah, according to the neighbors they don't remember hearing after six p.m. or so. But it could have just died down to a low level that the neighbors couldn't hear."

"Thank you, Deputy, I know what it implies," he lied. "All right, I'm done here. Call for a tow and get this wreck out of here once the coroner is done."

"Do you want to collect the jack?"

"Why, so we can process it for his own fingerprints? I'm not wasting any more of the lab's time on an accident."

35

The bright morning sun warmed Sarah's face, waking her from a restless sleep. She glanced at the clock: There was still ten minutes before the alarm sounded. Too short to sleep, too long to wait, she told herself. She had about two hours before the task force meeting began. Just enough time for a good breakfast and a workout, she thought.

Across the property, Daniel was already up and dressed. He turned the seasoned Dutch oven a half turn while squatting next to the pile of burning coals. Doc opened the cabin door and walked over to fill his coffee mug.

"Morning, young fella."

"Morning, Doc, how'd you sleep?"

"I slept fine. Didn't have you in there snoring like a chainsaw."

"I don't snore."

"Sure, sure, and that OJ fella's gonna catch the real killer soon. Couldn't help but notice you weren't around last night."

"Yeah, I couldn't sleep."

"Bad dreams again?"

"No, not this time. Just a lot of things on my mind," he said, moving the coals on the oven lid.

"You with Sarah?"

Daniel looked up to meet his gaze. "For a while," he admitted. "Then I went to the stables and took some time to think."

"You need to be careful," Doc said.

"I know, I will be."

"You can't let your personal feeling for her compromise the task at hand," he warned.

Daniel looked at Doc with the most serious expression he had ever seen. "I know what's at stake."

Huxley's arrival at the school caused a ruckus among the interns. The recent release of his best-selling book just added to the buzz around campus. It was a tawdry review of historical cases like Jack the Ripper, the Kennedy assassination, Marilyn Monroe, and even Elvis. He reviewed the cases, giving his assessment of the facts and offering his own theories and alternative suspects. It was armchair quarterbacking at its best. Students flocked to him, hoping to get their copy autographed. Jared ran interference and made sure that the prettier young interns got special attention, maybe even an invitation to dinner. It had long been rumored that Dr. Huxley was a drunk who used his celebrity status to take advantage of young college girls, hoping for a job recommendation.

Doc had no use for the man. After decades of dealing with criminals and con men he could see right through Huxley's facade. He was all show and no substance. Huxley charged $1,000 an hour to give sophomoric lectures on general forensic topics. Most of the interns at the Facility could do a better job of presenting the same material, he thought. Doc had been given the unfortunate assignment to escort the pair of pseudo-celebrities to the morning meeting. He found them finishing a posh breakfast in the Dolly Varden, the Facilities five star restaurant. A young female student was hanging on every word dripping from his mouth. Sitting on the table was a small stack of his books.

"Dr. Huxley, my name is Doc," he said, not extending his hand.

"Oh, right . . . I don't think I have a pen handy. Did you bring a book of your own or do you need to buy one of these?" Huxley asked.

"Excuse me?"

"My book, I assume you're here for a copy."

"I'm here to escort you to the meeting this morning."

"Splendid! Lead the way, my good man."

"I can wait until you pay the check," Doc said.

"Oh, I believe Art is picking up our tab this week."

Art will love that one, Doc predicted.

"Sandra, was it?" Huxley asked the young woman. "Why don't we meet back here for dinner and I can give you some advice on how to get into the business."

Sandra was all smiles and probably figured she had just won the lottery. The walk to the conference room was dull despite the heads that turned as they walked past. Doc couldn't figure out how such a loathsome man could garner the reputation that followed him.

"Ya know, I actually do own a copy of your book. Keep it right next to the toilet," Doc said as they approached the conference room door.

Toilet? What a cretin, Huxley thought. "Well, I suppose the important thing is that you're reading it."

"Who said I used it for reading?" Doc said with a wink and smile as he opened the conference room door.

Art began the meeting right at 9:00 AM with introductions around the table. The task force was comprised of members from the Colorado Attorney General's Office, the CBI, and the Facility, of course. Technically, the Attorney General's office was taking the lead in the investigation but Art still had the governor's ear and that constituted a lot of power to wield. John Finch of the Attorney General's office was sitting at the far end of the long conference table. Agent Tyler and Miles Johansson were to his right. Dr. Huxley and Jared made their way to the empty chairs across from them to Finch's left. Art took a seat at the other end.

Huxley had been brought in as a consultant at the behest of John Finch in the AG's office. Apparently, he felt the media and public would take their efforts on the task force more seriously if they had someone of Huxley's notoriety on the case. It also meant they had a convenient fall guy if the murders were never solved. After all, if Huxley couldn't solve them, who could?

Sarah was the only CSI not affiliated with a state or federal agency. She took a seat near the end of the table and out of the way. Miles had been a student of Dr. Huxley's in college and still felt the world revolved around the notorious scientist. She caught a conceited smirk from Miles from the other end of the wooden conference table. Sarah was betting she'd hear a lot from Huxley and his protégé.

"Good morning, everyone. I would like to welcome you all to our Facility and thank you for your time on this matter. I trust you all had a pleasant night's sleep?" Art asked.

"Jacob, why don't we start with the case overviews so everyone is on the same page?" Art suggested,

Jacob Tyler was a young but capable investigator with the Colorado Bureau of Investigation. He cut his teeth in a local police department and his reputation blossomed after handling several high-profile cases with the CBI. He was a serious investigator with a winning track record.

"Excuse me, sir," Miles said. "Should we have Ms. Richards step out?"

Art set his expression to look puzzled. "Why would you suggest that?"

Sarah burned Miles a look of annoyance. That sure didn't take long, prick.

"I thought we we're keeping case details inside the task force. Since Ms. Richards is here to just debrief the group on the events from her last encounter, I thought it might be prudent to ask her to step out," he said, looking smug as ever.

"You've been misinformed, I'm afraid. Ms. Richards is here at the request of the governor's office as the newest task force member. She will be given access to all case materials and information. Do you understand?" he asked.

"Yes, Dr. Von Hollen. Please excuse me, I was not aware of that development," Miles said.

"That's quite all right. The decision was made without your input. Please, Agent Tyler . . . continue with your briefing."

Agent Tyler briefed them on eight killings over the last twelve months thought to be associated with the Monarch Pass Killer, as they were now referring to him. None of the cases had even been associated until the victim from Monarch Pass was found. That victim remained unidentified. The earlier victims were discovered in small mountain communities and had never been connected. Their bodies had been dumped in secluded areas with little human traffic. "Our latest victim from the jogging path has been positively identified as a Ms. Amy Summers."

"How was she identified?" Huxley asked.

"Fingerprints from her driver's license record. She's divorced, with an eight-month-old daughter. She's the first victim that he's targeted in a major metropolitan area as best we can tell,"

It wasn't until Sarah chased the killer on the Pass that he began killing in the metro area, which signaled a major behavioral shift to Art. Few forensic clues had been recovered due to the advanced state of decomposition. The latest victims from Monarch Pass and the Littleton jogging trail showed peculiar red marks that looked similar to ligatures. Art had not yet debriefed the task force members on Doc's theory about the source of the red marks.

"So what we know to this date, thanks to Ms. Richards, is that we're dealing with a single white male subject in his thirties or forties, who displays aggressive behavior," Tyler concluded.

"Forensically we don't have a lot to go on, but there are a few leads to follow—" Art started.

Huxley interrupted him. "Excuse me, Arthur, but I do have a preliminary profile worked up on our subject here."

"You have a profile? Based on what?"

"Well, the evidence, of course, would you prefer me to use something else?"

Finch wanted to keep his options open. "Please, Dr. Huxley, I am very interested in your assessment. It's the reason we brought you on board."

Art took his seat, throwing Sarah a look of amusement.

This ought to be interesting, she thought.

"I think it's very clear that we're dealing with someone who is forensically insightful," Huxley began.

"I believe he is aggressive as Detective Tyler mentioned but he does not stalk his victims. I believe he picks his victims at random. In fact, it appears that he chooses the ambush site and then waits for the first victim who happens upon it, much like a spider might use its web. He is an orphan, estranged from any meaningful parent figure. He may never have met his mother and she is not in his life now, which explains why his victims are women.

"I believe you will find that he lives alone, collects a lot of firearms, and is obsessed with his body and appearance, He will be a smoker, despite the fact he is a body-builder. He will also be a current or former member of a radical militia or Tea Party-type group. Mentally, he is quite juvenile and incapable of complex tasks like using a computer for more than surfing pornography. He is not the type of person who will appreciate art or classical music, for example. I believe he will neglect his home, living comfortably in squalor. I think it is obvious that the killer lives in a small community in the mountains as evidenced by the dump locations."

"Excuse me, Dr. Huxley," Art said. "Most killers who dump their victims don't bring them closer to where they live . . . they transport them farther away. Knowing that, isn't it more likely that the killer lives in a metropolitan area, either in Denver or Colorado Springs, perhaps?"

Dr. Huxley sat reclined in his chair, looking at Art over the top of his glasses. The finger anchored over his upper lip barely hid the condescending smirk he aimed in Art's direction. "That may be the typical behavior expressed by many killers but this killer is atypical. I think the most recent murder scene gives us a glimpse of his ability to lure victims to his kill spot."

"I can speak to that issue, Dr. Huxley," Miles jumped in. "The evidence at the scene indicates that Summers was killed where her body was found. I believe that he used some kind of ruse to lure her to him."

"Any idea how he got her to leave the trail and go into the brush?" Finch asked.

"He may have feigned an injury or even posed as a law enforcement officer."

Unbelievable, Sarah thought. "Is there any evidence to support that theory?"

"Unfortunately, I was not immediately on scene and the local police may have compromised some of the evidence . . . but it seems the most likely scenario."

Sarah stepped into that one. It would do no good to start trading jabs with him, so she bit her lip. Sooner or later, though, she knew they would have a serious exchange of words.

"I'm curious, Mr. Johansson," Art said. "Did you use any reagents to rule in or out her location as the place she was first attacked?"

"Do you mean like a blood reagent?"

"Exactly," he said.

"I'm not aware of any blood reagent that would be able to detect trace amounts of blood in an outdoor setting like that. Remember, there had been significant precipitation in the area since the woman went missing. Any blood would have been washed away long before we arrived."

"Actually, studies have shown that Luminol can detect blood in the ground years after it was deposited."

"The CBI doesn't use Luminol because the State of California has ruled that it is a possible carcinogen," Miles reminded him.

California would regulate oxygen if they could get away with it, Art thought. "You still allow your agents to smoke cigarettes, though, right?"

"I don't think I understand your point, Dr. Von Hollen," Miles said.

"Well, your agency forbids the use of a product because it might be a carcinogen but does allow the use of a product that is a known carcinogen. Just seems odd to me."

"Art, I fail to see the relevance such a finding would have on the case," Huxley said, coming to his protégé's defense.

"I'm just suggesting that if the killer approached and killed the victim on the trail, it might require us to re-evaluate that part of your profile, Doctor," Art said.

"I don't think it would have any impact on my assessment," Huxley said.

Of course you wouldn't. "I'm curious about the evidence we have recovered from Ms. Richards home and the latest victim, what was her name, Amy Summers?" Finch interrupted.

"That's right, sir. The most promising evidence was the note he left behind at Ms. Richards home," Miles said. "First, there were no suspect fingerprints, only those of Ms. Richards and Detective Lopez" he said giving Sarah a condescending look. "We have analyzed the paper and found it to be a generic office brand with a common watermark found in a variety of retail stores. However, the suspect's handwriting was distinctive and if we can develop a good lead we'll have something meaningful to compare it to."

"The handwriting was distinctive?" Finch asked.

"Yes, it was," Huxley said. "I used the handwriting to help develop my profile of the suspect."

"Really, how is that done?" Finch asked.

"It's called graphology and involves an analysis of one's handwriting to discern aspects of a person's psychology."

"That is amazing!" Finch admitted.

"Unfortunately, it's a very controversial method," Art said.

"Oh, Art, I know it is chic to lament that which we do not understand, but the science is settled in this matter," Huxley claimed.

"Far from it, Reginald; in the very best light, most documents examiners consider it a pseudoscience," Art said.

"Gentlemen, please. We need to stay focused here," Finch pleaded. "I remember reading something in a report about shoe prints at Ms. Richards' home and also at the latest murder scene. Have those been compared to each other yet?"

"I examined the prints Ms. Richards cast at the Summers' murder scene by the Platte River and determined they were of no value. The ones at her home may have some value if we had something to compare them to, but they're in pretty bad shape," Miles said.

"No value, nothing we can use?" Finch asked.

"Nothing, I'm afraid. I examined them last night as well. Snow prints are of little or no value to begin with. The cast at the Summers' scene was devoid of any detail. Quite frankly, there's no reason to believe that they have anything to do with the murder," Huxley said.

"It's my understanding that the prints indicated the subject was standing and looking at the victim's position," Art offered.

"That may be, but I'm certain it's a coincidence. The shoe tread was completely gone which indicates that the prints are much older than the murder. It was probably some hiker that stopped to relieve himself a month ago," Huxley countered.

"Would anyone object to our footwear expert taking another look?" Art asked.

"It's your time to waste."

"So what else do we have?" Finch asked.

"Unfortunately, there's really nothing else of value to go on," Huxley said.

"That's not entirely true, Mr. Finch. What about the light bulbs at Ms. Richards' home?" Art asked.

"What are you talking about?" Finch asked.

"It's my understanding that the porch lights were out. It could be that the killer unscrewed the bulbs as he hid on the property. I'm just wondering what the fingerprint analysis revealed?" Art asked, putting Miles on the hot seat.

Miles sat in his chair plotting a response.

"What about these bulbs, Miles?" Finch asked.

"The bulbs were never collected, sir."

"What? Why the hell not?" Finch asked.

"Frankly, sir, there is nothing to suggest the killer did touch them. Secondly, it was very cold that night and the killer would have worn gloves," Miles said, trying to justify his decision.

"Perhaps we should process them just the same," Art offered.

"I can have them up here this evening if you'd like, Mr. Finch."

"Great, we need to do that. Who knows, maybe we'll get lucky," he said, hopeful of a possible lead. "Speaking of fingerprints, what did we find in the truck on Monarch Pass?"

"The truck was stolen from a north Denver neighborhood the previous day. Cigarettes in the ashtray did yield a DNA profile which didn't match the owner or his immediate family. The interior was so dirty we didn't find a single print," Miles said.

"Was there any blood lost during the accident?" Art asked.

"Not a drop," Miles said.

Art wondered how hard he had really searched. "What about the dog at the Summers' scene? Did you swab its teeth for DNA?"

"DNA?"

"The killer's DNA, perhaps the dog bit him while he was plunging a knife into his neck," Art suggested.

"The dog was too decomposed to hope for any trace DNA to be present."

He was right but it felt good to put the smug little shit in his place.

"Excuse me, Dr. Huxley. In your profile you suggest that the killer lives in the mountains?" Sarah asked.

"Yes, that's correct."

"So any idea why he would come all the way to Denver to steal a car then drive it back up into the mountains?"

"It's entirely consistent with his personality type. Magician's call it misdirection and obviously it is working with you, young lady," he said, in a condescending tone.

Art almost came to her defense but decided against it.

"Yes, but if the killer drove to Denver, that would suggest that he had to leave his own car in town while he dumped the body. Even if everything went according to plan he would have to come back to Denver to get his own car after dumping the victim then drive all the way back up to the mountains. It seems to me that leaving his car in an unfamiliar setting would increase his exposure. Plus which, he would have to bring the stolen vehicle back to a position close to his own car which would increase the chances that it would be found by police and processed for evidence." She had just found a major flaw in his "profile."

"Like I said . . . misdirection, young lady," he said, not conceding her point.

The tension in the air was thick as smog. Everyone knew that there was a problem with his profile . . . even Huxley.

"Why don't we take a short break and stretch our legs," Finch recommended.

36

Detective Vargas was grateful for getting called out to the shooting scene, even if it was just for a canvass. He spent most Mondays handling felony in-custody cases that had come in over the weekend. Detectives had to put together all the reports used to develop probable cause for the district attorney. They were a major pain in the ass for most detectives because the paperwork had to be completed within twenty-four to seventy-two hours from the time of arrest, so everything else had to be put on hold, except homicides, that is. He wasn't surprised that the young detective was requesting help on his first homicide. He rolled up on scene as the coroner investigator was getting out of his van.

"How's it hanging, Melvin?" Vargas asked, coming up behind him.

"Hey, Vegas, long time no see. Looks like we have another one, huh?"

"So they say. Are you the lead detective on this one?" he asked.

"Naw, I'm here for the grunt work. Bret Riley is handling point."

"I don't think I know him."

"He's pretty green so go easy on him, will you?"

"Sure thing."

"Gentlemen, what do you have for me on this beautiful morning?" Melvin asked.

"It's not so beautiful for this guy," Andy said.

"I can see that."

"I thought this was supposed to be a sniper case?" Melvin said, seeing the multiple gunshot wounds on the victim's body.

"There may be a change in M.O.," Riley said.

Melvin glanced up at Andy and could tell from his expression that he was not part of the consensus. "What do you think, Andy?" he asked, putting him on the spot.

"If it is the same guy, he's gone one hundred-eighty degrees from his previous tactics. The scene indicates an unskilled shooter who managed to miss his target from only a few feet away," Andy answered.

"We're not sure yet that they are misses," Riley said.

Andy looked at him the way a parent looks at a lying child. "Pretty sure they are."

Melvin squeezed the arm with gloved hands, looking for blanching of the skin. "Well, the lividity looks consistent with his position here but he's coming out of rigor so I'd say he's been here over twenty-four hours, based on the recent temperatures. The pathologist can give you a better estimate after the autopsy."

"So you're saying Sunday morning?" Detective Riley asked.

"Well, that's a minimum time. If I were a betting man I'd say common sense would steer us more toward Saturday evening or the early hours of Sunday since most tagging is done in darkness."

As Melvin rolled the victim over Vargas saw a familiar face beneath the caked blood and tangled hair. Up on the wall he could see the partial design of the familiar spider tag. The older detective crouched down to confirm his suspicions.

Riley didn't want the senior detective stealing the show. "Vargas, we need to start canvassing the neighborhood and try to ID this kid."

"No need, Bret . . . Say hello to Mario Duarte, aka, Spider."

"You know him?"

"Yep, he's a local punk street thug slash heroin dealer. He's small change in the drug circle but has displayed a lot of ambition . . . until now."

"Looks like twenty-six bucks, a lighter, and four condoms." Melvin reported as he searched the pockets. "No license on him, though. You sure about the identification, Vargas?"

"I'd bet my next paycheck on it. I picked him up on a domestic violence charge a few months ago. He beat the shit out of a middle-school girl he brought home on her lunch break. I would have had him on rape charges, too, but a neighbor called before he could get started."

"Sounds like a real winner," Andy observed.

"Oh, yeah, a real role model."

"Why isn't he in jail?" Melvin asked.

"You know our fabulous legal system. Little pecker is out on bail awaiting trial."

"What else do you know about him?" Riley asked.

"Not a whole lot. He pops up on radar every few months for something. The patrol guys may have a better idea on his latest escapades.

"Any known enemies?" "Not that I know of but I'll put a call into the gang unit and see what they have on him," Vargas said.

"Scratch that, Vegas. I'll handle the follow-up. I still need you to canvass the neighborhood for witnesses and evidence," Riley said, asserting his authority again.

"No problem, Bret. Should be a pretty easy canvass, seeing as how these warehouses were closed over the weekend."

Truth be told, Vargas was happy with the assignment. He got out of filing his in-custody felonies and now he could fill his day knocking on doors and looking busy. This might turn out to the best Monday I've had in months, he thought.

Art headed for the coffee bar with Sarah in tow. "I understand Doc told you about his previous cases involving bleach?"

"Yes! Very disturbing. I can't believe I haven't heard about those crimes before."

"I'm not surprised. They weren't well publicized and Doc isn't one to talk about it ."

"What's his story, then?"

"Who, Doc? Doc is the best criminal investigator I have ever seen."

"Really? Why does he work here as a handyman and not an investigator?"

"Just because someone is good at something doesn't mean they want to do it for a living," Art paused. "Doc's problem is that he cares too much. Every unsolved crime just ate away at him. When he did catch the bad guy, like with Mr. Everett, he watched as the system undermined truth and justice. Eventually Doc just burned out."

"But he still helps out here and there?"

"It's in his nature, I suppose. I don't think he can help it. He just can't do it all the time. He needs the solitude of his handiwork to maintain his sanity."

"He seems all right, to me," she said.

"He likes you. I'd take that as a huge compliment. Daniel has been good for him, too. They seem to connect on a lot of levels."

"What do you mean by a lot of levels?"

"Maybe you should ask Daniel,".

"All right, everyone . . . what do you say we pick this back up," Finch called out. Once everyone was settled, he asked, "What's next on the list?"

"We still have the issue of the red marks on the victim's body from Monarch Pass," Tyler said. "Does anyone have any idea what they are from?"

"Our lab has examined them in detail and can't determine what they are, or if they even relate to the murder," Miles said.

"I took the liberty of speaking to a colleague of mine and he feels that they may be a product of decomposition similar to lividity," Huxley said.

"Which colleague is that?" Art asked.

"The eminent Dr. Rosewood from the New York medical examiner's office."

Ah, another showman, Art thought.

"They don't appear to be related to the murder," Huxley added.

"That's too bad," Finch said. "I was hoping that there was something there."

"Actually, there might be," Art responded. "Ms. Richards reported smelling chlorine on the Monarch Pass victim. We took a closer look at Amy Summers' autopsy photos and found what appeared to be the same marks but with a much darker appearance due to the decomposition."

"I don't remember seeing any marks and I was at the autopsy," Miles said.

"You didn't note the smell of chlorine on the Pass victim either," Art noted.

"I don't make it a habit of smelling dead bodies," he countered.

"Well, thank heavens Ms. Richards did. I believe the marks are from a dousing of the body with bleach."

"Bleach? I've never heard of bleach doing that to skin before," Huxley said.

"We do have some documented cases here in Colorado from the nineteen forties."

"Amazing. Any idea why he would do that . . . some kind of DNA cleansing or something?" Finch asked.

"That's our thought, sir," Art agreed.

"I've set up an experiment to test the hypothesis. That should help to confirm or refute the nature of the artifacts," Art said.

Sarah noted that Huxley bit his lip. He didn't like being upstaged she figured.

"When is this experiment?" Finch asked.

"Tomorrow morning."

"All right, well, let's just put that discussion on hold until after the experiment , then. Okay, ah, what about these other possible cases I see on the list here?" Finch asked.

"We have reports of a woman missing from the Aspen area the day after the Monarch chase," Agent Tyler said.

"Are there any similarities with the other murders?" Finch asked.

"None whatsoever," Huxley jumped in.

"This woman is in the middle of a bad divorce and had gone to the family home in Aspen to get away from her husband for a few weeks." Tyler said.

"When was she last seen alive?" Finch asked.

"Last heard alive," Art corrected him.

"Yes, that's right. She was on the phone with a girlfriend talking about her plans for the day when the line went dead. The friend said she thought she could hear a dog barking and a struggle," Tyler said.

"What were her plans?" Finch probed.

"Apparently, shopping and spending every last cent her husband had," Tyler responded.

"What else?"

"Aspen PD hasn't seen her since and the friend can't get her on the phone. CBI initiated a track of the GPS on the phone with no results. The dog hasn't been seen, either."

"So what does that tell us?"

"I think it's pretty clear that the lady met up with a rich boy toy, as you call them, and is off to Aruba, tanning herself on the beach," Huxley said.

"You don't think it could be related?" Finch asked.

"Not at all. She's in a terrible divorce and went to Aspen to get away from reality. I'd wager she has already met a young ski instructor and whisked him off to some sandy beach. She'll likely surface in a month or two after she gets bored with him or runs out of money," Huxley commented.

"Aspen PD put a track on her credit cards and there's been no activity on any of her accounts," Tyler said.

"And if she's off on a tryst, why can't anyone locate her car?" Sarah asked.

"Perhaps she was murdered," Huxley said, conceding the point, "but she was not killed by our man. Without a body, we have nothing to examine. Every minute we spend chasing down the wrong killer puts us further from the man we want," he said.

The logic made sense to most everyone in the room.

"I don't like it," Art said. "Something about her disappearance bothers me."

"If there is some kind of lead in her disappearance you wish to follow up on, by all means, go ahead," Huxley said.

Even Art could see that Huxley had a good point: It was tempting to link every murder with a serial killer in the area but the truth was that serial killers didn't hold a monopoly on murder.

"Okay, what else?" Finch wanted to move on.

Everyone looked around the room for someone to speak.

"I think it would be prudent to allow everyone time to re-examine the information presented here as well as Dr. Huxley's profile, to see if we can elicit any new leads or observations in the case. Of primary importance is the processing of the light bulbs to see if we might be able to develop a viable suspect," Art said.

"Anyone else?" Finch asked. Hearing no reply, he decided to convene the meeting until the following morning. "All right, then, let's plan on meeting here at nine a.m. tomorrow to pick things up again."

"Please contact my staff if you need any assistance in the laboratories or research library," Art said.

Everyone rose and began filing out of the room, except Sarah. Art held back and waited for the door to close. "Are you sticking around for a while?"

"Yeah, I figured I'd use the time to get familiar with these previous cases," she said.

"You don't have anything to prove in here, you know."

"I know. I don't give a shit about Miles or Huxley."

"What is it, then?"

"You brought me into this thing for a reason. I know I have the least amount of experience in the room, but I'd like to contribute something here."

Art was beaming with pride. "That's why I brought you into the task force," he said. Art opened the door to leave but turned back to Sarah. "You know, Sarah . . . education takes you only so far in this business. More important is your ability to develop a *scene sense* or common sense as it relates to crime, and you are way ahead of most in that department."

As he left the room Sarah let the magnitude of the compliment sink in. A single compliment from Art meant more to her than all the criticism from the others. He was a good man, with a good heart. Sarah sat alone in the big room surrounded by file folders and photographs spread over the desk determined not to let him down.

Vargas found Riley sitting in his car, talking on the phone. Andy was leaning up against the open door with his arms crossed.

"Thanks for the information, Dwayne, I owe you one," Riley said as he hung up.

"What's up?" Vargas asked.

"Got a lead on a possible suspect."

"You're kidding . . . who?"

"Local shit bag named Reggie Winters aka Dope Bag. According to the gang unit he's been in a pretty big rivalry with the recently deceased Mr. Duarte."

"Oh, yeah, I know Reggie," Vargas remembered.

"You do huh?"

"Yep, the kid's old man had a classic porno mag collection."

"Wait, is that the kid with the scratch-n-sniff Hustler?" Andy asked, now interested in the conversation.

"September, 'ninety-three."

"You remember the kid because of a porno magazine?" Riley asked.

"Vargas here has what we call a pornographic memory," Andy said. "He never forgets."

"Well, we have his location as of a week ago, according to the gang unit. He's staying in a house over in Englewood. Seems to be a hangout for a lot of gangbangers," Riley said looking over his notes.

"We need to get SWAT involved on the entry. It might take a few hours to set up so let's plan on hitting the place tonight," Riley said.

37

It was 11:00 PM before the no-knock search warrant was signed. The Honorable Judge Larry Dawkins wasn't impressed with the evidence gathered thus far against Reggie Winters but allowed the search to proceed. He was aware of the political implications these sniper killings presented and he didn't want to be the judge who let a killer get a chance to strike again, especially on the cusp of an election year.

The SWAT team parked a half block away and sent in two officers to scout the location in front and behind the residence.

Like most nights, the house was crawling with partygoers. Neighbors had stopped complaining of the noise after several of their vehicles were vandalized and one middle-aged father was beaten half to death with a baseball bat. Most of the young punks considered themselves gang members although none belonged to any serious street gang. Tricked-out cars occupied every available spot on the street while beer cans littered the dirt-covered yard like weeds. Officers reported over twenty people in the house but had yet to see their target.

Reggie's 1973 Chevrolet Chevelle Laguna was in the driveway. The forward SWAT officer pulled a modified Smith and Wesson model 41 pistol from his thigh holster and screwed on a custom suppressor. The .22 caliber sub-sonic bullets didn't make so much as a whisper as he shot out the tires from twenty yards.

The officers advanced on the house in a classic echelon formation. Riley had instructed them to focus on the subject and not to engage the other partygoers unless absolutely necessary. The chilly air kept the rowdy crowd indoors playing drinking games and smoking bongs. The punks never saw the flash bang grenades lobbed in the windows until they exploded in a blinding light and deafening roar. In a flash, officers burst through the doors shouting commands at the stunned occupants.

Instincts took over in a few seconds and the young thugs scurried from the house throwing drug baggies in the air like confetti.

The grenades were bad enough, but Riley suspected the partygoers were more stunned by the officers who let them run from the house unmolested. The lead SWAT officer found Reggie in a back bedroom with a fourteen-year-old girl from a nearby trailer park. As Detective Riley entered the room Reggie was unleashing a torrent of profanities at the officers.

"Fuck you, pig, you got no right to bust up my Mom's place like this. I got a constitutional right to party with my friends, fool," he shouted.

"You don't have a right to rape young girls, Reggie, and you sure as hell don't have a right to murder," Riley lectured as he entered the room.

"Murder? I didn't murder nobody, cuz. Y'all got the wrong brother for that crime."

"This is a warrant to search the premises for a handgun and related evidence in the murder of one Mario Duarte, also known as Spider," Riley said with a smile.

"Spider, I don't know no Spider, fool. You cops just need a black man to pin something on, don't ya?"

"Skin color has nothing to do with this crime, Reggie."

"The hell it don't! It always does."

Riley noticed the reddened skin around the new tattoo below Reggie's lower lip. The word redrum stood out in bold gothic style letters. "I like your tattoo, there, Reggie. It looks new," Riley said, touching his chin.

"Yeah, what of it, pig?"

"What's that word there . . . redrum? What does that mean?"

"I ain't telling you shit! I'm calling Johnny Cochran and sue your ass for millions."

"Good luck with that. You want to tell us where the gun is, Reggie, or do we have to tear the place apart?"

"Go to hell."

Detectives Manny Lopez and Sal Vargas arrived a few minutes after the raid. Riley had tried to maintain his lead position in the case but Lopez was heading up the sniper killings and didn't like being kept in the dark.

The Scent of Fear

"Bret, what the hell are you thinking, running a raid on this case without me?" Manny demanded as he entered the house.

"I'm just following up on my case, Manny," the detective lied.

"Well, it ain't your case anymore," he said.

"It's my collar. I need to get back to the station and interview this punk," he protested.

Manny could pull rank on the younger detective but the situation presented an opportunity for Riley to learn something about interrogation. "All right, you can interview him, but I'm in the room with you, understand?"

"Sure, sounds good," Riley said, realizing he had caught a break.

"Where the hell are all the people from the party?" Manny demanded.

"Uh, Detective Riley gave us explicit orders to focus on the suspect Winters," the entry leader confessed.

"Well, that wasn't too bright, was it?" Manny said, looking at Riley.

"The priority was the murder suspect. I don't give a shit about some floozies smoking dope."

"I don't, either, Bret, but don't you think it might have been helpful to interview these shit bags? I don't know, maybe one of them might have some information on Reggie's whereabouts at the time of the murder, or maybe they know where the gun is?"

Riley hadn't considered that in his rush to grab his suspect.

"Sal? Stay here and conduct the search for the weapon and anything else that might be useful in our case," Manny said.

"Will do, boss. We'll turn the place inside out," he said. He kept two deputies to assist with the search while the rest either secured the perimeter or returned to the station.

Criminals like Reggie weren't clever when it came to hiding evidence. Vargas strolled into the bedroom Reggie had been using and pulled up the mattress. "Bingo." The pistol appeared to have blood on the front part of the frame from the head shot. Vargas wasn't about to end the search. He wanted to tear the place apart to see what else might be there. Besides . . . he needed the overtime.

The young deputies conducting the search were thorough and found several weapons and small bags of drugs stashed in the house. A small, portable fire safe was collected as well so it could be opened back at the sheriff's office. Vargas noted with amusement that all the cabinets in the kitchen were painted bright red. The phone, chairs, even a stapler were in the same color.

"They must really like the color red," one of the young deputies noted.

"It's their gang color," Vargas informed him.

"Oh, not too subtle, are they?"

"They don't do subtle."

Just then a patrol sergeant arrived and entered the scene. Frank Garrity was an old-timer like Vargas and had a reputation as a mean and tough-as-nails cop. He had been in three shootings, all of which were fatal.

"Someone finally kicked the door in on this shit hole, huh, Vegas?"

"You can say that again, Frank," Vargas said, shaking hands with the sergeant.

"So Reggie got picked up for the murder at the tool shop, eh?"

"Yep."

"You guys wrapping up soon?" Frank asked.

"I guess so. We have what we came for," Vargas admitted.

"What say we leave the little pricks a house warming present?" Frank stated with a devilish smile.

"What did you have in mind?"

As the two younger deputies entered the living room they found their sergeant peeing in a colorful water bong.

"Sarge?"

"Give me a hand, lads, I don't think I can fill them all," he said, laughing.

The two young deputies looked stunned as their boss began to fill another one.

"I can do you one better than that," Vargas said as he returned to the bedroom. After removing the pistol and placing it in an evidence bag he began urinating on the pillows. The two older cops laughed like children as they continued with their shenanigans. Not wanting to be left out of the fun one of the young deputies pulled out his Spyderco folding knife and began piercing the numerous condom wrappers lay about the room.

"What the fuck are you doing?!" Vargas erupted.

The deputy was stunned. "I . . . ah, I was just . . ."

"You were just what, numbnuts?" Vargas barked.

"What the hell's going on, Vegas?" Sergeant Garrity shouted as he rushed into the room.

"Deputy Numbnuts here was poking holes in the little fucker's condoms!" he said.

"Son . . ." Garrity said, placing his hand on his shoulder. "These little latex angels there are the only thing stopping the next generation of these shit bags from gracing our presence. You really want these dick weeds reproducing and making more dick weeds?"

"No, sir, Sarge."

"We don't defile them; we revere them. Got it?" Garrity said, holding up a condom.

"Got it, Sarge."

"Now get the fuck outta here before you screw something else up!" Garrity barked as the young deputy ran for the front yard.

Frank looked at Vargas. "Rookies." The two men erupted in laughter as they continued their exploits.

Sitting on her couch, huddled under a heavy blue comforter, Kim was surprised at the ease with which she was handling Jason's death. She was more saddened at the thought of being alone. Abuse came in many forms and verbal abuse was the silent killer of a woman's self-esteem. At least he never hit me, she reasoned. Jenny had promised to come over after her shift but that wouldn't be until after midnight.

Until then, she occupied herself by channel surfing the endless number of movies available on her Direct TV. She stared at the television with indifference. Aside from the dried tear tracks her face showed no emotion. She was dressed in pajama shorts and her long, silk- smooth legs peeked out from under the cashmere blanket, hinting at what lay beneath.

The killer would have given anything to know her thoughts at that moment. He had taken great efforts to ensure their union a success and yet still stayed an arm's length away from her. It was too soon for their date to begin, he thought. It would have been so easy to enter her house that night. In all of the hustle and bustle of the day's events she had left both her front door and back patio door unlocked. Soon she would be drifting off to sleep and he toyed with the idea of coming in and lying next to her like he did with his mother. Temptation raked his body as his fingers stroked the inviting door knob.

Too soon, he thought. He didn't dare risk an encounter the same day her boyfriend left this earth. She needed time to recover, he told himself. She needed time to recognize the emptiness of her soul. Then she would be ready for him; ready for him to fill that void one last time. He wouldn't have noticed how closely he had pressed up against the window frame were it not for his erection.

Go on . . . introduce me to the young lady, he imagined it saying. Too soon, repeated his antagonist persona. He was so engrossed in fantasy that he almost missed the headlights turning down the street. He darted behind a tree and gazed in despair as a familiar woman exited her car. It was the dyke cop! Her arrival made his decision easier. Much to his chagrin, a tactical retreat was in order. He picked his way between the trees, and vanished into the night.

38

Reggie Winters cried all night in his cell. He invoked his Miranda rights and waited for his court-appointed defense lawyer.

Manny and the other detectives went home to get a few hours of sleep. As Manny drove into work he assessed the status of the case against Reggie. All in all things were looking good. They had established a strong motive, found the weapon, and recovered compelling evidence from the crime scene. All he wanted now was a confession.

Sal Vargas was already waiting at his cubicle to discuss their strategy to get a confession out of Reggie. As Manny rounded the corner of his cubicle he found Vargas looking at a pornographic Web site on his desktop computer. The image on the screen was of two obese women engaged in sex with an anorexic-looking man.

"Jesus, Sal! What the fuck are you doing?"

"What?"

"Get out of that shit before IT flags my computer, you idiot," Manny demanded in a low hiss.

"IT can flag our computers? Thank God I'm using yours," Manny rolled his eyes and put his hand to his forehead as Sal Vargas exited out of the slutty site.

"How the hell did you get on my computer without a password? Never mind . . . I don't want to know."

"Good call."

"I trust you got enough sleep last night? Or did you have another one of your wild dates?" Manny asked, not sure if wanted to know the answer.

"Naw, nothing special . . . just a date with Palmela Handerson."

Manny looked confused until Sal raised his right hand and waved.

"You're sick, man, really sick."

Vargas shrugged.

"Patrol managed to snag a couple of partygoers last night when they came back for their cars. The statements don't tell us a whole lot but they do confirm a lot of bad blood between our Reggie and the deceased."

"Well, that's something, I guess. Not enough, I'm afraid. Bret is out checking on a local tattoo parlor to see when Reggie got his latest artwork done," Manny said.

"Okay, good. Forensics will be back on the gun soon so that should nail the coffin shut. In the meantime, we need to try and get another crack at him."

"Maybe a night in the slammer softened him up a bit," Manny suggested.

"Let's find out. Care to join me, Detective?"

"Love to."

The jail was located a block east of the sheriff's office across a small plaza from the district courthouse. Reggie was being held in a temporary cell off the main booking center. Manny drove into the huge sally port and waited for the heavy garage doors to close before exiting his vehicle. Before entering the building, the detectives locked their guns and knives in security lockers located in the garage. Movement within the jail was controlled by a few guards located in a control center two floors above. Doors had to be opened from that room and no two doors could be open at the same time in the same area.

This security protocol made traveling through the jail tedious and slow. Walking the fifty yards from the sally port to the booking center could take up to ten minutes even though there were just four doors to go through.

Vargas didn't mind the wait. He used his time to stare at the detainees adjusting to their new home.

"Hey, Tom, I'm looking for Reggie Winters," Manny said to the older booking sergeant.

"Winters . . . Winters . . . Oh, here he is: Interview room four," the older man said, consulting his screen.

"Thanks, Tom."

"Sure . . . Hey, Manny?"

"Yeah?"

"Keep him on a leash, will you? The last thing I need is another sexual harassment claim in my section," he said, pointing at Vargas.

Manny looked over to see Vargas talking to a young woman too young and too inebriated to be interested in the older detective.

"C'mon, Vargas, we got work to do," Manny said as he pulled Vargas by the arm.

"Some wingman you turned out to be. I was just about to offer her some throat yogurt." Vargas joked.

"I just saved you and the department one big lawsuit," he said.

Marie Sandstedt was as ambitious as lawyers come. At thirty-eight she had made a name for herself in the legal community with a take no prisoners approach to trial work. The euphemism, "bitch," didn't do her justice and detectives preferred a much more vulgar term.

Manny let out a long sigh after peering through the window. "Shit! Marie's in there,"

"Really? What's she wearing?" Vargas asked as he positioned for a better look.

"Keep it in check, Vegas. We can't afford to make any mistakes with her on the case."

"Roger-dodger."

Forty five minutes later Marie opened the door and paused as she eyed the two detectives slouched against the wall. "Detective Lopez . . . what a nice surprise. Come by to check on my client?"

"Yeah, I was real concerned with his well being."

"Oh, are you still mad at me?" she asked in an exaggerated baby voice.

In their last trial Marie had argued to the jury that Manny had made inappropriate sexual promises to a jailhouse snitch in exchange for information. It was an insult without any proof or logic. Vargas would have been flattered by the label but Manny took it as a direct assault on his character and hadn't forgiven her for it.

"Not at all, Marie; we all have our jobs to do, right?" Manny said.

"Glad to hear it, Detective. Now, as for Mr. Winters . . . What kind of deal do you think we can recommend to the DA?"

"How about a needle instead of a noose," Vargas commented.

"Glad to see you've got a sense of humor Sal. Must come in handy when you're standing naked in front of a mirror,"

"At least I have a reflection."

Marie's face pinched.

Vargas' phone rang and he excused himself to take the call.

"Look Marie, we got your guy dead to rights. You don't really want to take your chances in front of a jury, do you?" Manny asked.

"Oh, my dear Detective Lopez, I don't think this case will ever see the inside of a courtroom. Have you matched ballistics yet?"

"No, but I'm sure we will."

"Have any witnesses?"

"Just the dead guy for now, but the investigation isn't over."

"Doesn't sound like you have much to me."

"We got motive, means, and soon we'll prove opportunity. Hell, the victim was in the process of spray-painting over your client's moniker, for Christ's sake!" Manny blurted out.

"Have any forensics that can prove the paint had just been applied?"

"Look, Marie, if you want to play these games in court, be my guest but you and I both know that a jury just ain't gonna buy it this time."

"I just got an interesting phone call," Vargas said as he returned to the group. "That was Bret. Turns out Reggie got his tattoo done the day after the homicide."

"What tattoo?" Marie asked.

"You didn't notice the reddened skin under his lower lip with the word redrum?" Vargas asked.

"Yeah, so what?"

"Marie, redrum is murder spelled backward," Manny said. "And given the location on his ugly mug I don't think you'll be able to cover it up with a turtleneck sweater like last time," Vargas said with glee.

"Like I said, I still have an ace card to play, so I doubt this will ever be in front of a jury," she said with a self-satisfied smile.

"What ace? What are you talking about, Marie?" Manny asked.

"She's talking about the sniper killings," Vargas said.

"In a manner of speaking, yes," she confirmed.

"The sniper killings . . . are you serious? There isn't one shred of evidence that our sniper killer committed this murder. This was close and personal and has your client's fingerprints all over it. You can play that card all you want but a judge will never let it in," Manny stated.

"That's not what I had in mind," Marie said.

"What then?"

"What if I told you that my client saw your sniper right after the second murder?"

"What? You're full of it," Vargas said.

"Got a good look at him and his vehicle, apparently," Marie said.

"You're lying," Manny said.

"You willing to risk that with a killer on the loose? My guess is that when the media finds out you passed on the information they'll have both your heads on a platter." Marie was overtly confident now and it showed.

"I want to talk to him."

"No way in hell, Detective. Once we have a binding agreement in place then he'll talk, and not one minute earlier."

Manny couldn't believe what he was hearing. "Marie, you gotta give me something. I can't go to the DA without some kind of corroborating evidence that puts him at the scene."

Marie glanced back at her client, who nodded. "Mr. Winters was in the area with . . . let's just say an acquaintance. Apparently, this acquaintance of his, without Mr. Winters' knowledge, support, or approval, attacked one of your female officers in an alley just west of the crime scene."

Manny's eyes widened.

"According to Mr. Winters, one of the police officers on scene fired a shot at this acquaintance as he fled the alley," she said, her eyes darting to Vargas.

"Does he happen to know the name of this acquaintance?" Manny asked.

"What do you think? Now get us a deal or you won't get another piece of information."

"Okay, let's just assume for a moment that Reggie is telling the truth . . . what kind of deal are you looking for?"

"He'll plead to manslaughter, serve no more than three years, then limited probation," she said.

"Three years, for cold-blooded murder?!" Vargas exclaimed.

"Lady, let me know what you're smoking!"

"That's the deal . . . take it or leave it," Marie said with a shrug of her shoulders.

"His information would have to lead to an arrest," Manny protested.

"Provided you do your jobs, that shouldn't be a problem."

"You better not be pulling my chain, Marie. I'll sell it, but this information had better be worth it," he said.

Marie opened the door to go back in the room and turned back with a conceited look. "Tick-tock, Detective . . . tick-tock."

39

Art found Daniel on the pistol range at oh-eight hundred. He was into his fourth box of ammunition. "Hey, Uncle Art what's up?"

Art looked around to be sure they were alone. "Did you get a hold of your contact?"

"I spoke to him early this morning but you're not going to like the news"

"What have you found out?"

"I confirmed the mark on the base of the bullet is from a team of Russian assassins referred to as Gerovit."

"What do you know about them?" Art asked.

"The size of the group is a mystery. It's very covert; black on black, and untraceable. Most of the members are former Vyemple members of the FSB, as well as former GRU and Spetznas. These guys are all highly trained in counter-terrorism, sabotage, and espionage. They're well financed and highly skilled. It's believed that they use the lightning bolt symbol on the base of the bullet as a kind of calling card."

"What does the symbol mean?" Art asked.

"The lightning bolt is popular in Slavic mythology although we don't know if it has another meaning."

"Why would a Russian assassin be shooting small time taggers? It doesn't make any sense Daniel"

"I agree, these guys are serious. They don't come cheap and they don't play around with petty vigilantism."

"So what do you think is going on?" Art asked.

"He's planning something much bigger. He might be practicing a long-range shot and he needs to practice on live, moving targets. Let's face it, it's not like there's a thousand yard rifle range to practice on in the city."

"My God, and you think that the real target will be in the city?" Art asked.

"That would be my guess."

"Denver?"

"No way to know. It would make the most sense due to the altitude but he could be planning a shot in Fort Collins, for all we know."

"And we have no way of knowing who this guy is?"

"None. I doubt even the Pentagon knows who these guys are, if they ever did."

"That presents a problem then, doesn't it?"

"It sure presents one hell of a problem for his next target."

Art was dismayed. He had hoped that Daniel's sources could come up with more determined as he was to find out who this killer was and who his next target was. "I need you to make a road trip. Instructions are in the packet." He handed Daniel a manila folder.

"Where am I going?"

"Denver for starters, then to see an old friend," Art added with a touch of mystery. Daniel turned to leave but Art stopped him. "Daniel?"

"Yeah."

"No one can follow you. No one can know that you're gone today. They can't see you in Denver nor anywhere else, do you understand?"

"I understand. That Arapahoe sheriff's sergeant is keeping tabs on me, but he'll be easy enough to ditch. I'll need another car though."

"Take mine," Art said, handing him the keys.

"And Daniel… watch your six."

"Wilco, Uncle."

Art composed himself before entering the conference room. Everyone was sitting in their seats making small talk. There were two new faces at the table this morning. Richard Garske was the Facility's footwear examiner. Richard was one of 65 board certified examiners in the world and well respected among his peers. He was flanked by Samantha Meisner, a gifted and enthusiastic fingerprint examiner. Art had recruited her from the U.S. Secret Service, where she'd made a name for herself by identifying a deranged man who tried to blow up the presidential motorcade with a sophisticated, improvised explosive device, or IED.

Dr. Huxley was signing a copy of his latest book for the AV technician, who'd been setting up the projector.

Finch saw Art enter the room, and decided to begin the meeting. "Well, why don't we get started? Art, would you like to introduce your guests?"

"Certainly. Everyone, this is Samantha Meisner," Art said as Samantha waved at the members of the room. "Samantha processed the light bulbs from Ms. Richard's patio last night."

"It's already done? What did you find?" Finch asked.

"I got two partial prints on each of the bulbs, a thumb and index finger," she said.

"Were they of any value?" Huxley asked.

"They were a little smudged, but good enough to identify."

"That's great! Did you run them through AFIS, the fingerprint database?" Finch asked.

"I did, but there were no matches. I even ran it through the federal fingerprint database I-AFIS. If we had access to the DMV database then we might have something but as it stands, we're at a dead end."

"What about a call to the governor's office?" Finch asked the members of the room.

"I've talked to the governor before about this issue and he is dead set against sharing fingerprint data from the DMV database with law enforcement. It's a privacy issue with him," Art said.

Finch looked defeated as the glimmer of hope faded from his expression.

"I can tell you that the prints are not Ms. Richards', her friends that were over that night, or any of our people," Samantha continued.

"A lot of good that does us," Miles commented.

"Actually, we know quite a bit from this analysis," Art said. "We know he is not a cop, lawyer, teacher, stockbroker, or any one of a dozen occupations that requires fingerprinting."

"If you can develop a suspect I can place him there at the scene," Samantha stated.

"Let's not rush to judgment, shall we?" Huxley said. "Those prints could have been left by another family member or friend we haven't checked. At this point they don't prove anything."

"What about the note, Samantha?" Art asked.

"The note? CBI already tested the note . . . there were no fingerprints," Finch said, looking at his notes.

"Actually, there were. CBI treated the note with Ninhydrin and didn't get a print. Ninhydrin reacts with the amino acids in fingerprints, which are water soluble. I theorized that the snowfall that night might have diluted the amino acids just enough to prevent any prints from being developed. So I treated the note with the reagent Silver Nitrate. It reacts with trace amounts of salt in perspiration but is not as sensitive as Ninhydrin. In this case, however, I decided to give it a shot and it paid off. Based on the location of the print on the note I'm guessing it is a right thumb. I compared it to the prints on the light bulbs and determined that both prints were made by the same person."

"But we still don't know who the character is," Finch lamented.

"No, but it gives us more insight on his behavior, don't you think, Dr. Huxley?" Art asked.

Huxley was slumped in his chair biting his lower lip.

"Minutiae. This information doesn't alter my profile."

"Well, perhaps this might," Art said. "This is Richard Garske, our senior examiner in the impression evidence lab."

"That would be footwear and tire evidence, Mr. Finch," Miles offered.

"That's correct," Richard agreed.

"I had Richard examine the footwear impression photographed at Ms. Richard's residence, as well as the impression she cast at the scene of the Amy Summers' murder," Art said.

"I don't suppose you were able to match the impressions to anyone in a footwear database were you?" Finch asked.

"Well, sir, the footwear databases don't work like that. Those databases identify the manufacturer and model of shoe found at the scene. To that end I was able to confirm that the boot impressions left on Ms. Richards' porch were a size ten to twelve Hi-Tec Altitude hiking boot. They're widespread in the marketplace and affordable, unlike the Bruno Maglis you might remember from the OJ Simpson case fifteen years ago," Richard said.

"Can we use them to identify a suspect if we catch him?" Jacob Tyler asked.

"Maybe. The photographs were poor and whoever took them put the measuring scale on top of the snow, which complicates my efforts to resize them for comparison. Now if the investigator had made a cast of the impressions, then the sizing issue would be moot, but they didn't bother to do that," Richard said.

Sarah looked over to see Miles sinking in his chair.

"Whoever you had out there you might want to send them to remedial training," Richard offered to Agent Tyler.

"As for the print cast by the river, I've got some interesting news. I believe that it will be quite valuable for individualization should we ever find a suspect," Richard claimed.

"I thought you determined the impression was of no value, Dr. Huxley?" Finch asked with a raised eyebrow.

"And I stand by that finding. There was absolutely no tread elements in that impression, none whatsoever." He was not going to be embarrassed like Miles.

"Tread design is a reflection of function, Dr. Huxley. For example . . . hiking boots have multi-faceted elements which provide more surface area to grab onto rough terrain. Shoes designed for a tennis court, on the other hand, have smaller elements or tightly spaced lines and maybe a pivot ring to allow for greater movement on the court."

"Yes, but who on earth would design a shoe without any tread?" Agent Tyler asked.

"Fishermen," Richard stated.

Confusion draped the faces around the room as the members tried to understand what he was talking about.

Everyone that is, but Art. "You see, Mr. Finch, the outsole of the shoe is lined with felt; the felt lining allows fishermen to walk along the bottom of a stream without making a lot of noise which might spook the fish."

Sarah sat expressionless but was jumping for joy inside. She *knew* those impressions had looked new, but couldn't explain why at the crime scene.

"That's right," Richard said as he projected a digital photograph onto a screen at the far end of the mahogany table. "Here is a photograph of the cast," Richard said.

"I still don't see anything," Miles snorted, trying to avoid the unavoidable.

"Sir, I'm sorry. Here is the image at fifty times normal size," Richard said, projecting another image from his laptop. The fine hairs of the felt lining were unmistakable. "Judging by the lack of wear on the outsole, I'd say this boot was pretty new. Perhaps even brand new."

"I don't see how this helps us," Agent Tyler said. "Didn't you already conclude that the impressions might be from some passer-by, Dr. Huxley? I don't see how this evidence changes that."

Huxley sat silent, nodding his head, his chin resting in his hand.

"It changes things because the person who left the impressions was no fisherman," Art said.

Miles wasn't buying it. "How could you possibly know that?"

"Because, according to Ms. Richards' report, the river was frozen over," Art said.

"Maybe he was ice fishing?" Finch offered.

Sarah smiled, realizing Finch was a city boy.

"People don't ice fish on small rivers, Mr. Finch," Art said.

"Assuming you're right, why would the killer wear these shoes, then?" Agent Tyler asked.

"Well, for one, it would make for an innocuous disguise to the average jogger like Mrs. Summers. A fisherman walking near the river's edge or cutting through the brush would not be suspicious. Secondly, I presume his motivation was to leave impressions with no apparent tread design so that any future investigator would think they were as worthless as Mr. Johansson did," Art said, looking directly at Miles.

Home run! Sarah thought.

Miles glared at her. She failed to conceal her smile.

"Are you saying he wore these at the time of the murder?" Finch asked.

"No . . . these impressions are behind the brush from a concealed position but they do face the victim," Art said.

"So . . . What? You're saying he came back?" Finch asked.

"Exactly," Art confirmed. "Why he came back I don't know, but he did return to the scene. He may have been spooked before he could get closer to the body or he may have wanted to check the scene to see if the victim had been discovered," Art concluded.

"So what do you think that means?" Finch said.

"For starters, he's bold. Also, if he returned to this scene he may have returned to others as well. It's a long shot but I suggest you have the local agencies go back to their murder scenes and see if there is any new evidence around," Art said.

Finch was making a notation to do just that when Huxley said, "This is very interesting, indeed. I will need to evaluate this new information with my profile."

Sarah was sure he'd blame Miles for the misinformation to save his reputation.

"So where does all this leave us?" Tyler asked.

"Well, I believe this information sheds new light on our killer. He seems to be much more sophisticated than Dr. Huxley first suggested. I think we need to return to the scene and look for additional evidence, including blood evidence near the location of the running trail," Art said.

"Not that old broken record again, Arthur?" Huxley sneered.

It was clear that he didn't want any more of his conclusions challenged in front of the others, Sarah thought.

"I think we need to," Finch said. "Dr. Von Hollen, can you go with Ms. Richards and examine that scene this week?"

"Sir, that scene was processed by the CBI and I think we need to keep it that way," Miles protested.

Tyler avoided Finch's gaze when he looked over for support.

"I don't think a fresh pair of eyes is a bad thing, do you, Mr. Johansson?" Finch asked.

Miles knew he was beat, for now. "Of course not, sir."

"Great, then we're all in agreement. What's next?"

"This is a lot of information to take in. I suggest we take a short break and meet over in the biology building in fifteen minutes to see the experiment I have set up," Art suggested.

"Sounds good to me," Finch said.

As the lights came on everyone in the room seemed invigorated by the new findings. Everyone except Dr. Huxley and Mile Johansson. Those bruised egos would take time to heal.

40

Getting off the campus without being seen was easy for Daniel. He went into the Masonic Lodge, then followed a small underground tunnel to the opposite side of the hill where he was able to sneak back to Art's car undetected. Lester might spend hours peering in the windows of the lodge, hoping to catch a glimpse of Daniel while instead, he drove to Denver.

Daniel read the file Art had given him and learned he was to rendezvous with a retired Army officer at the deserted Federal Center in the western part of Denver near the intersection of Kipling and 6th Avenue. Daniel didn't drive straight there from the Facility. He drove on a number of small back-road highways and double backed on his route several times to see if he was being followed. He didn't arrive at the Federal Center until dark. As he pulled up to the entry gate, Daniel saw an older gentleman emerge from the bushes next to the guard shack. He waved off the guard in camouflage fatigues who was reaching for his M4 assault rifle.

"It's okay, Jim, he's with me," the older man said as he opened the car door. "You must be Daniel?"

"Yes, sir, Daniel Von Hollen."

The older man got in the front seat without saying another word and Daniel eased the car through the open gate. "Afraid they don't get many visitors here anymore since they shut the place down," the man said. "Just turn right on that road and follow it for a while."

Daniel noted the Masonic ring on his right hand. "Can I get your name, sir?" Daniel asked.

"Why don't you just call me Paul," he said.

Daniel knew it wasn't his real name but was used to dealing with false identities. The buildings appeared to be abandoned and another car was not to be seen. Daniel couldn't help but get an eerie feeling from the place.

"So you're Max Von Hollen's boy?" John asked.

Daniel couldn't believe his ears. "You knew my father?"

"Oh, yeah, met him in Germany before 'Nam. Interesting fellow."

"How so?" Daniel asked.

"I remember him being very proud . . . dutiful. Didn't seem to have much of a sense of humor, though," he said.

Daniel stared straight ahead, trying to imagine him.

"You look a lot like him."

"Thanks," Daniel said.

"I understand that you used to be part of that particular organization?" he asked.

"Yes, sir."

"Yeah, well, I read your file. Wasn't easy to come by, even for me."

Daniel didn't say a word, keeping his eye on the road.

"I gotta say it took some gumption to pull that stunt in Afghanistan," he said, hoping for a response.

"Yes, sir."

"Well, I don't care what those desk pokes at the Pentagon say, I'd have been proud to have you in my unit."

Daniel took it as a compliment and looked him in the eye. "I didn't accomplish my mission, sir."

"No, but you sure as hell did give it the old college try, didn't you?"

"I guess so," Daniel reluctantly agreed, his eyes drifting off into the horizon.

Five minutes later they arrived at a very small, nondescript building without any windows. It couldn't have been more than 200 square feet, Daniel thought.

"We're here," the older man said.

Daniel got out of the car and followed Paul to the small door. Paul punched a code into the digital key pad and put his thumb on a biometric scanner mounted on the wall. The heavy lock clicked and Paul opened the door and turned on a light. A plain metal staircase to the right of the door disappeared down into the darkness. Daniel followed the man down the dust-covered metal mesh stairs for at least four floors. Once at the bottom, Paul opened a heavy steel blast door that must have been six inches thick. Daniel spied a cement shooting bench and a tunnel that looked to be a gun range when he walked into a small laboratory. Paul flicked on the light and the range lit up as far as Daniel could see.

"My God, how long is this range?" Daniel asked.

"A pinch over three thousand meters"

"You're kidding? That must go halfway to the foothills."

"Pretty much goes right up to them."

"What exactly do you shoot here?"

"Name it. I was part of a secret project to develop advanced ballistics and weaponry for the army after World War Two."

"So I take it that you have a lead on the orange fragments we found at the sniper scenes?"

"I think so. Art sent me a sample and it looks a lot like something I was developing back in the 'seventies."

"What the hell is it?"

"It appears to be microscopic fibers of polyvinylsiliconcarbide, a kind of mutated soft ceramic material, if you will. Think of it as tiny bundles of spider webs dipped in liquid Kevlar. The strands are microscopic, but very strong."

"So how is it used by our sniper?" Daniel asked.

"I was hoping you'd ask." Paul pulled out a .308-caliber Marine sniper rifle Bravo-51 from a cabinet and handed it to Daniel. "Look familiar?" He held up an orange-tipped .308 cartridge.

"Amazing," Daniel said as he studied the tip of the bullet.

"This is just a crude approximation of what you've found at your crime scenes, you understand. I don't have quite the laboratory I used to."

"So he's using it like a paper patch?"

"Of sorts, but based on my examination of your fragments, he's programmed the coating."

"What do you mean, programmed?"

"By making certain . . . ah . . . seams in the coating it will peel off in a predictable manner and place each time it's fired."

"So the killer dips the bullets and ensures that the rifling marks from the barrel will be imparted on the coating but not on the bullet," Daniel said.

"Exactly . . . the coating peels off the bullet as it exits the muzzle and the small fragments scatter to the wind. Whatever the cops find in the victim can't be traced to any weapon. Here, see for yourself."

Daniel loaded a round into the rifle and sat down at the shooting bench. "Doesn't the coating make the bullet too big for the barrel?"

"It might if you used a factory bullet, but I hand-made this one on my lathe. The final product is a perfect match to the barrel dimensions."

Daniel donned a set of ear protection and pressed he rifle stock tightly against his cheek as he looked through the scope. After a few deep breaths he slowly pulled the trigger. The report of the rifle echoed through the tunnel. Daniel opened the chamber and set the rifle on a stand. Both men hurried around the bench to find the tiny, orange-colored fibers scattered on the floor a few feet in front of them. Daniel picked one up and held it up to his eye: The barrel's unique rifling marks were imprinted on the small fragments.

"I'll be damned. So mystery solved?" Daniel asked.

"Not quite."

Daniel looked at him and saw the concern in his eyes.

"This is advanced stuff, here. The technology is cutting-edge and expensive. These assassins have more money than a Columbian drug cartel and the smarts to make the most of it. If you're thinking of going after them you'd better have your wits about you."

Daniel nodded as they turned to walk back up the long stairway. The car ride back to the gate was quiet. Both men were contemplating the same question. Who was the shooter's ultimate target? When they reached the gate the old man unlocked his door and turned to say goodbye.

"It was nice meeting you, Daniel . . . I wish your old man was still around."

"Me, too," he said. The old man started to open the door, but Daniel caught him by the arm. "Sir . . . can I get your name please? Your real name?"

Daniel could see the old man thinking hard about his request. After several seconds he extended his hand.

"The name's Sprigg . . . Alan Sprigg, Senior."

"I hope we get to meet again someday, Mr. Sprigg," Daniel said.

"I think I'd like that, kid," Sprigg said as he shut the car door and faded back into the bushes.

The members of the task force had gathered in autopsy suite #1 where they found a dead pig on the stainless steel table.

"As you can see, we're using a pig to simulate humans in this experiment. The pig is at room temperature and was killed less than thirty minutes ago," Art announced. "Now I'm going to pour about a gallon of over-the-counter bleach across the pig's body." He held up the bottle.

Everyone gathered around the table to get a good look. One of Art's intern students was filming the experiment for the library archives. Art poured the bleach over the pig's skin, soaking it in the pungent solution. Sarah was disappointed at the lack of immediate results.

"We'll start seeing a change in the tissue in about five minutes," Art said.

Just then Finch's phone rang with a ring tone that sounded like the end of a Pac-Man video game when the character dies. Sarah watched him duck into a corner of the room to take the call. Sarah turned back to the experiment. Sure enough, the edges of the skin, which were in hard contact with the autopsy table began to redden in color. After ten minutes the margins of the skin were bright red. Art rolled the pig over and the small amount of bleach that had been trapped along the skin flowed down the drain. The researchers gathered around the table and studied the distinctive marks.

"That looks just like the marks on the woman from Monarch Pass," Tyler said.

Huxley produced a small magnifying loupe from his pocked and peered at the burned skin. "Arthur . . . there doesn't appear to be any hair in the burned area."

"That's right. The hair follicle is destroyed in the affected areas. The same is true of our murder victim," Art said.

"So that's what was used?" Tyler asked.

"This is just one crude experiment, Agent Tyler," Huxley answered. "*I'll* do some further analysis in my laboratory to confirm it."

"I look forward to seeing your results, Dr. Huxley," Art said

Art was the first to see that Finch had returned. "What is it, Mr. Finch?" Art asked, seeing the man's gleeful smile.

"I just got a very interesting call about another case of yours. It appears we have a witness in the sniper shootings."

"A witness? Was there another killing?" Art asked.

"No, the witness saw the suspect after the second killing," Finch said.

"The second killing . . . why are they just reporting it now?" Sarah asked.

"The witness was just arrested on an unrelated homicide," Finch said.

He filled the group in on the details of the Duarte murder as well as Reggie Winters' request to provide information.

"Are you considering the deal?" Sarah asked.

"Absolutely. Our office is drafting the paperwork as we speak. We expect to bring him into our offices tonight at seven to review them."

"Three years for premeditated murder . . . that doesn't seem fair," Sarah said.

"The Attorney General does, and that's all that matters; he's the boss. We're holding a press conference at noon." Finch said.

"I don't think you should do that, Mr. Finch," Art said in a very serious tone.

"Are you kidding? The political capital is priceless! There is no way we can pass up this opportunity."

"What about the victims?" Sarah asked.

"What about them? If the information pans out then we get a deadly killer off the street. If it doesn't then at least we look like we're doing something," Finch said.

"Mr. Finch, the press conference will alert the killer that we may be on to him. Also, it may put the witness at risk," Art warned.

"Good. I hope the killer thinks twice about shooting someone again. Maybe it's time for him to be on the defensive,"

"But, Mr. Finch—"

"Look Art, I thought you'd be happy about this. In any event, it's out of your hands now. The Attorney General has the final say and he's made up his mind. Deal with it,"

"I'm just suggesting that we take things slow," Art said.

"Duly noted, Dr. Von Hollen . . . duly noted."

Finch walked away to make another phone call, undoubtedly to a source in the media.

"So what do we do now?" Sarah asked.

"We still have a lot of work to do on *this* case. The sniper case is in the AG's hands for now."

Sarah rolled the information around in her head. "We're pretty well done here. You should head back to the Summers' crime scene tomorrow and see if you can find that blood trail."

"I'll head out after the meeting." Sarah started for the door but Art wasn't following. "Are you coming back to the conference room?"

Now it was Art who looked to be in deep thought. "I'll be there in a while. I need to get to my office and make a phone call."

41

Kim was happy to be home on a long-deserved day off. True, she had just been on vacation visiting family but spending time with her folks was hard work. She relished the alone time her house afforded her, even though it came at the expense of Jason's tragic death. She couldn't believe he was gone. She had always wanted him gone, but not that way. Not dead.

Kim planned a lazy day of soap operas and baking. A batch of Toll House cookies was already in the oven and she could almost taste the semi-sweet chips melting in her mouth. She was just about to settle into the couch when she heard a knock at the door. She wasn't expecting any company and her job kept her alert for danger. Many a home invasion occurred because someone opened the door to a stranger. She looked through the peephole and saw a normal-looking man holding a dog leash.

"Can I help you?" Kim called through the door. She was not about to open it to a stranger, even if it was in the middle of the day.

"Oh, hi. I'm sorry to bother you but my dog got loose and I saw him run under your fence. He's harmless but can you let me in the back gate so I can get him?"

She could see the man was worried. Losing a pet was a terrifying experience for a lot of people. Kim had fielded her share of panicked 911 calls reporting a lost pet. Perhaps it was her sense of duty, or perhaps it was the guilt she felt about not caring about Jason's death but whatever the reason she let her guard down and opened the door to the harmless-looking man.

"It'll be faster if you come through the house." He was dressed in green corduroy slacks, and a tan turtleneck sweater, which reminded her of Mr. Eberley, her fourth grade teacher.

"Boy, oh, boy . . . smells like someone is baking chocolate chip cookies," the man observed as the sweet scent filled the air.

"I'd offer you one, but they aren't quite done yet," Kim said, shutting the door behind her.

When she turned around he slammed his fist into the bridge of her nose; her knees gave way and she collapsed hard on the long entry rug before blacking out.

Kim awoke to the smell of chocolate chip cookies. The sweet-smelling treats were in sharp contrast to the bitter taste of blood in her mouth. She struggled to open her blood-caked eyelids. Her weary eyes searched the room but she couldn't see him, maybe he'd left, she hoped. It was then she realized her mouth had been duct taped. A pool of blood stained the rug by the front door and for a brief moment, she thought about making a run for it, but as her muscles came to life all hopes of escape vanished. She was tied to one of the kitchen chairs. The dog leash was tight and she could feel the burning ligatures forming on her wrists. She was still dressed but could feel that her bra was missing, which made her sick. Turning her head she gasped as she caught sight of the stranger in her kitchen. He stared at her, slouched in a wooden chair, eating a cookie.

"Hello, sleepyhead," he said in a low, terrifying voice. "You made my favorite . . . chocolate chip," he said, taking a bite. "It's almost like you were expecting me."

Kim's eyes darted around and her body struggled briefly against the restraints. The killer stood up and walked over to her. His big boots made a clunky sound as he lumbered across the wooden floor and came around behind her. He sprayed her neck with the lilac perfume as she fought to avoid the mist. Then he brushed his cheek against hers, letting his stubble drag across her perfect skin.

"You smell wonderful, Kim," he said

How does he know my name? He rolled his hand down her cheek to the nape of her neck. She recoiled from his touch.

"I've been looking forward to this meeting for quite some time now," he whispered with hot breath in her ear.

She screamed as hard as her lungs would allow but the tape muffled her cry to a low moan.

"There's no use in fighting it, Kim. This will be much more enjoyable if you'd just relax," he said squeezing her shoulder. "I have big plans for us, Kim" *STOP saying my name!*

The cruelty in his voice was palpable. Kim shook her head violently from side to side. Her wooden chair moaned as she rocked it back and forth. Panic had set in now. Fear was more powerful than any drug, more arousing than any aphrodisiac. Kim stared at the front door, willing someone to come. The killer must have read her mind.

"I'm afraid Jason isn't coming to your rescue."

She turned and glared into his eyes like a laser.

"Yes, that's right. I couldn't just let him lounge around here and spoil my plans," he said with a shrug of his shoulders.

Tears welled up in her eyes, now.

"You didn't like him anyway, Kim. He was a loser, way below your standards. I did you a favor if you think about it."

His eyes lingered over her feminine attributes as he munched on another cookie. Her stomach turned as she realized what he was thinking. He finished the cookie and wiped his mouth on his sleeve.

"Well, I guess we'd better hit the road," he said,

She tried to struggle again as he wrapped the remaining cookies in a floral-patterned paper napkin. Her struggle was so profound that her chair began hopping until she fell over onto her side.

He came up and knelt close to her face. "It's no use, Kim, we were meant to be together. I have a very special evening planned for you. But first . . . I want you to meet my mother."

"I don't like this one bit, Vegas," Manny uttered as they arrived at the doors of the booking Facility. The Colorado Attorney General had accepted the terms of his offer, much to the chagrin of the seasoned detectives.

"I know, man, but think of the trade off. We get a solid lead on our serial killer and we still get to put Reggie behind bars," Vargas said.

"Yeah, for three years," Manny spat.

"With any luck he'll discover a new definition of love. Plus which, my money is on somebody shanking his ass," Vargas said with a glimmer of hope in his eye.

After several minutes, the detectives were able to make their way through the labyrinth of doors to the interview rooms where Marie Sandstedt and her client were waiting.

"Detectives. So nice to see you again," Marie said.

Reggie Winters sat reclined in his chair, his feet up on the table, with a smug expression on his face.

What an arrogant prick, Manny thought.

"Marie, you and your client will ride in the transport van with the deputies while we follow in our car. That is, unless you would rather take your own vehicle?"

"Nonsense. I'm going to be by his side every minute until this paperwork is signed," she said, holding his hand.

The affectionate speech was enough to even make Vargas puke.

"Whatever . . . just follow the guards and we'll see you down there," Manny said.

Vargas was so disgusted with her that he didn't even check out her shapely figure pass him in the doorway. She could see the resentment in his eyes and winked at him.

Daniel didn't have much time. After his show-and-tell at the Federal Center, he high-tailed it down to the attorney general's office. Art had filled him in on the news of the witness over his satellite phone. He and Daniel agreed; there was no way the Gerovit sniper would let this kid live long once word got out. Art's efforts to postpone the plea agreement had fallen on deaf ears. He had tried in vain to convince the governor about the possible threat without exposing details of Daniel's knowledge of the assassin. Without solid proof, however, the governor had not been convinced the threat was real. It was a fanciful tale that sounded too much like a Hollywood movie and the governor's chief of staff was unmoved by the desperation in Art's plea.

Daniel knew there was a good likelihood that the Gerovit network had moles in the government to alert them of just such a threat.

Daniel scouted the area around the AG's office for several hours. The busy cityscape offered way too many options for a skilled sniper to take advantage of. Worse still, Daniel didn't know the approach the witness would be taking, what side of the building he would enter on, or the time he'd arrive. This was critical information he was used to having supplied to him in the past. The assassin could be anywhere, he thought. Would he be perched on a rooftop, sitting in a hotel room or office building, or just walking on the street? Daniel had tried thinking like the assassin but there were just too many options to make an educated assessment. It would have to be a guess, then.

The assassin was in his element. He had performed this task countless times before. He wasn't nervous or impatient; he just rehearsed the shot in his head over and over again. He adjusted his Leupold Mark 4 ER/T rifle scope with a gloved hand while sitting in a comfortable desk chair. The rifle was resting on a bipod along the length of the cheap wooden credenza he'd repositioned at the back of the room. It was a great nest. The setting sun behind him blinded anyone looking toward his window as he set up his perch. Most of the hotel guests would be at dinner when the shot was taken. It didn't matter anyway, he thought; he would long gone before the police could arrive.
The attorney general's office was a mere four blocks away.

It was a drab-looking government building situated north of the state capitol. The closest intersection at Colfax and Sherman was bustling with traffic. The numerous cars, buses, and pedestrians would provide ample confusion in their panicked scattering after the shot. With any luck, police would rush into Civic Center Park, believing the shot came from there, and waste precious time. But there was always a chance some over-zealous cop might start stopping people at random. He had stashed his pistol, fake ID, and two thousand dollars in cash in a used book store two blocks away just in case. Once the shot was taken he couldn't afford to get stopped in the hotel with a gun.

His pre-paid cell phone vibrated across the wooden laminate top. He answered without speaking.

"Target just left the jail. E.T.A. thirty minutes."

The killer hung up the phone and snatched a bottled water from the room's mini-bar.

42

Manny looked comatose as he steered his Chevrolet Impala through the city streets. Sal Vargas stared at the passing motorists with uncaring dullness as he tried to think of anything but Reggie Winters. This wasn't the type of justice either had signed up for.

Manny's phone went off just as he pulled away from a red light. The caller ID showed it was an extension at the Facility. "Detective Lopez," he answered.

"Manny, this is Art Von Hollen. Have you left for the AG's office yet?"

"Art? How did you know we were going down there?" he asked, surprised.

"Have you left?"

"Yeah, what's up?"

"Where are you now?"

"Uh, on Broadway, coming up on I-25. Why, what's going on?"

"Listen, Manny . . . I don't have a lot of time to explain. I have reason to believe that your witness may be at risk from assassination."

"Assassination? What the fuck are you talking about, Art?"

"You need to abort the arrival."

"Art, calm down. Tell me what this is all about."

"Manny, your witness is in danger."

"Yeah, I heard you the first time. What are you basing this threat on?"

"I can't get into that now. Just trust me and abort the arrival."

"You know I can't do that. The AG is waiting for us. The sheriff and district attorney signed off on the deal. Have you tried calling the AG's office?"

"Yes, of course, and they're not listening to me."

"I hear what you're saying, but this is way above my pay grade. I can't jeopardize this plea agreement based on some hunch."

Vargas leaned in closer, trying to hear the conversation through the cell phone.

"Manny, you know that I don't trade in hunches."

Manny was beginning to worry a bit now. He didn't know Von Hollen well, but he knew enough of his reputation to know that he wouldn't be calling without good reason. "I don't know what you expect me to do about this."

"Just abort the arrival. Meet at some other building or something," Art pleaded.

"All right, I'll see what I can do."

"And Manny, one more thing."

"Yeah?"

"Watch your ass."

"What the hell was that all about?" Vargas asked. Manny was concerned.

"Seems Art is convinced that Reggie is going to get whacked at the AG's office," Manny said.

"Finally . . . some good news."

"I'm serious, Vegas."

I am, too, Vargas thought. "Where did he get that crazy idea from?"

"He won't say, but I could tell he was dead serious."

"Well, that and a dollar might get us a cup of coffee," Vargas said, looking ahead.

Manny reviewed his options. "I'm going to call the sheriff."

"You sure you want to do that?" Vargas asked.

"No, but I'm going to do it anyway."

"Something tells me the old man ain't gonna be too happy to hear the news," Vargas predicted.

Sheriff Westin was sitting down to an early dinner with friends when he saw Manny's name on his Nextel. "Yes, Detective Lopez, everything on schedule?"

"Sorry, to bother you, sir, but I just got a call from Dr. Von Hollen," Manny said.

"Jesus Christ, not this crap again. He's been calling everyone from the governor to the mailman!" Westin blurted out.

"So you're aware of the threat?"

"Of course I am. I've talked it over with the staff and no one is taking this seriously, Manny."

"Yes, sir . . . but what about changing the arrival location, or the time, maybe?" Manny suggested.

"There is no way this sniper could know about Winters. Hell, we just found out about him a few hours ago. Just get him to the meeting and find out what he knows, all right?"

"Will do, Sheriff."

"Call me when you get something to go on." The sheriff hung up the phone without saying another word.

"So we're proceeding as normal, then, eh?"

"Seems so," Manny said his eyes darting around the streets.

"Okay, then."

"Look Vargas, keep a sharp lookout, all right? I don't want to get caught off guard out here. Maybe Art is right."

"I'll keep an eye out all right, but just to be on the safe side, let's not get too close to Reggie."

It was five minutes to seven when the two sheriffs' vehicles arrived downtown.

"You sure about this deal?" Reggie asked.

"I'm sure. The language I've written is iron-clad," Marie boasted.

"I really didn't see shit, you know?" he whispered from his seat at the back of the van. Marie patted his leg.

"Just let me do the talking until we sign the agreement, all right? It's just like we practiced it," she said, trying to calm him.

"But ain't they gonna be pissed when I tell 'em I didn't see nothin'?"

"Oh, I'm sure they'll be plenty upset, but their desperation to get a lead in this case was an opportunity we just couldn't pass up. It's not our fault they accepted a deal on such vague assurances. Trust me, Reggie, they can bitch and moan all they want but there's nothing they can do about it," she said as a wicked smile turned the corners of her mouth up.

The two jail deputies opened the door and helped the lawyer and her client out of the van. Marie insisted that Reggie be allowed to wear street clothing and he'd chosen to wear his favorite sports jersey for luck. The light blue and yellow Denver Nuggets jersey sported the number 15. It was gaudy and too ironic a choice for the young thug who was about to start snitching.

The deputy attorney general stood in the doorway to the building with the public information officer.

The Scent of Fear

Reggie stiffened as he saw the important-looking men in fine suits.

"Don't worry, Reggie, it'll be just like we practiced," Marie assured him.

The pair walked along the sidewalk.

Daniel had made an educated guess and settled on the rooftop of the Adam's Mark Hotel on 15th and Cleveland. It wasn't the best position for the shot, but it offered some good buffers between the target and the shooter. Searching the rooms would have been impossible so Daniel headed for the rooftop to see if he could spot the assassin before he took the shot. Of course, it would have been better had he brought a rifle with him. As it stood, he had his .45 pistol and a small duty bag filled with minimal gear from his car. He would trade it all for a scoped rifle.

The sun had set and the streets were awash in the colored, artificial lights of the city. Daniel surveyed the west entrance to the building with his powerful Swarovski SLC 56 binoculars. The expensive and high quality optics was just the tool he needed in the dim light. He spotted the sheriff's van pulling into the parking lot and watched in disbelief as a young man emerged wearing a bright blue shirt. Jesus, why didn't you just wear a neon sign, kid? Daniel had resigned himself to the notion that he couldn't stop the killing . . . all he could do was try to catch the killer.

Reggie's nerves settled with each footstep and he began to smell the sweet scent of victory. The thought of outsmarting the cops made him cocky but he knew he had to play the part of the concerned citizen a while longer. When it was done, though, he would bask in the joy of seeing the faces on those two cops.

"You know what I'm gonna do when I get out?" Reggie asked Marie.

"No, wha—?"

Reggie's head exploded in a shower of blood, bones, and brain matter. Marie was a step behind him on his right side when the massive 250 grain bullet struck. Her face was now spackled with the wet remains of her former client. Worst still, several small chunks of brain entered her open mouth. She gagged when she reflexively swallowed one of the chunks in her panic.

As Reggie's body crumpled to the ground in a heap, the rifle report echoed between the buildings. A flock of pigeons scattered from the rooftops as the concussion wave struck.

Manny and Vargas saw the bullet strike from twenty-five yards away and both detectives hit the deck as the report of the rifle reached them. The two jail deputies were not as quick but managed to grab the lawyer and hustle her back into the van.

"Where the fuck did that come from?" Vargas yelled.

"I didn't see a muzzle flash," Manny screamed as they both took cover behind a car. .

The two detectives could hear the jail deputies screaming over the police radio. "Shots fired! Shots fired! Witness is down!"

43

Daniel was startled by the rifle's report even though he knew it was coming sooner or later. His hunch had paid off and he knew the killer was close. The shot came from the southeast corner of the hotel and Daniel scanned the top floors for a broken or open window. He found what he was looking for after shining his bright, Stinger flashlight at the windows below. A window cracked open. Daniel pulled a small rope from his bag and after securing it to the railing, he repelled down the building and broke through the window. Glass shattered across the carpeted floor and credenza when he swung through coming to a stop atop the credenza. It was easy from there to spot a Lapua .338 magnum rifle resting on its bipod.

Looks familiar, he thought as he drew his pistol from the holster. The room was empty but he quickly searched under the bed and in the shower. "Damn it!" he cursed as he sprinted to the door. The fire alarm went off as he entered the hallway and within seconds he was confronted with guests streaming out of their rooms like ants in a flood. Daniel sprinted to the nearest stairwell, hoping to catch the killer in flight, but as he opened the door all he saw were hotel guests flooding the stairs. There was about three feet between the winding stairwell railings and Daniel could see all the way to the bottom floor. He smashed the small glass cabinet holding the fire hose and jerked it free from its lock. He plunged over the railing without thinking and dropped down the small opening.

He winced in pain as the flesh was torn from his palms while trying to control his descent. It was impossible to see faces as he slid past, blood streaking a trail behind him. He reached the end of the hose with a violent jerk and almost lost his grip. A woman screamed as the bloody man launched himself onto the landing. Daniel grasped the railing, trying to orient himself. The cold metal pipe relieved the pain of his torn skin. He looked up the stairwell, wondering if he had fallen past his prey when he turned and looked down the next flight of stairs.

Neither man knew what the other looked like but each had the ability to find their own kind in a crowd. The tall man with short black hair stared in disbelief at Daniel as the two made eye contact. While others were looking down the stairs in a panicked rush to leave, this man stood still. The look lasted just a second before the man leapt to the next level and pushed through the door.

Daniel sprinted after him, knocking an elderly woman down. It was the worst tactical move he could make; chasing after a trained killer with no idea what he was going to confront, but he had to catch this man. Punching his bloody hands against the push bar, he blasted through the door and onto the 13th floor in dogged pursuit of the assassin.

Kim had no idea how long she'd been unconscious. The last thing she remembered was being lifted into a car trunk in her garage and having a cloth placed over her nose and mouth. Her mouth was still duct taped and the room seemed dim. As her eyes adjusted to the dark she could see a window well leaking light through a dirty plastic dome cover. She was lying on her side in a very uncomfortable bed, she thought. As she lifted her head she could feel a tingly sensation of hair being pulled across her cheek. Then she caught the odor of dank death filling her nostrils.

She adjusted her eyes and discovered with horror that she was lying in a coffin with a decomposing mummy!

The exposed end of the duct tape had pulled flesh from his mother's face, which now dangled against her cheek. The fresh opening in her skin let out a moldy smell she could not escape and Kim let out a wild scream muffled by the tape. Kim looked around the room in a panic and saw the killer smiling at her from a recliner chair a few feet away.

"Good, I'm glad you two were able to meet," he said.

Tears rolled down Kim's cheeks.

"I hope you don't mind, but I took the liberty of dressing you up a bit. Isn't she beautiful, Mother?" he asked the corpse.

Looking down, Kim could see that she was wearing a white ornate dress stained with his mother's decomposition. Is this a wedding dress she wondered? *Oh, God, it is*!

"Do you like it?" he asked.

Kim shook her head from side to side in retaliation. The thought of him undressing then re-dressing her in this outfit was repugnant. God knows what else he did.

The killer got up and stood next to the coffin near Kim's head. He stroked her messy, stained hair with his hand as he whispered to her. "Shhh, shhh, shhh; it's all right, Kim, it's all right. I'm here now. "Fuck you!" she screamed, muffled under the tape. Her throat was dry and raspy. "Good, I'm happy to see you're excited too," he said.

Kim kicked and struggled with all her strength but it was no use. Her bindings were tighter than ever.

Her stomach churned with terror. She had heard the stories told by detectives of sociopathic killers and the things they would do to their victims. They were horrible . . . unfathomable. She was looking into the empty eyes of evil and saw them staring right back at her. She trembled as the shiny knife blade was slowly dragged across her breast. No one from the street would ever hear her desperate cries from under the layer of gray duct tape.

The darkened, empty hallway was illuminated every few feet by bright emergency lights. A deafening fire alarm made it all but impossible to hear the assassin's footsteps, the sound of a door closing, or a pistol being cocked. Daniel drew his Sig Sauer .45 and advanced down the hallway in the combat-ready position. He never looked in a direction the gun was not pointed.

Tactically, this was worse than bad. He was stalking a trained killer in a sensory overloaded environment, with no backup. For a moment he wondered if it was worth it to risk his life over the death of a street thug but pushed the thought away. This was more important than Reggie Winters. This assassin had his sights fixed on someone important and Daniel had a chance to stop it.

The main hallway split off to the right near the elevators and Daniel focused his attention on the corner leading to the new hallway. Then the overhead sprinkler system came on. He was drenched as the cascade of water streamed from the sprinkler heads above. Great, he thought.

He moved along the far left side of the hallway to gain as much distance as he could from the opening. If the assassin were waiting down the new hallway he could pick off Daniel with ease as he crossed in front of the opening. Daniel rounded the edge of the wall inch by inch, with his Sig Sauer extended in front of him. If it weren't for the blaring alarm and the downpour of water he might have heard the service room door open behind him.

The heavy glass ashtray came crashing down on Daniel's head with no warning.. He dropped to a knee as his mind fought back the darkness. Another blow came and Daniel rolled into a somersault and fired his gun blindly at the location of the assassin behind him.

Anticipating the move, the assassin side-stepped the doorway as two hollow point bullets tore through it. He kicked Daniel's gun hand to the side and landed another heavy blow across Daniel's temple before sprinting down the adjoining hallway.

Water and blood were streaming over Daniel's face as he tried to find the killer with his illuminated night sights. All he could make out was a dark figure at the end of the hallway when he fired a single shot. The figure stumbled but disappeared through the stairway door. Daniel was in pain. He felt like he had just gone three rounds with Evander Holyfield. All he wanted was to fall to the floor and pass out but his survival instincts kicked in. Wiping the blood from his face with his shirt sleeve he moved down the hallway. Within seconds his training took over and he regained his dedication to finding the killer. He was close . . . closer than anyone had been during the investigation and Daniel needed to end this now.

Arriving at the door Daniel saw the crimson stain tattooed over the elegant white-and-blue wallpaper. He's hit. Judging from the height of the stain he figured it might have been a shoulder or upper arm injury. Daniel knew the importance of the blood evidence from his time at the Facility and assumed the DNA might be very valuable in identifying the assassin so he un-tucked his undershirt and smeared the blood along the bottom edge before tucking it back into his pants. Daniel could hear people stampeding down the stairs before opening the door. An older woman wearing a soaking wet purple terrycloth nightgown screamed as she saw the muzzle of his gun pointed in her direction. Daniel lowered his gun as the mass of people began shoving him to the side as they fled the building like rats on a burning ship. It would be impossible to spot him again in this crowd. Daniel was sure the killer would get out of the building as soon as possible so he made his way to the lobby, fighting the mob of guests every step of the way down.

He burst into the lobby with the other frightened guests and looked around for his prey. The lobby resembled an adult version of a Chuck-E-Cheese restaurant with flashing lights from the emergency vehicles and panicked adults running in all directions. Where the hell did he go? He got a good look at the sniper but it was nearly impossible to study people's faces in their panicked rush. He didn't even know what to look for.

At that moment Daniel remembered something Art had told a classroom full of students once: "A name or a face is trivial data to the forensic scientist," the voice in his head repeated.

He was looking for a face when he should be looking for something else. Daniel re-trained his mind to look for the one thing that would distinguish this killer from all the other hotel guests—and then he saw it. The bright crimson bloodstain streaked across the glass of the south lobby exit door. Gotcha! As he moved toward the door, Daniel caught a glimpse of the elderly woman in the purple nightgown talking to a police officer and didn't put it together until it was too late.

"Stop right there, asshole!" the police sergeant yelled, drawing his weapon.

Shit!, Daniel thought. He was not about to fight a cop even if it was to pursue a killer. He had to try reason first. "Sergeant, please, there's a killer escaping from the scene . . . out those doors there," he pleaded.

The sergeant was unmoved and direct. "Show me your hands, asshole!"

Daniel stood frozen. Cops were not trained like soldiers. They didn't face down real shooters every day so they were somewhat unpredictable in how they would react to the capture of a gunman. The old woman must have told them of Daniel's gun and the cop assumed he was responsible for Reggie's death. Judging by his looks Daniel couldn't blame the cop for being on edge. One sudden move and this cop might just pull the trigger.

"HANDS!" he yelled.

Daniel had no choice but to comply. "Okay, okay. I'm no threat, Sergeant."

"Down on the floor NOW!"

As Daniel knelt to the ground he saw two more officers trained on him with shotguns. "I'm down, I'm down," Daniel said as he flattened out prone on the floor.

He felt a knee in his back as the handcuffs were snapped on his wrists. They snatched his gun from his hip holster.

"Officer . . . the sniper is escaping out those doors to the south. Look at the blood on the door for God's sake!" he pleaded.

44

Governor Tim Hoines was in his private office enjoying a glass of Octavius Estuche Lujo brandy in a fine crystal hardball glass. The Boettcher Mansion was the governor's private residence on Logan Hill and was a monument to wealth and prosperity in the early 20th century. It was still early in the evening but the governor was exhausted. He had had a very long week. Although the next election was still two years away, his re-election campaign had already begun. Soon the airwaves would be filled with mud-slinging campaign ads that painted each candidate as despicable thugs. He was a shoo-in for the next Democrat primary and most would consider him a lock in the next election, but Hoines knew that every politician was just one scandal away from the lecture circuit. He was a good family man, married to his high school sweetheart but the state's economy was sluggish. Most taxpayers could forgive infidelity more than high unemployment rates.

Some days he had wished an affair was the worst of his problems.

News of the shooting spread like wildfire through the press, no doubt fueled by insider information from Marie Sandstedt. The Attorney General called the governor on his personal line within five minutes of the shooting.

"How in the hell could you let this happen, Mike?" Hoines yelled. "Jesus, do you know the political fallout that could come from this? . . . I don't care; just get over here so we can figure out how we're going to respond to this thing!" Hoines slammed the phone down. Within thirty minutes his chief of staff, public information officer, and the attorney general, Mike Copeland, had joined him in his office. Lanny Miller, brother to the popular local newscaster, was busy fielding calls from the media on his cell phone. Hoines had hoped that hiring the brother of a local newscaster would give him an edge on major stories before they were released to the public and an inside voice to a major news outlet, but he soon learned that Maggie's devotion to work was greater than to her brother.

Gregory Spencer, his trusted chief of staff, escorted the attorney general up to the private office.

"What do we know, Mike?" the governor asked.

"Not much, sir. It appears that the sniper was aware of our meeting with the witness and took him out before we could talk to him."

"How in the hell could he have known about the meeting?"

"Not sure, sir. He may have had . . . a mole in the government."

"Is the leak in your office?"

"Honestly, sir, I don't know. It could have been us, the sheriff's office, any number of people could have known about this transport. Hell, the jail deputies could have mentioned it and some prisoner overheard the conversation."

"Well that's just fucking great!," Hoines said, slamming his fist down on his mahogany desk.

"Governor, no one could have predicted this killer could act so quickly. We didn't even know about Mr. Winters' eyewitness information until a few hours ago. Frankly, it never occurred to us that he would be in any danger."

"Well, I'm sure that will be a big comfort to his family," Hoines blasted back. It was a mistake, and he knew it. Everyone was under a lot of stress and what was needed in this situation was level-headed decision-making. "I'm sorry, Mike, I shouldn't have said that. But the ramifications of this could be disastrous. People are going to want to know how this could have happened and there will be a witch hunt for the leak that will stain all of our offices."

"Believe me, sir, we'll find out who this guy is and how he got the information."

"See to it that you do, Mike, and kick the afterburners on," Hoines said.

Copeland's phone rang. "Copeland, here . . . Are you serious? Give me the bullet points." The AG began scribbling on a notepad. "What's the suspect's name? Get me everything you have on him and fast. Do we have a motive yet? . . . All right, get back to me in fifteen minutes," he said as he hung up the phone. "Governor, I think we may have caught a break."

"What is it?"

"Denver Police have made an arrest," he said.

"Already? What do we know?"

Lanny Miller hung up his phone and joined the other men.

"Apparently, the suspect was apprehended fleeing the Adam's Mark Hotel. Police believe he set off a fire alarm in order to blend in with the crowd and disappear from the scene in all the chaos. They searched the upper floors and found a room with a rifle propped on a table or something, facing my office," Copeland reported.

"So that's it? We got him?"

"It looks that way, sir. The suspect was armed, had pointed the gun at some of the hotel guests during the escape and had several bleeding injuries when police caught him."

"Injuries . . . Please don't tell me some rookie officer tuned this guy up," the governor said.

"No, sir, the police assure me that he was already injured when the caught him in the lobby," he said.

"Thank God, for that."

Lanny broke into the conversation. "Mike, what are the police doing with the suspect now?"

"They took him to Denver General Hospital for his injuries . . . that's where they are now. I'm guessing they will book him into the Denver Jail after that. The Chief is going to call me with an update in fifteen minutes."

"Do we have an identity on the suspect yet?" Lanny asked.

"Yes, I wrote it down here . . . Daniel Von Hollen," he said.

"Von Hollen?" Hoines asked, perking up at the answer.

"Yes, sir," Copeland confirmed,

"What is it?" Lanny asked. "You look like you just saw a ghost."

"Dr. Art Von Hollen is the director of The Rocky Mountain Forensics Center near Steamboat Springs," Hoines explained.

"Yes, I know about the Facility. We've done some PR stuff for the state, touting their contributions to the law enforcement community," Lanny said, still looking confused. Hoines looked up at his PIO with deep concern. "You don't think he's a relative or something do you?" Lanny asked.

"Art Von Hollen called me a few hours ago warning of an assassination attempt on this Winters kid," he said.

"What?" Copeland asked. "Why wasn't I told?"

Hoines ignored the tone his AG took with him and wrote it off as frustration. "Art spoke with your chief deputy, who is reviewing another set of murders up at the Facility," Hoines said.

"Finch?" Copeland was seething inside that his chief deputy had not called him with the warning. The three men stood in silence for several seconds, considering the onslaught of information that had besieged them.

The governor spoke first. "All right. Lanny, not a word to the press until we get some further information. If someone asks about a suspect, refer them to DPD. Mike, call the chief of police and tell him to keep his mouth shut, at least until we can get some additional information on this Von Hollen character. I want updates every half hour and let's get the main players in this case in here by oh eight-hundred hours tomorrow for a debriefing."

The men gathered their things and stood to leave.

"I've got to make a few calls," Lanny said as he headed for the door.

"I need to make a call as well," the governor said as the two men hurried out the door.

It was late when Art's phone rang in his residence. He had been waiting for Daniel to call with an update and grew concerned that he hadn't checked in yet. News of the shooting was on every local television channel.

Art snatched the phone off the base. "It's about time."

"Art, its Tim Hoines."

"Governor? I'm sorry, sir, I was expecting someone else."

"Daniel?"

"Yes, sir. I assume you take the threat seriously now?"

"That would be a colossal understatement, Art."

"I'm sorry, sir, but I did try to warn you."

"I know, and I should have listened to you but now we have bigger problems."

"What is it?" he asked.

"It's about Daniel," Hoines said.

"He's all right, isn't he? Did he catch the sniper?"

"Art . . . as far as the authorities are concerned, Daniel *is* the sniper," Hoines said bluntly.

"What? What are you talking about?"

"Daniel's been arrested for the shooting."

"How in the hell did that happen?"

"The police caught him fleeing the hotel the sniper used. He was bleeding and he had a gun on him."

"Tim, you know that Daniel didn't do this."

"I know, but the optics of this suck."

"Well, debrief him and find out what he knows," Art suggested.

"Art . . . you don't get it. The police are going to interrogate him. I can't get in the middle of this. The press would have a field day . . . not to mention my opponent in the next election."

"Don't make this political, Tim . . . you owe me, remember?"

"I'm sure the investigation will prove he's innocent, but for now he's going to have to be treated like a suspect. If the press finds out that I had prior warnings of the shooting and then I'm perceived to help the one suspect we have . . . I'm done."

"You do what you have to, Tim, but remember one thing . . ."

"What's that, Art?"

"Daniel is family," he said as he hung up the phone.

Art stared at the firelight as Prokofiev's "Sonata for Solo Cello in C#" played through his Cambridge Soundworks speakers. Staring out the old wood-framed window, Art watched a light snow fall against the backdrop of a full moon illuminating the snowfield outside the house. It was surreal. It was at times like these that he missed his wife's counsel. Treacherous times lay ahead and for the first time in years, Art had no idea what to do next.

45

Sarah woke from a deep sleep. She had dreamt of Daniel and the tension between them. She felt unusually alone and she didn't like it. She was making a big mistake and wanted to talk about the other night after dinner. She wanted to confess her fears and hoped he'd open up to her. She didn't need the details of his past, just the essence. After showering and a light breakfast, Sarah began searching for him around campus but he was nowhere to be found. She found Art typing on his computer in his office.

"Art . . . have you seen Daniel today?"

"Ah . . . no, I haven't."

"I've looked everywhere. Doc hasn't seen him and he's not answering his cell phone. I'm starting to worry about him. He didn't go out hunting alone, did he?"

Art slid his chair back from the desk. He couldn't hide his troubled face.

Sarah could see it, too. "What is it? What aren't you telling me?"

"Sarah...there's no easy way to say this. Daniel's been arrested."

The news hit her like a truck.

"Arrested? Arrested for what?"

"Last night there was another sniper shooting in Denver and the police think Daniel did it. But he didn't do it, Sarah, I know it for a fact," he said, hoping to soften the news.

"Denver? A shooting? Daniel was up here yesterday. How could he be in Denver?"

"I sent him there."

"*You* sent him there?"

"Sarah, look at me," Art said. "I will take care of this, okay? I wouldn't lie to you about that I'm going to have Ed drive you back to the city in your car."

The words were like dull thumps against her head. She didn't hear any of them. Was Daniel the sniper? It didn't make any sense. And then she began to recount how easily he had found each of the sniper nests. How he spoke professorially about the evidence. Could it be? Is this what he's been hiding?

Sarah was jolted back into the room as Art shook her shoulders.

Art knew she needed a task to get her mind off of Daniel. "Sarah. You need to set this aside. I am handling it alright? We still have a killer out there that will kill again if we don't stop him."

It was enough to get her attention. "What do you want me to do?" she asked.

"Get back to the Summers' murder scene. We need to find out if the blood trail began at the pathway or not."

"Art . . . I need to go see Daniel," she said.

"Sarah, please listen to me. You need to focus on catching this other killer. Daniel will be out of jail before you know it. I'm sure this is all one big misunderstanding. Besides, they're not going to let you just walk in there and visit with him," he said.

She knew he was right, of course.

Those present at the 8:00 AM meeting were a virtual Who's Who of state and federal law enforcement officials. Sheriff Westin and Detective Lopez sat together near the far end of the oak conference table. Others included the director of the Colorado Bureau of Investigation, the local FBI Senior Agent in Charge, and Attorney General Mike Copeland, as well as their respective staff members. The Arapahoe and Denver district attorneys sat near the head of the table while the Denver chief of police sat across from Sheriff Westin with two of his deputy chiefs and the Denver sheriff. The governor came in last and took a seat at the head of the table with his chief of staff sitting to his left. Lanny Miller remained standing at the back of the room.

"All right, gentlemen, thank you for coming on such short notice. I know you all have work to do so I'll keep this brief. Where is the suspect now?" Hoines asked.

"He's being held in solitary confinement," the Denver sheriff announced.

"What do we know from the shooting scene?" Hoines asked.

The Denver police chief sat up in his chair and reported to the group. "My people have determined that the suspect fired a single shot from a room in the Adam's Mark hotel that struck the witness in the head, killing him instantly."

"The Adam's Mark?" the CBI director commented. "How far away is that?"

"We're still getting the trajectories confirmed but it's over four city blocks away," the chief said. "The suspect, a Mr. Daniel Von Hollen, was apprehended while trying to flee the hotel. He tripped a fire alarm in an attempt to conceal his escape with the rest of the hotel guests. My officers found a high-powered rifle set up in a sniper's nest in one of the rooms. My people are still working the scene, but that's pretty much the findings in a nutshell. I should have a final report in a few days."

"Has the suspect made any statements?" Lanny Miller asked.

"Nope, he's quiet as a church mouse. I gave strict instructions not to question him until we decided on a course of action."

Hoines rocked in his chair, digesting the information. "Sheriff Westin?"

"Yes, Governor?"

"What is your agency's position on this arrest?"

"Sir, I feel my agency should take the lead on this case. The majority of the killings were in my county."

"I'm not sure that's the best idea," Copeland said. "Denver PD has the guy in custody and they're more than qualified to handle the interrogation."

"Chief, what's your position on this?"

The Denver police chief was a practical man. His staff was capable of handling the case but he saw no reason to burden his already overworked detectives with a complex serial murder investigation originating from another county. "I agree with Sheriff Westin. His detectives are already up to speed on the other killings and it would take my guys days to get ready for the interrogation."

"Governor, I don't mean to question the professionalism of Sheriff Westin's deputies but this is a major investigation and I think we need to bring in some big guns," Copeland said. He could feel Sheriff Westin burning him a look from across the table.

"What did you have in mind, Mike?" Hoines asked.

"Sir, I've asked George Buckley, the FBI senior agent in charge of the Denver Office to lend us some resources. He has a man well suited for the task at hand.

"You're not going to water board him are you?" Hoines asked, chuckling. It was a small poke at humor that lightened the serious mood in the room.

"No, sir, but he will get him to talk."

"Governor, I must insist that my men conduct the interrogation," Westin said.

Hoines was a shrewd politician. He saw the benefit of involving the FBI. No one would be able to suggest that they weren't doing everything they could to bring this man to justice. After all, the FBI must have the best people for this type of work, he thought. "I tell you what Brian, you can have one of your men present in the room with the agent. Would that be acceptable?"

Westin wasn't used to others telling him how to do his job but he was not about to argue with the governor. "Thank you, Governor. We can coordinate the details when we speak to the agent. In the meantime, I would like to have my people come up and take custody of the prisoner," he said.

"I'll have him ready for you, Brian," the Denver sheriff said.

"Gentlemen, I want to keep a tight lid on this. We've got three dead kids on our hands and we can't afford any screw ups at this stage of the game."

The morning sun struck his bloodstained face as it crested the horizon of the grassy field. It had been a very long night. Kim had been better than he had ever hoped, the best so far, he thought. He stood next to her cold, lifeless body, taking digital photographs to remember the moment forever and relive their first date when the need arose. He had gotten carried away in the throes of passion and lost control of himself. Her mutilated body resembled nothing of the pretty girl he had abducted from her kitchen the day before. At least you got to meet Mother, he thought as he stroked her tangled hair.

He could hear the high-pitched screams of coyotes as the packs readied for the morning hunt. "They'll be here for you soon, my dear," . A small cattle trough lay a mere twenty feet away and the killer stooped down to wash his hands and face. The water was icy cold but refreshing. A small, solar-powered agitator kept the water circulating for the cattle. He watched as the deep-red blood swirled in the crystal clear water. It was a kaleidoscope of death, beautiful in his eyes. With one last look at his girl, he bid her farewell

The trip back had been uneventful and Ed tried in vain to keep a conversation going, but Sarah was just too preoccupied with her thoughts about Daniel and the sniper killings to keep up. It was a roller coaster of emotions rivaling the mountain roads they were traversing. Once home, she checked messages and ate a small sandwich. Andy had stopped by the laboratory and made a fresh batch of the chemical reagent Luminol. It was an effective reagent for finding trace amounts of blood, but the mixture was only good for about eight hours after mixing.

Andy was leaning against his crime lab truck in the shopping mall's parking lot when she pulled up. "Hey, Sarah, you sure picked a good time to be out of town, huh?" "I know . . . I'm really sorry about all that, Andy; thanks for covering my shift."

"No problem. You're doing me a big favor by covering my vacation dates. I think my wife might smother me in my sleep if I miss another anniversary."

"You ready for this?" she asked.

"Yeah, but Manny wanted to be here and he's dragging Vargas along, too. They should be arriving any minute."

It was another fifteen minutes before they arrived. Vargas had a sourpuss look on his face as he exited the vehicle.

"Ready for the light show, boys?" Andy hollered.

"I bet we don't see shit," Vargas grumbled.

"Don't mind him. He's upset that he had to cancel a date tonight," Manny said.

"Hey, look at the bright side, Vargas . . . just think of all the penicillin you'll save," Andy quipped.

Vargas was not amused.

"Have you ever done this before, Andy?" Manny asked as they walked the path down to the Amy Summer murder scene.

"I've used Luminol on all kinds of surfaces but never in soil."

"No way the blood will be there," Vargas said.

"Art swears that it will work. Apparently, they've done some research on the process up at the Facility," Sarah said.

"Yeah, but there's an inch of snow on the ground. Is the Luminol going to go through it?" Vargas argued.

"No, according to Art, we'll have to scrape it off the area we want to test," Andy said.

"I don't see how the blood can still be there after all the snow we've had," Manny said.

"There's one way to find out," Andy said as they reached the site.

As Sarah and Andy set up their camera equipment, Vargas continued griping. "Tell me again why we're out here at night?"

"The Luminol reaction is chemo-luminescent," Sarah said.

"Okay . . . so what the hell does that mean?"

"It means that when it reacts with the blood it will glow a bluish-green color. It's a lot like a glow stick. The reaction isn't real bright so we have to photograph it in the dark," Andy explained.

"Seems like a lot of trouble to go through," Vargas complained.

Sarah tried to keep busy with her assignment so her mind wouldn't drift. She cleared a patch of snow ten feet square ahead of where they thought Amy might have been standing.

"Shouldn't we be a bit farther up the path?" Manny asked.

"I thought about that, but if we overshoot the area we're looking for then we'll just be trampling down the snow, making it harder to clear off. It's better to move into the area little by little," Andy explained.

Manny nodded. Andy pulled two 16 ounce bottles of the reagent from his pack. The bottles were glowing like futuristic night lights.

"Let's get started, shall we?" Andy said.

He was in too good a mood for being out in the dark on such a cold night. Vargas assumed he must have gotten laid before coming out.

Andy began spraying the bare soil with no reaction. "Nothing so far."

Sarah took his cue and began clearing another patch of snow. This area looked to be closer to where the victim may have been if the killer dragged her to the opening in the brush. Andy again sprayed the solution over the entire area without any reaction.

"I told you this was a waste of time," Vargas said.

Sarah had to admit she'd been hoping for more. Criminalists weren't supposed to hope for any outcome but Sarah prayed for a reaction.

"Well, we gave it a shot," Manny said in defeat.

"Hold on a second. I'm not ready to give up yet," Andy said.

"C'mon, man . . . we ain't gonna find nothing out here. I'm freezing my balls off," Vargas blurted out.

"Go wait in the car, then," Sarah said, annoyed with his complaining.

"What if we're going about this all wrong?"

"What do you mean?" Sarah asked.

"Well, we're assuming that the killer attacked her on the trail, right?" Sarah nodded. "But we're just guessing about where it happened. We should be starting our search in the one area we know she would have been dragged."

"The opening in the brush!" Sarah said.

"Exactly."

The team approached the opening from the side, hoping that they wouldn't disturb the drag path, assuming one was there.

"Okay, Sarah, work your magic," Andy said as Sarah began clearing another patch of snow.

As Andy sprayed the reagent on the soil the four of them watched in amazement as the ground began to glow.

"I'll be goddamned," Vargas blurted.

It was a clear trail of blood, not more than twelve inches wide, angling back toward the trail.

"Keep going, Sarah," Andy told her, indicating for her to follow the apparent path of the drag mark back toward the trail. In a mere fifteen minutes they had revealed a glowing river of trace blood from the opening to the trail.

Manny watched as two distinct blood pools formed on the edge of the trail. "One for the girl, and one for the dog."

"We've gotta get a photo of this," Andy said.

Sarah set the Nikon D2 digital camera on a bulb setting and focused the image.

"Guys, we're all going to have to spray to make this work. Manny, there's another four bottles in the bag there. Can you get them, please?"

Manny retrieved the glowing bottles and handed them out.

"All right, as soon as Sarah trips the shutter we all begin spraying," Andy instructed the team as he spaced them out along the trail.

The first image was dark so Sarah set the exposure to two minutes and the resulting image was amazing.

"The prosecutor is gonna love this," Vargas said.

"Sounds like someone is in a better mood?" Sarah asked.

"I think I'm getting a high from the fumes," Vargas explained.

That explains it, Sarah thought.

"Hey, guys, I hate to play devil's advocate, but what does this do for us?" Manny asked.

"It sure adds a dimension to the profile," Sarah said.

"Yeah, but are we any closer to finding out who this guy is?" Manny continued.

Sarah had to admit that while the discovery was interesting, it didn't exactly break the case wide open. It did, however, throw a kink in Huxley's profile and that might be good enough, she thought.

Manny and the two criminalists milled around the new evidence as Vargas announced he was heading off into the woods to relieve himself.

"Sure, you'll be okay out there by yourself?" Manny joked.

"I hope so, last time it was stuck in my shoe! I'll call you if I need any help," he said, winking at Sarah.

She burned him a crusty look.

"I wish we had found something more to go on," Manny admitted.

"These cases are about assembling a puzzle, Manny, you know that," Andy said.

"I know."

"Each piece may seem like nothing by itself, but put them all together and pretty soon you start getting a clearer picture. We'll get a break; I can feel it."

Twenty yards away Vargas was attempting to write his name in the snow as his bladder evacuated the day-old beer and bourbon. His urea-laced penmanship was akin to a convulsing blind man writing in an earthquake but he was proud of his artwork nonetheless. As he attempted to deposit a period at the end of his name, Vargas caught a glimpse of something out of the corner of his eye. Turning, he walked a few feet through the crunchy snow to a tall ash tree. It took his brain several seconds to realize what he was staring at.

46

"Hey, guys . . . I think you'd better get over here!" Vargas called out through the crisp cold air.

"Couldn't find it, eh?" Manny yelled as Sarah burst out laughing.

There was no reply from the dirty old detective.

Sarah finally spoke. "Don't look at me, Manny, no way in hell I'm going out there."

"Me, neither. I may be naive at times but even I'm not stupid enough to fall for that one," Andy said.

"Vargas! Are you all right?" Manny called out into the darkness.

"Get over here, man! NOW!" Vargas yelled back.

Hearing the concern in his voice, Manny started trudging through the shin-deep snow.

"Watch out for the one-eyed snow snake," Sarah warned him.

Manny found him leaning against the old ash tree with his arms crossed. The smug look on his face told Manny that he had discovered something worthwhile.

"What is it, you old goat?" Manny asked. Looking down he saw the crude moniker in the snow. "This? You called me over to look at your name in piss?"

Vargas stepped away from the tree and held out his arms like a magician showing the beautiful woman he had sawed in half.

Manny stared at the odd box and blinking red light as he tried to make sense of what he was seeing. "What the hell is that?"

"It's a camera!"

"A camera?"

"You know, like one of those trail cameras hunters use," Vargas explained.

"Holy shit!"

"Yeah, and look where it's pointed," Vargas added, looking back at the two criminalists standing by the glowing trail.

"Holy shit!" Manny repeated.

"All right, maybe you should sit down or something . . . " Vargas began saying.

"Andy! Sarah! Get over here now!" Manny yelled out.

The two criminalists ran toward the detectives, expecting to see them with their guns drawn.

"What the hell is it?" Sarah asked as they came upon the pair of detectives standing in the trees.

"Check it out," Vargas said as he pointed to the square box camera.

"What is that?" Andy asked.

"It's a trail camera," Sarah answered.

"Holy crap! Do you think it could have caught the murder?" Andy asked.

"These things can run for months," Sarah said.

"It's pointed right at the section of the trail where the blood pools are," Vargas said.

"It's pretty far away. These things are designed to take photos of something within thirty or forty feet," Sarah said.

"Hey, kid, don't rain on my parade. I say we take the thing back to the lab and let Matt take a crack at it," Manny said.

"Don't we need a warrant or something?" Sarah asked.

"A warrant . . . screw that! We're in the middle of public open space!" Vargas said. "For all we know, that thing is abandoned property," he added.

"It belongs to somebody," Sarah said, trying to make a point.

"Who? You see a name tag on that thing? I'm with Manny . . . let's take it and roll," Vargas said.

Even in the darkened trees Manny could see the concerned look on Sarah's face. She didn't want their find thrown out of court on some legal technicality. "Hey, Sarah, no one can claim privacy here. We're on public land. If somebody comes to find this thing and it's missing they'll just call the cops . . . which is us," Manny assured her.

Andy had been studying the device while the other three talked. "Looks like the owner chained this thing on with a locking cable."

"Bolt cutters . . . I'm on it," Vargas said as he sprinted towards the cars.

"Why do you think someone put this thing out here?" Andy asked.

"You can't hunt here," Sarah said, pondering the question.

"Maybe some student tree hugger trying to document deer humping. Hell, it might even be from the State Park Rangers," Manny said.

"Can Matt even access that thing?" Sarah wondered aloud.

"If anyone can do it, he can," Manny assured her.

"This might just be the break we've been waiting for," Andy hoped.

"A good picture of this guy might be more valuable than a fingerprint," he surmised.

"If Matt can pull an image we can get it on Crime Stoppers by tomorrow night," Sarah offered.

Manny and Sarah were all smiles at the hope of obtaining a valuable clue from the digital camera.

"Hey, guys, you wanna know the best part?" Andy asked.

Manny and Sarah stared at him, waiting for the answer.

"Vargas was taking a leak right next to this thing."

Manny's lips spread into a broad smile as he realized the valuable blackmail contained in the small, camouflaged box.

Daniel had slept in worse places. Under an Abrams Tank in 120-degree sand, a filth-laden brothel in Amsterdam . . . He had even slept one night in the crux of a small tree above alligators and poisonous snakes in a South American jungle. A night in the Denver jail would be a cakewalk. Better still, he didn't have to share his cell with some steroid-puffed Nazi looking to assert his dominance. Daniel knew he could take care of himself but he didn't need assault charges piled onto his current situation.

As he lay on the ultra-thin cardboard sheet passing for a mattress he thought of Sarah and wondered if she was aware of his current situation. He wished she'd never find out but he knew that was a fantasy. He didn't know how he was going to explain this to her. Maybe now was the perfect time to tell her the truth, he thought.

"She'll understand; she's a good woman," he mumbled, trying to convince himself.

He stared at the dull, dark ceiling and closed his eyes. He imagined the stars of Cassiopeia and for a brief moment Daniel hoped Sarah would understand.

Matt Harper was getting ready for bed when his Nextel went off. As the forensic video expert he was rarely called after hours.

"To what do I owe this pleasure?" Matt asked as he eyed Manny's name on the caller ID.

"We may have a break in the Amy Summers murder," Andy said.

"Really . . . surveillance tape?"

"Not exactly . . . " Manny said as he explained their find.

"How soon can you get to your lab?"

"I'll be there in thirty" he said.

Sarah, Andy, Manny, and Vargas were already waiting for him when he arrived. Matt took the sturdy device in his hands and studied it.

"Do you think you can get the images off that thing?" Detective Vargas asked.

"I've never worked on one of these, to be honest, but these cameras are designed for the general public so it can't be that tough," Matt said as he opened the door to his laboratory.

The Digital Evidence Laboratory, as it was known, looked like the bridge on the Starship Enterprise.

"Jesus, now I know where all the budget money goes," Vargas said as they settled in.

The room was cold to keep the electronic hardware from overheating and Manny shivered a bit.

"Now you know why I drink so much coffee," Matt said, seeing Manny's expression.

Racks of component hardware featured everything from the latest DVR recorders to an antique beta recording device. "All right, let's see what we have here," Matt said as he took a seat in his comfortable chair. "Looks like a simple USB connection," he said, opening a small drawer full of cables.

Six dozen thumbnail images filled the screen when Matt opened the file folder. Many were of deer or coyotes. The images were dark and didn't show much detail past the range of the tiny infrared flash.

"How far away would your suspect have been?" Max asked.

"Thirty or forty yards," Vargas said.

"The sensor probably doesn't reach that far," Matt said and Sarah nodded in agreement. Then he stopped talking as a human figure could be seen walking toward the camera.

"Wait a minute . . . we might have something here," Manny flipped the light switch off so they could see the screen better. Matt scrolled through three images of the man as he walked past the camera.

"It looks like dawn or dusk. There's some ambient light present," Max said.

"It's him," Vargas announced.

Andy wasn't so sure. "How can you tell?"

"He just looks guilty."

"We're going to need more than that, I'm afraid," Matt said.

"Matt, can you enhance the images?" Sarah asked.

"You read my mind. Let me just copy these over to my workstation." Matt's fingers danced across his ergonomic keyboard as the image transformed before their eyes. He switched between contrasts, various exposures, and made custom adjustments to the color elements of the image until he was satisfied he had the best picture possible. "Okay, I think this is the best I'm going to get," "That's him," Vargas repeated.

"Could be just some guy out walking," Manny said.

"Yeah, but look where he's walking from. He's coming straight from the murder scene," Vargas said.

"Maybe he's just some guy cutting through the woods?" Max suggested.

"Cutting through to go where?" Vargas asked.

"He's right, there's nothing in that direction but more trees and fields.," Manny said.

"Look at these images, guys . . . look at the way he's dressed," Andy said.

"Sweat pants and a sweat shirt," Sarah said.

"Look lower," Andy said.

"What? His shoes?" Vargas asked.

"His boots! The guy is wearing big ol' clutter boots with sweat pants."

"It does seem odd if he's out there running or something. He should be wearing sneakers," Manny agreed.

"Matt, can you zoom in on his boots?" Andy asked, getting more excited.

"I'll try, but this is only a three-mega pixel image."

"There! Right there, and along the side of the toe!" Andy said, pointing to the screen.

"What? Those dark spots?" Sarah asked.

"Exactly! That's blood . . ." Andy said.

"I don't know, man, the resolution isn't that great."

"It's not the resolution, Matt, it's the pattern. That's a bloodstain pattern; I'd bet my life on it."

Sarah could see it, too, but wondered if her mind was filling in the details she wanted to see.

"Matt, can you tell when this pic was taken?" Manny asked.

Matt opened the file and looked at the unique file information known as metadata.

"According to the clock in the camera unit it was about seven twenty-five a.m. on the day of the murder."

"Fits the timeline the mother gave us of when she left the house," Manny said.

Vargas patted Manny on the shoulder. "Let's not get ahead of ourselves. I'll warn you guys now that date time stamps are notoriously in error. Unless we can establish the time by some other means the defense can argue that this isn't even the same year as our murder. You need to find the owner and get a statement of how he set it."

"We should be in the last images before we collected it, Matt, and I wrote down the time we collected it," Sarah said.

"Perfect," Max said.

"Sarah, can you test this thing for fingerprints?" Manny asked.

"No problem, but maybe you guys should call the manufacturer and give them the serial number. It's possible the owner mailed in his warranty card," she suggested.

"Good idea, I'll take care of it," Manny said.

"I've got a tentative briefing on this case at oh-nine hundred. Max, do you think you can have these in some kind of a presentation for me?" Manny asked.

"No problem. I just need to get a cup of Joe."

"I'll get it for you, stud . . . you've earned it," Vargas said.

47

Senator Aaron Barclay was worse than the typical politician. A fourth-generation Colorado Democrat; his ambition was insatiable. His family had occupied prominent political positions since the founding of the nation and they used their considerable power and influence to enrich their own lives. Until now, Aaron Barclay had relished his role as a United States Senator. He had power, wealth, and very little responsibility. Recent events had changed all that though and he had set his gaze upon a higher office. His limousine pulled up to the governor's mansion a few minutes before 9:00 AM. Shoulders back and chin slightly raised, he carried an aristocracy about him as he strolled into the foyer.

Gregory Spencer, the governor's chief of staff, greeted the senator at the base of the grand staircase.

"Senator Barclay, welcome," he said, extending his hand.

"Gregory. Thank you for accommodating me on such short notice,"

"Well, we have a pretty full plate today but I managed to squeeze you in for a few minutes. I can get you a longer meeting tomorrow, if you wish?"

"No, a few minutes are all I need."

Spencer led the senator into the governor's library admiring his tailored suit. Spenser poured a cup of coffee before closing the ornate wooden doors behind him.

Barclay thumbed through the pages of a *Newsweek* magazine and didn't notice the governor enter through a side door.

"Good morning, Aaron; to what do I owe the pleasure?"

"I was in the neighborhood and thought I'd stop by to talk politics."

"I don't believe you were just in the neighborhood." Although they were of the same political party Hoines loathed the man. Hoines always said the Senator's moral compass was more like a weathervane. Barclay got right to the point.

"I couldn't help but notice you've started up your re-election team."

The Governor nodded. "The election will be here before we know it. We need to be sure that the Democrats maintain control of this office, wouldn't you agree?"

"I do. I just don't think you're the right man for the job."

"Excuse me?"

Barclay offered a wicked smile. "Come now, Tim." Hoines hated his lack of demeanor and cut him off.

"You think you can win the primary over a sitting governor?"

"You've had your term, and the economy isn't improving, crime is rising, and the people want results."

"And I suppose you're the one who's going to turn it all around?"

"Correct." Barclay's answer laced with contempt.

"The party will never stand for it Aaron."

"The chairman will do whatever I tell him to . . . and you know it. Most of those hacks owe their coveted positions to me and I intend to cash in my chips."

"You are one monumental back-stabbing son-of-a-bitch you know that Aaron?".

The Senator smirked a bit at the Governor getting emotional.

Hoines did his best to maintain his composure "So, you came by to intimidate me, is that it?"

"I rather hoped you'd listen to reason and simply announce you weren't seeking a second term," Barclay said, sipping his coffee.

"Listen, Aaron, I have a very busy schedule, so if there's nothing else?"

"I take it that's a no then?" "You can go to hell. I'm running, and if you want to sit in this office you're going to have to get here over my dead body."

"I'd expect nothing less," Barclay said as he rose and began walking to the door. "Oh, and Tim?" he said, stopping halfway across the room. "I was so sorry to hear about the death of you sniper witness. I sure hope those killings get solved soon. I'm sure the press is going to have a field day with this latest incident."

Hoines knew Barclay would make sure of it.

With a smug smile the senator showed himself out.

After the door closed Hoines took a deep breath and steadied himself. He walked to his desk and snatched the phone from the receiver. Punching the intercom button Hoines spoke to his secretary. "Janice, get me Special Agent in Charge George Buckley ."

George Buckley was a career agent in the FBI. After serving in several conflict zones he chose Denver as his final station before retirement. Denver was a lot different from Chicago or Puerto Rico. The field office was busy but not chaotic.

"Agent Buckley, I have Governor Hoines holding on line two," his secretary announced over the intercom.

"Governor Hoines, this is George Buckley. How can I help you?"

"I need a favor from you, George."

"Certainly, sir, just name it."

"I assume you've heard about the arrest of a suspect in the sniper killings?"

"Yes, sir, Mr. Copeland gave me a head's up that you would be calling."

"Well, I think the local authorities are going to need some help interrogating this suspect. Do you have someone who is skilled in getting confessions?"

"As a matter of fact, sir, the perfect man transferred into this office two weeks ago. He just got back from a tour overseas in the sandbox," Buckley said, referring to the wars in the Middle East. "But sir, we would need an official invitation from the local agency before we could intercede—law enforcement agencies guard their turf in these high-profile cases. We don't want the FBI to get blamed for aiding in the case just so we can take credit for solving it."

"Don't worry about that, George; Sheriff Westin is on board."

"Well, that's good to know."

"George . . . this is time sensitive. I need your man to get a confession."

"We'll get one, Governor," Buckley said, even knowing it was promise he couldn't guarantee.

Buckley hung up the phone wondering if he had just walked through a door he'd soon wish he hadn't.

Special Agent Oscar LeMorley was a true professional. He saw himself not as a mere civil servant, but as an agent of good, fighting evil. He had put himself in harm's way more times than he could remember and would do it again at the drop of a hat if it meant nailing a bad guy. He wasn't happy about this assignment, though. While he had received some very interesting information regarding the suspect's past it didn't seem to fit the man he was going to interrogate.

Flashing his badge at the security guard Agent LeMorley walked through the magnetometer setting off the alarm. Detective Manny Lopez had been waiting in the sheriff's office lobby for his arrival and greeted him with a warm handshake.

"Agent LeMorley, I'm Detective Manny Lopez. I've heard good things about you," he confessed.

"I've heard good things about you, too, Detective," he lied.

"Have you been brought up to speed on the investigation?"

"I've had a briefing and read the file, yes."

"How about I take lead until you get acclimated to the case history," Manny said.

The agent stopped him in the hallway. "Detective Lopez, I wasn't called down here to get acclimated, as you put it. I was sent down here to get a confession and I will be taking the lead in the interrogation. I understand that you will be present during the interrogation but I expect you to keep quiet." The icy words sliced through the seasoned detective. "Interrogation is an art and I don't need you butting in at an inopportune moment to spoil the momentum."

That sure was a short honeymoon, Manny thought. "This is your interrogation."

"Glad to hear you're on board. Now . . . please show me to the suspect," he said as Manny led the way.

Walter opened the package, retrieved the small container inside, pulled the fired bullet from its protective case, and held it under the light. "Just like the others, no rifling marks," he said.

"What else do you see?" Art asked.

"It's in better shape than I would have expected. How far away was the shooter from this kid, Reggie Winters?"

"The investigators estimated a half mile or so as the crow flies," Art said.

Walter mounted the bullet so he could examine the base. Art could hear Walter mumbling as he mounted the bullet beneath the microscope.

"What?" Art asked, prodding him.

"See for yourself."

As the monitor powered up Art stared at the screen trying to make sense of what he was looking at.

"Here, let me reorient the image and zoom in a bit," Walter said making the adjustments. There on the screen was the lightning bolt.

48

After missing two shifts, Kim's dispatch supervisor became worried and sent a deputy to check on her welfare. Several knocks on the door later the deputy decided to look through a crack in the dining room curtains. He eyed the blood pool by the door, before kicking in the front door. Within a few minutes the dispatch center was erupting in panicked calls over the radio.

"Dispatch, we need some detectives and the crime lab out here,"

Deputies formed a strong, almost familial, bond with the dispatchers. They often talked to dispatchers more often than they talked to their real family. It wasn't long before Captain Karl Evans' phone rang.

"Sir, this is Becky in dispatch. We sent a deputy over to Kim McFadden's residence on a welfare check and there is evidence of foul play. Patrol is requesting investigators and the lab to respond," she said in the most professional tone she could muster.

The call took him off guard. "Kim McFadden? What kind of evidence?".

"Sir, there's not a lot of information at this point but deputies found a large pool of blood by the door and signs she was tied up."

"Is she dead?" he asked.

"We don't know, sir. The deputies on scene have searched the residence and Kim is not there," she said, her voice beginning to tremble.

"Tell patrol to secure the residence. I don't want them in there finger-fucking all the evidence. I'm sending detectives right now," he said as he slammed the phone down. Stepping to his office door he looked around the bull pen at the available detectives when Manny walked by with a stranger. "Lopez, get over here!"

"Sir?"

"I need you to go over to Kim McFadden's place. Patrol went over for a welfare check and found a blood pool."

"Sir, I was just about to begin the interrogation of Daniel Von Hollen with Agent LeMorley here," he said.

"I need you over at the scene. Vargas can cover your part in the interrogation. Take Detective Riley with you and let me know as soon as you find something out."

"Yes, sir. I'm on my way," he said as he hurried off to find Vargas and get his field gear.

Andy Vaughn had beaten Manny to the scene by a good ten minutes and he didn't like what he found. "Hey, Manny, this doesn't look good,"

"Homicide?" he asked, not wanting to know the answer.

Andy nodded.

"Are you working this one?" Manny asked.

"I'm just here as an advisor. Since Kim was an employee the sheriff felt that CBI should do the processing."

"Does Sarah know?" Manny asked.

"I don't think so, but it's just a matter of time before she finds out," Andy said.

"I'll give her a call once I get the CBI folks oriented."

Forty-five minutes later Andy was happy to see Julie Knowles and Jacob Tyler. There was another, younger woman with Julie in the crime scene van. Andy figured she was a rookie learning the ropes.

"Hey, Julie, glad you're here,"

"Sorry it had to be under these circumstances," she said.

"This is Teresa, our new fingerprint examiner. She's shadowing us for a while until she can take calls on her own," Julie explained.

"What can you tell us?" Tyler asked.

"The residence belongs to one of our dispatchers, Kim McFadden. She hasn't reported to work in two days so patrol came by to do a welfare check and this is what they found," Andy explained, opening the front door for them to see in.

Agent Tyler took in the scene and noticed small wood chips saturated in the blood pool. The door's wooden molding was broken and lying on the floor.

"This door was kicked in. Was that from the suspect or the officers?" Tyler asked.

"The deputies kicked the door in. According to the first on scene the front door was locked so he looked in the window over there," Andy continued.

Julie stared at the pool of blood, trying to imagine the blitz attack on Kim as she opened the door.

"Do you think she surprised a burglar or opened the door to a stranger?" Julie asked.

"Too early to tell, but my hunch is she wouldn't open the door to someone she didn't know. Kim was on the other end of that phone call too many times," Andy said.

"So we need to figure out how he got in," Julie said.

"I did a walk around the house before you arrived and couldn't find any evidence of forced entry," Andy said.

"Looks like she was tied up to this chair here," Agent Tyler said, looking at the duct tape still sticking to the armrests.

"What was he doing while she was tied up?" Andy wondered aloud.

"I can smell cookie dough and there are some chocolate chips melted into this pan," Teresa noted, trying to be helpful as she canvassed the kitchen.

"Her car is still here," Manny said, returning from the garage.

"There's a blood trail between the garage and kitchen. It looks like he took her out that way," Manny continued.

"Jesus Christ," Julie said, staring at the kitchen table.

"What?" Andy asked. Julie pointed to a pale-blue envelope resting against the fruit bowl. Agent Tyler, Teresa, and Andy stopped what they were doing and gathered around the table to see what she was looking at. Andy used his gloved hand to pluck the envelope from the ornate doily it rested on. He brought the envelope up to his nose; he could smell fresh lilacs and something sweet. Manny smelled it, too, as Andy held it closer.

"This is the scent she described on the Monarch Pass victim," Andy said.

"*Ay, Dios mia,*" Manny blurted out.

Teresa felt like the odd man out. Seeing the name written on the outside, she asked, "Who's Sarah Richards?"

Daniel was escorted into the room by two goliath deputies from the jail's notorious goon squad. A special division enforcement team, they were called in to handle any prisoner who might present a security risk. They usually dealt with barricaded subjects or prisoners coming into the jail who were drunk or high, but they also guarded murderers. Daniel was wearing a full body red jump suit signifying him as a high risk inmate. His feet shuffled in the leg irons. His hands were cuffed and he had an electronic stun device attached to his waist which deputies could activate by touching a red button on their utility belt.

"Mr. Von Hollen, I'm Special Agent Oscar LeMorley of the FBI . . . please take a seat," he said. pointing to the one available chair in the room. "This is Detective Sal Vargas with the Arapahoe County Sheriff's Office. He'll be observing the interview," he said.

Interview . . . right, Daniel thought. Daniel recognized an interrogation room when he saw one. They were designed to intimidate the subject but civilian versions were plusher than the military and militia versions he had used. The walls were bear with the exception of a wall clock meant to focus his attention on the time. A small thermostat and electrical socket were camouflaged audio microphones and a camera—he could tell that by their unusual height and locations on the wall. Clever, he thought, as he took his seat. Daniel noticed that the front legs were about an inch shorter than the rear legs, an old trick to make the subject feel uncomfortable.

"I've heard a lot about your uncle. Sounds like a real stand-up guy," Agent LeMorley said as Daniel scanned the room. "Your father was a genuine war hero, according to our files," he said, touching his finger to a manila folder lying on the desk.

Daniel paid him no mind as he examined his handcuffs for the tenth time.

"Then there's Daniel Von Hollen . . . " LeMorley said. "An Army mechanic who seems to know a lot about sniping. Daniel kept his poker face. His eyes were open but he almost looked to be in a trance.

"You know, I got the door slammed in my face pretty hard when I requested your service record. Not many mechanics get protection from a one star general at the Pentagon". Daniel's expression remained flat.

"Why do you think that is Daniel?"

"Maybe he's afraid I'll become an FBI agent and waste my life away"

LeMorley laughed as he adjusted his position in the chair. He glared at Daniel as his smile evaporated. "You really want to go down this road with me?" Daniel didn't reply. "You were dishonorably discharged from the army . . . is that right?" LeMorley asked, trying to get under his skin.

It must have worked, he thought, as Daniel's expression changed.

"It was an administrative discharge."

"Oh, my mistake. So how does one get an administrative discharge?" he prodded.

"Why don't you just read my file?"

"Well, that's just it, Mr. Von Hollen . . . I had agents go out to your last post and no one there seems to remember you."

"I'm a private guy."

"Yes, it would appear so. You know, normally when we find you military types with, how should I say this, unusual backgrounds I always think black ops."

"You should stop watching so much television. I'm just a hunting guide."

LeMorley's gut told him he was on to something. "So I contacted some sister agencies and made some inquiries. Do you know what I found out?"

"No, Agent LeMorley, I can't imagine."

"One of two things; either the United States Army is secretly training it's mechanics in sniper schools . . . or your former position was so classified that it doesn't even flag as classified when your name is run."

"Like I said, Agent LeMorley . . . you watch too much television."

"What I can't figure out is why you snapped"

"Snapped?"

"War can do that to some men, you know?" he said fishing for a response

"How would I know? I watched the war on Fox News like most folks"

"Maybe you just enjoyed the killing too much, and when you got booted from the Army, you had to feel that rush again. Is that it?"

Daniel leaned forward in his chair and stared directly into his eyes. "You've got some fucked up imagination man"

"Do I?" LeMorley thought he might actually be getting somewhere.

"What makes you think I could shoot some innocent kid?"

"It wouldn't be the first time would it Mr. Von Hollen?"

Daniel cocked his head as he tried to figure out what the FBI agent was implying

"Technology is an amazing thing isn't Daniel?"

"Yeah, I just love my new iPad"

LeMorley smirked.

"I'll bet you didn't know that the FBI keeps a database of photographs taken by our soldiers overseas"

"You don't say?"

LeMorley thought he sensed a bit of tension in Daniel's answer.

"Thousands of them. Civilians, hadjis, live, dead, doesn't matter. After Abu Ghraib the Justice Department decided to scan everything into a big database so we could run facial recognition software on everyone"

"Fascinating, but what does this have to do with me?"

LeMorley had hoped for just such a moment. Keeping his eyes locked on Daniel he slowly flipped through his folder and pulled out a half-dozen photographs, tossing them onto the table.

"Recognize anyone?"

Daniel leaned over the photos pretending to study them. He didn't have to.

"Nope"

"Funny thing you see. I ran your photo through the system and the computer says your facial features are a match to the man in those photos"

Shit. Daniel thought.

"I'd say you better check your computer then" Daniel said trying to keep his composure.

"No, I think the computer is working just fine"

"The guy in those photos looks nothing like me" Daniel lied

"I don't know" LeMorley paused studying the photos. "You take away the beard, the hat, the glasses in that one, I think it's a dead ringer" Daniel sat expressionless.

"I've had our people go over these photos with a magnifier. No name tags, no insignia, nothing to identify the soldier's unit" he admitted.

"Hell, the ARMY won't even confirm those are our soldiers" he said throwing up his hands.

The tension in Daniel's legs eased a bit.

"So that leaves just one question Daniel" Their eyes locked, Daniel raised his eyebrows in anticipation.

"Just who the hell are you?"

Manny took the envelope from Andy's hands while opening his pocket knife.

"Wait . . . what are you doing?" Andy asked.

"I'm opening it."

"You think you should do that?" Andy asked, worrying about disturbing the contents.

"What do you suggest? Slip it in her mailbox for God's sake?"

Julie helped steady the envelope as Manny cut along the top seam. Inside, he found a single, tri-folded purple-colored page Opening it, the criminalists stared at the ornate calligraphy gracing the Victorian-style floral stationary.

"What does it say?" Teresa asked, trying to look over Andy's shoulder.

Manny stood frozen, unable to speak.

Julie took the note and read aloud; her voice stumbling over the words. "Roses are red, violets are blue, this time it's Kim . . . next time it's you."

The foreboding poem sickened the hardened professionals who recalled Amy Summers' fate, and now Kim McFadden's. At the bottom of the page Julie read a set of GPS coordinates.

"I need to get Sarah on the phone right now," Manny said as he pulled out his portable radio. He called the patrol watch commander and ordered a protective detail back out to Sarah's home. "Andy, get with dispatch and find out where these coordinates are," he said, handing him the page.

"You think he's going after Sarah?"

"What do you think?"

There was a desperation hanging in the air. No one seemed focused on the crime scene around them.

Teresa inched closer to her mentor and whispered a question into Julie's ear. "You don't think Ms. McFadden is still alive, do you?"

The seasoned criminalist turned and looked to the younger analyst with grave concern. "For her sake, I certainly hope not."

Sarah sat hunched in a chair staring at the small video screen. If any of the supervisors caught her watching Daniel's interrogation she be suspended. She was sure everyone else was watching the interrogation on the large flat screen monitor in the conference room. As long as she left before it ended, she shouldn't get caught. Sarah caught herself biting her nails as LeMorley continued his questioning. She was still trying to figure out how they could possibly think Daniel was the sniper. There was no way she could fall for a killer and not know it, she assured herself. No, it had to be a mistake.

"You've been using Ms. Richards, haven't you?" LeMorley asked.

The question was unexpected and it showed. "What are you talking about?"

Sarah mouthed the same words in unison.

"You've been feeding her information the whole time, haven't you? Leading her to the evidence, stringing her along as you killed those innocent children . . . and then there was the seduction," he said, turning the page in his file. "She's quite a bit younger than you. Was it easy to take advantage of her; so young and naïve?" Daniel's icy stare even gave Sarah a slight shiver. "That first night after dinner with her . . . What was the name of that quaint restaurant? Ah, yes . . . Romano's," LeMorley said rolling the name out.

Sarah's face squished, not comprehending the agent's implication.

"That was your big move wasn't it? The night you finally got her into bed?" LeMorley asked.

Daniel's face was expressionless, but this proved his suspicions about being followed.

"Or perhaps Ms. Richards knew all along about your crimes?" LeMorley asked, raising an eyebrow. "Is that it? Sort of a, oh what do they call that, a symbiotic relationship." Daniel wasn't biting. "You know, you help her career, and she returns the favor so to speak".

Daniel yawned, acting bored with the conversation.

Seeing that he was not going to get anywhere with this line of questioning, LeMorley closed the folder. "Maybe we should take a break. Deputies . . . take the prisoner back to holding until he's ready to talk. Maybe a few hours in a cell will change your mind about talking to me."

Daniel stood in his confining suit and headed for the door when LeMorley called out, "Daniel . . . I really do want to help you, but I can't if you won't talk with me. I do hope that you won't drag Ms. Richards though what I'm sure will be a lengthy investigation of her role in all of this."

The threat was subtle as a chainsaw but Sarah knew that Art would have her back; and Daniel's. Cracking open the door to the video room Sarah scanned the empty hallway. As quietly as she could, Sarah eased the door shut and headed for the nearest stairwell.

Detective Vargas waited until Daniel was down the hall before speaking. "So what's your read on him? Is he telling the truth?"

LeMorley tapped his finger against his lips as he considered the question.

"About shooting the kids...I can't tell yet. About his past...no way in hell".

49

Julie Knowles and the others tried to focus on the task at hand. If they could find some clue left behind by the killer they might be able to find him. It was maddening to them that even though they had his photo and fingerprints they were no closer to catching him; and now one of their own might be at his mercy. Julie examined every inch of the kitchen chair and duct tape, hoping for some revelation.

"It looks like he tied her up, but I can't figure out why," she said.

"The chair is pointed toward the kitchen, maybe he was watching her from in there," Teresa theorized.

"The chair could have been moved as he took her from it. We can't assume the current orientation has anything to do with anything," Julie lectured. Even as the words came out she regretted uttering them. The worst thing a criminalist can experience is despair.

"I've got it!" Andy called out as he hung up the phone with dispatch. "The coordinates are just south of the town of Deer Trail at the east end of the county," Andy relayed.

"Do we have deputies en route?" Manny asked.

"As we speak," Andy assured him.

"Then let's get rolling. Jacob, I suggest we seal this scene up and head out to the position of the coordinates. I can have deputies guard this location until we get back," Manny offered.

With any luck they'd get to Kim before it was too late.

News of Kim's abduction spread like wildfire through the department. Tony had spent nearly an hour searching for Sarah. Her truck was there but she wouldn't answer his repeated pages. He had staked out several bathrooms hoping she was simply hiding in a stall but no one had seen her. He found her sitting at a small table in the corner of the lunchroom obscured by a large support beam.

"Jesus, Sarah, where have you been?" Tony asked.

"I . . . I . . . had my phone turned off." Sarah lied. She knew Tony would understand why she watched the interrogation but there was no reason to drag him into it. It was better for both of them. She could see the concern in their eyes. "Why, what is it?"

"You haven't heard about Kim?" Tony asked.

Sarah raised an eyebrow.

"Kim in dispatch," he said.

"I have no idea what you're talking about," Sarah said.

"She's missing," Max said.

"Missing? What do you mean missing?" Sarah realized he was white as a ghost. "Just spit it out."

"It's the killer, your killer, he's taken Kim," Tony said

"What?"

"They found blood at her house and it appears he took her," Tony explained.

Her hand clamped over her mouth as she felt her stomach drop. She knew what this fiend was capable of. Sarah began shaking her head from side to side as tears began to stream down her cheeks. "I can't…I can't hear this" she said. Her words were broken by a gasp of air. Her mind was racing. Why Kim? It couldn't be a coincidence she thought. Then she thought of Kim's Chesnutt hair. Oh god, did he think she was me? Did I somehow lead him to her? It was more than she could handle. Tony's hand on her shoulder was little comfort as she began to cry uncontrollably.

It took over an hour to reach the crime scene. Patrol deputies on the perimeter looked both horrified and furious. It was not a good sign, Manny thought, as he threw the gear shift into park. He and Andy a few steps behind the CBI team as they approached the security tape.

"Manny, I don't think you boys want to go down there," a gruff old sergeant said as they came close.

Manny would have ignored such a comment on most days, but today he wasn't so sure. He saw the sheriff pull up in his trademark Chevy Trailblazer. With a dozen antennae poking through the roof the car was nicknamed the Porcupine. Captain Evans exited the car with sheriff Westin and Manny imagined the conversation those two had on the ride out.

The Scent of Fear

"What have we got, Lopez?" Evans called out.

"I was just about to head down and check it out, sir," Manny said.

Evans stopped at the bright yellow crime scene tape. Twenty years on the job, he knew better than to step over the tape and risk winding up in court.

As for Manny, his job lay across the tape. All investigators experienced a sensation when crossing that barrier. Time seemed to slow down as you got closer and closer to the aftermath of mayhem. Training had taught seasoned investigators to approach a crime scene carefully. The purpose was to reduce the chances of missing evidence. Today, however, he was trying to avoid the inevitable. Manny made it about halfway down the marked trail before hearing the screams.

He took off at a sprint and ran smack dab into Teresa. The young analyst was bent over a bush, retching her lunch to the ground. There was nothing he could do for her now, but it was a tell-tale sign that Kim was dead.

He spotted an old wooden barn as he rounded the trail past some small pinon trees . The roof was caved in and the deep-brown wood looked a hundred years old. Manny could see that the people were gathering on the opposite side of the barn so he skirted along the walk line, trying not to overlook any evidence the killer may have dropped. His heart skipped a beat as he came into view of the murder scene and he stood speechless, along with the other members of the team.

What was left of Kim was hanging on the side of the old wooden planks like a side of beef. Her arms were outstretched and tied with old, musty rope to rusty iron pegs nailed into the wall decades earlier. Her battered wrists were worn to the bone from struggling against her assailant. At first, Manny thought she was wearing a dark-colored shirt but as he got closer he could see it was just the dry, caked blood clinging to her naked body.

As disturbing as her corpse appeared it was the commotion at her feet that caught his attention. Julie Knowles and Andy Vaughn were crouching next to Agent Tyler, who was screaming in pain. Blood was gushing from his lower leg as the agent hollered for the others to set him free. Manny rushed to the small group.

"Julie, what the hell is going on?" Manny yelled.

"It's a fucking bear trap!" Jacob screamed.

Manny took his shoulders and tried to keep the agent from struggling out of control. Looking down at his left leg Manny saw the old, rusty jaws of the #15-sized spring-loaded trap. The iron teeth were embedded into the flesh of Jacob's calf; his foot was turned the wrong way. It was clear that both the fibula and tibia bones were broken.

"Get it off! Get it off me!" Jacob screamed.

Manny helped to free the massive jaws of the 40-pound trap. As his leg came free the flow of blood doubled and the lower part of his leg fell backward. It hung by strands of tendon and skin.

It seemed like hours but paramedics arrived at their side within seconds of freeing Agent Tyler.

"Hang in there, Jacob," Manny said as he gripped the agent's hand.

The fear in his eyes was unmistakable. The paramedics dragged him onto a field gurney and cinched a tourniquet onto his leg. Thirty seconds later they hauled him up the trail and out of sight.

The investigators stood in shock as Manny struggled to catch his breath

Secondary devices had been employed at crime scenes in the past but those were at bomb scenes. Deputies shut down the scene while investigators searched the layer of tumbleweeds pressed against the barn wall; Kim's corpse waiting patiently above.

"Looks like that was the only one, Detective," a patrol deputy told Manny as he waited off to the side of the commotion. "Have you ever seen anything like that?" he asked.

"Never," Manny said, wondering if it might be a sign to come.

"We're going back down there, Manny," Julie called out.

Julie's intern, Teresa, was nowhere to be seen and Manny assumed she was hiding in the crime scene van. Standing in the background for the last thirty minutes Manny had stared at Kim's body with the clinical discipline of a doctor looking at a patient with a horrible disfigurement. The problem was that Kim no stranger. They didn't talk often but he knew she was a good person and no one, not even a criminal, deserved to die this way. She had been disemboweled from her sternum to her cervix, her entrails dangling down onto the ground. The ghostly white bird droppings on her shoulders were a bleak reminder of nature's dispassionate march to reclaim death. The dried blood caking her body looked to be moving but upon closer inspection it was an army of carpenter ants marching into the cavities of her damaged body.

"Looks like her fingers have been removed," Andy said as Manny stared in disbelief. "If I were a betting man, I'd say he walked them over there." He pointed to a fenced pig farm a hundred yards south.

"She must have scratched him and he's cleansing his DNA by removing her fingers," Manny said.

"She's got some item of clothing or fabric stuffed in her mouth," Julie announced as she photographed Kim's battered face. Her tangled red hair was matted with blood and covered most of her once beautiful face. "Jesus," Julie whispered as she contemplated Kim's final minutes.

After thirty somber minutes of investigation, Manny broke the silence. "Are you seeing any similarities with the Amy Summers' scene?"

"The ligature on her neck looks to be the same and she has been raped with a foreign object; probably a knife. That and the poem at her house all seem to suggest the same killer," Julie said.

"Anything different?"

"Andy and I were just looking at these marks on her body," Julie said, pointing to her torso.

"What are they, can you tell?" Manny asked.

"They appear to be a group of superficial cuttings. I'd describe them as violent doodling for lack of a better description," Andy said.

"Was she tortured?" Manny asked.

The two seasoned criminalist looked back at the detective with raised eyebrows.

"Okay, dumb question," Manny said as he scribbled in his notebook. "We've got to find something here to connect the killer," he said, stating the obvious. "Make sure we swab her vaginal vault for DNA."

"That's going to be a problem," Andy said as he looked closer at her body.

"Why is that?" Manny asked, thinking the criminalist may not have brought the right supplies.

"It's gone," Andy noted.

Julie moved closer to confirm that.

"What do you mean, it's gone? Gone, gone?" Manny asked as if there were another kind.

"He's right," Julie confirmed. "Deputy!" Manny called out. The young patrolman sprinted down the trail anxious to be of help. "Get over to those pig pens and look around for any body parts," the detective ordered.

"Seriously?"

"Don't I look serious, numbnuts? Get going," Manny barked.

The deputy sprinted off with his partner trying to keep up.

"You know that those parts are long gone if they went to the pigs," Andy said.

"I know, but we have to try," Manny answered. His phone rang as a local news helicopter began buzzing overhead. "Detective Lopez!" he yelled into the phone, waving at the helicopter to go away. Julie and Andy watched as trace evidence began flittering in the gust of wind from the rotary craft. He could barely hear over the chopper.

"Manny, it's Sarah!" he heard. "Is it true? Is Kim dead?" she asked.

"Sarah . . ." He didn't know what to say. His inability to form the right words angered him but not as much as the news helicopter. Manny yanked his portable police radio from his belt. "Dispatch! There's a news helicopter flying overhead. Tell the pilot if he doesn't get to an altitude of at least five hundred feet I'm going to have him arrested!" he yelled. He turned his attention back to his Nextel phone. "Sarah . . . I'm sorry. I don't know how to say this. Yes, Kim's gone."

He could hear her crying on the other end and wished he were there to comfort her. She said something to him but he couldn't hear her over the roar of the Bell 407's engine as it hovered overhead. It took several minutes for the pilot to receive the ominous threat which could revoke his license but when it did, the pilot climbed in elevation much to the chagrin of the reporter riding shotgun. Manny tried to get Sarah back on the phone but she didn't answer.

Manny had spent the last twenty minutes looking for some other note from the killer. If he were lucky, the killer might reveal his next move. He searched the barn, the tumbleweeds they had moved, and everywhere else he could think of. Nothing. Maybe the bear trap was the message, he thought . . . a message taunting them in another way. He could lead them to clues, or he could pick them off one at a time. The killer was asserting his control of the situation.

He watched from a distance as Melvin loaded Kim's body into the ubiquitous black body bag. Several deputies gathered near the edge of the clearing to assist Melvin in loading her body. The uniformed pallbearers were saddened but honored to deliver her to the coroner's van; it was the least they could do for her.

Manny watched as the gurney passed by the back of a patrol car. There, emblazoned on the rear panel were the words *To Protect and Serve*. It was a daunting pledge. Most of the public was on their own when it came to personal safety and they didn't even realize it. Cops just clean up the mess a criminal leaves behind and he was angry about it. Someone must have known that this man, this killer, would be a danger to society. No doubt he had been in and out of the legal system numerous times as judges and lawyers played their dangerous game of chance with the public trust. Feeling defeated, Manny promised that Kim's death would not be in vain . . . no matter the cost.

The crime lab staff was given the rest of the day off but Sarah couldn't bring herself to leave. Kim's murder still didn't seem real. She called Jenny and the two cried for their friend and cursed the man responsible. It was the same with her co-workers. She even wandered into dispatch, and stared at Kim's empty chair. She returned to the lab and carried on in a zombie-like trance, finishing reports, checking her gear, anything to avoid dealing with Kim's death directly. Her Nextel rang. It was Jenny again.

"Hey."

"Hey."

"Sarah, you shouldn't be alone tonight. Why don't you come over here?"

"I don't know."

"*I* don't want to be alone tonight," Jenny clarified.

Jenny's tough SWAT exterior was crumbling. Sarah looked up toward the window and realized it was already dark out. How long have I been sitting here? she wondered.

"Sarah?"

"Yeah, Jenny, all right, that sounds like a good idea. I could use the company, too."

"Thanks."

"I just need to stop by the house and pick up a couple things."

"Just come over, I've got everything you need."

It was a nice gesture but Sarah wanted to change out of her work clothes and maybe take a quick shower. "I won't be long. I'll call you when I'm on my way up to your place."

"All right, drive safe, and call me if you want to talk during the drive."

"Okay, thanks, Jenny,"

"See you soon," Jenny said, dropping off the line.

50

Sarah's drive home was a blank. It wasn't until she was a half mile away that she seemed to recognize her surroundings. The streets looked dark, darker than normal, she thought. The street lights were on but things just seemed darker. It was her mood, she decided. It wasn't like this neighborhood had a lot of traffic, she reminded herself. Sarah eased up to a stop sign a few blocks from Sterne Park. Her Nextel announced a new text message. It was from Jenny. Sarah looked down and began to read *Sarah, don't forget to . . .* BAM!

Her tires screeched like burning cats as her truck skidded into the intersection. Her head snapped back even before she slammed into the airbag. The big, Chevy truck bed crumpled in half as the cargo van pushed her back wheels, bouncing off the ground. It seemed like several minutes passed before she felt the deep pain in her chest from having the wind knocked out of her. She slowly moved her joints to see if anything were broken. Her ears were ringing from sensory overload as she tried to assess her surroundings. The cab started rocking. Someone was tugging at the driver's door to get it open, she thought. With a crack she felt a breeze of colder air rush in. A man grabbed her arm but Sarah didn't want to move. The next yank wasn't so gentle. Sarah flew from the cab and tumbled onto the pavement.

"Goddamnit! Are you trying to rip my fucking arm off?"

The heavy work boots stopped a few inches from her face as a powerful hand grabbed a tuft of her hair and yanked her head a foot off the ground. "I told you I was coming for you, didn't I?"

Holy shit!

It's him.

He grabbed her collar with his left hand and yanked her to her knees as he began dragging her toward his van. Sarah began fighting with every ounce of strength she had, but he was too powerful. She went limp, hoping he'd lose his grip on her dead weight. It didn't work. His beefy fingers were the size of cigars.

"Let go of me, you fucking prick! Help! Somebody help me!" she screamed.

She had to act. Sarah spun her legs around and dug in her heels. The twisting motion pulled her hair so hard she thought it would come out. The move made him pause and she kicked his knee as hard as she could. She felt some relief as he stumbled down to his good knee.

"You fucking bitch!" he snarled.

Sarah didn't hesitate and immediately went for his face. Her right thumb gouged his eye as her fingernails raked his face. It must have been painful because he released his grip if only for a few seconds. This was her chance. She stumbled toward her truck and abruptly ran head-on into another man.

"Lady, are you okay?"

It was a passerby. He must have seen the accident and stopped, she thought. She didn't have time to explain. The killer let out a barbaric yell as he ran up to the pair. Sarah had barely turned around when she caught a glimpse of his fist rushing toward her. She dodged her head to the left and launched her body, knee first, into his chest. She might as well have been body-slamming a cement wall. The killer caught her mid-air and threw her into the side of the pick-up. The passerby wasn't so lucky.

After Sarah hit the ground she looked up in time to see the killer smash the young man in the face. His head jerked back and he collapsed to the ground in a heap.

Sarah could hear his moans as the killer grabbed her by the collar and shoulder and began dragging her toward his van again.

If he gets me in that van, I'm a dead, she realized. She twisted left and right but his grip was solid. She tried twisting her legs around again but he anticipated the move and side-stepped her kick. She didn't avoid the punch this time. She struggled to stay conscious as he yanked her up and put her in a bear hug from behind. Adrenaline surged and snapped Sarah from her dizziness. She kicked her legs into the air trying to find something for leverage. Then she saw it. The primer-gray van had a large metal cattle guard across the grill. It was barely dented from the impact with her truck. As he brought her across the front of the van, she planted a foot and let her legs take up the slack. In one deft move, she pushed hard against the guard while thrusting her head back into his face. She felt the bones of his nose crunch as he released his grip and she fell to the ground again.

Landing on the asphalt a second time wasn't doing anything for her back. She lay motionless for a second, inhaling a deep breath in pain.

The killer recovered quickly and with blood streaming down his face he pulled a large Buck knife from his boot. His evil stare froze her in place and Sarah realized in an instant the fear all his victims must have felt. He was just taking a step toward her when she heard someone yell.

The passerby ran from the shadows and struck the killer across his back with a wooden baseball bat. Had he aimed for the killer's head it might have made a difference. The killer arched his back in pain but turned in time to block the second swing with his left arm, locked up the bat with his elbow and drove the knife deep into the man's chest. The man gasped in pain and knew his death was seconds away. The killer spun and tossed the man into the van's grille. Clutching his chest, the man fell to his knees and collapsed onto Sarah, facing her. She watched the light in his eyes fade away as his last breath tickled her cheek.

The killer went into a rage. Sarah saw the knife blade coming over the man's shoulder and took cover under his body. She could feel the impacts on the man's body coming over and over as the killer stabbed at her in a frenzy. It was all Sarah could do to keep the dead man's body between her and the killer. She grabbed at his sides using anything she could use as a handle. Sooner or later he'd connect with her.

Then she felt the metal clip of the dead man's pocket knife. She grabbed it and swung the blade open in one awkward motion. Her timing just happened to be lucky. She planted the blade in the side of his neck as he came down with another blow. The killer recoiled in pain, blood spurting from his neck wound. Sarah hoped she had severed an artery.

Wasting no time, she rolled the dead man off and went for the bat. The killer was still on his knees, grasping his neck when she landed the first blow to the back of his head. He crumpled forward to the ground, writhing. She struck at him again, and again. With each swing she saw the faces of his victims as she bashed his head against the road with the wooden bat. She lost track of how many times she hit him as another man, maybe a neighbor, rushed up and pulled her off.

"Lady! Stop! What the hell are you doing!" he cried.

Sarah fought against him until she realized the killer wasn't moving. The man snatched the bat from her hands and tossed it to the sidewalk. She collapsed to the ground in his arms as another man rushed up and began checking on the other two. "Call a doctor, Becky!" he yelled into the darkness. "Call 911!"

Sarah let out a deep breath as she looked up at the man holding her.

"Lady, are you hurt? Are you all right? What the hell happened here?"

Sarah had nothing to offer but labored breaths as she tried to make sense of what had just happened.

51

Sheriff Westin wasted no time in calling the Governor with news of Sarah's killer. "Have we confirmed this information?" Hoines asked

"Yes, sir, the local coroner has confirmed his death and says he looks a lot like the man in the trail camera photo our CSI found yesterday, at least what's left of him. Although he cautions that he has not confirmed the killer's identity."

"Brian, do we have any idea who this joker is?" Hoines asked.

"Well, sir, we're trying to trace his van but the license and VIN are not on record with the state DMV," Westin said.

"What? How can that be?" Spencer asked.

"I have no idea, sir. The coroner has found some credit cards and a license in the name of John Rogers. I've got investigators heading over to the address on the driver's license right now."

"How long until we get some kind of forensic evidence linking this guy to the murders?" Spencer asked.

"It'll take a few days for the DNA but we have some partial prints from the note and the light bulbs at Ms. Richards home. The coroner will bring us the man's prints within the hour and we should have an answer shortly after that," Sheriff Westin explained.

"How is Ms. Richards?"

"Pretty banged up but she'll live."

"Thank God for small miracles," Hoines said.

"Yes, sir."

"All right, Brian, thanks for the update. Please call me the minute you get any information on his identity."

"You can count on it, Governor," Westin said before Hoines disconnected the line.

Gregory Spencer stood and walked toward the window overlooking the mansion grounds. "Governor?"

"What is it, Greg?"

Tom Adair

"I think we need to take advantage of this situation. It holds tremendous political capital for you, sir."

"What did you have in mind?" Hoines asked, always interested in gaining a political advantage.

"I think we need to make an announcement during the ten o'clock news," he said.

"Sir, I think we need to wait until we have more facts," LeMorley offered.

"I don't know, Greg, maybe we should wait until tomorrow. Give Westin and his detectives some time to put the facts together."

"Governor, I think we should seize this opportunity, before your adversaries have time to weigh in," Spencer argued.

Spencer had a point. If they played it right, Hoines And his task force could take credit for stopping the killer.

"Set it up, Greg," Hoines said. "And let's get as much information on the suspect as we can before we go live," Hoines added.

Detectives Lopez and Vargas arrived at the killer's home and were surprised at the neat and tidy appearance of the yard. It didn't look like the home they expected a cold-blooded killer to occupy.

"Fuck me. Looks like a house from downtown Mayberry," Vargas observed.

"Remember, this might be a phony address, let's tread lightly until we know for sure," Manny said.

The detectives drew their guns and headed for the front door, with four deputies in reserve. Manny banged on the door.

"Sheriff's Officers! Search warrant!" he yelled. There was no response. "All right, kick it in."

A young spit-fire deputy shattered the door jamb with one kick. Wood splinters showered the floor as the detectives entered the living room with guns trained straight ahead. The detectives moved into the living room as the patrol deputies breezed past to clear the house.

A red collar on the fireplace mantle caught Vargas' attention and he picked it up, looking at the tags. "Check it out, Manny," he said, handing him the dog collar.

352

Manny read "Amy Summers" on the tag and knew they were in the right house. The home was immaculate. A photo of a younger woman was on the fridge in a frame labeled world's greatest mom.

"Pretty hot lady," Vargas said, looking over Manny's shoulder.

"Looks like it was taken in the sixties," Manny observed.

"Detectives!" a patrol deputy yelled from the basement.

"You'd better get down here!" he yelled in a panic.

Manny and Vargas scrambled down the old wooden stairs.

An ornate Mahogany coffin sat perched on a two-foot-high stand positioned carefully in the center of the unfinished basement. Two red carpeted stairs stood next to the coffin base. The lid was open but the detectives couldn't see the contents well. The small window wells were covered in dirt. The casket was illuminated by one deputy's flashlight.

"Tell me there's not a body in there," Manny said.

"Female . . . elderly," he said as he suppressed a gag. "Looks like a mummy," he said just before clasping his hand over his mouth and running from the basement after dropping his flashlight. Vargas picked it up.

A dank odor of death hung in the room. Most detectives were accustomed to the smell, but this was like none other they had ever experienced. As the pair got closer they could see the elderly woman in a light blue dress.

"You think it's the mother?" Vargas asked.

"Sure looks like it," Manny said.

"What the hell is she lying in?" Manny asked.

"Looks like rock salt or something," Vargas said, taking a closer look with the deputy's flashlight.

Manny looked over to see Vargas peeking up the old woman's dress with his flashlight. "Jesus, Vargas! You are one sick bastard, you know that?"

Vargas paid him no mind and instead continued his examination.

"Sal! Knock that shit off . . . someone is going to see you," he said.

Tom Adair

Vargas looked up from his light with a penetrating gaze. "Check out her vagina, Manny. Now I'm no expert . . . but I think this woman has recently been violated."

"There's a press conference scheduled for ten oh-five p.m. on the west steps of the capitol," Spencer said in a hushed tone. "The governor is going to highlight the death of the serial killer and take credit for orchestrating the investigation. I'm sure his poll numbers will surge."

The phone line was silent as Senator Barclay considered his options.

"I think we need to act now, sir. If we give the authorities a chance to look into this situation they might discover our true intentions."

"All right . . . stay by your phone," Barclay said, hanging up without waiting for an answer. He had hoped by now that Hoines had been taken care of. He should have stopped the sniper after the first boy was killed. Barclay didn't buy the excuse that they needed to make Hoines death look like the work of a serial killer to mislead the police. It was a cockamamie idea that put the whole operation at risk. He had spent a small fortune recruiting the elusive team of assassins and he was beginning to wonder if they were worth it. This whole thing is getting out of hand he told himself. Barclay punched in the number he had promised never to call again.

"You don't listen well," the assassin said.

"We have to talk!" Barclay pleaded. "Hoines is going to be giving a press conference a little after ten tonight—"

"I'm aware of that, Senator," he said, cutting him off.

"Well, what are you going to do about it?" he demanded.

"I intend to fulfill the contract, Senator, plain and simple. The details are not something you should be burdened with."

"Look! My ass is on the line here, too, you know," Barclay snapped.

"Your ass is never on the line, Senator. The closest you come to danger is dining in the Congressional cafeteria. Now stop interfering with my operation and keep your mouth shut," he demanded. The assassin turned off his cellular phone and tossed it in the pedestrian trash can as he walked by. That weasel . . . I should be killing him, he thought.

354

The bank of news cameras was the largest he had seen since the State of the State Address. A cool breeze drifted across the steps outside the State Capitol as Maggie Miller inched closer to Gregory Spencer. Maggie was kept her at arm's length from the Governor's office so as not to appear to have special access because of her brother. That forced Maggie to get creative. She had worn her best perfume and showed just enough cleavage to look professional while still attracting attention.

"So, Gregory, have you thought about my offer?" she asked.

"I'm still mulling it over," he said, smiling at the attractive newswoman.

"Anything I can do to sweeten the pot?"

"Hmmmm . . . how about dinner Saturday night?"

"Where did you have in mind?"

"I thought the Oceanaire Room would be nice," he said, speaking of the five-star seafood restaurant downtown.

"And I suppose you want drinks afterward?"

"I was thinking of breakfast."

Maggie gave him the most seductive smile she could muster to seal the deal.

The press core erupted in questions as the governor walked up to the podium. Police had blocked the surrounding streets to muffle the traffic noise. Holding his hands up the press settled down to hear his prepared statement.

"Ladies and gentlemen. . . please . . . I will answer your questions following a brief statement," he said. He was stoic and poised in appearance and speech. His tailor-made dark blue suit and red tie projected an image of the leader he imagined himself to be. "Tonight . . . evil has been vanquished from our community," the governor announced. "For the past year our state has been plagued by a malevolent agent of death who has extinguished the life of nine women and tried just today to kill another," he said. "But I am happy to report that good has triumphed—"

The 250-grain bullet ripped through his head from close to a mile away. It struck with the force of a fifty-pound sledgehammer as blood and brain matter were spattered across the podium and unlucky staff members standing close by. His lifeless corpse collapsed to the red carpet as the squelch of the microphone screeched through the sound system. Before anyone could register the horrific event that had just occurred the rifle report echoed like thunder. Most people had the good sense to hit the deck but Maggie Miller stood alone, screaming with a fine misting of blood coating her face.

From his elevated position the scene resembled and ant hill after a good stomping. People scattered in every direction as news crews tried to convey the chaos while running for cover in the parking lot. Satisfied his mission was complete, the killer headed for the freight elevator. After dropping the rifle down the shaft it would take approximately three minutes to reach the loading dock exit. By this time tomorrow he'd be halfway around the world.

Sitting in his lofty conference room, Special Agent in Charge George Buckley sat alongside Oscar LeMorley and stared in disbelief as the image flashed on the screen and the networks went to break. Seconds later their pagers erupted in punctuated yelps confirming that what they saw had been real.

"Sir, this is an act of terrorism," LeMorley said as the two stared in awe at the televisions, waiting for an update. It was LeMorley's way of suggesting they get down there to take over the investigation.

"We don't know what we have yet, Oscar. I'll wait for more than your hunch," he said.

"I don't understand, sir . . . are you implying that I've been wrong about something?"

"Art Von Hollen has been calling everyone under the sun trying to convince them that his nephew had nothing to do with the sniper killings . . . kept saying the killer had a bigger objective," he said, giving LeMorley a blank stare. "Looks to me like he might have been right," the senior agent said.

Tilly ran into Art's private office to turn on his television. "Governor Hoines was just assassinated." Doc and Art hurried over in front of the flat screen television as Tilly scanned the Denver news channels. After watching several minutes of coverage Art's fist pounded the table.

"Damnit! I should have seen this coming!" he snapped.

Doc put a hand on his shoulder but Art shrugged it off.

"No one could have predicted his real target, Art . . . not even you," Tilly offered.

Art dropped his head into his open hands; he couldn't look either of them in the eye. "Daniel warned me it would be a high-value target. You don't get much higher than the governor," he said.

"There's a hundred such targets, Art. The wealthy, politicians, sports figures, hell, we don't even know the motivation of the guy who hired him," Doc noted.

Doc was right of course. No matter how sophisticated their technology, how complete their dedication to catching him, without a motive they would always be one step behind.

Doc took a seat in a leather chair as Art sat in another. Neither man spoke as the disheveled news anchors looped the same video coverage and theorized about the motive in the assassination. There was speculation about the linkage to the earlier sniper killings and at least one newscaster wondered aloud how this assassination could have happened if the right suspect were in custody.

Senator Aaron Barclay did his best to act shocked as his staffers gasped at the live assassination unfolding on television. Senator Barclay had been working on his response speech to the assassination when it unfolded on television. The people would need a leader to help them get through this tragedy and he planned on filling that role. While technically the Lieutenant Governor would take over the office, Barclay knew he didn't have the political power to win the next election. He was an unknown junior politician with neither the proper drive nor funding to hold the highest office in the state. It was a foregone conclusion that the party would have to back him in the next primary election and he would walk into the office with relative ease. There were no serious challengers from the other parties and if one emerged he would do what he had always done. Bribe, cheat, or intimidate them into submission.

His idealistic staff called dozens of sources to get the latest information for the senator. What none of them could have known was that he didn't need any updates. He already knew all he needed to about the killing. By tomorrow his private off shore account would be depleted $1,000,000 in fulfillment of his contract. Just the cost of a few prime time campaign ads he thought. A bargain.

It took less than an hour for the senator to get interviewed on the major networks. Art and Doc watched as he spoke to reassure the public that the government would function as normal and that they would track down this killer and prosecute him to the fullest extent the law allowed.

"Typical politician. Always trying to jockey for the limelight during a crisis," Art observed.

"With him there might be more to it than that," Doc said.

"Why do you say that?"

"Don't you remember who his grandfather is?" Doc asked, surprised that Art had forgotten.

Art recalled the story of Roger Everett and how the then Denver mayor had fixed the trial for his nephew in the killings Doc had investigated so many years ago.

"You can't think Senator Barclay had anything to do with this, Doc," Art said, looking amazed he would even suggest it.

"You're the one always talking about the killer genes and such, aren't you?"

"It's just a theory Doc . . . don't go all conspiracy theory on me, all right?" Art said, dismissing the preposterous idea.

Doc sat rubbing his upper lip as he watched the television. It didn't seem so farfetched to him.

52

It was two days later before the bullet that killed the governor was examined at the CBI ballistics laboratory. The director allowed Walter Haruki to observe the examination as a favor to Art. Paul Rippley mounted the bullet on his microscope pedestal and noted that the rifling was absent. Walter shared photos and reports of his previous examinations and the two experts agreed that all the bullets shared the same characteristics. When Walter had Agent Ripply examine the base of the bullet all doubts were put to rest: by an act of pure luck, the base of the bullet was pristine. There on the base coated in a thin film of dried blood was the unmistakable lightning bolt.

Sarah broke out into shouts of joy when she looked through the peep hole at Daniel standing on her front porch with a small bouquet of roses. She disengaged the alarm and threw open the door and embraced him with all her strength.

"You're out!" she said, relieved.

"Yep, thanks to Walter and Uncle Art, the lieutenant gov saw fit to pardon me of any further involvement in the killings.," he said, smiling.

"And Agent LeMorley?" she asked.

Daniel shrugged. "He's still pissed" Sarah hugged him and kissed his cheek as he lifted her off the ground. "So, can I come in?" he asked, flashing his pearly white teeth at her.

"Of course," she said, flustered by his unexpected arrival.

"We have a lot of catching up to do."

As Daniel brushed past her Sarah found herself looking across the lake at the empty park bench under the spruce tree. He might be dead but there were others out there like him; men who would terrorize and torture innocent women to fulfill their own petty pleasures and fantasies. She might not be able to see him now . . . but he was out there . . . somewhere.

Daniel came up from behind to embrace her. She felt secure and wrapped her arms around his. She smiled as he kissed her head. He could tell she was still seeing the dead. He was quite familiar with the phenomenon and knew that she would need time to learn to cope with it. The truth was that the faces never went away. They were always there, just below the mind's conscious awareness, waiting below the surface for the right conditions to rise again. For now all he could do was comfort her and listen. Sarah could sense his benevolence. He was a man unlike any she had ever known before. She felt safe in his arms. Looking back across the lake she saw the beauty of nature. It was clean, unspoiled. She turned toward him and planted a passionate kiss on his lips. In that moment she knew that everything would be all right.

THE END

ABOUT THE AUTHOR

From investigating the shootings at Columbine High School to locating gravesites in the remote back country of the Rockies, Tom Adair has lived a life most crime authors only write about. An internationally recognized forensic scientist, he has a Bachelor's degree in Anthropology and a Master's degree in Entomology. He has served as the president of the Association for Crime Scene Reconstruction, Rocky Mountain Association of Bloodstain Pattern Analysts, and the Rocky Mountain Division of the International Association for Identification. While in law enforcement he was board certified as a senior crime scene analyst, was one of only 40 board-certified bloodstain pattern analysts and one of 80 board-certified footwear examiners worldwide. In addition to writing over 60 scientific papers, he has served as the editor of an international peer-reviewed science journal. Over his 15 year career he has been interviewed by and consulted for television, text books, novels, magazines, and newspaper articles including documentaries on the Discovery Channel and National Geographic. He continues to teach and conduct research in the forensic sciences. When he's not writing he enjoys hunting, hiking, and camping in Colorado's back country with his wife and chocolate lab.

Tom Adair

Connect with me Online

Website: www.authortomadair.com

BLOG: www.forensics4fiction.com

Follow Author Tom Adair on Facebook

Follow CSI Sarah Richards on Facebook

Follow me on Twitter @AuthorTomAdair

Made in the USA
Charleston, SC
01 March 2012